Murderess
by
Moonlight

THE TORVAN TRILOGY
2

ELIZABETH NEWSOM

Summary: "Lady Selene is living a double life as an assassin. Her current
mission is to hunt down Draven, the man who killed her mother. But her new
guard, hired by her parents, continues to get in her way. The more time she
spends with him, the more she realizes that he could be the very man she's
been hunting."

First published in the United States of America in November 2020 by Fayette
Press.

ISBN 978-1-953419-05-7

Library of Congress Control Number: 2020920384

Printed in the U.S.A.
Cover design by Kiff Shaik

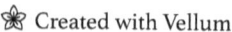 Created with Vellum

Soli Deo Gloria

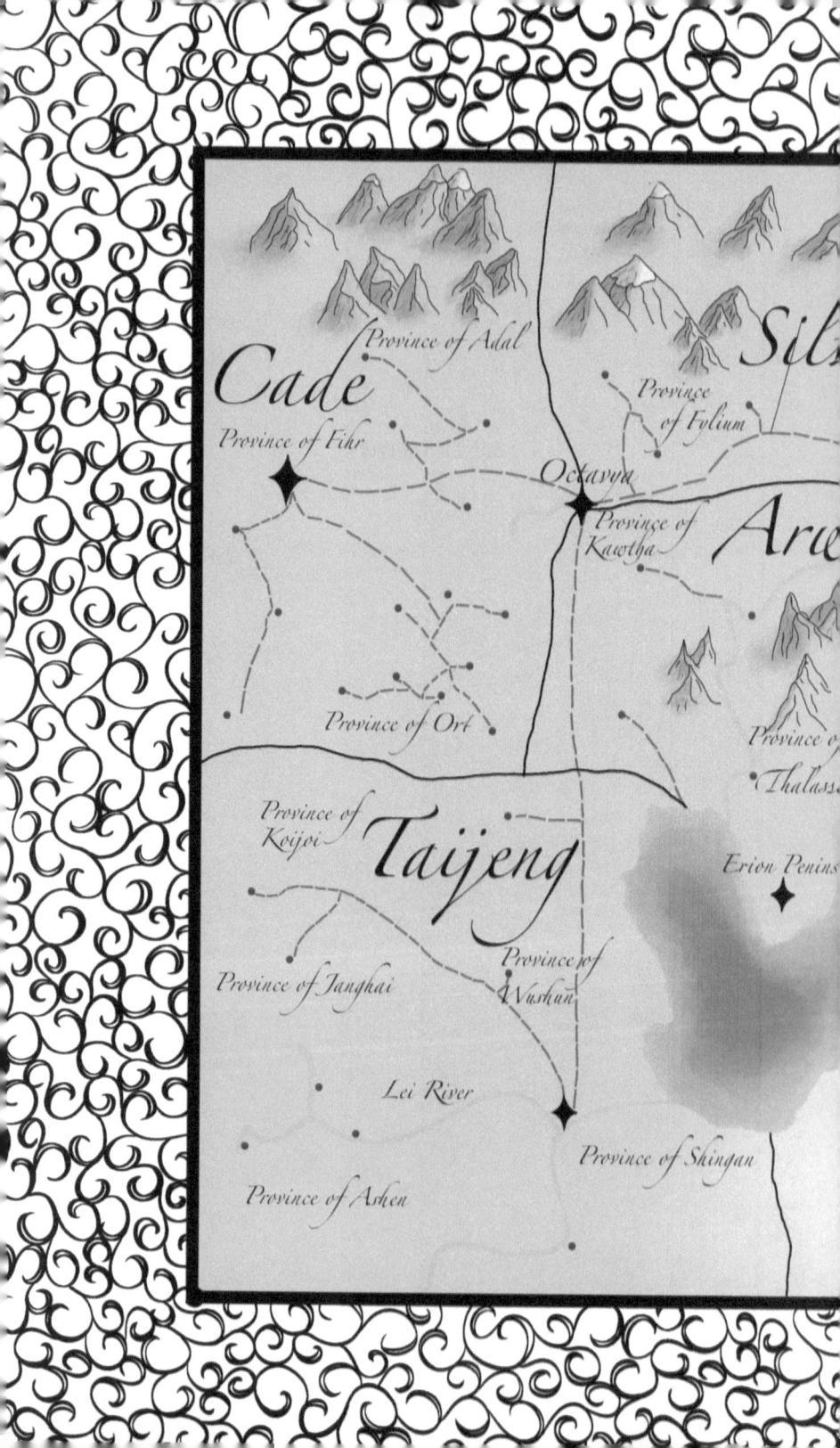

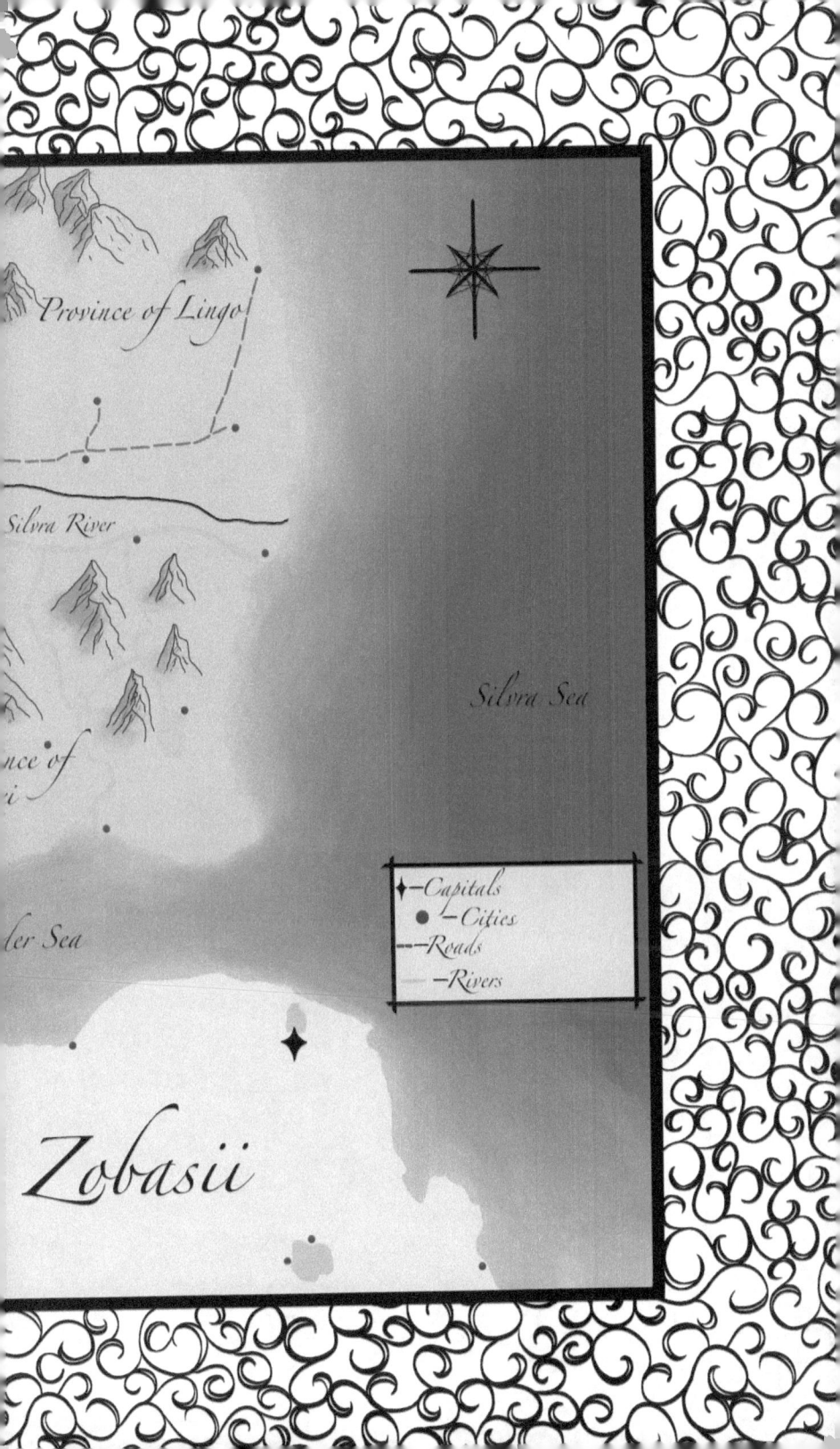

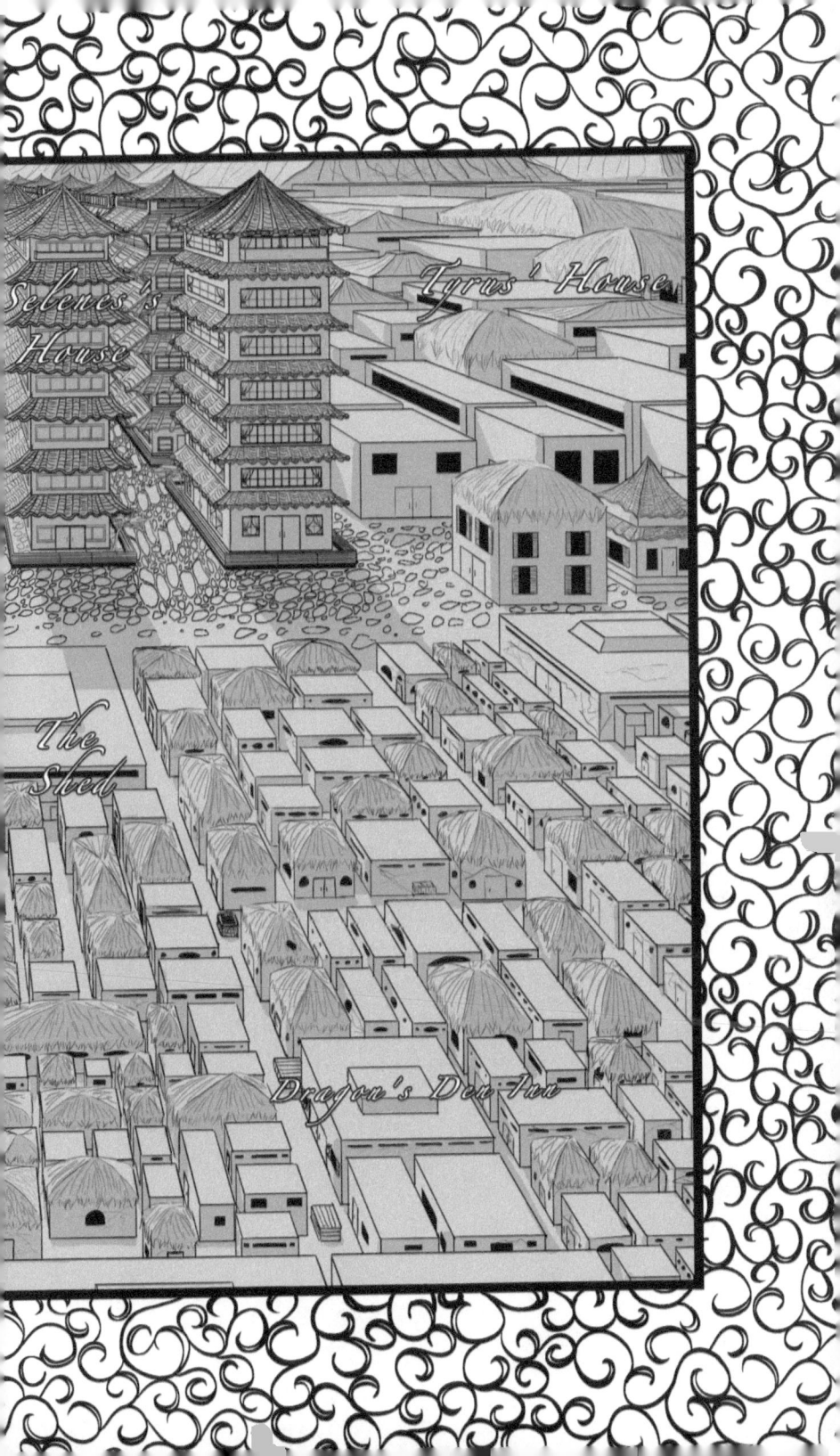

1

TO KILL A KING

Selene spent the rest of the night in the base, revising her plan to kill the King.

She reread the ink-smudged note the messenger had handed her a few hours earlier:

The King sent out a missive to the country of Cade, hiring several highly trained bounty hunters and elite soldiers for his New Year's trip to Taijeng. I'm not certain what positions they'll be assigned to in the Taijese palace or if they'll remain as the King's and Queen's personal bodyguards.

I've discovered little else; it seems they're keeping the details of their visit under wraps. These particular bounty hunters all adhere to some sort of honor code, and if we offer to bribe them, I think it unlikely they'll be turned against their initial employer.

No doubt, the Queen's coming had instigated this. Up until the last two weeks, it had been announced that only the King was to travel from the Octavian palace to the Empress' New Year's ball in Taijeng. Selene had heard how protective he was of his half-blood bride.

With the added protection, killing the King would be that much harder. Selene's stomach twisted at the thought of failure.

Her motivation to kill the King stemmed as much from the reward as it did her thirst for revenge. She needed the 80,000 aurum in order to escape the Scorpio and flee to Arwa—a feat many before her had died trying. Onden, a highly skilled bounty hunter, was the only man who'd managed to successfully smuggle former Scorpio assassins to Arwa. Hiring him would be expensive but worth it.

Even without the reward, killing King Alaric would be a noble goal. After all, he was the reason her mother had died. It was *his* fault that Draven, a former Scorpio assassin, had gotten away and murdered her mother.

To return and kill a fellow assassin was unthinkable, but to inject her with Evanescence poison meant Selene hadn't even been able to give her mother a proper burial. Of course, Selene had taken lives too, but she was different. Her targets had been people worthy of death—and she'd ended their lives quickly. While her mother might have been cold at times, she hadn't deserved such a cruel end.

"Master?" a quiet voice asked from behind her.

Selene suppressed a startle. Lyra's stealth continued to impress her. If only her other skills were as well-developed. The girl was fifty-two and had yet to make her first kill. What would that be in human years? Fourteen? Torvans lived almost three times as long.

Sometimes Selene envied Lyra's innocence and naivete. The girl could sleep at night without seeing the dying light in her victims' eyes as they thrashed in a pool of their own blood. At least Selene had only assassinated those worthy of death, those who had cheated their servants or abused their wives or neglected their people. Like the King, who had chosen to ally himself with a monster like Draven.

"I'm not your master yet," Selene said to Lyra.

"But you're going to be." Even without looking, Selene could hear the grin in Lyra's voice. "Arzil said that you'll be promoted to master as soon as you kill the King. And I'll be your apprentice."

"Well, the King's not dead yet." And at this rate, he wasn't going to be unless she figured out how to sneak past these new guards. "What did you come to tell me?"

"Master Arzil says you're late for your sparring lesson."

A wave of cold washed over her. Tuteno. Arzil did not like tardiness. And there were severe consequences for making the first-in-command of the Scorpio wait.

She pocketed the note and rolled up the blueprint of the Taijese palace before tucking it back among the other scrolls on the library's stone shelves. The whole place emanated a cold aura, but that was to be expected from an underground location chiseled from stone. Wrought iron chandeliers dangled from the ceiling, the Lux stones embedded in them casting the library in a stale light.

Selene headed toward the wooden double doors. Though the girl didn't make a sound, she could sense Lyra trailing behind her.

"Perhaps you could spar with me afterward," Lyra said. "All the other apprenticelings would be so jealous if I got to spar with the third-in-command."

Third-in-command was a high rank for someone of Selene's age. She had only been awarded that status when she'd become Arzil's apprentice. Serpent was the mysterious second-in-command intelligence agent. Selene had never met him, since Arzil was Serpent's main point of contact.

Selene entered the hallway. The interior was much the same as the library, the primary differences being the tighter space and the sconces protruding from the walls. The air here constantly felt stuffy, as if it'd been breathed too many times. Sometimes Selene could swear that the passage grew a hair narrower every time she traversed it.

But after she killed the King, she wouldn't have to wander these halls again. She would be free.

Her biggest concern was keeping her escape plans a secret from Arzil. As her master, he was irritating and arrogant. But as her enemy, he'd be cruel and vengeful. She'd seen what had happened to other assassins who'd been caught trying to run away: the skin peeled from their flesh, their eyes gouged from their skulls, their fingernails yanked from their hands.

"Selene?" Lyra asked. Only then did Selene realize the girl had been waiting for a response.

"Perhaps another time." She ignored the jab of guilt.

After Selene killed the King, there wouldn't be a next time. Lyra would feel abandoned. For a brief moment, Selene considered trying to smuggle Lyra out with her. But to think such a plan would work would be naïve. Not only would she have to trust that Lyra wouldn't report her, but she'd have to give Onden double the payment.

"Oh." Lyra's voice withered in disappointment. "Well. May I watch?"

"If Arzil permits it."

The passageway forked into three. Selene took the left, climbed up a spiraling set of stairs, and opened the door to the training room.

Though straw softened the ground, she knew from experience that it did little to cushion a fall. Mounted weapons lined the stone wall, gleaming in the Lux light. Arzil was battling an invisible opponent but stopped upon seeing her.

He lowered his weapon, his chest heaving. "Selene." His eyes were so pale they seemed to glow.

As always, Selene was tempted to squirm beneath his piercing stare, but she quashed the urge and bowed. "Master Arzil." She had to act natural. If she showed any indication of guilt, he might use a truth serum on her until he discovered what she was hiding.

"You're late. There will be no time for a warmup," he said.

She'd better be careful not to pull anything—or her family would ask questions. "I understand." She whipped out her daggers from where they dangled by her hips. Emeralds adorned the pommel of the right dagger and the top edges of the blade; it was all she had left of her mother.

Arzil raised his sword. "Begin."

Neither of them moved, both of their gazes assessing the other.

Arzil casually circled her, his gait slow and predatory. "Does your tardiness have anything to do with the plans for your mission?"

"Yes. But I assure you it won't be an issue," Selene said.

He tossed a lock of his white hair behind him. It was so damaged from bleaching that it appeared thin and brittle. After Draven had betrayed the Scorpio, she'd heard that Arzil had changed his appearance radically lest Draven decide to give a description of Arzil to the authorities. Some said he'd even changed his name. Even though Selene was his apprentice, she'd never heard his old name before.

Arzil lunged forward, as fast as a snake's strike. Selene leapt to the side.

She dared to flash Arzil a grin. "You'll have to do better than that if you want to best me."

Frustration flared in Arzil's eyes. "Is that so?"

He charged her. As she raised the dagger, he knocked it from her hand.

He'd used this series of moves on her too many times before. His next step was to get near her, until their bodies came in contact. Somehow, she'd never been able to get over her revulsion to physical touch.

Arzil grabbed the sleeve of her shirt, yanking her forward as he slipped behind her. She could practically feel his arms closing around her. She ducked and sliced at his ankle before rolling away from him.

He darted backward. "Nicely done, Selene. I'd hate to see you freeze in the middle of another duel."

She clenched her jaw, trying to douse her frustration at the reminder. All weaknesses could be overcome with enough time and willpower. She surged forward, deflecting Arzil's swing and delivering one of her own. She slashed and jabbed until her clothes grew sticky with perspiration.

She thrust her dagger forward—and went too far. Arzil dodged and, while she was off balance, grabbed her arm. He yanked her backward, until his chest met her back.

Every muscle in her body turned to wood. Her heart sped so fast that she could barely breathe in enough air to keep up with its pace. A chill feeling slunk down her spine as her vision narrowed.

Just before it winked out, Arzil stepped back, leaving Selene to collapse to her knees and haul in deep breaths.

"Remember, Selene. Assassins don't feel fear; they only incite it," he said.

As her vision cleared, she kept her gaze fixed on the ground, unable to stand the sight of Arzil's smirk. Hearing it in his voice was enough.

"You still have much to learn." Metal rasped against leather as he sheathed his daggers. "But I'm certain you'll do well in your mission... so long as you don't let the King touch you."

She waited until Arzil had left, the door clattering shut behind him, before gaining her feet.

Lyra hurried toward her, handing her a waterskin. "I can't believe he did that. That was hardly a fair fight when he knew—"

"Hush, Lyra. Even these stone walls have ears. Besides, assassins don't fight fair."

Selene uncorked it and took a deep drink, feeling sensation

coming back to her lips and fingertips. What was wrong with her? Why couldn't she will her way through the panic that ensued after someone touched her?

Selene handed the waterskin back. "Thank you. I'd best return home before sunrise." Her father and stepmother had recently hired a new guard for her and were insistent that she meet him this morning. He was supposed to be able to keep her confined to her room at night—a task her past thirty guards hadn't managed to accomplish.

Lyra nodded. "Of course. Don't let me keep you."

Would she still say that if Selene told her that she was going to leave, forever?

Selene entered the maze of passages. She stopped by the women's room to peel her black clothes off her body and exchange them for a commoner dress.

She climbed up the stairway leading to the entrance of the base. The passage wasn't lit, and though she could see, the colors were muted and dim. At least she wasn't a human. Climbing this stairway, a human would be blind, helpless. At the top, she pushed against the fake bookshelf disguising the entrance. It swung open, revealing a dilapidated one-story house.

The broken remains of a chair sat in a heap in the corner. A film of dust blanketed the wooden floor. As apprenticelings, all the assassins had been taught how to not disturb the dust. Selene pushed the bookshelf back into place and slithered past the broken window, careful not to let the glass shards touch her.

The pitch-black sky was already a few shades lighter. Selene scanned the streets and set off at a brisk jog to the abandoned shed, halfway between her house and the Scorpio base. Her house was in the middle of Renshi, where all the nobles' houses were, while the Scorpio base was swaddled in the darkness and chaos of the slums.

Her steps were soft, noiseless. Even this early in the morning, the streets were filled with people.

Beggars lingered on the sides of the streets, their empty palms and cups outstretched. Merchants hauled their wares to the market to open up their stalls. She even spotted a few nobles on a morning walk, accompanied by a half-dozen guards.

The buildings grew taller as she ran past, stretching up toward the sky. With land becoming increasingly expensive in the crowded city, most chose to build upward rather than outward.

Selene dipped into a small alley, stopping in front of the shed. It was a forgotten little building, affixed to the backend of a shop. The paint on the door was bleached from exposure to the sun, long strips of it missing from the wood.

Selene grabbed the key in her pocket and unlocked the padlock before disappearing within. The shelves held nothing but folded squares of clothes. She'd first found it littered with broken pottery and molding bread. It had taken her hours to scrub the shelves clean.

Selene pulled down her lady's gown from the shelf and shook it out. It was of nicer quality than the commoner dress she wore, but the cut was unflattering and the color plain. Just how she preferred it. After all, there was no reason to attract too much attention. Nothing disgusted her more than feeling men's gazes sticking to her as she walked by.

She tugged off her dress, folded it, and stowed it on the highest shelf. It was a pain to have to change twice, but the extra precaution was worth it.

Selene tugged on her gown, its design simple enough that she could change in and out of it on her own. A necessary feature for as many times as she changed a day.

The cloth rubbed against her hair, and she could feel it frizzing. She huffed and smoothed a few wisps back. The humidity here was bad enough by itself; she didn't need a change in clothes to further muss it.

She emerged from the shed, locked it, and pocketed the key. The sun was peeping above the horizon, as if deciding whether or not it was safe to come out. Selene stuck to the streets for the rest of the walk back home.

Now, it was time to meet her new guard.

The Channing family appeared to be normal—for the most part.

A mustached father, who thought too highly of himself.

A petite wife, who feared wrinkles so much she rarely smiled.

A handsome, spoiled son with a cruel bent.

An uncommonly vivacious grandmother, who didn't seem to care for social convention.

While exchanging a few pleasantries with the family, Draven had studied each of their expressions carefully. The father and mother seemed delighted to meet him, while Shonn and the grandmother seemed less than pleased.

Once he'd been properly introduced, Draven strode over to the wall to better observe them as they chatted. The solar was spacious, with the seating arrangement forming a half circle around the fireplace. A window against the wall behind Draven flooded the room with light. Shonn also chose to stand, leaning against the wall by the fireplace. The smell of lemony incense thickened the air, likely to keep blood-sucking skimmers at bay.

All of the family members were present except for one: the daughter, Selene. Once she appeared, Draven would have seen all the potential suspects. His intuition told him to keep a close eye on the son, but he knew better than to trust intuition alone. Judging from his information, it was a highly ranked, experienced assassin he was after, which left the father, mother, and grandmother. It could take weeks to be certain which of the three was the assassin.

But time was a luxury he didn't have. Alaric and Evelyn were to arrive at the end of the month. Though the Channing family wasn't by any means a wealthy or prominent household, they were still noble, giving them access to the party and festivities taking place at New Year's. He needed to root out the assassin before then to keep Alaric and Evelyn safe.

The irony of the situation struck him like a gauntleted fist, and he fought a smile. Instead of being the Scorpio assassin, he was hunting one. And instead of plotting to kill King Alaric, he was working tirelessly to protect him.

Much had changed in the last seven years. After helping Evelyn and Alaric escape from the Octavian Scorpio base, he'd come to Taijeng to make amends with Faina. He could still hear her biting words ringing in his ears. But it was no worse than he deserved. The Empress of Taijeng had found him wandering the streets and offered him a chance to redeem himself by hunting down the rest of the Scorpio assassins. Since Faina had resolutely rejected his help, aiding the Empress seemed like the next best option.

He'd spent the past four years training with the samurai and ghosting through the city, looking for clues as to where the rest of the Scorpio had gone. And he'd found none—until now.

There was a knock at the door, and the father said, "Enter."

The door glided aside, revealing Lady Selene, and everyone's attention shot to her. Draven quickly observed the family members' expressions at her entrance. The father appeared unimpressed, even a bit annoyed. The wife's face tightened with envy. Something dark glinted in the son's eyes. It made Draven's gut twist, even though he wasn't the subject of that gaze. The grandmother smiled with a subtle pride.

Interesting.

Finally, he glanced at Lady Selene as she strode to the front of the fireplace.

She was plainer than most ladies, and she made no effort to disguise that fact, even going so far as to wear a too-large dress colored a muted yellow. The shade reminded him of street-lights he'd seen on Earth. Her figure was unremarkable, though her hips were a touch wider than most Torvan's. For a brief moment, his thoughts were drawn to Evelyn, but he turned away from there.

Even though Lady Selene's Taijese skin was darker than his own northerner skin, the bruise-colored bags beneath her eyes were clearly visible. Her thick, black hair was heaped into a bun, making it impossible to determine if it would fall straight or in waves. Her lips were thin. Her nose had a slight bump on the bridge—an unpleasing feature on a woman's face.

But her eyes were remarkable—more in expression than color. They were so dark that one had to search to see the rich shade of brown. They sparkled with life and intelligence. When they met Draven's, he sensed thoughts flickering behind them but was unable to read any.

It was like someone drawing translucent curtains over a window. One could see the shifting of darkness and light behind them but couldn't discern the shapes and objects casting those shadows. It made Draven want to draw the curtains back and see what lurked behind.

But that was a rather dangerous desire. The last time he'd allowed himself to become involved with the object of his mission, he'd fallen for her—hard. He couldn't afford to make that mistake again, especially when Lady Selene could be the cold-blooded assassin he sought. Either way, he refused to become entangled with another woman. He'd ruined Faina's life, and that was enough.

Lady Selene broke their locked gazes first, looking to her father. "I'm sorry for being late. I was just—"

"Enough with your excuses!" Her father lunged to his feet.

Draven only realized he'd tensed after the fact. Subconsciously, it seemed he'd already assumed the position of Selene's guard.

"You sneak out every night, cause your stepmother and me needless worry, cause shame to our family. You are a disgrace!"

Her eyes went dim, the translucent curtains becoming opaque.

"If we had a good, obedient daughter, we wouldn't have to find a new guard for you every few months. But instead, we have you."

Lady Selene showed no reaction.

"If your mother could see you now, she would be ashamed."

Selene flinched. Sympathy and anger clenched Draven's chest. Using Selene's mother as a means of eliciting a reaction from her was despicable. His own grief and guilt after his mother had died had kept him awake for nights on end, the agony tearing through his chest.

The father released a long breath and sank back down to the divan. His ensuing smile left his eyes untouched. "Selene, this is your new guard." He gestured toward Draven.

Lady Selene's eyes flickered to him briefly before returning to her father.

Draven was glad her gaze didn't linger. She seemed completely uninterested in him, which meant she suspected nothing. Keeping his identity a secret from his young charge could be difficult, but he had taken precautions, especially since he'd stopped that group of assassins in the Taijese palace.

He'd shaved his jaw clean and smooth, dyed his hair brown, and rubbed dark-tinted ointment into his skin. He doubted even Alaric and Evelyn would recognize him.

Shonn, her stepbrother, straightened from where he'd been leaning against the wall. "Once I'm head of House Channing, I won't tolerate such insolence from Selene. She wouldn't sneak out every night if I were given charge of her."

Shonn thought that Lady Selene would still be his charge by then? He didn't think she would marry? Draven glanced at Lady Selene. She'd started shivering, though when her gaze met Draven's, she went still.

"In fact," Shonn continued, "I'd use my money to hire the best guard, perhaps a former commander or palace guard."

"Now, Shonn, show respect for your elders," his mother scolded without heat. "And you know we don't have that kind of money..." The woman smiled apologetically at Draven.

As far as they knew, he was just a common man with some light experience in the city watch. Draven suppressed a smile. If anything, he was overqualified for this position.

Shonn's lip curled. "We'd have plenty of money, Mother, if Uncle Tyrus had helped us when your first husband—"

"Enough!" the father said. "I am your mother's husband now, and you would do well to respect my authority. As I was saying," he turned to face Selene, "Selene, meet your new guard, Raban."

Draven stepped forward and bowed. "Lady Selene."

She inclined her head, a smirk flitting across her lips.

"Selene," her father said, "I expect you to behave for him. Do I make myself clear?"

"Crystal clear, Father." Sarcasm rang in her tone.

"Excellent." He rose. "Your stepmother and I care for you. You know we just want to keep you safe."

All evidence of the smirk was gone; both the curtains and windows had been drawn and shut tight. "Am I dismissed, Father?"

"Yes, Selene. You may go. I expect to see you at dinner tonight; no more sneaking out."

"Of course, Father."

When she left the room, Draven wasn't certain whether he

ought to remain with her parents or go with her and begin guarding her. Shonn was quick to follow her with a strangely possessive look in his eyes, making Draven's decision for him. Draven offered a brief bow to her parents before leaving and opened the door Shonn had disappeared through just as he said, "I wasn't done, Selene."

They'd stopped by the spiraling stairwell that accessed the many floors of the house, and Shonn was standing far too close to her for Draven's liking.

"Don't be angry." A subtle fear underlined her tone.

Her parents were obviously able to hear what was happening. Draven glanced back to see if they intended to do anything. But the wife had turned her attention back to her cross-stitching, and the father back to his ledger. Neither seemed concerned.

"If you don't wish me angry, then be quiet and let me speak," Shonn said.

Draven shut the door and approached the pair. If her stepbrother so much as touched her—

When Shonn gripped her arm and hauled her closer, white-hot fury stormed through Draven. There were few things he loathed as much as physically abusive men.

Shonn continued, "I think your guard has ulterior motives, motives that our parents aren't—"

"Unhand her," Draven said, tamping down his fury into those two words.

Shonn glanced over Selene's head at him, his eyebrows rising. "You obviously don't know who I am, *Guard* Raban. I am Lord—"

"I know who you are, and I don't care." He took a final stride toward them, until he stood at Selene's back. "The lady obviously doesn't want your touch. Unhand her."

2

HUNTING THE HUNTER

Shonn's expression scrunched into a snarl, his grip tightening on Selene's upper arm. "Listen here, Guard—"

In the blink of an eye, Draven grasped Shonn's wrist and yanked his hand off of Selene. He peered down at Shonn, thankful for his height. "I told you to unhand her."

Shonn tore away from him, his face turning purple. "You dare touch me? To manhandle me? I am heir of House Channing, you fool."

"And I am Lady Selene's guard, tasked with keeping her safe. You'd do well to remember that."

Shonn jabbed his finger at Draven's chest. "I refuse to tolerate such insolence, especially from an inferior. My mother and stepfather will be told of your behavior." He stormed past Draven before disappearing into the solar, like a juvenile throwing a tantrum.

A small part of Draven was concerned. After all, his mission was dependent upon his ability to hold his position here as Selene's guard. That meant he would have to make himself indispensable by doing what the other guards couldn't: keeping Selene in her room at night.

"Perhaps that wasn't your best choice of conduct, given they hired you today," Lady Selene said. But the glint in her eyes suggested that she was at least a little impressed.

"They hired me to guard you," he said evenly, "and I intend to do so." But, even outside his duty, there was something that made him feel... protective. Perhaps because he knew what it felt like to be unwanted in one's own family. In many ways, she was like he'd been as a younger man.

And then there was the vulnerability he sensed in her, like an abused flower keeping its bruised petals furled protectively around itself. He had a weakness for trying to aid distressed maidens—which had gotten him in trouble with Evelyn.

She met his eyes. "Have my parents told you about the other guards?"

"They have."

"And you still wanted this position? Why?"

To capture the Scorpio spy and save Alaric's and Evelyn's lives. "The pay."

"Other positions pay more." When he didn't reply, she continued, "I just thought I should warn you that your fate will be the same as the other guards'. Perhaps you should resign before Shonn can persuade them to fire you."

A slight grin tugged at his lips. She might be plain, but she was filled with fire. "Encouragement isn't your strong suit, is it?"

Her own lips turned upward in a smile before she smoothed them back into a straight line. Unfortunate. A smile made her appearance verge on lovely. "You could say that. And I don't mean to be rude. I just wanted to warn you."

"Why?"

"Because if you fail to do your job, your reputation will be damaged. If you resign—"

"No, I meant 'why do *you* care?'"

Selene glanced at the door to her parents' solar, and for the first time, Draven heard muffled shouts and exclamations behind it. "I appreciate what you did for me. Just now."

Draven clenched his jaw until pain shot up his cheeks. "Did the other guards not do the same?"

"I don't blame them." Her smile was a twisted reflection of the one he'd seen earlier. "Their position was at stake, after all."

"So they placed the security of their position above their duty." Her former guards had better hope and pray that they would never cross paths with Draven; he would teach them a lesson they wouldn't easily forget.

More thoughts flickered behind her eyes, and for a moment, he hoped that she would continue to engage him. Instead she said, "It doesn't matter now. Good day, Guard Raban."

She turned and marched up the stairs. Draven followed closely behind until she entered her room and shut the door.

When Selene awoke, it was evening again. It seemed like she hardly saw the sun anymore. Assassins truly were creatures of the night.

After taming her hair, she slid her door open. And nearly startled when she saw her new guard standing there. His hair was a dark brown, so dull that she could find no shine among his locks. His eyes blazed green against his deeply tanned skin. What was his name? She couldn't quite remember. "Guard Rabar, wasn't it?"

"Raban."

"Right. Have any notes been left for me?"

"Yes."

Selene extended her hand, and he placed a slip of white paper into her palm. Suspicion lined his forehead. Her heart beat a bit faster. Could he have read the note? Did he suspect something? Selene forced a smile and told herself that was ridiculous. Even if he had, the note was coded.

"Is everything all right, Guard Raban?"

"Of course, Lady Selene." The suspicion cleared from his expression.

Selene fingered the edges of the note, running her thumb along the paper. "Would you like to know a secret?"

"If you're so inclined to share one."

"My parents often wonder where I go at night. Where do you think I go?" She let her smile slop at the edges, turning it into a goofy grin. "You'll never guess."

"As your ladyship has said, I'd never guess, so what's the point in trying?"

His words startled a genuine laugh from her, but she quickly recovered. "I've fallen deeply in love, so deeply that I never have any hopes of recovering. I suspect that I may love him forever."

"Is that so?" His expression remained carefully neutral. She couldn't tell if he was merely being polite or suspected that her story was fabricated.

"Yes. He's terribly handsome."

"What does he look like?"

Clever. Another question that could either be a polite enquiry or searching for more information. Selene ran images of men through her head. The noblemen she knew were out of the question. Given that her family was among the lowliest of nobles, none would dare become her lover lest it led to marriage.

She'd once met a patron at a brothel Arzil owned. He could work in a pinch.

"He has a thick beard of velvety black hair and eyes the color of dirt."

"Dirt?"

Thankfully, she was better with a dagger than she was with

words. "I mean wood. No, chocolate. Yes, rich, sweet chocolate. And naturally, since he's not a noble, my parents wouldn't approve of the relationship. Which is why it's necessary to sneak out."

"And why bother telling me? I'm your guard, not your confidant."

"Well, perhaps you can be both. Now if you'll excuse me, I have a note to read." She waved it in front of his face before retreating back into her room.

She was simultaneously proud of herself and dismayed. Proud because she played a rather convincing lovestruck girl. Dismayed because she would have to maintain that persona until the guard was fired.

Selene broke the seal, unfolded the paper, and smoothed it against her desk.

Dearest Selene,

I do hope you'll wear the maroon dress again; it looks quite lovely on you. I hope to see you soon because I find myself missing you more with each passing hour. But please be careful. An unexpected storm is coming, and I wouldn't want you to be caught in it.

Your Love

Selene reviewed the code words in her head, piecing together the true message.

I do hope you'll wear the maroon dress again: meet at the Maroon Maidens.

I hope to see you soon: she was to come as quickly as possible.

An unexpected storm is coming: there was a new, unforeseen threat.

An unforeseen threat? Could someone have discovered their plans to kill the King? Had one of the assassins been captured?

After ensuring her door was locked, Selene pulled the rope out from under her mattress and tied it to the bedframe. She tossed the remaining length out the window after looping it around her like a harness. By the time her guard thought to check on her, she'd be long gone.

Draven waited until the room was completely silent before pulling out his lockpick and tension rod. He tucked the edge of the tension rod in, twisting the lock slightly to the side. He dug around in the keyway with his pick, pushing each pin into place with a nearly inaudible click. It took a surprising amount of time, which made him wonder what kind of locks Lady Selene had installed in her door... and why.

To be fair, since she was a lady, she likely wanted to protect any jewelry within. Perhaps he was being too suspicious. But she didn't seem like the jewelry-wearing type.

He pulled on the tension rod and the keyway turned smoothly. He opened the door.

Selene was gone—of course.

A rope was tied to her bedframe and tossed over the windowsill. She was highly motivated to see this lover of hers, if that was indeed her motive.

A quick search of her desk and bed revealed that she'd taken the note with her. Draven scanned all the nearby streets —just in time to see her dash into an alleyway. He wrapped his hands around the rope, tempted to slide down, but if it burned his hands, it would make climbing difficult later. He wrapped his legs around the rope and climbed down, hand by hand.

When he reached the bottom, he sprinted into the alley she'd disappeared into. Mud between the cobblestones revealed some of her footprints. Either she was arrogant or unaware.

Draven followed the alley until it poured out into a main street. This would make things more difficult.

He began to approach a street vendor to ask if he'd seen a lady of Selene's description when he spotted her dark hair as she wove through the crowd. He could run her to ground and drag her back home. Or he could see where she was going.

Draven quickly decided on the latter option and pulled his hood over his head as he trailed her.

After changing into a commoner dress in her shed, Selene walked the rest of the way to the Maroon Maidens. A translucent red curtain clothed the doorway. Pushing it aside revealed a room cluttered with tables below and red lanterns overhead. The lack of doors was highly impractical in the chilly month of Cedembre.

Arzil wouldn't want her to enter through the main entrance, so she walked past it and around the corner to a little door practically indistinguishable from the wall. One might not know it was a door except for the rusted handle protruding from the wood.

A prickling sensation clambered up her arms, and Selene scanned the alleyway. She couldn't shake the feeling that someone was watching. Surely her guard hadn't managed to follow her.

Selene performed her routine second scan of the area, just as Arzil had taught her. She searched for potential escape routes and weapons, in case a situation arose in which she might need them. She could climb the rooftops, but that would take a while. Her best bet was to dart down one of the many alleyways filled with broken shards of pottery and bottles that could be used as weapons.

When a few more moments passed without disturbance, she rapped against the door.

A little wooden panel slid aside and a blue eye peeped through. "Sel—I mean Raven?"

If Corsicanna was using Selene's codename, that likely meant that there were others in the room with her. She was thankful her friend had avoided using her true name. "I hope you'll let me in sooner than later. The alley is quite eerie at this time of night."

The door swung open, revealing Cori. Most people would have been so distracted by her beauty—her frosty blond locks flowing over her shoulders, her maroon dress cupping her curves—that they wouldn't have noticed the weariness aging her eyes. She wore a matching ribbon as a choker necklace. The golden chain of a second necklace disappeared beneath her collar.

Selene entered before closing and locking the door behind her. "Are you all right, Cori?"

Cori swung her arm to gesture to the pallets full of sick girls. "What do you think?"

Dusky red wallpaper, peeling away at the edges, revealed yellow-painted wood. Dust had wormed into the cracks between the wooden floorboards. A chandelier dangled from above, its crystal so dirty that it appeared opaque. A large bed was the only piece of furniture in the room, pressed flush against the wall. A faded red quilt, patched with different colors of cloth, covered the bed and the several girls occupying it. The air was saturated with the sour, musty smell of vomit and sweat.

One girl covered her mouth and her body trembled as she coughed.

Cori rushed to her side and poured her a cup of water. "Some of the girls aren't doing very well. I'm not able to tend to them all the time, since Arzil still requires me to work. And when I do work, I'm not able to get any clients."

"What?" Selene knelt by her. "How could you not get any clients? You're lovely."

Cori righted the cup. "There's been this cloaked patron who just watches me, and it scares the other clients away. I've told Arzil about him, but he won't do anything. I don't see how you can stand to work for a monster like him, Raven."

Cold flashed over Selene's skin as she searched the room for Arzil—or anyone who might report to him. "Don't speak like that, Cori. And you know I hardly have a choice." Until she earned enough money for the bounty hunter to smuggle her out of the country. But she couldn't tell Cori that. "This is my way of life now, and you can't just quit..." *being an assassin*. She didn't dare say so with so many around, but Cori would understand.

"I think you're just not looking hard enough." Cori helped the girl drink before setting the cup down with a *clank*, water sloshing over the brim.

"I didn't come here to argue with you. Where's Arzil? I need to speak with him."

"Of course you do," she muttered. Before Selene could reply, Cori rose and glided out of the room, slamming the door shut behind her.

Selene pulled the door open and followed her down the dark hallway, only lit by small Lux stones. Though Cori was shorter, Selene had to lengthen her stride to catch up to her.

Cori stopped before the door to Arzil's office and gestured with a flourish. "Your master awaits." She promptly turned and marched back to the sickroom.

Selene fisted her hands, resisting the urge to chase her down. When Selene was younger, before her first kill, she and Cori had been close friends. Her mother would take her to the Maroon Maidens to speak to Arzil, and while they were talking, she and Cori would play together.

Selene remembered her confusion when she'd realized that Cori couldn't always play. Sometimes she disappeared into the bedrooms with strange men and didn't emerge until hours later.

But no matter what had happened, she'd always greeted Selene with a smile—even if it was a little strained at times.

Selene knocked on Arzil's door. "Master Arzil?"

When the door swung open, Arzil stood in the doorway. His frail bone-white hair fell straight, all the way down to his chest. As usual, he kept the top half tied back.

"Selene. You arrived rather quickly."

She managed a short bow. "You've trained me well, Master."

"That I have. Come in. I have some rather unfortunate news."

She entered and Arzil closed the door behind her. Paraphernalia crowded shelves and tables. Her gaze landed on a single infant-sized shoe, nearly worn through at the heel, placed on top of a sheaf of documents. Perhaps it was a personal item once belonging to a debtor.

Occassionally, Arzil accepted personal items from debtors as payment. His one requirement was that the item had to be the object they most valued; somehow, he had a way of telling if it wasn't.

"What's happened? Is the King still coming to Taijeng? Has someone been caught?"

"Yes and no. Are you familiar with the former Duke Draven?"

Selene stiffened. The man who had *killed* her mother, leaving her with only an emotionally abusive father? "Of course."

Arzil had ranted about him many times, especially when she was younger. Master Sephtis and Apprentice Draven were the ones who'd betrayed the Scorpio to King Alaric, leading to Arzil's master's capture. They were the reason the Scorpio had to flee and live in abandoned tunnels, concealing themselves in the cracks and crevices of the city. Though Selene hadn't lived in the base by Octavya, many of the Scorpio had before it'd been stormed by King Alaric's knights.

"He's not only in the country of Taijeng—he's in this very city, in the Taijese palace," Arzil said.

Tuteno. He'd been in the Taijese palace all along? That was only a half-hour's walk outside the upper-class district, where her family resided. "He's here?" She gripped her mother's dagger tightly through the hidden pocket in her dress. It would be so fitting if she could slay him with the dagger of the woman he'd murdered.

"Yes. And apparently, trying to find the remaining Scorpio."

"What are we going to do? Do you think he'll find us and expose us to King Alaric as he did last time?"

She saw the slap coming and did nothing to block it. Her cheek tingled with pain, and she resisted the urge to rub it. Arzil usually wasn't violent without cause; news of Draven's presence must have really upset him.

"I didn't teach you to be so fearful, Selene. Remember, an assassin feels no fear."

"Apologies, Master."

"We are Scorpio. We are assassins. We are hunters. We will find him before he finds us. And when we do, he'll rue the day he was born."

3

OUTSMARTED

What was Arzil proposing? That they hunt Draven down? Excitement and fear jolted through Selene at the thought. She'd dreamed of doing just that for quite some time. She let her gaze wander the cluttered shelves of Arzil's study, trying to conceal her eagerness with nonchalance.

"And what would you have me do?" Selene asked.

"I would have you track him down and kill him—before the King arrives."

Just as she'd hoped.

Arzil picked up the infant shoe he'd been using as a paperweight and tossed it from hand to hand. "We can't have Draven meddling in our plans as he did last time."

"Where did you find this information on Draven? Do you have any leads?"

"This information came from one of our spies in the Taijese palace. Draven revealed himself to foil the capture of a noble residing in the Taijese palace." Arzil set the shoe down, ripped a corner off a piece of paper, wrote on it, and handed it to her. "Ask for a man who goes by this name. Say that you're his sister.

And inquire about Draven's appearance. No doubt he's changed it in order to disguise himself."

She took the paper from him and read it: *Gushvin Gacheru.* "I will."

"Report back on your findings within two days' time. Meet me here again."

"Why not at the base, Master?"

"With people about looking for the Scorpio, it's best that I not be seen making mysterious excursions to an abandoned house."

"With all due respect, Master, if we fear being caught, wouldn't it be best that I not make mysterious excursions to a brothel?"

"Anyone watching would assume that you're here to meet a lover. Or perhaps to hire a brothel worker for the night. Or even to make some coin yourself."

Selene buried a cringe. After seeing what Cori went through, she'd never participate in brothels—neither the giving nor receiving of favors.

"That is all, Selene. You're dismissed."

Selene bowed and left the way she'd entered. As she passed through the sick room, Cori placed a hand on her shoulder, stopping her.

"I don't like that glint in your eyes... Raven."

Selene stiffened at her touch until Cori lifted her hand. "It's nothing to concern yourself with."

Cori toyed with the chain of her necklace, rolling it between her fingers. Though she'd worn it as long as Selene could remember, Selene had never seen the necklace's pendant. Cori always kept it tucked into her bodice. "I just worry about you. And I've missed your visits here."

"Arzil's been keeping me busy."

"And that's why I worry." Cori smiled softly. "You truly are a kind person, Raven. I fear what this line of work will do to you."

Cori was one to talk. Selene bit down on her lip before the answer could escape. There was no need to be harsh with the one person—aside from Lyra—who truly cared for her. "Thank you. I appreciate the concern."

Perhaps if she told Cori that she was plotting to leave the Scorpio, it would ease her concerns. But then Selene's attention drifted to the walls. Knowing Arzil, he would have a way to eavesdrop on every room, whether that was a discreet peephole or a passage near a grate. It was best that she kept her secrets to herself.

"I know it won't change anything, but thank you for listening," Cori said, her ocean blue eyes darkening.

"Of course. Now, the night grows late, and I'd best leave." She should probably visit the Taijese palace tonight, while she was out.

Cori saw her to the door and locked it behind her.

Selene emerged into the alley and let the cool breeze brush against her cheeks. It reeked of vomit and urine. Some of the patrons of the Maroon Maidens came back here after they'd imbibed too much but didn't want to reveal to the other men that they couldn't hold their drink.

Selene pinched her nose. The smell here was stronger than when she'd first come. Someone must have been here recently. It reminded her of the reek of illness in the sick room. Which reminded her of Cori. She knew Cori disapproved of what she did and who she worked for—but Cori was a prostitute herself. Who was she to judge?

As Selene padded across the stone alley, the slight whisper of cloth was her only warning before a hand clamped down on her arm.

Hot anger washed over her—anger at herself for letting her thoughts wander so far that she'd let her assailant grab her from behind. Arzil would whip her if he could see her now. She had to get this man's hand off of her *now*—before her panic took over.

"What do we have here? A maiden escaping from the brothel?"

His breath brushed her ear, so damp it bordered on soggy. She reached down to pick up one of the broken glass bottles she'd seen earlier and slammed it into his head.

He staggered left and clutched the side of his face as shards of glass showered the ground around him. The tinkling of it hitting stone sounded like musical rain.

The man straightened, his cheek bloody. He was bigger than she'd initially realized—and recovering from the blow faster than expected.

Though anger darkened his expression, she saw a flicker of amusement. He latched onto her wrist in a surprisingly quick motion and yanked her backward so hard that she feared her arm would pop out of its socket. The movement pressed her into his chest and belly, his flesh warm at her back. The contact was enough to make her stomach heave and memories spiral through her mind.

As her breath grew tight, Selene fought panic. No, not here. Not now. She'd been trained for these situations. She had to get ahold of herself, especially before he got her on the ground. Once she was on the ground, there'd be no controlling her panic.

"What's a pretty lass like you doing out all alone on a night like this?"

Breathe. In. Out. She needed distance from her attacker. His position was sloppy, his stance too narrow to be stable. She could trip him.

She drew her elbow back, ramming it into his gut. His arm around her waist loosened, giving her an opportunity to step to the side, skate her foot around his, and trip him. He fell, as she'd expected. What she didn't expect was for him to keep ahold of her, dragging her down with him.

Selene landed on top of his sizable stomach. She tried to gain her feet, but his grip tightened on her middle, hard enough to squeeze the breath from her.

"You little twit. Trying to get away, eh?" He rolled, so that he was on top, his immense weight pinning her like a trapped butterfly. "Let's see you get away now."

Her past years of training evaporated in an instant, and she could see someone else looming above her, pinning her to the ground, hurting her as he used her for his pleasure. She remembered little else but darkness and frustration and help-lessness and tears. And the feeling of someone else's skin pressing against her own.

She had to get a grip on herself, or else this man would repeat what was done to her decades ago. She was flat on her back, the man straddling her waist. As he reached for her, she realized he'd left his groin unguarded. She raised her elbows above her head and slammed them between his legs.

He roared and doubled over, but his weight didn't shift off of her.

Selene reached back until she felt a cracked wooden mug lying on the street. She curled her fingers around it and slammed it into his temple. The man's weight finally tipped to one side, and he thudded to the ground, his immense body going limp.

Raban was standing a few scevola away, daggers drawn.

She blinked hard, to see if her panic had caused a hallucination. But the vision of Raban remained. Tuteno. He'd *followed* her? But how was that possible? It had to be pure luck. Perhaps he'd been on his way to the Maroon Maidens anyway once he'd realized that she was gone, and he'd just happened to be been in the right place at the right time.

Raban approached her and offered her a hand.

She ignored it as she wriggled out from between the man's legs. "I don't require assistance."

Raban stared at the unconscious man but spoke to her. "You nearly did. When I saw you, I feared..." Instead of continuing, he shook his head and withdrew a loop of slender rope from his pocket before binding the man's hands and feet. "Even if you did manage on your own, I'm glad I was able to follow you."

So he had trailed her to the Maroon Maidens. Impressive. Perhaps she'd underestimated this guard.

She glanced from Raban to her assaulter. The drunk reminded her of the men she'd killed. He deserved death, just as they had. After all, who knew how many other women he would prey on after her? She absent-mindedly touched her dagger, concealed in a hidden pocket.

But she wouldn't. Not only was Raban watching, but a part of her squirmed at the thought of an unnecessary murder. Killing for a mission was one thing. Killing a man on the street was another.

Raban yanked the last knot tight and stood. "That should hold him until the city guard comes by."

"The guard?" Had Raban summoned the city guard? Though they couldn't know she was a Scorpio assassin, the thought still made her chest squeeze.

"Yes. I'll go speak to them before returning you home."

Home? But she needed to go by the palace; she only had two days before she reported to Arzil again. Perhaps she could escape from her guard while he made the report. "An excellent idea."

Raban merely raised his eyebrows before walking out of the alleyway. He glanced behind him, slowing his steps when she didn't move. After a moment of hesitation, she followed him. She would try and escape from his watch when he was distracted. Raban walked to the nearest guard post—a tall stone fortress circumscribed by a wall—one of four in the city.

Raban rapped on the latticework metal gate, past which was a small stone courtyard. "This is Guard Raban. I have a report to make."

"What's your report?" someone shouted above them.

Selene tipped her head back. A guard on the wall peered over the edge, his leather armor gleaming in the moonlight. As Raban shouted back the details of the attack and a description of the man, Selene slipped away until she stood on the brink of an alleyway.

Then Raban's voice caught her. "Don't take another step, Selene."

She burst into a sprint, pumping her legs for all she was worth. She knew this city better than any prissy noble's guard. Even if she couldn't outrun him, she *would* outsmart him.

Footsteps pounded behind her, closer than expected. Selene's breathing roared in her ears as her slippers thudded against the cobblestone. She needed to find some obstacles to slow him down.

Selene veered back onto a main street and leapt over a stand of kabobs, eliciting a surprised shout from the vendor as she caught a whiff of grilled meat and spices. There was a pub nearby.

She dipped back into the shadows of an alleyway before dashing into the pub. She wove around tables, the wooden floorboards groaning beneath her feet. Her dress snagged on the splintery edge of a table, the cloth tearing as she ran into the kitchen.

A wave of heat crashed over her, making sweat bead on her hairline. The cooks were too surprised at her appearance to yell —though she did hear an explosion of glass as someone dropped a plate. She spared them a little wave before disappearing out the back door.

She slowed in an adjacent alley, trying to catch her breath. The cold air stripped her throat dry. She straightened, studying the empty alley. At least she'd managed to outrun—

"Can you truly not run any faster?"

Raban's voice! Her heart lurched, knocking against the underside of her ribs. Tuteno. But where was he?

"Now, if you're done running, it's time for you to go home."

She glanced up. Raban perched on the edge of a roof. How had he gotten up there? She couldn't help but admire his agility. Given his skills, he was rather underemployed as her personal guard. If he charged what he was truly worth, there wasn't a single chance that her parents would have been able to afford him.

Which brought about her question from earlier: why was he working as her guard? There had to be another motive besides pay.

"Selene? Have you lost your tongue?"

"That's *Lady* Selene. And no, I have not."

"Apologies, Lady Selene. Now, do you yield?"

She glanced up at the moon. The night was still young, and she hated to surrender so easily, but it seemed that Raban had her. She would have to invent a more sophisticated plan if she wanted to escape his watch tomorrow night. "I... yield." She had to force the last word through gritted teeth.

"A sensible decision."

She expected him to whip out a rope and rappel down the building. Instead, he began climbing down, his hands and feet somehow finding holds where she thought none existed. Where had he acquired such skills?

He let go when he was still a few scevola off the ground and landed in a crouch. He straightened and offered Selene his arm.

She passed by him and pointed down an alley. "This way." She'd had enough physical contact for one night. Hopefully he had assumed the cause of her behavior was anger with him rather than fear of—

Lock the lid tight, she reminded herself.

She had to lock the lid tight and not look inside. She'd promised herself that she wouldn't. And she'd already lost her control once tonight; she wouldn't let it happen again.

Raban followed behind her in silence. Now he knew the Maroon Maidens' location. What else did he know? Selene let her hand drift into her pocket, brushing past her sheathed dagger to touch a glass vial. Perhaps she should use the Manasseh on him, make him forget all about this night. But the substance was rather expensive, and it would be nearly impossible to force him to drink it.

As they neared her home, the city changed, the buildings growing taller with ornate roofs and glass windows. The streets were cleaner. There were more carriages and fewer people walking on foot.

They stopped before the gate to her house. Though she knew it to be polished gold, beneath the moonlight, it gleamed silver.

A guard approached the gate from the other side. "Who goes there?"

"Lady Selene and Guard Raban," she said.

"Lady Selene?" The guard froze with shock. "Incredible. Guard Raban has done it!"

She seethed within, her frustration heating to a boil. "If you'll just let us in—"

"Of course." The guard fumbled with the keys for a moment before unlocking the gate and letting it squeak open.

Selene entered the courtyard, and as they passed, the man slapped Guard Raban on the back.

"A job well-done," the man said. "You might keep your position here yet."

There were more similar exclamations of surprise and

congratulations as servants and guards saw Selene walk into the house with Guard Raban trailing behind.

Selene finally made it into her room, and she'd nearly managed to shut the door when Guard Raban edged his foot into the crack.

She narrowed her eyes. "If you don't remove that foot, Guard Raban, I just might be tempted to crush it."

He positioned his face by the crack, a slight smile on his lips. "I don't blame you."

Her thoughts stuttered, and when she opened her mouth, only silence came out.

"If I were in your position, I would loathe myself." He released a one-beat laugh. "Well. Not loathe myself. Loathe whoever my guard happened to be. I just wanted you to know that my intent tonight wasn't to humiliate you."

"Then it seems you've done so regardless of your intentions."

"I'm afraid you're right. But I'll endeavor to make it up to you." His grin was genuine, his vividly green eyes brightening with a sparkle. The sight of it knocked the breath from her chest.

She mentally shook herself. A reply. He was expecting a reply. "How do you intend to do that?"

"I will think on it. I'm certain I can come up with something."

Intriguing. What could he possibly stand to gain from befriending her? "Goodnight, Guard Raban."

He withdrew his foot. "Goodnight, my lady."

4

A DEAL

When Selene emerged from her room just before noon, she was almost disappointed that Guard Raban wasn't standing outside her door. It was a different guard, who often stood outside her room during the day. It made sense. Guard Raban had to sleep too. And really, she should be grateful. The other guards were ridiculously easy to escape from; no challenge at all.

Selene climbed up the stairs to the dining room, trying to let the nightmares ebb away as she grounded herself in reality. She wasn't on a mission, staring into the glazed eyes of a corpse; she was here, safe in her house. The smell of freshly baked bread and cooked meat wafted from the room, washing away the phantom smell of blood. She inhaled more deeply as she crossed the threshold.

Rice-straw tatami mats cushioned her footfalls. A panoramic window swept across the wall to her left. The remaining walls were made of yellow screens with inky black swirls forming the slithering ridges of mountains and the plump tufts of clouds. Servants flowed in and out of the room via a door in the back.

She performed her second scan of the room. If she had rope, she could break out the windows and rappel down in an emergency. The plates would serve well as weapons, heavy enough to stun her opponent, and the glass shards could prove effective as well.

When she turned her attention to the people, she found four widening gazes meeting her own.

"Selene," her stepmother said, "you're up rather early."

Father leaned back in his seat with his hands clasped across his belly and a smile stretching his lips. He reminded Selene of a cat that had just lapped up the last of the cream. "I heard that Guard Raban successfully retrieved you last night."

Retrieved. As if she were an object to be fetched. Selene mentally smoothed her ruffled feathers. "Yes, he did."

She seated herself at the table, and a servant placed a platter in front of her. She picked up her pike and meal dagger before sawing away at a thick slab of fish.

Shonn leaned forward, his forearms on the table. "Did he happen to mention where she'd been going?"

Father shook his head. "I've only heard reports from the servants and other guards. Guard Raban is still within his chambers, as far as I'm aware."

Shonn's dark eyes pierced hers, but he didn't ask questions. He knew better; they all did. She would tell them that she'd wandered into the Howling Jungle or had walked to Octavya or had swum with a mermaid. The story changed, depending on how she felt.

The conversation veered to other matters, and Selene lapsed into her own world as she ate. She had to visit the palace tonight. Or... during the day, while Guard Raban wasn't on shift.

Selene tucked the last crumbs of Coran bread into her mouth. "May I be dismissed?"

Father nodded before returning to his conversation with

her stepmother. Whatever the topic, they both must have found it enrapturing. Or perhaps it was each other they found enrapturing.

Selene rose and left, her stomach knotting. He'd never looked at her mother like that. She supposed she should be happy that Father had found someone else to love, assuming he'd ever loved her mother in the first place.

As she descended the steps, a faint creaking behind her announced that she was being followed.

She stopped at the landing to her room. "Do you require something, Shonn?"

"I was just going to inquire about your new guard."

"What about him?"

Shonn stopped at the landing by her side and made a point of looking up and down the empty stairwell. "I don't see him anywhere."

"He can't guard me perpetually."

"No. He can't."

Chills skittered up her arms. "What are you trying to say?"

"A mere observation." He continued down the stairs.

Selene walked into the hallway and slid open the door to her room. Shonn's behavior bothered her, but she couldn't imagine him being much of a threat. Not anymore.

Selene closed the door and locked it. Enough thinking about Shonn. It was time that she made her way to the palace.

She decided against using the secret passage. She and her mother were the only ones who knew of its existence, and she wanted to keep it that way. She'd just sneak out a window when the guards weren't looking—which happened more often than not.

It was almost enough to make her wish Raban were up; at least he presented a challenge.

On the street, Selene cast a smile at a passing guard, and he nodded in reply. The closer she'd gotten to the palace, the more frequently she'd seen guards. She touched her mother's dagger, comforted by the cold kiss of the metal hilt. She tugged it halfway out of its sheath and ran her fingers along its length, feeling the tiny emeralds that ran along the top of the blade.

She stopped a few scevola from the stone wall of the palace, her eyes climbing up its height. This near, she could only see the curved green roof of the palace, glistening with gold paint at the tips.

She followed the wall until it was interrupted by a large golden gate, flung wide open as a steady flow of people, horses, and carriages surged toward the palace.

Once within the walls, the crowd forked off, some going straight into the palace, while others approached the back. The former were likely petitioning the Empress, while the latter delivered supplies.

Selene tipped her head back as she entered the palace. Golden tiles covered the ceiling, forming a mosaic of precious metals. The smell of incense hung thickly on the air, causing a faint headache to pulse at her temples. Marble pillars towered above her. Doors, every few scevola, embedded the straight, broad hallway. Each remained closed, leaving the throne room as the people's only destination.

Her family had visited the palace a handful of times, usually for the New Year's Ball. But that had only been after Father had married her stepmother. When her mother had been alive, Selene could only remember them visiting the palace on one occasion.

Selene broke away from the crowd and approached a guard standing near a pillar. "Excuse me."

He turned toward her, his shockingly blue eyes contrasting with his darker Taijese coloring. "What do you require, citizen?"

"I have a brother here by the name of Gushvin Gacheru. I wanted to visit him."

The guard strode toward one of the side doors. "This way."

He entered, and she followed to another hallway, this one narrower and far less luxurious. The floors were plain stone, and there were no grand pillars. People in work clothes bustled about with bundles of cloth, platters of food, and cleaning implements.

The guard pointed to a rickety wooden chair. "Remain here."

She seated herself, eyes trailing the bustling servants. Their footsteps echoed against the stone, tapping like a heavy rain.

When he left her, she was tempted to get up and explore this section of the Taijese palace. She'd never been back here before. And this was her opportunity to explore unsupervised.

But it was more important that she meet Gushvin Gacheru. He could have valuable information about Draven. Once she had a description, it was only a matter of time before she found him. As much as she'd like to kill him by herself, she doubted she had the ability. Hopefully, Arzil would allow a few other assassins to accompany her.

The guard returned, a stout man with a swaying goatee following him. The guard halted before her. "I've brought you your brother. I'll leave you be and return to my post from here." He vanished back into the main hallway, the door clattering shut behind him.

"Sister!" Gushvin Gacheru pulled her into a hug.

Every muscle in her body went stiff at the feel of him while nausea churned her stomach. The man likely had no idea how close she was to throwing up on him.

Gushvin released her with a frown, likely thinking she wasn't a very good actress. "You are Raven, are you not?"

"Yes. What information do you have for me?"

He glanced at the bustling servants before heading down

the hallway. Selene trailed him until he stopped at a tiny wooden door. Though Gushvin entered with ease, Selene had to duck her head slightly. She was taller than most women, but not nearly as tall as Raban.

She closed the door, taking a moment to absorb her surroundings. A pallet in the corner held a straw-stuffed mattress and a blanket coarse enough to be better suited for a horse than a person. On the left stood a square table, squatting low to the ground, and a chest.

Selene played out a scenario in her head as she scanned the room a second time. The window was too narrow to squeeze through if she needed to escape, so she'd remain close to the door. As far as weapons went, she could possibly use the table —or throw the blanket to temporarily blind her opponent. But her mother's dagger was a better option than either of those.

When she returned her attention to Gushvin, he was smiling. "I see Arzil taught you well."

She nodded. "Your information on Draven?"

"Of course." Gushvin sat by the table and gestured for her to sit across from him.

She remained standing. She didn't know this man, which meant she didn't trust him.

"Very well. I saw Draven about a week ago."

"Then why did it take so long for you to report this to Arzil?"

"Because all the servants were being carefully watched. Leaving the palace would have aroused suspicion that could have seen my head severed from my body. I was on a mission with three others to capture a marquess' son, so we could hold him for ransom.

"Everything was going smoothly until Draven appeared. He wasted no time in dispatching the other two Scorpio. I was masked, thankfully, so he didn't recognize me. And in truth, he was so changed that I almost didn't recognize him. He wore a thick beard, obscuring his entire face. His eyes were the same shade of green. His hood was pulled up, concealing the color of his hair. It used to be gold-colored, but he may have dyed it since."

"If this man was so different," Selene asked, "how did you know it was Draven?"

"His voice. He told me that if I dropped my weapon, perhaps he'd show me mercy."

Wonderful. So he had a beard, which could be shaved, and had been identified by his voice—which she'd never heard before. At least green eyes were a start. But the color was common enough that it'd be hard to track him down based on that alone.

An image of Raban flashed to mind, his brilliant green eyes boring into her. That seemed almost too coincidental. But it couldn't hurt to ask. "Gushvin, what was Draven's skin tone like?"

Gushvin grunted out a laugh. "He was a pale one. He'd be like a glowing candle among the native Taijese people."

Raban had dark skin, the shade far too dark to be a tanned northerner. And Raban was too kind to be Draven, anyhow. She couldn't see him as a cold-blooded murderer. "Is there anything else?"

"As I said before, all the servants were closely watched within the palace after the incident. Since then, I've done some investigating, and I've found that Draven has been personally serving the Empress for the past five years. I intercepted a note from the Empress to Draven, telling him that hunting down the remaining Scorpio should be his first priority."

"And you're certain that no one suspects that you may be a Scorpio?" If so, she was now in danger as well.

"Of course, or I wouldn't have given my report to Arzil."

"I'll take my leave, then."

Gushvin rose as she headed toward the door. "One more thing, Raven."

She stopped, her hand on the knob. "Yes?"

"Draven is not someone to be trifled with. He was among the best of the assassins before he and his master betrayed the Scorpio. For all our sakes, I hope you find him before he finds us."

"Thank you for the warning." But with enough other assassins, she had no doubt Draven would fall easily. And she intended to deliver the killing blow. "Now, I'd best leave before I'm missed."

Draven shifted his weight as the Empress and her daughter stared at him in silence, wishing she would give him permission to rise. Kneeling on marble floors was quickly becoming his least favorite pastime.

If only he was reporting directly to Alaric and Evelyn. They never required subordinates to remain kneeling while they spoke—even though they ruled an entire collection of countries while the Empress only controlled one beneath their reign.

Back when he'd been a duke, he and the Empress would have had the same rank. There was a head duke and duchess of each country, and this woman was no more than a glorified duchess who preferred to be called "Empress." He tightened his jaw as his knees began to ache.

When he'd been a duke, he'd been in a room nearly as lavish as this one. Roses bloomed across the red wallpaper, so lifelike that they appeared to have depth. Golden crown molding flowed between the wall and ceiling. A chandelier loomed over them, each candle topped with a faceted Lux stone, giving it a quaint appearance.

A fountain with a dragon sculpture dominated the middle of the Empress' sitting room. Ironically, water poured from its fanged jaw into the awaiting pool. Chairs were scattered across the room, their frames golden and their cushions the same maroon as the wallpaper. The Empress was seated on a divan of a similar design.

"You've found no evidence indicating who the Scorpio assassin might be? None at all?" The Empress crossed her legs, making light ripple across the silk of her magenta gown.

The Empress' daughter mimicked the motion, staring at him with blue eyes as expressive as her mother's were cold.

"No, Empress," Draven replied.

"This is troubling, Draven. I need you to root out the assassin before the King of Torva arrives." She tucked her lower lip between her teeth, her lip paint staining their white surfaces red. It was a habit that only emerged when she was very distraught. "If he arrives and there's an assassination attempt, he might suspect that I have been slack in my duties. He might strip my title or—"

"Empress, if the King knows of the situation we've been facing in Taijeng, I'm certain he'll be empathetic."

The Empress' hand sliced through the air. "Silence! I didn't give you permission to speak. And the King has other concerns; he does not need to worry about the happenings in Taijeng."

Draven clenched his jaw. "Empress, what happens in Taijeng is very much his concern. He's the King of—"

"I will not tolerate this insolence, Draven. You were nothing before I plucked you out of the gutter and employed you as my spy."

Just remembering that day made a hollow pang reverberate through his chest. To a degree, both the kingdom and the Scorpio viewed him as a traitor. Though he'd been pardoned for his crimes, he was left to drift in the wind, purposeless.

Especially after Faina had crushed him so hard that his soul had splintered.

Draven bowed his head deferentially. "Forgive me, Empress."

"I will think on it."

Her tone had enough salt to season a feast.

"As you were saying," she continued, "you have no evidence pointing to one member as the Scorpio assassin, but do you have any suspicions?"

Selene. She snuck out every night, for reasons she wasn't particularly forthcoming about. But the Empress already knew that was why the Channing family had hired him, and that thought stayed his tongue.

"No, Empress."

"Then rise and return to your post. I'm relying on you to find this assassin before the King's arrival. Should you fail, the consequences will be dire."

Of course they would be. Draven lumbered to his feet, wincing as his knees creaked. "Yes, Empress."

He strode to the marble wall and pushed aside a tapestry, revealing a narrow wooden doorway, no higher than his chest. He hated using this passage. He hunched down and began the long journey to Selene's home. He should be back within the hour—long before his shift was due to begin.

The passage was so dark that his eyes ached from trying to pierce it. Without his night vision, he would have taken a wrong turn several intersections ago. He finally reached the exit and opened the door, which emerged from the palace wall itself.

Draven closed it, marveling at how well it blended with the wall—it was nearly invisible. He interlaced his fingers behind his back and stretched until he heard several pops in his spine.

His first instinct was to dash into an alley and take cover. After all, Taijeng was swarming with Scorpio, and someone might recognize him. But then he reminded himself that he was well disguised. With his dark skin and hair, it was unlikely even M'rithun would recognize him.

Draven strolled down a narrow street and saw a cloaked figure a few strides ahead of him. He kept completely still, his eyes trailing the figure.

Something about him seemed familiar, something about the fluid swagger in his walk. No, it wasn't a *him*. It was Selene. What was she doing in the city by herself? It hadn't taken her long to escape once he'd left.

It only took a few minutes of shadowing her for him to realize that she was headed home. Which made him wonder where she'd been before he'd seen her. She only wandered about the city at night; what could prompt her to do so during the day?

She rounded the corner, and Draven paused a beat before following. But when he glanced the way she'd gone, he saw nothing. A brief prickling sensation skittered down his spine, and he turned back.

A hand slammed into his throat, thrusting him against the wall of the building behind him. Pain burst in the back of his skull, and he was preparing to snap his attacker's arms in half until he peered beneath her hood.

Selene was staring back at him, her dark eyes glittering in her pale face. Though her skin was still darker than his, she was a few shades lighter than most Taijese.

"Guard Raban?" Selene's grip on his neck slowly loosened before her hand fell away.

He cleared his throat, rubbing the area her hand had been. "You have a very strong grip."

Judging from her pursed lips, his efforts to lighten the mood had failed miserably. "What are you doing out in the city? Father was under the impression that you were in bed asleep, as was I."

"Interesting. I was about to ask you the same question.

Visiting your lover again, I assume? Did you go to that same brothel?"

Her lips tipped into a smirk. "Perhaps."

But judging from that smile, he'd guessed wrong and she now knew that he hadn't been shadowing her for long. "You were near the palace. What for?"

"No, now it's my turn. What were you doing in the city?" she asked.

"I was just walking. I used to be a city guard, you know, and these were some of my old routes." He was almost embarrassed at how easily the lie slid off his tongue, like oil off water.

"No one saw you leave the house. Did you sneak out?" She tapped her chin. "For what reason would you want to keep this excursion a secret?"

"It's not a secret; you're welcome to tell anyone. I told your parents that I was a former city guard when they hired me."

Her brown gaze was made of steel, stubborn and unyielding. Strong. Yet something within him sensed vulnerability, a need for protection. The longer he looked into her eyes, the more they melted, softening until her eye contact felt more like a caress than a slap.

She stiffened and jerked away from him, her slightly imperfect nose in the air. "Perhaps I will bring this up to my parents. Combined with your spat with Shonn, I think they'll be most displeased. Perhaps even displeased enough to relieve you of your duty as my guard."

Draven lowered his eyebrows. The only reason she'd threaten him like this was if she wanted something. "What do you want?"

"You allow me another excursion from the house tomorrow night, and I'll let you sneak back into the house and act like you never left. This meeting here will be our little secret."

"Tempting. But if I just let you disappear one night without making an effort to stop you, they'll fire me regardless."

"Then pretend to make an effort." She tilted her head, her eyes sparkling as if she knew she'd won. And perhaps she had. "Do we have a deal?"

"Deal."

He extended his hand, and she clasped it in a surprisingly firm grip. He hadn't noticed before but her hands were rough and calloused, both fingers and palm.

She jerked her hand back and wiped it against her dress, as if she couldn't stand touching him. "Excellent."

Draven didn't bother offering his arm again as she took the lead. Did she loathe any touch? Or just his? And why? He recalled Shonn's grip on her arm yesterday. Something sour coiled in his stomach. Could Shonn have something to do with her aversion to touch? He'd have to keep an eye on their interactions in the future.

And how could she possibly have a lover if she didn't enjoy physical touch? Perhaps it was different with her lover. Or perhaps that was a cover hiding a much darker secret.

When Selene arrived home, her entire family expressed their displeasure at her venturing into the city unescorted. She wondered whether they were more concerned for her or for their reputation.

Once she'd appropriately expressed her remorse, they finally released her.

As she climbed the stairs, she reviewed the information the palace spy had told her. Apparently, Draven had been charged by the Empress to kill the remaining Scorpio.

She would never let that happen; she'd kill him first.

She heard Shonn before she saw him. His room was on the sixth floor, while hers was on the seventh, which meant she couldn't bypass him. Her heart pattered a little faster, but she forced her spine straight, reminding herself that she was no longer a little girl.

When he came into view at the landing, Selene nodded politely. "Shonn."

He was leaning against the wall, arms folded against his chest. "Selene. You didn't tell me that you had plans to leave the house today. And in broad daylight, nonetheless." He pushed off the wall. "You're getting quite bold, aren't you? Sneaking out whenever it pleases you."

Something in her shrank back at his words, begged her to retreat, to protect herself. But the best way to protect herself was to show Shonn that he wasn't capable of hurting her anymore. She lifted her chin. "My plans are none of your concern."

"No?" He descended the stairs, until he was one step above her. "You forget that I'm to inherit House Channing, which means you'll be completely under my control. And there will be no guard to save you."

"You're not the head of House Channing yet, Shonn, and I'm perfectly capable of defending myself."

"Like you defended yourself last time?"

Her body flushed hot, then grew cold. The darkness skittered out from the corners of her mind, the memories begging her to drown in them, to lose herself. No, she wasn't going to lose control in front of Shonn. Not again.

She'd almost shoved the darkness back into the recesses of her mind when Shonn bent down, his lips hovering above her ear, his warm, moist breath grazing her cheek.

"Do you remember what I said, Selene?"

Her mouth was numb, her lips frozen together.

"I said that you will never escape me, no matter how hard you fight or how far you run. And when you least suspect it, I'll—"

"Forgive the intrusion, Lady Selene, but I was told my shift had started."

They both glanced down the stairs where Raban stood. He must have been coming up to her room to start his shift. His anger was more tightly contained than it'd been the last time he'd confronted Shonn, but it still sparked in his eyes.

Despite herself, Selene felt relief wash over her so potently that she nearly trembled. As long as Raban was here, she was safe, even if she panicked and froze.

"Guard Raban," Shonn said.

Raban nodded—not bowed as he should have, given Shonn's position.

"My sister and I were having a private discussion—"

"But we're finished," Selene said, padding down the handful of steps between herself and Raban.

Guard Raban offered her a bow, which was Shonn's due, not hers. "Lady Selene." He straightened. "Perhaps you'd like an escort to your room."

"I would." When he extended his arm this time, she gripped the crook of his elbow and offered him a faint smile. Though merely touching him dampened her palms, at least her skin wasn't coming in contact with his.

But his eyes were completely fixed on Shonn. They appeared to be communicating something, and the message seemed far from friendly.

Finally, Guard Raban led her up the stairs, past Shonn, to her bedroom door.

She turned to face him. "I assume you snuck back into the house without hinderance?"

"I did. With all due respect, your guards are rather lax in their duties."

"Not *my* guards, my parents'. Or perhaps grandmother's would be more accurate, since she's the one in charge of hiring them."

"If so, she's done an exceptionally poor job. I can see why your parents would want to oversee the hiring of your guard personally."

Raban was right, which had made sneaking out ridiculously easy. In fact, she was even able to bribe one to look the other way when she had a spare bottle of korosasth on hand. Perhaps her grandmother's mental faculties were failing her, leading to her poor choice in guards.

When she glanced at Raban, he said nothing, but continued to look at her expectantly.

"What is it?" she asked.

"I keep thinking about something Shonn said."

"What?"

"He implies that you'll be his, once he's the head of House Channing. And the only way that could happen would be if you never wed."

She raised her eyebrows. It was a rather personal observation. "What are you asking?"

"Why don't you intend to get married?"

Marriage. The mere word made her stomach twist. "I'm not fit for it, Guard Raban." She sank her teeth into her lower lip. She should have told him it was none of his business. Instead, she'd given a glimpse of the truth.

"Why not? You seem perfectly suitable— " Color raced across his cheeks. "I mean, aside from the fact that you sneak out every night. Wouldn't you be interested in marrying this lover of yours? Even though he's a commoner, at least it would keep you from Shonn's grasp."

Few things seemed as unappealing as marriage—and the expectations that came with that. Running away before Shonn inherited House Channing was her best option. Once she'd successfully killed the King, the money she'd make would be enough to escape the Scorpio and live in comfort for the rest of her life. She'd finally be free of Shonn.

But she couldn't explain that to Raban.

"My lover and I don't need to be married to express our love for each other."

Raban's brows slammed downward. "Selene, love is a choice, and marriage is a commitment to that choice. If he has refused to consider wedding you—"

"Guard Raban, this is hardly any of your concern." She offered him a thin smile. "You and I made a deal that benefitted both of us. That doesn't mean we're friends."

"Sel—Lady Selene, I'm just trying to help. Nothing can come of your current choices but pain."

Anger flickered, then flared. The sheer audacity of him telling *her* what she should do, when he knew nothing about her. He didn't know how few options she had, how helpless she felt. She was taking the only escape route there was; anything else would result in her death.

"Good day, Guard Raban." She shut the door, then leaned against it, sinking to the floor.

As much as she didn't like his meddling, she couldn't help but hear his words play over and over. But it wasn't as if the path she was on was entirely of her own doing. Her mother had trained her as an assassin, even helping with her first kill. And once her mother had died, Arzil had become her new master. And all members of the Scorpio knew that there were dire consequences for betrayal. Leaving the Scorpio wasn't an option... not until she had enough money to hire Onden.

Selene chuckled. That hadn't been what Raban was talking about—he was talking about her decision to become involved with a lover who had no intentions of marrying her. And yet her mind wandered to her involvement with the Scorpio.

At times, being an assassin did bother her. But Arzil allowed her to say no to some of the jobs presented to her. Yet she was still part of a larger whole, an organization that slaughtered those who didn't advance their cause.

Selene released a harsh breath and stuffed her unease into a tight container before clamping the lid shut. Just as she'd done for the past thirty-seven and a half years. Or eighteen human years. She didn't have the luxury of second-guessing her path. Now that she was here, there was no going back. She had to finish what she'd started.

The Next Day

Night approached, spreading its star-dusted cloak over the sky. Shadows spilled from buildings and light from windows. Tonight, she was to report her findings to Arzil. Her next challenge would be finding Draven in-person. She needed to ask Arzil if he wanted her to capture Draven or kill him herself.

Given her arrangement with Raban, sneaking out tonight would prove to be easy. At least she hoped so.

She considered rappelling down her window again but decided to go right out the door. After all, Raban had promised to leave her be. This would test his word.

She opened the door. Raban stood at his post, his eyes following her movement, his jaw pulsing as he clenched and unclenched it. But he made no move to stop her.

"Don't look so worried, Guard Raban. You need only keep your promise for this night."

His gaze was intent and solemn. "Lady Selene, I do hope I'm wrong about you."

Wrong about her? In what regard? Perhaps he was referring to his earlier comment, that her choices would bring her nothing but pain.

She entered the gardens and escaped over the wall. Child's play, as usual.

The humid warmth clung to her, tempting her to shed her thick cloak. But she needed it as a disguise until she could wear her other clothes. She entered the shed and changed into her commoner garb. After going back outside and securing the padlock, she made her way to the Maroon Maidens.

Once in the alley by the brothel, she paused, searching for signs of movement. No men here to pounce on her this time. Without Raban's protection, she'd have to be extra careful.

A prickling sensation crawled up her neck—just like it had last time. Could Raban be watching her from somewhere? Or someone else? Though it would break his promise, she hoped it was Raban. She considered waiting outside a few minutes to see if she could spot her stalker, but after the event two nights ago, she couldn't work up the courage. And if it wasn't Raban, she'd best get inside to safety as soon as possible.

She paused at the back door, her hand poised to knock. She didn't want another confrontation with Cori but going around the front wasn't an option. She rapped twice. The eyehole opened for a second, closed, then the door swung outward.

Cori pulled Selene inside before shutting the door and locking it. The sour smell of vomit wafted over her, and a few girls stirred in their pallets. Cori's blue eyes were wide, catching every bit of dim light in the room.

"Raven," Cori said, "do you remember the man I mentioned last time? The one who watches me?"

Selene vaguely remembered Cori mentioning it. What about the man had Cori so worked up? Could she harbor feelings for him? "Of course. He sounds rather smitten."

She shook her head, her golden hair swirling around her. "No. I've offered my services before, and he denied me. But I have a way to find out what he really wants."

"Perhaps he fancies himself in love with you and would rather have his affection returned than your services."

Cori's expression remained doubtful. "And he wears a mask and hood, so that you can only see his eyes, which look far from lovestruck. I feel like—like he's a predator circling me."

"If you're truly concerned, tell Arzil."

Frustration sparked in Cori's eyes. "As I said last time, I've told Arzil and he's done nothing. But perhaps you can help me."

"What? Me? How?"

"You can go where I can't. You can follow him, find concrete evidence against him. There has to be something. And Arzil would trust your word over mine. Once you can inform Arzil of whatever dark secret this man has, I'm certain he would ban him from the Maroon Maidens."

Selene felt a pinch of sympathy. She hated the idea of a man preying on her friend... but she doubted that was the case, and she had matters to tend to other than her friend's paranoia. "I... will think on it."

Cori's face melted in disappointment—a punch to Selene's gut. She wanted to help Cori, but this man didn't truly seem to be a threat. She had bigger concerns at the moment.

She thought Cori would give her a tongue-lashing, but instead, she silently led Selene to Arzil's office. Guilt tugged at Selene's chest.

Even if Cori's concerns weren't legitimate, they were friends. The least she could do was ensure that Cori felt safe. And she could go to Onden and make some casual inquiries about this man; he'd likely know something. Once Cori realized that this was just an ordinary commoner from off the streets, she wouldn't be worried.

As Cori began to walk back to the sickroom, Selene said, "Cori, wait."

Cori stopped in the empty hallway and glanced over her shoulder, a fragile hope glowing in her eyes.

"I can't promise anything, but I'll do what I can."

The tension fled her in a single breath. "Thank you, Selene. That's all I ask."

Selene nodded, knocked on the door, and entered when she was bidden.

Arzil had a pen poised midair, its end glistening with fresh ink. "Selene. You have news?"

"Yes, it appears Draven is working directly for the Empress and has done so for the past five years. The servant described him, said he had a full beard and green eyes. I'll watch various places around the palace until he appears, then follow him. When I have him, would you rather me kill him or bring him to you?"

Arzil's eyes crinkled in a smile, and he set his pen down. "How thoughtful of you to ask. I'd like him to be brought to me. I have some personal matters to settle with him."

So perhaps she wouldn't get the killing blow. Disappointing. "When should I report back?"

"It may take you some time to find him if you're simply having to watch and wait. See me within a week's time."

"Yes, Master."

He raised his pen again. "If that's all, Selene, you're dismissed."

"Actually, I have a rather unusual request tonight."

"Oh?"

"I would like to do some spying within the Maroon Maidens. Of course, the only women in the Maroon Maidens—"

"Are my prostitutes." His eyebrows nearly kissed his hairline. "Are you proposing you disguise yourself as a prostitute?"

5

A PROSTITUTE IN DISGUISE

Arzil's question made her heart go into a nervous flutter, her palms dampening at her sides. Did she want to disguise herself as a prostitute? What if she actually had to spend the night with some man to keep up the charade? Bile clambered up her throat, and she thrust it back down.

No, she would find out what she could about the masked man and leave before anyone could request her services.

"Yes, I am suggesting that I disguise myself as a prostitute," Selene said. "Few positions would be more advantageous for collecting information. I would be in the midst of a crowd of drunk men with loose tongues."

"I'm not opposed to the idea, Selene," Arzil said. "But in the past, you've always seemed to hold a certain... disdain for coming into contact with men. As a prostitute, you'd attract a certain type of attention."

"I'm aware, and though it's not ideal, I'm convinced that this is the best way to find more information about Draven." Unlikely. But at least she could abate Cori's fears.

Arzil stared at her, his pale eyes seeming to peel back her outer layers to reveal her soul.

Selene held very still. She knew from experience that he couldn't actually see her true motivations—unless she showed signs of discomfort.

"Very well. I'll summon one of the prostitutes to find you more appropriate attire. But you have to understand that you'll be responsible for your own safety. If I intervene, it will look suspicious."

"I understand, Master. Thank you."

Arzil went to the door and rang a little bell on the doorframe.

Light footsteps skittered over the floorboards, followed by a timid knock. "My lord?" The wooden door muffled the voice.

Arzil opened it to reveal a woman in the hallway. She was short with generous curves that flowed as if drawn by an artist.

"Just for this night, this woman will join your ranks," Arzil said. "Find her a dress and let her take a shift by the bar."

"Yes, my lord." The woman extended a hand to Selene. "Come. We'll have you spruced up and ready for the men in no time." Her smile was genuine, crinkling her eyes until their color was no longer visible.

Selene slipped her hand into the woman's, suppressing a cringe at the brush of her warm skin. The woman led Selene down the hallway, chatting the entire time. It faded into background noise as Selene reviewed her plan.

She *would* indeed search for information on Draven, but her primary goal was to find out what she could about this cloaked man that had so disturbed Cori. If he refused to talk to her, she would watch him from a distance, perhaps even stalk him. And tomorrow night, she could visit Onden and ask what he knew. Since she was a potential client, he'd likely comply.

The woman led her up a flight of stairs, a red carpet muffling their steps. Candle flames rippled as they walked past, making light and shadow flutter along the walls. Perhaps it was to create a more romantic ambience.

The woman opened a door, gesturing for Selene to enter first. The room was filled with racks of red dresses, vanities sandwiched in between them. A few of the women were swiping color onto their eyelids or lips in front of the mirrors.

The woman scanned Selene's figure before she plucked a dress from the rack. "This one should fit you just fine."

The maroon dress had a broad V-shaped neckline that exposed an indecent amount of cleavage. Black lace stretched across the neckline, creating the illusion of modesty. There were no sleeves, and the slit up the side of the dress would expose her leg well above the knee. The whole dress appeared a few sizes too small, and she feared it would be tight enough to squeeze the air from her lungs.

A fuzzy light feeling swelled in her head. There was no way in Torva that she was wearing *that*.

Worry built inside Draven's chest. He hadn't wanted to betray Selene's trust by breaking their deal. But he couldn't bear the thought of letting her venture into the city at night alone. He hadn't seen her emerge from that building in quite some time. Last she'd visited the Maroon Maidens, she'd been in and out within minutes. It'd now been nearly an hour.

Ideally, he would have watched from afar as she went about her business, nothing would happen, and she'd return home by morning without ever knowing he'd broken their bargain.

Draven paced back and forth on the rooftop. What could she possibly be doing in there? Could her lover be a male prostitute? Was that why she'd gone within? Perhaps she was visiting him at this moment, which was why she was taking so long.

The thought bothered him more than he cared to admit. But he couldn't sincerely believe that she had a lover in the first place, not with her aversion to touch. But what else could she be doing?

Perhaps she *was* the Scorpio assassin. Could she be in the building killing her next target? But why return to the same place? Could this be a Scorpio base in disguise?

Draven stopped pacing, glancing at the door where he'd last seen Selene. Either she was in trouble or was involved in some sort of nefarious work. Regardless, it was his duty to discover what was happening and protect her or stop her.

He wasn't sure whether he preferred the former or latter scenario.

Draven anchored his grappling hook to the roof and used the slender length of rope to rappel down the building. Though he could have climbed down without it, using the rope was faster. The only advantage to doing it without a rope was to flaunt his climbing abilities, as he'd done with Selene.

When his feet hit the ground, he jerked the rope until the grappling hook came loose, clanking onto the stone street next to him. Once he'd stored the hook and rope back into his pocket, he circled around to the main entrance of the Maroon Maidens. Most people probably wouldn't be allowed in through the back entrance as Selene was.

In the building, men huddled along a bar against the far wall. Clinks of metal and glass announced that this brothel served food as well. Alcoves lined the other walls, each crowded with a circular booth wrapped around a circular table. Red curtains framed the alcoves—some curtains had been drawn closed.

A few women smiled at him, their maroon dresses cut low to display their wares. Feeling a flush of heat, Draven averted his gaze, tugging his hood a bit lower. Once, he would have gladly accepted their implied offers. When he visited Taijeng as a young duke, he and his friend Daiyu would patronize brothels. But he'd never entered a brothel again after he'd ruined Faina's life.

Selene had entered through a backdoor, so there had to be a hallway leading there. Draven brushed past a merry crowd of drunks, his attention fixed on a doorway next to the bar.

He'd almost made it to the back when he spotted a prostitute flirting with a man in the corner of the room. The man was cloaked, his face hidden in shadow. There was something familiar about the prostitute's figure and the spill of straight dark hair over her shoulders, like a waterfall at midnight.

When she glanced to the side, he caught a glimpse of her face. Dark eyes. Slender brows. Thin lips. His heart stopped beating.

Selene.

She was here. As a prostitute.

Perhaps her aversion to touch was an act. Or perhaps it was genuine, but she was somehow being forced into this role. Though Draven couldn't imagine why. She was a lady, after all, and her parents had enough to provide for her. Perhaps this was why she wasn't suitable for marriage: because she wasn't chaste.

A slender woman glided up to him. "How may I be of service, my lord?"

"Actually, I was wondering if I could see that girl. In one of these curtained areas. And bring us two drinks of gemen." Draven gestured to a booth.

The girl beamed. "Of course. And I'm certain she'll be thrilled." She set a hand on Draven's arm. "She's rather new at this, and I'm certain she'll be excited to have someone as handsome as you for one of her first customers. But do be gentle with her. I hear she's still adjusting."

Pity and anger warred inside him. Pity that she'd resorted to prostitution. Anger that some of the other men might not have been gentle. Or had even touched her in the first place.

"If you'll seat yourself at the third table," the girl pointed, "I'll have her join you in a moment—and I'll bring those drinks."

He seated himself at the circular booth and drew the curtains closed. He didn't want her to see him from afar and try to take off. He tilted his head back, absorbing the noises wafting past the curtains. One man was talking about his bad luck fishing. Glasses clinked. Girls tittered. Men laughed.

There. A pair of footsteps neared his table.

The curtain was swept aside, revealing... the same girl from before, two glasses of gemen in hand. She set them down and shot him an apologetic grimace. "I'm afraid she's otherwise engaged at the moment. She refused to leave the man she was already talking to. Perhaps once they're finished—"

"No." He wasn't going to let that man have anything to do with her. He released a long breath. What was getting into him? This was Selene's choice, not his. And where had all this protectiveness come from? Was it merely out of concern for her safety as her guard?

"P-pardon?" the girl asked, furrows interrupting her smooth forehead.

"What I mean to say is that I will talk to the girl myself. Perhaps she can be persuaded if I tell her of how much I'm willing to pay."

"Oh. Of course." Her lips pinched, jealousy oozing from her. No doubt she wanted whatever coin Draven had to offer. But she glided away without another word.

Draven rose from the booth and approached Selene. Her back was to him, and he found himself once more studying how the dress fit her. She'd not worn anything remotely like this since he'd known her. Her other clothes were drab, shapeless. And he hadn't seen her hair down before, with her black locks flowing down over her shoulders, so straight and glossy that every light in the room seemed to dance upon her tresses. A tight maroon ribbon ran around her neck, highlighting its slender length, and a slit ran up her dress, revealing a well-toned thigh.

Once more, she appeared as an enigma to him. She seemed repulsed by touch and avoided drawing any undue attention to herself. But here she was: a prostitute in a skin-tight dress flirting with a man. Why? If she were the Scorpio assassin, could she be seducing the men before she killed them? And if so, was the brothel owner aware?

Draven tapped her shoulder.

She whirled around, hand dipping into the slit of her dress. For what? A weapon? Interesting. She straightened, her eyes widening in recognition. "Y-you! You promised—"

"I'm not going to drag you back home—and that's what I agreed to. However, I would like to speak with you privately."

She narrowed her eyes at him. "For what purpose?"

"Follow me, and you'll find out."

"Can't you see I'm busy?"

"It'll only be for a moment. Please?"

Selene turned toward the other man, donning a sweet smile. "You don't intend on leaving anytime soon, do you?"

He stared back at her blankly. "I'll leave when I please."

Draven suppressed a grimace. He was rather prickly. Why would Selene waste her time on him?

Selene sighed and glanced at Draven. "You'd best make this quick."

Draven grasped her hand and began to pull her to the private booth. When her hand went stiff in his, he released it, chiding himself for touching her without thought. At the booth, he swept aside the curtain and gestured for her to seat herself first.

Color played across her face. She was almost pretty when

she blushed; it softened the contrast between her dark eyes and milk-tea skin. "I-If you want to hire my services—"

"Just hear what I have to say first. Please. Then I'll leave you alone for the rest of the night." Or watch her from a safe distance, rather.

She slid into the booth and Draven sat next to her, yanking the curtain closed.

He released a slow breath. "I can't allow you to run off into danger alone, Selene. Is this where you've been going every night? To work as a prostitute? What about your lover?"

Her face turned several shades of pink before settling on a lovely magenta hue. "This isn't—I'm not—" A sigh gusted from her lips, and she narrowed her focus to the goblet of bubbling gemen in front of her, her finger circling its glass rim. Finally, she glanced at him. "I don't have a lover. I figured that was a better tale to tell than revealing that I'm—that I—" Color washed over her face again.

When he placed a hand on her bare shoulder, she tensed. "Even now, you can hardly stand my touch, Selene. How can you stand theirs?"

Her skin felt like delicate silk against his roughened palm. It was almost painful to remove his hand. As soon as he did, the tension seeped from her.

She picked up her goblet of gemen, rotating her wrist to swirl it. "I know this probably seems like a foolish decision to you, given that I'm a lady and my parents are able to provide for me. I can only imagine what this has done to your opinion of me."

"Selene, I just want to understand. And to help you." He suppressed the urge to reach out to her, knowing it would only bring her discomfort.

She glanced up at him, curiosity sparkling in her eyes. "You would? I mean, you do?"

"Yes. Of course."

A smile teased at her lips, and she took her first sip of the drink. "Let me guess: your duty as my guard requires it?"

Admittedly, this was not within his duties as her guard. But even so, he had to do what he could to help her. As atonement for the girls' lives he'd ruined, perhaps he could make hers a bit better... And she reminded him too much of his younger self. He wanted to be the friend that he'd never had, protect her when even her family had abandoned her.

He answered, "I'll do whatever I can to keep you safe."

Her smile faded. "Though I'm provided for at the moment, I don't want to remain in House Channing when Shonn becomes the head of the house. I want to leave. But leaving would cost money that I don't have. So I'm saving in preparation for my eventual escape."

Draven raked his fingers through his hair, trying not to think of what her occupation required her to do to earn that money. "There are other ways, Selene. You could work for a merchant or—"

"Guard Raban, do you have any idea how profitable this is? I could earn far more as a prostitute than most any other profession."

"Most any? What profession could earn you more coin? And why aren't you doing that instead?"

She hesitated, then shrugged. "I was just making a generalization. Now, if you'll excuse me—"

"Wait." He reached out to grasp her wrist, only to let his hand drop.

Her slender brows dipped as she frowned. "Guard Raban, you promised that you'd let me go tonight. Even though you followed me, the least you can do is not drag me back home. I know my profession bothers you, but—"

"No, Selene. I'm not proposing that I take you back home."

He clasped the back of his neck, felt its heat nearly sear his palm. "I was sincere when I said that I wanted to help you."

She nodded slowly and took a long drink of the gemen.

When she set it down, he asked, "C-could I purchase your services for the night?"

6

REVEALED SECRETS

Selene inhaled sharply, only to begin spluttering and gasping.

Fear washed over Draven, and he grasped her hand. "Selene, what is it?" Was she acting like this because she was shocked? She had just been drinking gemen. Could it have gone down the wrong way? What if it had been poisoned?

Thankfully, he had the antidotes for most poisons tucked away in hidden pockets sewn into his cloak—most poisons too. Draven was reaching for the first antidote when Selene released a final cough and drew in a deep breath.

She stared at Draven. "I'm sorry. What did you say?"

Not poisoned. That was good. But she also didn't seem too thrilled about his proposal.

He let his hand fall back to his side, and the heat on his face nearly burned his skin. "I-I mean, not so that I can—so that we can..." He made a circular gesture and wasn't sure himself what it meant. "I understand that you need the money. I could provide the money you need for tonight, and I could give you a reprieve from... your usual work."

She stared at him for so long that he began to rethink his words, wondering what he'd said wrong. "You're saying that you'll pay me what I would normally make in a night, but you wouldn't... want anything from me? At all?"

Draven nodded.

When she continued to stare at him, he suppressed the urge to squirm beneath her gaze. But he wouldn't retract his offer. She could refuse it if she'd like, but he wanted to present her with a way out that didn't involve selling herself.

Selene feared she'd melt into a puddle right in the booth. She hadn't known that men like him existed, men who were genuinely kind and noble.

She was more than tempted to accept his offer. The coin would truly be helpful. Even once she hired the bounty hunter, she'd still have other expenses to consider. And besides, it would give her an opportunity to learn more about this mysterious guard of hers.

But what about the promise she'd made to Cori? To find out who the cloaked man was and where he was from?

But if he had come here every night, he'd likely be here tomorrow night. Or the night after. She could accept Raban's coin now and still tail Cori's cloaked admirer.

"What is it, Selene? Surely that man wouldn't be opposed to me stealing you for the night."

"That's true; I could just offer my services to him tomorrow night."

A grimace flashed across Raban's features, and she hated the lie she had to spin. She couldn't imagine working in this profession, letting a man's hands crawl where they pleased. She'd rather sell her soul as an assassin than her body as a prostitute.

She scooted out of the booth and thrust the curtain aside. "Come. Let's make our transaction elsewhere."

As Raban rose with her, she wove around the tables as she headed toward the entrance of the Maroon Maidens.

"Selene!" someone called.

Selene stopped her retreat and glanced over her shoulder just as Cori rushed up to her.

Cori placed her hands on her slender hips. "*What* are you doing here?"

Raban's brows dipped in confusion, and she could practically see the wheels turning in his mind.

Selene pulled Cori close and whispered, "I told you I'd find out about that cloaked man."

Cori—thankfully—lowered her voice as well. "But by disguising yourself as a prostitute? And who is *this* man?" Cori cast a dark look at Raban, the blue in her eyes a churning ocean. "Is he trying to—to hire you?" Cori approached him, burying her pointer finger into his chest. She kept her voice low and sharp. "I don't know who you are, but I'll have you know that *Lady* Selene is not for sale. That's right—you were about to pay a lady as your prostitute. You ought to feel ashamed—"

Raban was staring at her, his mouth open, his face scarlet. He seemed like he was trying to speak but couldn't manage to interrupt Cori's tirade.

Selene pushed Cori back from Raban. "No, you don't understand. This is my guard." She leaned in closer, her voice dipping. "And he truly thinks that I'm employed here."

Cori's gaze darted between the two. "I see."

Selene raised her voice slightly, enough so that it would be audible to Raban. "And he has generously offered to pay me for a full night without... requiring me to do any work."

Cori blinked. "Oh. My." She cast Selene a knowing smirk. "And to think you supposed that *I* had a potential beau."

Heat shot to Selene's cheeks. She hoped Raban hadn't heard that part.

"But you can't just leave together. The other women will get suspicious, as will the men. Even if he doesn't intend to use your services, you should at least go above stairs and pretend to..."

And if Selene wanted to come back and track the cloaked man, it would be best if she not arouse suspicion. "How do I know if a room is free?"

"There are candles on either side of the door. If they're both lit, the room is occupied. If one is lit, a woman is waiting within for a man who's reserved her services."

Selene nodded. "Thank you, Cori."

"Of course." Cori threaded her fingers through Selene's, and though her hand went rigid, Cori didn't release her but instead leaned closer to whisper, "You know that I don't want you to risk your life or wellbeing by helping me, don't you? If you discover that man is truly dangerous, perhaps you should just leave him be."

Selene blinked, as if getting a clearer view of Cori would help make sense of her words. "No. I wouldn't abandon you."

Cori studied her feet. "I've suspected this might happen eventually. And it was selfish of me to involve you." She squeezed Selene's hand. "And don't worry about me; I can protect myself better than you realize."

Selene was too numb to feel further discomfort at Cori's touch. Questions danced on the tip of her tongue. How could Cori protect herself? Why had she suspected this? What was going to happen?

Who was she?

Before Selene could ask, the piano trilled with an upbeat tune. It seemed one of the drunks knew how to play. Singing swept over the crowd, but Cori kept her lips tightly pursed. If Selene knew one thing about Cori, it was that she hated singing.

Cori released her hand and mouthed, *go*. She turned toward Raban, shot him a narrow-eyed glance, and strode through the sea of men. Their eyes trailed her as if they'd fallen under a trance—a few even stuttered in their singing.

She'd have to ask Cori what that was all about when there weren't so many people around.

Selene glanced over her shoulder, arching her brows in a silent question.

Raban nodded. Though she didn't look back as she traversed the main room and ascended the stairs, she could feel subtle vibrations in the wooden floor as his steps shadowed hers. A surprising number of candles were already lit. She had to walk to the back of the hallway to find a door with two unlit candles, where the sounds of the bawdry song were so muted that she could no longer distinguish the words.

She stopped in front of it, twisted the knob, and pushed the door open. The room was small though richly decorated. There was only room for a bed and two wing-backed chairs next to a narrow window.

Selene immediately went to the window. She might be able to squeeze through, but she doubted Raban would. A quick scan of the room revealed a rather small selection of weapons. A candelabrum squatted on the nightstand, which could potentially be wielded like a club. A narrow strip of decorative fabric adorned the bed. It could be wrapped around someone's neck to choke them.

She glimpsed Raban, and the sight of him broke her concentration. The room suddenly seemed to shrink. She tried taking deep breaths and focused on the buildings beyond the glass window. She could feel the effects of the gemen cascading down her body, making her head feel light.

The door clicked shut behind her. The lock snicked, and she nearly startled. Selene released a sharp breath. She'd been trained better than this; why was she so nervous?

She whirled around. "I was thinking we could leave

through the window, so we wouldn't have to remain here all night."

Raban strode toward her until he stood by her side. His cloak was gone, likely set on one of the chairs. "Wouldn't it look suspicious if you're not here come morning?"

That was true. She'd best remain here for a few hours. Selene drew her hands up her arms, trying to rub away the chill there. She was shaking so hard she feared her teeth would chatter.

Now that they were alone—and likely would be for the next few hours—she wasn't sure what to say.

Raban, for once, seemed equally uncomfortable. He glanced out the window, at the city of Renshi. "Have you and your family always lived here?"

"Yes." She began to fiddle with the edge of her sleeve—only to remember that this ridiculous dress didn't have sleeves. "Have you always lived here?"

"No."

"Then what brought you?"

"A debt owed for a mistake I made."

There was a note of finality in his voice, and she suspected he would speak no more on it.

He swallowed, his throat bobbing. "I forgot to ask; how much do I owe you?"

Hang it. She should have asked Cori for the rates she charged. What was a decent amount of money to earn in a single night? "What about 200 aurum?"

Raban's eyes widened. "Two hundred? Selene, you need not charge me so little. I said that I would pay the normal price for a night of your services."

Which meant 200 wasn't enough. "Four hundred, then."

His brows hovered low over his eyes. He withdrew a coin purse from his belt and counted out 700 aurum-worth of coins before funneling it into her palms. "There."

She stared at the pool of coins glistening between her hands. Seven hundred aurum. Not the 80,000 aurum she would make slaying the King, but a generous sum. "Thank you." She glanced down at her dress. No pockets. "Could you possibly keep this for me for a while longer? I don't know where I'd put it at the moment."

"Of course." Raban pocketed the coins once more. "If you're tired, you're welcome to take the bed. I prefer to sleep in a chair anyhow."

Obviously a lie. Who would prefer a chair over a bed? But she appreciated the chivalry. "Thank you, Raban."

She made her way to the bed and peeled back the covers. The sheets were so smooth they gleamed, and the mattress felt like it'd been spun out of clouds. She settled into the center and pulled the covers up to her chin. Though the bed was comfortable and she was tired, her mind denied her sleep. Perhaps it was because she was in an unfamiliar bed, there was a man in the room, or thoughts about Cori kept circling around her head.

What secrets could Cori be hiding? It almost sounded like she was an assassin as well. But she couldn't be a part of the Scorpio; perhaps she was in another assassins' guild.

The frame of the chair creaked as Raban shifted. Only a minute later, he shifted again. He only partially muffled his sigh before rising to his feet. While pacing the floor, he held his arms behind his back.

Selene sat up in the bed. "You're welcome to use the other side of the bed. Though you prefer chairs, I can assure you that the bed is more comfortable."

Raban stopped pacing and shook his head emphatically. "No. You are a lady."

"I'm also a prostitute."

"Regardless, I shall endeavor to treat you as a lady. And I don't want to..."

"What?"

"To make you uncomfortable." He continued pacing, as if the discussion were over.

"Given my occupation, you can assume that I wouldn't be uncomfortable."

"Is that so?" He stopped before the bed. "Why do you flinch whenever I touch you? Wouldn't a prostitute be comfortable with a man's touch?"

She only noticed how tightly she was gripping the sheets when her knuckles began to ache. "It's different with my clients."

"So now that I'm your client, you'd be comfortable with my touch?"

"Of course."

"Is that so?" He lifted his hand, and she shied away from his touch—even before she realized what she was doing.

"Raban, don't play games with me. I'm tired, and I'm trying to be kind in offering to share the bed."

"I'm not the one playing games, Selene." He lowered himself to his knees, his chest at the same level as the mattress. "What's truly going on? Why are you leaving your house come nightfall?"

"What's a man with your skillset doing as a personal guard to a lady of a poor noble family?" She arched her eyebrows, daring him to reply.

His jaw went tight.

"See? We both have questions that we don't want to answer."

"Perhaps you would consider a different question, then."

Selene tilted her head, letting her hair pour over her shoulder. She was curious what else he could want to know, but something warned her to refuse him. "Perhaps."

"Why do you fear touch? And don't try to deny that you do."

She barely kept her mouth from dropping open. He wanted

to know *that*? Surely that would be much less interesting than her mysterious nightly activities.

"Selene? Will you tell me?"

She glanced away from him and closed her eyes. In that brief moment, in the darkness behind her lids, she saw memories flash before her. She opened her eyes again before the thoughts could take hold of her. She turned back toward him. "Why do you want to know this?"

"I want to understand you, Selene. And I want to help you." His brilliant green eyes were kind, their appearance further softened by his brown eyelashes.

Before this night, she wouldn't believe someone could be so altruistic. But after he'd paid her 700 aurum, she couldn't help but trust him. And even though she'd only known him for a short time, it was obvious he was a good man of noble heart and character. Someone who deserved better than to guard the likes of her.

"A few years ago, Shonn happened upon me a-alone." The memories grew stronger, until she could smell her own fear and taste the drug that had muddied her senses. Her throat clamped up, denying her both breath and words.

"He hurt you, didn't he?" Anger sparked in Raban's eyes.

Somehow, it was gratifying to see that he was upset, to see that he cared. It was more than many others had done. The pressure on her throat eased, and the words seemed to spill from her. "Yes. I was asleep. Ever since my father was wedded to his mother, he's preyed upon me. It started off with small pranks that soon became cruel."

She was tempted to glance at Raban and see his reaction, yet she also feared what she might see. So she kept her eyes on the bedsheets. "As years passed, I became smarter and more adept at avoiding his tricks. I thought a prank was what he intended that night. I decided to pretend to be asleep until he was nearly upon me. Then I would defend myself and show him that he could no longer prey on me like he used to. But when I turned toward him, he shoved a cloth dampened with Somnus sap over my mouth and nose. My limbs went numb, and when he started to touch me, I couldn't s-stop—"

Her chin wobbled, tears welling in her eyes, and she turned away. Deep breaths. She had to take deep breaths. It had been a long time since she'd recalled those memories—and for good reason.

When she glanced back, Raban was gripping his own hands tightly, his chest rising and falling fast. Were Shonn here, she had no doubt that Raban would beat him to a pulp. The thought made her flush with warmth. Just the idea that someone else would protect her was comforting.

"And did you tell your parents?" he asked.

A sour taste filled her mouth. They were both more Shonn's parents than hers. "I did. But they didn't believe me. My step-mother dotes on Shonn, which means Father does as well."

Raban just knelt there, fire in his eyes, tension in his expression. "I am very, very sorry, Selene. What they all did was wrong." He shook his head. "I'm sorry I wasn't there."

He was sorry? She wasn't quite certain what to make of all his apologies. It was in the past, and it wasn't his fault. But somehow, even though a few words seemed paltry in comparison to what she'd suffered, it helped. His apology was salve on her battered soul.

"Thank you." She sniffed hard and turned from him, embarrassment and relief melding together. She felt tender and raw. She could hardly believe that she'd shared that when she'd only known him for a few days.

He nodded solemnly, and, for a moment, questions flickered in his eyes, but he didn't ask them. Likely, he still wondered why she would have resorted to prostitution, given her past. "Now you can see why I can't share the bed with you, though I appreciate the thought."

"Raban, I truly don't mind. You're different from Shonn. And I trust you." As soon as the words escaped, she regretted them. Those were dangerous words for anyone to speak—much more an assassin. And yet they rang true.

Something in his eyes changed, softened. Like the colors in a meadow ripening as summer approached. "You keep addressing me without a title."

So she had—and not just now but throughout the night. She let her hand curl into a fist, digging her nails into the meat of her palm. Hopefully the pain would snap her back to her senses. She'd made far too many mistakes tonight. If Arzil ever found out, he'd whip her hard enough to peel the skin off her back.

"Are you certain, Selene?" He rose to his feet, towering above her.

For a moment, she felt small, helpless. It reminded her of when—

"Forgive me." Raban stepped back. "I didn't mean to startle you. Judging from your reaction, I think it best that I avoid the bed this time."

She tamped down her embarrassment long enough to ask, "*This* time?"

Raban inhaled sharply. "I didn't mean—Apologies, Lady Selene. I misspoke." He returned to his pacing more vigorously.

Selene buried a smile. There was something endearing about seeing him flustered. She shook the thought from her head a moment later and pulled the covers back over herself. A good night's rest would set her thoughts aright.

But that would only happen if she weren't interrupted by her routine nightmares. She hoped they would abate, at least for tonight. Even though Raban couldn't possibly suspect that she was an assassin, she didn't want to arouse any suspicion.

A distant sound echoed in her ears, bouncing against her head. It reminded her of a buzzing fly.

"Selene..."

She burrowed more deeply into the covers. For once, she had slept wonderfully and had no recollection of any nightmares. Perhaps if she stayed in bed long enough, she'd fall back into a deep, blissful slumber.

"It's time to wake up, Selene."

She furrowed her brows, trying to block the persistent, annoying noise.

"Come, Selene. The sun is about to rise." A hand gripped her shoulder.

She bolted upright, heart thundering in her chest.

Raban stepped back, raising the offending hand. "Forgive me. I—"

"No, you must forgive me." She had become far too reactive as of late. "I shouldn't have startled. I'm stronger than that."

Raban's brow crumpled, and he opened his mouth as if to contradict her.

Someone rapped on the door. "Selene. Are you in here?"

Arzil.

7

CAUGHT BY THE SCORPIO

Selene rolled out of bed and glanced at Raban just in time to see the last drop of color drain from his face. "Tuteno," he muttered.

No doubt he feared being caught—and what it would do to his reputation.

"Selene?" There was a metallic scratching against the door, then the click of a lock.

"I'm here," she replied.

By the time she'd glanced back at Raban, he was gone. But where? Just as well; it was best for his own safety. Selene rushed to the door and pulled it open just as Arzil pushed it.

She stepped into the hallway, shutting the door behind her. It was best that what she and Arzil said wasn't heard by Raban. If Raban learned about the rest of her past, she would receive no more sympathy or kindness from him.

Arzil examined her from beneath lowered brows, which were a shockingly dark contrast to his bleached hair. "Selene. What are you doing here? I was told by the other women that you'd disappeared upstairs with a man."

She kept her face perfectly stoic as she nodded, stepping a

bit farther away from the door. "I met a man that I thought might have a potential lead as to Draven's whereabouts, Master Arzil. Since I was playing the part of the prostitute, I came upstairs with him and—and I did as he paid me for in hopes of coaxing information from him. He must have left sometime last night, once we were... finished."

Surprise bloomed across his face. "Impressive. I admire your determination, Selene, and how you've recovered from your squeamishness. You'll be the best assassin of the Scorpio yet, my dear."

His words kindled a pride within her, but she tempered its flame, knowing his praise could as easily turn to criticism.

"What did you discover?"

She flipped through possible lies in her mind and considered telling him she'd discovered a secret passage to the palace. But he'd demand to know its location. "Nothing. The man kept hinting that he knew something, but I think that he was pretending as a ploy to... get up my skirt."

Arzil's lips barely twitched, but she could tell he was displeased. "Disappointing. All that effort, gone to waste. Well, no matter. I'm certain you'll have Draven run aground soon enough. There's no one else I would trust to lead the hunt for him."

"Lead, Master?"

"Yes. I have two other assassins who will assist you in finding Draven. He isn't a man to be easily subdued. He was among our most skilled before he turned traitorous."

Good. She was hoping that she'd have backup when she confronted Draven.

"Come to the base tonight. I will make the appropriate introductions. You will all scout the palace in search for a secret passageway. Lyra has asked to accompany you."

"Lyra? Master, she's not even an apprentice. She's not ready for a mission."

"You would question my judgment, Selene?" He strode around her, like a predator circling its prey, and feathered his fingers down her back as he passed.

A shudder wrapped around her bones. She still bore faint whiplash scars from one of the few times she'd failed a mission. "No, Master. I would never question your judgment."

Arzil returned to standing in front of her. "Excellent. This is a safe mission, and Lyra needs the experience. Perhaps it will give her the motivation to make her first kill. If she doesn't prove herself to be useful *very* soon, I might need to replace her."

Selene forced her breathing to remain slow and calm. She'd never allow him to hurt Lyra. Perhaps good could come of this mission. After they'd finished scouting, she could visit Onden to ask about Cori's admirer. But how would she escape Raban? Regardless of the technique she used, he always seemed to find her.

"Is there a problem, Selene?"

She was shaking her head before she could even think of a reply. If she told Arzil that her guard could be a problem, he'd suggest that she kill him. She couldn't stomach that task.

"There'd best not be. Now, you should change unless you also wish to work a morning shift. And prepare yourself for your mission tonight."

She suppressed a flare of irritation and bowed her head. "Yes, Master."

Arzil strode down the hallway. Most of the candles were now unlit. The passage would have been bathed in darkness if not for the window at the end of the hallway. Hinges squeaked, and Selene turned just as Raban peered out from the room.

"Why did you hide?" she asked. "Were you embarrassed?"

Raban rubbed the back of his neck. "It would ruin my reputation as a guard if it were known that I frequented brothels."

As she'd thought. "But you still came here last night."

"Because I was concerned about you. And I was cloaked last night to disguise my identity. Is it safe to emerge now?"

She nodded. "We'd best leave separately. And before I go, I still need to grab my other clothes."

Raban nodded and left the room. "I'll wait for you outside."

She retraced her steps to the backroom with the rows of dresses. Her commoner dress was folded neatly on the edge of a vanity. The room had been teeming with women last night, but this morning it seemed deserted.

While she yanked off the ridiculously tight dress, she began scheming of ways to go to the Scorpio base that night. She had to be particularly clever about this escape attempt.

Draven strode outside in a daze, still reeling from the fact that Selene knew M'rithun. Not only knew him but was *employed* by him. He must have changed his name after Draven and Sephtis had betrayed the Scorpio—or Draven would have heard of the man by now. But he'd recognize that man's voice anywhere.

The breeze carried a whisper of cold with it. Even in winter, the tropical environment wouldn't get much colder. The street wasn't as crowded as it had been last night. Most of those walking past did so with purpose, their strides quick and determined as they headed to work, perhaps at the docks, the market, or a wealthy noble's home. The aroma of baking bread wafted past the scent of ale and urine that drenched the brothel.

Draven kept his head down as he crossed the street, afraid M'rithun would appear any moment and recognize him. If M'rithun discovered him, Draven would suffer a long, torturous death. The man still blamed him and Sephtis for the capture of his master, Lord Dalgar. If M'rithun was the owner of the brothel, he was obviously wealthy and in a position of power.

He remembered when both he and M'rithun were mere apprentices. Draven had been an anomaly when he'd joined the Scorpio. He had been admitted as a teenager, still maintained his noble status as a duke, and become apprenticed to the most powerful Scorpio lord, Sephtis.

The others had kept their distance, except for M'rithun, who had helped Draven throw his first dagger. In return, Draven taught him how to use the most obscure poisons. But that had stopped when the others on the Scorpio Council began plotting to oust Sephtis. Then Draven had used M'rithun as a means of spying on Master Dalgar. M'rithun had likely caught on and ceased requesting to meet Draven.

Now Draven was a traitor to the Scorpio and, in order to save his own skin, Sephtis had given King Alaric instructions on how to capture all of the other Scorpio leaders, including Dalgar. Draven had heard rumors that M'rithun was now leading the Scorpio. He suspected them to be true. Which meant the Maroon Maidens served more than one purpose.

He would have to mention this to the Empress and have the man captured immediately. As the new Scorpio leader, M'rithun was a threat to King Alaric and Queen Evelyn.

His heart grew heavy when he thought of what would happen to Selene. She was part of House Channing and she knew M'rithun, who was a part of the Scorpio. It all seemed too coincidental; she had to be the Scorpio spy.

He remembered what M'rithun had told her: *Now, you should change unless you also wish to work a morning shift. And prepare yourself for your mission tonight.* Who was she to meet tomorrow? Other assassins? If only he had hurried to the door earlier.

Someone gripped his shirt by his shoulder, snapping him

back to the present. "If I hear that you went back on your word and abused Selene's trust—"

Draven turned and found the small blond woman from last night. She was as different from Selene as the sun from the moon. Her hair was nearly white, her eyes a chilled sapphire. Her curves couldn't have been better placed even if she were a marble statue in the hands of a master sculptor.

But there was something enchanting about Selene that he couldn't put his finger on. Something about her thin figure, the flare of her hips, the dark glitter in her eyes. Even the slight bump in her nose was—

The woman's eyes flared in anger and disgust. "I knew it. You're just like all the other men. Openly ogling any woman who passes your way, just like you were doing to Selene last night."

His cheeks blazed with heat. "I hadn't intended to stare. I was just thinking—"

Her jaw firmed. "Oh, I *know* what you were thinking." She snorted. "Men. And I had such high hopes for you. You're going to crush Selene's heart when she realizes why you want her. Not that you'd care. You've probably already taken what you want from her and—"

"*Stop.* Stop. Just please, stop." He rubbed his temples as a headache writhed beneath his skull, likely a result of last night's lack of sleep. "First of all, I'm not going to crush Selene's heart. She hardly cares what I think of her, and I'd have to have her heart before I could even be capable of breaking it. And secondly, nothing untoward happened last night. If you don't believe me, wait until Selene comes out and ask her."

"Oh." Her anger seemed to deflate, and she shot him a sheepish grin. "Why didn't you just say so?"

"I would have, but I wasn't prepared to be verbally assaulted so soon after awakening." He ran his fingers through his hair and worried about the state it was in. He'd need to tidy it before returning to the Channing's house.

The woman toyed with a necklace chain that disappeared into her bodice. "I apologize. I just intended to check on Selene... and get a closer look at her new guard."

The woman's comment reminded him of what she'd said last night. She'd called Selene a lady. Apparently she knew Selene was living a double life. Did she also know that Selene was an assassin?

And if Selene truly was an assassin, why pose as a prostitute? Perhaps it was a guise, a means of obtaining information.

A figure headed toward them, and Draven glanced up. Selene was striding out of the Maroon Maidens, garbed in a plain brown dress with an apron around her waist.

The woman followed Draven's gaze. "You say she hardly cares what you think. She cares more than you know. I see it in her eyes. No one has protected her in a very long time. I think that you could be the one to save her."

Draven was getting whiplash from this woman's moods. "Save her from what?"

"From herself."

The woman left and met Selene halfway across the street. They spoke for a moment, and the woman swept back into the brothel. Selene glanced from Draven to the woman and back as she walked toward him.

"What were you talking about?" she asked.

"She told me that she was going to kill me if I'd gone back on my word and... slept with you."

Selene nodded, a sad smile on her lips. "That sounds like Cori. I assume we're going home now?"

Draven nodded and gestured for her to take the lead.

Selene strode forward, leading them into a narrow alley. She walked slightly in front of him with confidence and grace. But beneath that façade, he saw her wounds, her vulnerability.

It reminded him of himself. Once he had been a young duke, hiding the fact that he was an assassin while struggling with his mother's death. He'd buried so many dark secrets and hadn't had anyone to share his burdens with.

What if he could be that for Selene? What if he could help her? Protect her? Save her? Perhaps he could turn her from the Scorpio, prevent her from walking the path to her own destruction.

He released a harsh breath, letting the hope inside him wither and die. In the end, he could help, but he couldn't save her like the prostitute had suggested. Only Selene could do that.

And he wasn't supposed to become so emotionally invested in a charge. The last time he had, he'd failed his mission. Though in truth, that was a mission he was glad he'd failed. Alaric and Evelyn deserved to be together. There were few who would be as worthy of ruling Torva as they.

And even if Selene changed, turned away from the Scorpio, he'd sworn off marriage since... A face appeared before him. It took him a moment to realize that he hadn't merely conjured her; she was *here*. Faina. The woman he'd completely ruined.

Selene slowed when she realized Raban had stopped walking. She turned to face him. "Raban?"

No response. He just stared blankly at... a woman? She appeared to be a streetsweeper, her dress little better than sackcloth, and she was staring back at Raban.

Selene strode over to him and tugged at his sleeve. "*Raban?*" When he glanced at her, his face tight and pale, she said, "Are you coming or not?"

What was so fascinating about this woman? Upon closer inspection, past her drab clothes, she was stunning, her features delicate, her skin so pale it nearly shimmered, lashes framing liquid-gold eyes.

The streetsweeper scanned Selene before returning to her work, dragging the broom across the ground in large strokes.

Raban shook his head and continued walking, his pace a touch too fast.

Selene had to maintain a light jog to keep up. "Are you all right?"

"Yes. Just thinking. Will your parents be upset when we return?"

She glanced up at the sky, giving it thought. "Perhaps. If we arrive together, you should pretend to drag me back, so they assume you made an effort."

His smile was genuine, though she couldn't imagine what he found so amusing. "An excellent idea." He glanced at her and abruptly slowed his pace. "You should have told me I was going too fast."

Selene shrugged, and for the rest of the walk Raban fell into a contemplative silence, the furrow between his brows growing deeper and deeper.

When they neared her house, he lightly wrapped his hand around her wrist. "Is this all right?"

Warmth washed over her, and she suppressed a smile. She'd never had a kinder guard; she'd miss him when she fled to the country of Arwa. She focused on the sensation his touch created. It felt normal, not disturbing in the slightest.

At her nod, Raban tugged her toward the house. She fell behind as if she were being unwillingly dragged. When he stopped at the gate, the guards opened the door, casting Selene severe looks.

One said, "Your parents want to see you in their solar, Lady Selene."

Raban gave her wrist a brief squeeze, and she appreciated

the comfort. But she knew what was coming and didn't fear it. She'd faced it a thousand times before, after all.

Selene stood in the solar before her family, enduring a half-hour tongue lashing—more boring than hurtful. At least, that was what she told herself.

When Father had demanded to know where she'd been, she told them she'd snuck into the palace and stolen a gem from the Empress' circlet. She'd spent the rest of the night finding a place to hide the gem until Guard Raban had found her and dragged her here.

When he was done with her, Father cast his glare toward Raban. "Well. Do you know where she wandered off to?"

A cold sweat bathed her skin. What if he—

"No, I'm afraid not. I found the lady wandering the streets aimlessly this morning and brought her back. As far as the gem goes, I found no trace on her person."

Father leapt up from his seat, the veins at his temples bulging. "Which means that she's *lying*."

"*Or*," Selene said, "that I've hidden the gem so well that Guard Raban was unable to find it."

Father clenched his fists, advancing. Did he mean to strike her?

Raban tensed, and Selene prayed that he wouldn't try to interfere. Doing so would mean the loss of his job, and at the moment, he was the only friend she had. But Father stopped a stride away, jabbing his finger toward the door. "*Get out!*"

She was all too happy to comply. Raban trailed behind her as she began the three-story trek to her room. She glanced back at him, preparing to ask him how she'd done.

But he was already staring at her, a strange look on his face.

She stopped a few stairs above him. "Raban?"

The look cleared. "Yes?"

"What's wrong?"

"I was just thinking about what happened earlier this morning."

"Do you mean when you were almost seen at the brothel? Or the encounter with that woman?"

His laugh fell flat. "Both?" He continued walking up the stairs, and Selene resumed as well.

Though she could understand that he was afraid of being caught, she didn't understand why he was so fixated on it. Could he have possibly heard her conversation with Arzil? Or had something happened between him and the streetsweeper?

One glance at his closed expression revealed that it was unlikely that she'd gain any answers from him.

If he'd heard her conversation with Arzil, would he report her? A chill shot across her arms. He hadn't thus far, but maybe he was just waiting for an opportunity to leave and tell one of the city patrol. Bile clambered up her throat. Imprisonment would be far too merciful a sentence; death would be her end.

They stopped in front of her door. Raban reached out to her, only to drop his hand. "Are *you* all right, Selene? Did something happen between you and M'rithun?"

"Who?"

"The man who you spoke to outside the room."

"His name is Arzil. And no. Everything was fine. He just wanted me to wake up and get out."

Several emotions flitted across Raban's face, each one too fleeting to comprehend. "Ah. I heard his voice, and I mistook him for someone else."

Was that why Raban had been so afraid? Because he thought that Arzil was this M'rithun? What had M'rithun done to strike such fear into a man like Raban?

"I see," she said.

If Raban hadn't heard her call him "Arzil," then he mustn't have heard their conversation.

Before crossing the threshold to her quarters, she turned to Raban. "I suppose you'll be pursuing me in earnest tonight."

"I will—for your own safety."

Selene smiled. "I look forward to the challenge." And for once, she meant it.

Escaping Raban this time would not be as easy. She needed a new plan. Time to make use of the secret passage.

The difficult part would be keeping Raban from discovering it or she'd never be able to use it again.

She peered out the door to ensure that the other guard was still outside her door and that Raban wasn't on shift yet. Her family was upstairs having dinner, and Selene had asked to remain in her room, claiming that she didn't feel well.

Selene retreated back into her room and opened a hidden compartment in the side of her desk. Her mother had possessed a similar compartment within her wardrobe.

Two bottles of amber liquid glistened at the bottom of the compartment. She'd been saving the korosasth for a special occasion. Selene grabbed the bottle, pushed the compartment back into place, and opened her bedroom door.

"Excuse me?"

The guard glanced her way. His eyes instantly fell to the bottle in her hands. "I take it you're venturing out tonight?"

"Yes. But as far as you know, I'm still abed in my room."

"Well..." He rubbed his spongey beard. "Your parents have been rather insistent that you remain within your room as of late."

Selene rolled her eyes but returned to her room to retrieve the second bottle. She presented both to the guard.

He grinned and took them from her. "Yet somehow, even though I was watching you carefully, you just magically disappeared from your room."

She pointed her finger at him. "Exactly. Have a good night."

She strode past him as he popped the cork off the first bottle. Hopefully her parents wouldn't catch him drinking on duty. She navigated the halls carefully, ducking back when she heard someone approaching.

Finally, she reached the storage room, which smelled faintly of dust, salt, and fruity jams. Jars of preserved food lined the shelves, and the floor was littered with hefty bags of Coran flour, beans, and three varieties of rice. Selene dragged a few aside before flipping over the rug and raising the trapdoor.

She snuck into the passage, pulled the rug back over, and let the trapdoor fall shut. Dirt filled her nose, tempting her to sneeze. The crawl space was small, so narrow at times that she had to completely flatten her body and pull herself forward. When she reached the end, she shoved on the top of the tunnel, pushing aside the stone that sealed the exit.

After she pulled herself out, she emerged into an alley and set the flagstone back before dusting herself off. Selene jogged to the next alley and scanned the streets before making her way to the Scorpio base.

There was no way that Raban would be tracking her now.

Wherever Selene was going, she wasn't headed to the Maroon Maidens.

Draven had seen her stop by the shed to change into her commoner dress and now she was heading south, toward a poorer district of town. Once he saw her destination and brought her safely home, he'd go to the Empress in the morning and arrange for M'rithun's arrest. After all Draven had done against Evelyn and Alaric, it was time he did something for them.

Why couldn't Selene simply stay in her room? What could propel her to leave every night? What if she were truly a prostitute? Maybe she was meeting a special client tonight, one who paid extra to have her go to him.

Something clamped tight onto Draven's gut. It took him a moment to realize that it wasn't foreboding—it was jealousy. He wanted to be the only man that Selene had opened herself up to, and eventually, the only man who was able to touch her in a manner she found pleasing.

His own thoughts made his face warm. Fool. If he continued to harbor feelings for her, he might compromise the mission. And it was unlikely that she was going to see a special client anyhow, at least in the poorer district. No one here would be able to afford a private visit.

When she darted across the street, Draven withdrew a coiled rope from his cloak pocket. A grappling hook sparkled from the end. He tossed it across the street, yanked to ensure it remained stable, and took a step off the edge of the building. Wind tugged at his clothes. He landed silently against the building's wall with his knees bent. By the time he glanced down at the street, Selene had disappeared.

Hang it. He climbed the rope to the rooftop and disengaged the grappling hook. After taking a running leap, he landed on the next building. He traveled that way for a few minutes, searching the alleyways and streets for the raven-haired maiden.

Many of the buildings here were low, more shacks than houses, their roofs threatening to cave in on themselves. Some even had a red X painted over the door—a sign that the household had been infected with Bloodburn. A few frail-boned children wandered the streets, silent and solemn as tiny wraiths. Whenever a gang swept by, they were careful to tuck themselves into hiding places that seemed little more than cracks and crevices.

A few minutes passed with no sign of Selene.

What if she were an assassin, as he'd suspected? And she was in the Scorpio base this moment? He'd just missed his opportunity to discover the base's location. Draven secured his grappling hook and was preparing to rappel down to the ground. Until he saw four forms, clad in skin-tight black—the standard clothes worn by a Scorpio assassin.

Though they were masked, he recognized Selene's fluid gait, the way she routinely scanned her surroundings. If she were alone, he would have confronted her. But now he was forced to change his plans.

They spoke in low tones as they headed down one of the alleys. Draven tugged his hood to conceal his face. He was about to follow when he spotted a man in loose black clothing trailing them. His movements were slow and cautious, and Draven lost him amidst the shadows more than once.

Who else could be trailing Selene tonight? Hopefully no one that wished to do her harm.

Draven checked to ensure his daggers remained at his side and rappelled down the building, following Selene's stalker through streets and alleys. A few times, the man stopped and glanced back at Draven's hiding spots but never for long.

After a few turns, Draven realized they were nearing the palace. Did the assassins plan to sneak within? Kill the Empress? If that was the case, then Selene's life was forfeit.

There had to be some way that he could warn her or pull her out of this scheme entirely. No matter how skilled she was, the Empress' samurai would catch and slaughter her.

Draven shook his head. He'd gone soft. Even now, he was plotting ways to save Selene instead of hunting and capturing her. He wanted to save her—and would if given the opportunity. But he also wasn't going to allow her to kill another soul.

After all, once he'd been just like her. With some help, she could still change and choose a different path.

The stalker darted to another alley, and Draven followed. When he arrived, the man had disappeared. No matter. Surely he'd left some clues in his wake. Draven could track—

A blade pressed against the back of his neck. Though it was through his cloak, he was familiar enough with a dagger's kiss to recognize it.

"Who are you and why are you following us?" The voice was fluid and surprisingly feminine. A quick glance revealed that it was one of the assassins who had been with Selene. Scorpio assassins were mostly men—though the females who did join often became highly skilled and were assigned to many of the difficult missions.

Draven raised his hands, affecting a commoner accent. "I mean no 'arm. Was just wanting to see where you was going, is all."

"Stand up. Moonwing, Raven, Sparrow, come here. I've found our little spy."

Which meant that their other "little spy" was still out there somewhere. And now their stalker was likely watching Draven *and* Selene.

Selene and the other man ran back down the alley until they surrounded him. A smaller, slim figure trailed behind, her eyes so wide he could see their golden flecks. Despite her profession, she emanated innocence and youth—not more than a girl. He guessed that she was Sparrow.

Selene was pale, her lips parted slightly as she stared at him. Did she recognize him through the disguise? Could she be afraid for him? Perhaps he could use that.

The man looked him up and down. "Doesn't seem like such a little spy after all. Rather big, if you ask me."

None of their voices sounded familiar. That was good. He didn't want an assassin from the Octavian base to recognize him. If they knew he'd betrayed the Scorpio, they'd likely kill him where he stood. Or bring him to M'rithun.

"I can pay you," Draven said, "if you release me. I truly didn't mean any 'arm, and I certainly don't want trouble."

"Remove your hood and let us see your face," the woman said, circling him and pressing the dagger against his throat.

Draven lowered his hood. Selene's eyes grew a bit wider, but neither of the other two older spies reacted. The girl's gaze ran up and down his form curiously.

"Look at his clothes," the woman said. "He resembles a guard—and not a very important one. Perhaps we could kill him here. Plenty of people are disposed of in Renshi's alleys."

The girl, Sparrow, sucked in a breath, and the woman shot her a look of disgust.

"Or we could bring him in for interrogation. Find out what he really knows," the man said.

"No," Selene said.

Everyone faced her.

She had her arms folded over her chest, looking smaller than she usually did. "He—he's my guard."

Sparrow regarded him with a question glowing in her eyes.

"Your what, Raven?" the man asked.

"My guard. When I'm not an assassin, I'm a lady in a noble household, as Master Arzil already knows," Selene said.

Master Arzil. She was his apprentice. A fuzzy feeling poured through Draven's head. If she knew his real identity, she wouldn't hesitate to gut him.

"My parents have hired a guard to protect me when I go out at night and to bring me back home. He must have just followed me," she continued.

"And now he knows you're an assassin," the woman said, pressing the dagger more firmly against his neck. "It's imperative that we kill him and let this knowledge die with him. Perhaps we can use Evanescence and dispose of the evidence."

Evanescence? Draven shoved down a shudder. When the fuchsia-tipped flower was liquified, it could be injected into the victim through a syringe. It ensured a slow, torturous death as it disintegrated the victim's body like acid, leaving a mangled, unidentifiable corpse behind.

Selene grasped the woman's arm. "No. There's another way."

Draven wasn't certain if he should be relieved or worried.

"What are you proposing?" the woman asked.

"Manasseh," Selene said.

Manasseh. A drug.

As an apprentice to the man known as the "Master of Poisons," Draven was quite familiar with the rare substance. Only a drop would render someone unconscious—and make them forget everything that had happened an hour prior. It's one weakness was that it didn't work on those with human blood. Unfortunately, he had no human blood to speak of.

However, he did have antidotes hidden in his cloak.

"I can assure you," Selene continued, "that if you torment him, capture him, or kill him, it will be noticed by my family. The only way to truly ensure that we don't arouse any suspicion is by erasing his memory and returning him to my home."

"But by then, the guards will have been changed out," the man said. "We'll have lost our opportunity to scout for a secret passage."

"Then we'll have to do it another night," Selene said. "We don't really have an option at this point. If we let him go, he'll report us. If we hurt or kill him, someone will notice and look into it. The passage can wait a day. Dealing with him cannot."

The woman nodded. "Her reasoning makes sense." She repositioned the dagger at Draven's neck. "Now, open your mouth and take whatever she gives you."

8

HER CAPTIVE

Draven's foot shot out, kicking the dagger from the woman's hand. Before the others could react, he was taking off down the alley. Likely, they would capture him again. But that was all right. He tucked his hand into his pocket, withdrew the pill, and popped it into his mouth, using his tongue to tuck it against his cheek.

A moment later, they hauled him backward and slammed him against the ground. A slight figure landed on top of him, straddling him with an astonishing amount of strength.

"I have him." To his surprise, it was Selene's voice that rang out.

He looked up at her. "Selene, please don't do this. There's always another way. Let me help you escape the Scorpio."

Selene shook her head. "It's too late for that, Raban. I'm truly sorry."

The other assassins caught up, and a blade was once more pressed against his neck. "Open your mouth or I'll slit your throat," the woman said.

It was a rather cliché threat, but Draven refrained from saying so. Instead, he opened his mouth wide. Selene uncorked a vial and let it hover above his mouth as she tilted it. A single drop dangled from the edge of the glass before falling into his mouth.

Raban went limp instantly.

She looked down at him. He appeared younger when he slept. Though he couldn't hear her, she murmured, "I'm sorry," low enough that the assassins wouldn't hear, and lifted herself off of him.

Mace drew his leg back and delivered a blow to Raban's side, catching him right in the ribs. When Raban remained still, he said, "It really did work."

Selene grabbed Mace's arm and yanked him backward. "What are you doing? If he wakes up with a bruise or broken ribs, he'll become suspicious and realize that his memory was erased."

Lyra knelt next to Raban, tugging up the hem of his shirt. There was a red mark where Mace had kicked him. She gently prodded his side. "It doesn't feel broken, but he'll likely have a bruise," Lyra said, tugging his shirt back down.

Perhaps Lyra would have made a better healer than an assassin.

Mace narrowed his eyes at Selene. "I'm beginning to think you're truly concerned for this guard."

"Not at all. I just want to ensure that we won't be caught. Now, help me take him back to the house." If they were carrying Raban, it would likely take them between an hour and a half-hour to reach it.

They found a broad plank of wood to set him on. Selene positioned herself in front, carrying the edge of the board by his head. Imalda took up the left side, Mace the right, and Lyra walked ahead of them, scanning the alleyways.

They hauled him back to the house unseen, careful to go down a different alleyway whenever they heard the sound of people up ahead.

Mace said, "When will we meet again to scout out the Taijese palace?

"Tomorrow night," Imalda replied. "We need to begin as soon as possible, kill Draven before he kills us."

Selene shook her head. "I don't think I'll be able to make it tomorrow night. Perhaps the next night." She needed to find a fool-proof way to escape Raban—and for that, she needed time.

Imalda arched her eyebrows at Selene. "Are you antici-pating trouble shaking your guard off your tail, Selene? Why not just dispatch him, here and now? He won't feel anything."

"No," Selene said. "This is my mission, and Arzil has assigned me as the leader. If either of you doubt me, you're welcome to take your concerns to Arzil."

At that, both of them fell silent. Until something moved in an alleyway.

Mace stopped walking. "What's that? Perhaps we have another stalker?"

"I'll go check." Imalda drew out a dagger; using that weapon was her first response to everything. As Imalda began to loosen her grip, the board wobbled.

"No," Selene said. "If you let go, he'll fall."

"Then we'll put him down. After all, we wouldn't want to hurt your precious guard." Before Selene could contradict her, Imalda began lowering her side of the board.

Something black shot out of the alley, whizzing between Imalda's legs. She squeaked and lost her grip on the board.

Selene darted forward, just in time to cushion Raban's body with hers. He was heavy, built as solidly as a brick. The feel of his weight pinning her to the ground made bile singe the back of her throat. If she vomited, it'd be all over herself and him—

not to mention in full view of her colleagues. She began to shove at his chest, trying to lift him off of her as Imalda continued to squeal, hopping from foot to foot.

"Did you see that?" Imalda said, continuing to whirl around, her dagger extended.

She bumped into Raban, and Selene's arms collapsed, letting Raban flop forward onto her once more. Nausea swirled in her stomach, her fingertips and toes tingling. She was *not* going to pass out like this. She was preparing to ask Mace for help when Raban's eyes flickered, then opened. For a breathless moment, they fixed on her. Then they closed.

He was awake. He was *awake* and pretending to be unconscious. He'd just heard everything they'd said.

Selene's breath froze in her lungs, panic washing over her. Every curse word that she'd ever heard flitted through her mind.

He. Was. Awake.

Tuteno. He knew everything. He'd report her once he had the opportunity. She was a very dead woman unless she could come up with a plan—fast.

Mace gripped Raban's arms and hauled him backward. Even though he was off of her, uneasiness swirled in her stomach. He knew everything. Mace let Raban fall limply onto the alleyway, his head bouncing on the ground.

Selene flinched. To think he'd been awake when Mace had kicked him. "*Careful.*"

Mace snorted. "I believe the response you're looking for is 'thank you.' I doubt you would have been able to lift him yourself."

Lyra extended her hand to Selene and pulled her to her feet. Selene couldn't pry her gaze from Raban. He must have had a rare immunity to Manasseh. She ran the last few lines of their conversation through her head. He knew that she was supposed to kill someone named Draven and that she was an apprentice to Arzil. And he already knew who that was, though he'd called him M'rithun at first.

Sweat beaded along her hairline, and her clothes suddenly felt suffocating. How was she going to get out of this? She just had to make sure that they didn't talk about something else incriminating.

Mace nudged Raban's side with his foot. "If you can't even kill this skimmer, it makes me wonder how you'll manage to kill the King."

The blood rushed from her face, her head going light. And now Raban knew she was plotting to kill the King. Wonderful. Should she continue to pretend he was unconscious, so the other assassins wouldn't kill him? Or perhaps they should bring him to Arzil. The sooner she let Raban go free, the sooner she'd meet her death.

"What's the matter, Selene? Does thinking about killing someone make you a bit woozy?" Mace asked. "Have you even had your first kill yet? Or are you as inexperienced as your apprentice?"

Lyra folded her arms, shooting Mace a glare. "Everyone in the Scorpio knows she has more kills than *you*. That's why Arzil made her the leader of this mission."

Tuteno. Raban would hate her now, knowing the darkness that tainted her soul. She should tell Mace that Raban was awake, let Mace finish him off. But she couldn't stomach the idea. She could kill, but murdering Raban would be different.

Selene withdrew a slim rope from her belt and began to fasten Raban's wrists. With the other assassins around, Raban wouldn't dare resist her and reveal that he was awake.

"What are you doing?" Mace asked. "He's asleep."

"Just a precaution, in case he wakes up early."

Mace nodded and withdrew his own rope to fasten Raban's ankles. Lyra parted his hair and pressed her fingers against his scalp, likely seeing how hard his head had hit the ground.

Imalda approached them. "Did you see how fast that skimming cat was?"

"Yes—and we saw how you panicked," Mace said. "I'm not sure any of you *girls* are best suited for the upcoming mission. I'll have to talk to Lord Arzil about getting replacements."

Selene felt heat pour into her face but she ignored the jab. What mattered most was keeping Raban alive and ensuring that he didn't have her arrested. They rolled him back onto the board and lifted him, heading toward her home. They stopped at the edge of the alley. A broad stone street separated them from her house. A nearby stable caught Selene's eye, and suddenly, she knew what she'd do with Raban.

"You can stop here," Selene said. "I'll take him the rest of the way."

Imalda and Mace lowered him to the ground.

"We'll meet the night after tomorrow?" Imalda asked. "And in the same place?"

"An excellent idea," Selene said. When she turned back toward them, they'd both vanished. Selene suppressed an eye roll. A rather dramatic exit.

Lyra was in the same spot. "Do you need help, Selene? Or someone to cover your back?"

Selene shook her head. "I'm nearly to the house, Lyra. I can take him from here." She thought about setting her hand on Lyra's shoulder but feared that the physical contact would make her uneasy. "You've done well tonight, but in the future, please don't ask to accompany us on a mission."

Lyra's face sagged in disappointment. "But I thought you said that I did well."

Selene's chest constricted. She remembered being like her, so desperate for affection and approval. "You did, but as you can see, things don't always go according to plan. I don't want you to be caught in the crossfire."

Lyra's jaw firmed. "How am I going to become an experienced assassin if I never take that risk?"

Perhaps Lyra shouldn't become an experienced assassin. Though it paid well, it wasn't worth the secrecy, the nightmares, the sense of guilt, and being trapped in the Scorpio. Once Arzil realized Lyra's value, she'd never be allowed to leave. But Selene kept her lips seamed. She couldn't risk Lyra reporting her if she voiced traitorous ideas.

"Lyra, on this mission, I don't want you involved. Understood?"

Lyra's struggle was visible in her expression, until her chin dipped down to her chest. "So long as you spar with me after you've finished this mission."

Not possible, since she'd be leaving soon. But if it would keep Lyra out of danger... "Of course."

Lyra bowed and strode away, disappearing around the corner of a building.

A prickling sensation cascaded down Selene's body, and she whipped around, preparing to see... someone. Raban was still there. Perhaps he'd opened his eyes and she'd sensed his stare.

Selene dropped her pack, withdrew her commoner dress, and pulled it over her assassin clothes. She hoped Lyra would understand, one day, that Selene had only been trying to protect her. She picked up the edge of the board and dragged Raban to a nearby stable, pushing him just out of view. She rapped on the stable door, and a boy opened it.

The stable smelled of fresh hay and horses. Wooden beams ran overhead to support the triangular ceiling, and a broad walkway connected the stables, out of which peered curious horses—and even a unicorn.

Selene batted her eyelashes at the boy. "Greetings, good sir."

He drew himself a bit taller. "Greetings."

"Me and my beau need somewhere to stay for the next few

hours." She withdrew a few coins and extended them to him. "If you could clear the stable, it would be much appreciated."

He nodded. "I could do that. But if someone wanted to enter the stable, I couldn't stop them."

"That's all right. Just... make a bird call if someone is about to come in. That will be my signal to leave."

At his nod, she dropped the coins into his palm. Once he'd left, Selene returned to Raban. He was tugging at the rope binding his ankles, though he froze when he saw Selene, a hard glint in his eyes.

Selene pulled out her dagger. "Stand slowly and walk into the stables."

"With my ankles bound, I can hardly walk."

"Nice try, but I'm not about to untie them, so you'd best figure it out."

Raban scowled at her. He'd never looked at her with such darkness in his eyes until now. Before, they'd been adversaries; now they were enemies. He slowly rose to his feet before taking a short series of hops into the stables. She followed him, closing and locking the door behind them.

The stable had two exits, the second being a door on the other end, which presumably connected to a house or another building. Potential weapons abounded: nails, pitchforks, reins, lead ropes, and hoof knives.

She gestured with her dagger to an empty stall. "Get in."

He hopped inside before turning back to her. "Now what? Do you intend to keep me here or torment me until I promise not to say anything?"

She walked into the stall after him and closed the gate behind her, latching it into place. "Of course not—or I wouldn't be shoving you into a stable, now would I?"

He leaned back against the wall. "Then what do you intend to do with me?"

"You'll see."

The first step was to find out how much he knew. Had he been following her the entire way? Did he know where the Scorpio base was? If he reported the location to the authorities, the Empress would send her samurai to slaughter all the assassins at the base, young and old. Lyra's youthful face came to mind, and Selene's stomach knotted. Perhaps she could be at peace with Arzil dying, but not Lyra. The girl trusted her, and Selene wasn't about to feed her to the wolves.

"What did you hear?" she asked.

"Nothing of importance." When she squinted at him, he smirked and continued, "Aside from the fact that you're a Scorpio assassin, Arzil is your master, you're plotting to kill the King—and someone named Draven." He arched his eyebrows. "Which makes me curious: what did this Draven character do to warrant being killed?"

Murdering her mother, the only person who'd remotely cared about her. And he'd used Evanescence to do it. It was hard to conceive of a more painful end than dying by Evanescence. "I haven't killed him yet. And that's none of your business." She kept her dagger raised and a few scevola of distance between them.

"Are you afraid of me, Selene?" Raban took a single hop toward her.

His approach was simultaneously amusing and threatening. "Remain where you are."

Raban stopped his advance. "You have quite the dilemma, don't you?"

She tightened her grip on the dagger.

"On one hand, you don't want to kill me, but on the other, you fear what I'll do with the information I know."

"You do know quite a lot. Did you see where the Scorpio base was hidden?"

"Perhaps."

"If you want to live, you'd best prove to me that you won't

speak of this to anyone. Perhaps I can keep you locked up somewhere until this all settles down."

"You mean until the *King* dies." Determination sparked in his eyes.

"Well. Yes." Judging from that look, there was no way she could persuade him to voluntarily agree to keep the Scorpio's plot to kill the King a secret. But if she enlightened him about what the King was really like, how he'd allowed Draven to kill her mother, perhaps he'd understand.

"I think you'd be pleased to know that I also have a dilemma," Raban said.

"And what's that?"

"I don't want to see you killed or arrested. But I can't let the King be murdered either."

"Why are you so loyal to him?" she asked. "Not only has he made some rather foolish decisions, but there are many laws he's promised to change—laws he hasn't even mentioned to the Council. He's a terrible King. And he let Draven…"

"He let Draven what?"

"He let Draven go, enabling him to—to kill my mother."

Raban's eyes grew round. "K-kill your mother?"

As a common city guard, he likely wasn't used to dealing with murders. "Yes."

Raban fell silent for a moment, apparently still reeling from shock. "You're certain?"

"She was definitely killed. She—"

"No, not that she was killed. That *Draven* was the one to kill her."

"Most definitely."

"So you saw this Draven character kill her?"

"No. But Arzil said they found her remains after Draven used Evanescence on her." Selene's throat grew tight. "He said that she was so… so mangled that they didn't bother bringing her body back; they just threw her into the Lei River." She breathed deeply. "I know that I'm an assassin, and I've killed people... many, many people. But she was my mother. And the least he could have done was end her life mercifully."

Raban seemed to struggle for words before finally saying, "Selene. I am so, so sorry that happened. From what little I've heard about Arzil, he doesn't seem to be the most trustworthy. You're certain he's telling the truth?"

"Of course. What reason would he have to lie?"

Raban's lips thinned. "Many reasons—none of them good. And why would Draven kill your mother? And in such a cruel manner, nonetheless. What could he have against her?"

"She was a Scorpio—the third most highly ranked after the destruction of the Octavian Scorpio base. Of course he wanted to kill her. After she died, I received her rank."

"If Arzil is in command, and you're third, then who's the Scorpio's second?"

Perhaps he just asked out of curiosity, but Selene wasn't about to reveal anything about Serpent. It was imperative that as few people knew about him as possible. "Raban, the more you know, the more likely it is that I'll have to detain or kill you. As I was saying, Draven is now hunting down the remaining Scorpio members, dragging them before the Empress so that she can slaughter them."

A war raged across Raban's face before his expression settled into one of resignation. "I don't suppose I know enough about the situation to convince you one way or the other."

"No. You don't. Now tell me, do you truly know where the Scorpio base is?"

Raban shrugged in response.

"Then you leave me no choice." Selene unbuttoned a small compartment on her belt and withdrew a vial of clear liquid. She neared him, dagger extended.

He eyed the vial. "Truth serum."

He seemed to know his way around drugs. "Yes. Take it

peacefully, and I won't have cause to hurt you."

He snorted. "As if you would."

Selene stopped before him. "Raban. The Scorpio are my *family*. I like you, but I love them, and I will do what's necessary to protect them."

Compassion softened his gaze. Or perhaps she was mistaken. "I understand. But I can't just allow you to have access to all my secrets."

Which meant that this wouldn't be accomplished easily. Selene lunged forward, knocking him to the ground.

Raban was quick to roll over, pinning her beneath him. Tuteno, he was fast. The warmth of his body against hers made her stomach heave. She clenched her mouth shut, praying the nausea would subside.

Raban flinched. "I'm sorry, Selene."

A weakness. One she had to exploit if she had any hope of making him take the truth serum. She closed her eyes, letting her breath come hard and fast. "J-just please get off of me. *Please*, Raban. Every time someone touches me, I can feel Shonn's hands on me, hurting me."

"Selene..." His voice was steeped in concern and pity. Perfect. "I'm not going to hurt you, and I don't want to remind you of Shonn. But I can't just let you go." Even so, he lifted himself off of her.

She knocked him flat on his back in an instant and shoved the end of the vial between his lips.

When he coughed and spluttered, she removed the vial and stood back. He spat onto the hay, but they both knew it was too late. It didn't take much serum to have an effect.

He narrowed his eyes at her. "I hate you."

She was almost hurt—until she sensed that there was no heat behind his words. The truth serum should be taking ahold of him now. Perhaps it was time to test her first question. "*Do you hate me?*"

9

SHONN'S ASSASSIN

"No, of course not. I-I care about you. Far more than I should," Draven unwillingly answered Selene's question. Heat poured into his face, so hot it felt like he was being burnt. Hang her. He hadn't wanted to answer that question truthfully.

He didn't miss the smile that flickered across Selene's lips before she smoothed them back into a straight line. She took a step nearer. "I see. And what do you know about the Scorpio base?"

"Only that it's somewhere within Renshi. I was unable to follow you to the base, and I don't know it's exact location." The truth streamed from his lips without his consent. He had an antidote for truth serum, but bound as he was, he hadn't been able to access it.

Selene sighed, relief softening her tense expression. "Excellent."

"You're truly worried about risking the lives of the other assassins, aren't you?"

"Yes. But I don't expect you to understand that. Not all assassins are cold-blooded and heartless."

But he did understand, more than she knew. "This doesn't

have to be your path, Selene. You don't have to be a part of the Scorpio or kill the King."

"Yes, I do." She drew closer. "It's the only way that I'll truly be free to make my own decisions."

She thought that killing the King would set her free? What kind of twisted logic was that? Pain knotted in his chest. He hoped she wasn't too far gone; he still wanted to change her as he'd been changed. "How will killing the King give you freedom?"

The shutters in her eyes slammed close. "It doesn't matter."

"I could help you, Selene. I can give you protection. I have allies."

She arched her eyebrows. Even though her figure and features lacked feminine grace, her eyebrows were slender. "Allies more powerful than the *Scorpio*? Like who? The Empress? The Queen and King of Torva?" Before the serum could prompt him to answer, she laughed and said, "I don't think so."

Revealing who his allies were would bring about questions, ultimately revealing who he was. And if Selene found out that he was Draven, she'd kill him. "Selene, if you leave the Scorpio, I won't report you—and I'll do what I can to protect you from Arzil's wrath."

Selene shrugged. "If you don't report me, then I won't kill you. It seems like it's in your best interest to stay quiet."

Out of the corner of his eye, he studied the position of her legs. She'd drawn nearer than she'd realized. "You're in no position to kill me, my dear."

"I'm a highly-trained assassin, and you're on the floor of a stable, tied up, completely at my mercy. I have one more question: how were you immune to the Mana—"

He swept his bound legs across the floor, hitting her ankles so hard that her feet flew out from under her. She fell back, slamming her head against the stable door. He inwardly flinched but didn't let that stop him from lunging toward her and falling on top of her, pinning her to the ground.

That had been close. Had she completed her question, she would have discovered a vital clue about who he was.

She blinked hard, staring blankly up at the ceiling, and Draven's heart lurched. Could the fall have given her a concussion?

"Selene," he asked, "are you all right?"

She blinked once more, focusing on him. He suppressed a sigh of relief. Their noses were a hair's breadth from touching, and he took a moment to study her face, the subtle knot in her nose, her thin lips, pressed tightly together. Her lashes were short and surprisingly thick, casting her already dark eyes in shadow. Her hair splayed across the hay, its silky black length contrasting with the coarse golden material. Upon first seeing her, he'd thought her plain, but the more he saw her, the more he'd realized there was a prettiness about her.

Her eyes grew hard and fierce, like flint that only needed the strike of steel to create flames. "What do *you* care?"

Bitterness saturated her tone. He felt a pinch of guilt for tricking her, but it wasn't any worse than she'd done. "You know that I *do* care; I just admitted it. I don't want to report you, Selene, but I will in order to save innocent lives."

Her eyes fluttered close, and her chest heaved beneath him.

Sympathy washed over him, but he didn't dare remove himself from her. "You remind me far too much of myself. I can help you leave the Scorpio, Selene. I know it won't be easy, but it's possible."

A slight smile graced her pale face. "If you think it's possible, then you've obviously never had to leave the Scorpio."

Though the serum only worked on questions, he still desperately wanted to tell her the truth. But to do so would mean losing her trust completely. She thought that he'd killed her mother, and there was no way that his testimony would have more weight with her than Arzil's would. "Don't return to the Scorpio. Don't come in contact with Arzil again. If they do contact you, tell me. I know you don't believe me right now, but trust me, I *will* protect you."

A frown flickered across her forehead, but she kept her eyes closed. "I have my own plans to escape the Scorpio. I know from experience that this is the only method that will work, Raban."

"What are your plans?"

She paused, then said, "The money I'll get from killing the King will give me enough coin to pay this bounty hunter. He's the only one who's been able to smuggle Scorpio to other countries."

"There's another way to escape the Scorpio, Selene. Go to the King and appeal for his protection."

Selene laughed, the sound weakened by the nausea she was obviously battling. "As if he'd trust a Scorpio assassin."

She'd be surprised. "I'll be with you, Selene. He'll trust my word. And even if you don't trust the King's mercy, trust me, Selene. Haven't I proved that I'll protect you?"

The furrow between her brows deepened. She opened her eyes, and for once, the curtains weren't drawn. "Yes, you have."

"Then you'll try to leave the Scorpio?"

She nodded slowly. "But if something goes awry, if the King decides to kill me instead, then I make no promises about what I will or won't do to defend my life and freedom."

That wouldn't happen. But if it did, he'd take care of her. "Fair enough. So you agree?"

She nodded.

He tried to conceal his excitement. Once she realized he was capable of protecting her, that the King would pardon her, she'd have no need to return to the Scorpio. Finally, he was able to do some good. "Excellent. As part of our bargain, could you also untie me?" Draven lifted his bound wrists.

"Only if you get off of me."

"Right. Sorry." He rolled off of her.

She sat up, considered him for a long moment. "I can't believe you've persuaded me to agree to this." She shook her head, running her hand through her thoroughly mussed, straw-filled hair. "I'm a dead woman."

"No. You're not. You'll be fine."

"I suppose we'll see."

She withdrew a dagger, and Draven's eye caught on the emeralds in its hilt. It was almost gaudy in comparison with Selene's usual sense of style.

"Is that your mother's?" he asked.

She sobered slightly, nodding. "She never actually gave it to me. I just took it after she died." She began to saw at the rope binding his wrists.

"I'm sure she'd want you to have it."

Selene shrugged.

"You don't think so?"

"I don't know." The last strand of rope snapped, and Selene brushed the broken pieces aside, freeing his hands. She started on his ankles. "She wasn't a very sentimental person."

Had her mother not cared for her either? He hoped that wasn't the case. "Yet you obviously cared for her very much."

"I suppose. She was the only person I had, and I was hoping that, as I rose through the ranks, she'd be proud of me. That she'd... love me back." A blush stormed across her pretty features and she sawed more vigorously at the ropes.

"And you were angry that Draven stole that opportunity." Or Arzil. That was the likeliest option. Heat built inside his chest. Arzil would pay for what he'd done—for killing her mother and lying about it.

Selene nodded, and the last rope broke. Draven rose and offered his hand.

When she eyed it skeptically, he remembered her distaste of

touch and almost withdrew it. But he let it hover in the air: there for her to take or refuse.

She finally placed her hand in his, and Draven pulled her to her feet, basking in the warm glow of triumph. "I suppose you should change back into your lady's dress before returning to your home."

Selene nodded. "Smart thinking."

Together, they walked out of the stable in a drastically different fashion than they'd entered. Draven fell in a step behind her and allowed himself a smile. Selene was on a new path now, one of hope instead of destruction.

Selene slid her door shut after bidding Raban goodnight. Her eyes were dry as dirt and her mind was buzzing. She pressed her back against the door.

Raban was a fool. A noble, kind-hearted fool.

He didn't truly think that he could change her allegiance in a five-minute chat, did he? And though he appeared confident, she knew for a fact that he couldn't help her. No one could but herself. And she wasn't going to be truly free until there was no one trying to control her.

A part of her wished that she were naïve enough to believe Raban's hope-infused promises. She could change sides, focus on rebuilding her life instead of destroying others'. The King would pardon her and reward her richly for her service to him, and Raban would be happy that he'd changed her immoral ways. They could save Lyra and deliver her to a family that would adopt and love her.

Of course, that was ignoring the fact that the King would likely execute her or sentence her to life imprisonment for her crimes. But more likely, Arzil would kill her before the King had that opportunity. Yes, Raban had concocted nothing more than a grand fairytale she doubted anyone aside from himself would believe.

Selene performed a routine scan of her room, searching for abnormalities. On the right side of the room, cushions were scattered around a little table, little plates and teacups were placed in front of each cushion, and a teapot crowned the table's center. She'd used it as a little girl, before her mother had taught her how to be an assassin. There was her wardrobe, rather small for a noblewoman's.

Her bed was flush against the window in the back. She'd insisted on the arrangement, preferring to be closer to an escape route in case Shonn ever—

She didn't bother finishing the thought. Best she not.

Her search ended on her desk, its wooden surface carved into an image of a whimsical forest. A slip of white placed on it caught her eye.

Selene plucked the folded piece of paper up. A note. A wave of cold crashed over her. Could Arzil have seen her and Raban leaving the stable together? Or one of the other assassins? She unfolded the note.

Dear Lady Selene,

It only took a bit of searching to find out who you were. And for your sake, I'm glad I did. I've come to warn you about your guard. He has a past that you might be unaware of. Meet me at the Yare Wolf's Serenade the evening of Cedembre the twenty-sixth.

And though I hate to ask, please bring 20 aurum of coin in return for the information. I'm desperate for money, and the man who led to my financial ruin was your guard. I look forward to seeing you there.

-Faina

Faina. Financial ruin? Could that have been the streetsweeper? The woman who'd stared so strangely at Raban when they were walking back from the Maroon Maidens? Normally, Selene would have dismissed such a note, but given Raban's strange reaction, meeting this woman might be worth her while. What dark secrets could Raban be hiding beneath his honorable exterior? If she found blackmail that she could use against him, perhaps she could use that to ensure that he never reported her.

Guilt knotted beneath her chest, and unease sloshed in her stomach. Raban had been so kind to her, and she was preparing to unveil information that she could use as blackmail. Selene strode to her bed and fell back into its embrace, not bothering to remove her dress. This really wasn't her choice, nor her fault. As usual, she was simply taking the only option presented to her.

If she left the Scorpio early, she wouldn't have enough coin to escape.

If Raban found out she still planned to be an assassin, he'd report her.

If he reported her, she'd die or be imprisoned.

If she found blackmail against Raban, he wouldn't report her.

Selene fisted her hand, crumpling the note, and shoved it beneath her mattress. She stared at her bed for a moment, dreading sleep. She kicked off her shoes and tugged her blanket to her chin. As she drifted from consciousness, the memories closed in around her.

Selene inhaled deeply, only to spew out the blood-scented air in a cough. Some of her kills would have been clean, but this one had been amateurishly sloppy. On her first few missions with Arzil, he'd stand back as she assassinated the victim and then carefully critique everything she did.

She could imagine him in the room now, pinpointing her mistakes with a sharp eye. Her first mistake: She should have tested the floor before choosing her hiding place. Then she would've avoided making the floorboards creak when she'd approached.

That led to her second mistake: The noise had given the man enough time to rise to his feet, knocking back his chair. Thankfully it had fallen onto the thick wool carpet, muffling the sound.

Her third mistake: When she'd gone in for the kill, the man had stared at her with wide eyes and breathed three words, "But my daughter..." She'd seen a mural of his daughter on the wall, with her gap-toothed smile and pink cheeks. His words had thrown her off, and she'd stabbed the side of his neck instead of in between his vertebrae. The man had panicked and leaned back against his desk as he tried to stop the bleeding.

Her fourth mistake: When his body collapsed to the floor, she'd been too stunned to let it down gently, soundlessly. It had thudded against the carpet without her aid, the soft wool fabric lapping up his blood.

With her hands shaking, she'd finally managed to stab between the vertebrae, and he'd gone still instantly. Though he'd suffered for only a few seconds, to him it must have seemed an eternity.

Sloppy, sloppy, sloppy. Most of her victims hadn't even realized they'd been attacked. Death was instant, painless. But not this one.

Selene studied the mural again, and the little girl seemed to be staring back at her. Mere hours ago, her eyes had seemed to shine with glee and sunlight. But perhaps they were shining bright and glossy with tears.

But my daughter...

But his daughter needed him.

But his daughter would wake up the next morning without a father.

But his daughter would be an orphan.

Selene fled, bile singeing the back of her throat, blood

burning her hands. She rode her horse hard and fast back to the city. Found a narrow alley and dry-heaved. Stared at the blood drying on her palms for hours. If she went back to Arzil and refused another mission, she'd be killed. Death seemed to be her only means of escape, but there was nothing she feared more.

She washed her hands in the river and made her report to Arzil that night only to walk home with images of her victim's daughter dancing in her mind. Occassionally, the phantom pitter-pattering of little feet caused her to check over her shoulder. The longer she walked, the slower her pace became. The tiny footsteps tapped closer, until a petite hand wrapped around her wrist. Before Selene could turn back, someone yelled:

"I demand that you step aside!"

Selene startled awake, bolting upright. A sheet of hair flopped over her face, and she shoved it behind her ear. A quick glance outside the window revealed that the sun had yet to rise. It must be early morning. And judging from the pulsing pain in her head, she hadn't slept nearly long enough.

Old memories made inescapable nightmares.

She pressed a hand to her vibrating heart, trying to ignore the chill washing over her.

The person outside her door continued, "If you don't step aside, you'll be stripped of your position in this house and tossed into the streets." *Shonn.*

Raban's reply was a low, deep murmur, the tone significantly cooler.

Shonn was outside her door.

The sheets rustled as Selene yanked them back and rose. She strode to the door, unlocked it, and opened it. Both men had their focus locked on each other, though they glanced at her when she approached.

"Shonn. Guard Raban. Is everything all right?" she asked.

Shonn began to step toward her, but Raban blocked him. "Selene. Tell your guard to stand down."

"Do you require something, Shonn?" she asked.

"Yes. I would speak with you."

Was he manipulating her or telling the truth?

"May I come in?" he asked.

The skin on her arms prickled, her muscles going stiffer than ice. The last thing she wanted was to stir up bad memories or freeze in front of him alone. And after her nightmare, she feared she'd be more likely to lose control than normal. She barely suppressed a shudder.

"Have a good day, Shonn."

Selene went back into her room. She was stronger than she used to be, but she wasn't about to test that strength unnecessarily.

Though the door muffled Shonn's voice, his tone exuded anger. Raban's replies remained low and even, but the steel in his voice reinforced them.

Hearing their argument put her on edge. She exchanged her clothes for a nightgown and collapsed back into bed, covering her ears with her pillow.

When she emerged a few hours later, Raban held out a note for her.

Arzil? Already? She took it slowly, without making eye contact.

"Shonn handed it to me when I refused to allow him entry into your room," he said.

The dread within morphed from a dark, slimy feeling in her chest into a cold, hard knot. "Thank you." She retreated back into her room and opened up the note.

Selene,

Or should I address this to a "loyal servant of the Scorpio?"

The coldness within her unfurled, spreading to her fingertips. Tuteno. He knew she was an assassin. But how? She quickly eliminated the possibility that Raban had told him—that would never happen. And for all Raban knew, she was no longer a part of the Scorpio. It continued:

I've hired a spy to follow you for quite some time now.

All those times she'd felt like she was being watched—she'd assumed it was Raban.

I've always suspected that there's been more to your wanderings than you've revealed. Imagine my surprise—and intrigue—when my spy saw you wander into a small house and emerge with two others, all of you dressed as assassins. Now, I not only know that you're an assassin but also the location of the Scorpio base. I wonder how much the Empress of Taijeng would pay for such information.

I have yet to share this with anyone, but don't doubt that I will unless you do exactly as I say. And since you're an assassin, I might as well put you to good use. I have a mission for you.

10

BETRAYING RABAN'S TRUST

Selene stared at the note long after she'd finished reading it, wishing she could reduce Shonn's words to ash.

Tomorrow night, he wanted her to kill his uncle Tyrus, a man who'd refused to give Shonn and his mother aid after his father's death. She felt the tiniest smidgen of pity for Shonn. She'd never really thought of what it must have been like for him to lose his father.

Tyrus was a commoner in the middle-class district of Renshi. Killing him would be easy enough. But... did he truly deserve to die? Her typical targets were people who viewed commoners as animals and abused their servants.

Now she'd be killing a man who could be a loving husband, a loving father. Someone who had denied Shonn and his mother aid because perhaps he couldn't afford it.

But if she didn't follow through, Shonn would report her. Didn't leave her much of an option. She either had to face execution or complete Shonn's mission.

But if Raban knew about her mission to kill Shonn's uncle *he'd* report or arrest her.

Unless... she could convince Raban to "help" her.

Selene opened her bedroom door and glanced outside. It seemed Raban's shift had ended; another guard stood in his place. She considered leaving Raban alone, since he'd had a long night as well. But time was of the essence, and she needed his aid.

The guard smiled crookedly at her. "Got any more korosasth?"

"If you stay here, I'll owe you a bottle." She swept past him and padded down the stairs, to the third floor, where the servants lived.

She'd never actually visited Raban's quarters. In fact, she hadn't often wandered here at all. The hallway was narrow, tiny rooms crammed together to preserve space. Given that it was midday, the hallway was empty. The servants were likely up and cleaning the house or cooking their meals or helping haul bathwater for her stepmother.

A number marked each door. Which was Raban's? She didn't want to go knocking on random doors.

A servant girl emerged from her room, freezing when her gaze alighted upon Selene. "Lady Selene." She dipped into a deep curtsey.

Selene nodded. "Greetings. Do you know which door belongs to Guard Raban?"

The girl's eyes brightened with interest, but she said nothing, simply pointed out a room on the right side of the hallway.

"Thank you." Selene strode to his door and knocked.

No answer.

She used the side of her fist to bang harder.

The door swung back, revealing a very disheveled Raban. His green eyes flared in surprise, a stunning contrast with his darker skin. "*Selene*? I—I mean, *Lady* Selene?"

"May I come in?"

He grimaced and glanced back into his tiny room. "Wouldn't that be unseemly?"

"Just for a moment."

His brows plummeted, and he opened the door wider, stepping aside to admit her entrance.

She walked in, and he closed the door behind her. She had thought that Gushvin's room in the palace was small. This was a mousehole.

The entire place was barely wider than the door. Beneath a tiny square window sat an unmade bed with a chest underneath. The rumpled covers revealed Raban had just woken up. She stood occupying the only clear area of the small space.

A second scan revealed that the door behind her was the only escape route. In an emergency, searching the chest for weapons would take too long. The blanket could be used to choke an assailant and the pillow to smother him. Of course, her dagger would still make a better weapon.

"Selene? What's wrong? Has Shonn... Did he do something?"

She faced Raban. He still lingered by the door, as if preparing to charge outside and hunt down Shonn if she answered "yes."

She shook her head. "I read his note." She held the note out to him.

He took it from her, his jaw muscles tensing as he read it. "I see." He handed her the note back.

Selene pocketed it to later store in her desk's secret compartment.

"I would recommend that you turn yourself in right now, but..."

"But what?"

"I would trust the King with your life, but not the Empress. You've heard the rumors?"

"That she was driven crazy with grief after her husband died and the miscarriage?"

"Yes. They're true."

Suspicion niggled at the back of Selene's mind. "It sounds like you know the Empress personally."

"Oh. No. But I have friends who are Taijese palace guards."

That explained it.

"As I was saying, the King hasn't arrived yet." He strode past her and sank onto his bed. "What should we do?"

Selene leaned her hip against the wall. "Perhaps I could act as though I were truly going to kill the uncle, and we could make it look like you stopped me. I could tell Shonn that there's no way I can complete the mission he's given me as long as you're my guard."

"If you make it seem as though I'm the only reason that you can't kill the uncle, you think Shonn won't report you?"

"Right. If you stop me, then it's not *my* fault."

"It's mine," Raban replied. A smile teased his lips. "You're an excellent tactician. And I think we're an excellent team."

Selene returned his smile, feeling the tug of a connection between them. A warning blared in her head: *too close, too close.* She straightened. "Well, thank you for your time. And I apologize for disturbing your sleep."

He waved off her concerns with a swipe of his hand. "It's fine. I'm glad you did."

Selene stopped at the door. After yesterday, Arzil would expect a report tonight. She had to go to him without Raban suspecting anything. "And one more thing." Her fingers began to fidget with the cloth of her dress and she splayed them.

"What?"

"Tonight, I need to go scout the house, act as if I'm truly planning to kill the uncle. That way, Shonn's spy will see and report back to Shonn. If you're all right with it, perhaps you should remain here and pretend that you didn't 'notice' that I snuck out." And while she was out, perhaps she could make some other stops.

Raban nodded. "And then I'll 'catch' you tomorrow night."

"Precisely."

Raban released a sharp sigh. "But if I'm not guarding you tonight—"

"I'll be safe. I've gone out plenty of nights on my own, believe it or not."

Raban's expression grew tense. "If something happens to you—"

"I'll be fine." Selene stretched her lips into a smile. She desperately hoped he didn't decide to follow her anyway. If he saw her enter the Scorpio base, she was sunk. "Trust me, Raban."

Raban nodded slowly. "All right. I don't suppose you'll be able to wish me 'goodnight' before you leave, will you?"

Her heart beat out a strange rhythm. "It's best that I not speak to you right before I leave, in case the spy sees and becomes suspicious. But I'll find a way." She opened the door. "Sleep well, Raban."

"Stay safe tonight."

Selene's room had gone silent.

Draven fisted his hands, everything inside him telling him to track her down and follow her. What if something happened to her? Or she was cornered in an alley again? Or someone touched her or pinned her to the ground?

But she'd said to trust her. And he would. After all, she'd put an enormous amount of trust in him to agree to turn herself over to Alaric when he arrived. Doubt tugged at the back of his mind.

What if... what if she'd lied to him? What if she had no intentions of turning herself over to Alaric? What if she still intended to be an assassin? But if that was the case, she wouldn't have brought up Shonn's attempt to coerce her into murdering his uncle. She wouldn't have sought out Draven's help at all.

He glanced down at his feet, his eye catching on a white slip next to Selene's door. It hadn't been there when he'd begun his shift.

Draven picked it up. It read, "goodnight" in a flowing, feminine script. Thankfully no one was around to see him grin while he pocketed the note.

Could he be developing romantic feelings for her? His smile evaporated. Surely not. He just liked her, as a colleague and friend. And sometimes, when she blushed or gave him a certain look or flashed him a smile, he might think she was beautiful, but so would any other man. They were on the same side now, so it made sense for him to feel a connection to her.

He fingered the edge of the note, permitting himself a small smile. It wasn't easy, but he could trust her to be by herself for one night.

Selene finished writing down the last detail about Tyrus' house and reviewed her list.

Two-story house.

Six windows on first floor, two on second.

First story appears to be a living room, kitchen, and carpentry shop in the back.

Second story appears to be bedrooms and washroom.

Beneath that was a small diagram, with different symbols to indicate windows, doors, and stairs.

Selene scanned the area. Though she felt a chill snake up her spine, she didn't see anyone. But she had a hunch Shonn's spy was there.

How was she going to report to Arzil with the spy watching? On second thought, perhaps it didn't matter. Shonn already knew she was a part of the Scorpio—he had no idea that she'd made an agreement with Raban to "leave" the Scorpio. In addition, the spy already knew where the Scorpio base was. As long as she could convince Shonn of her act tomorrow night, he wouldn't report her or the location of the Scorpio base.

Selene removed a rope from her belt, swung the grappling hook over her head, and tossed it over the lip of a roof above. Her arms were burning lightly by the time she reached the top. She hauled herself onto the building and leapt from rooftop to rooftop until she neared the Scorpio base.

After scanning the area, she climbed down the building and snuck into the "abandoned" house. She slid the false bookshelf open, then raced down the rough-hewn spiraled stairs and through a long passageway.

The passageway ended in the door to Arzil's study. The wooden door was perpetually damp from being in the cold tunnel. The handle hadn't been polished in decades, leaving it as dull as the wood.

Selene knocked.

"Enter."

She opened the door. Arzil sat like a king in his grand armchair, its back stretching outward and upward to frame his pale figure. A low table stood in front of him, a map of Taijeng splayed across its surface.

Stubby white candles were placed at regular intervals around the circumference of the room. Their once smooth surfaces were knobby and warped with melted wax. Trophies and memories, hinting at Arzil's nostalgic bent, plastered the wall. There was a piece of burnt wood—a remnant from the Octavian Scorpio base. Selene didn't know what sentimental value the other tokens held: a string of golden beads, a wooden dagger, and a peacock masquerade mask.

Though there was only one visible exit—the door behind her—Selene knew Arzil well enough to suspect another somewhere within the room. No shortage of weapons within reach, either.

"Have you finished, my little raven?"

Arzil's expression was carefully blank, and an icy sliver of fear pierced her chest. "Yes, Master."

"And where are the potential escape routes? The weapons?" Arzil reclined in his chair, settling his right foot on his left knee.

"The door behind me is the only one I see, which makes me wonder where you're hiding the others. As always, there is a variety of weapons on the wall."

"Excellent job. You have yet to disappoint me... though I fear that will change soon."

Selene remained silent, waiting for more information.

"I was told that your guard interfered the other night. He was able to trail you all the way to the Taijese palace."

Selene nodded. "Yes. I should have noticed him sooner. We used the Manasseh on him, so he doesn't remember—"

"I know what happened, Selene. But even with his memory wiped, I wonder if he'll become an issue again, an issue that requires my attention."

If Raban was killed because of her, she'd never forgive herself.

"None of the guards your parents have hired for you over the years has ever presented a problem. Which makes me wonder, who is this new guard of yours?" Excitement flashed in Arzil's frosty blue eyes. Like her, he enjoyed a challenge. But where Selene liked the challenge of outrunning the hunter, Arzil preferred to be the hunter.

11

A WARNING

If Arzil made Raban his prey, Raban wouldn't stand a chance. And Selene wouldn't allow that to happen. Why not was a question she didn't dare examine too closely. She blanketed her nervousness with cold indifference. "The only thing I know of note about Raban is that he was a city guard."

"A city guard? I suspect more to the story. Do you truly not know anything else, my dear?" Arzil asked.

She shook her head. "I don't ask my guard about his past. We're at odds most of the time and aren't on speaking terms." The lie glided off her tongue.

"Should you find out any more about him, I'd like to hear of it. And if he interferes again, I won't hesitate to dispatch him myself—no matter how fond you are of him."

Only decades of training kept Selene from blushing to the roots of her hair. He made it sound as though... as though she were in love. Ridiculous. If she didn't trust Raban enough to let him touch her, how could she love him?

"Do I make myself clear, Selene?" Arzil leaned forward.

She bowed her head, as much a show of deference as a

means of escaping the icy grip of his eyes. "You always do, Master."

"Perhaps, as a show of loyalty, I should have you dispatch him yourself."

Disgust and fear descended on her like vultures on carrion, and a thousand urges assailed her at once: to swallow, to stiffen, to clench her jaw, to inhale sharply, to purse her lips, to frown, to narrow her eyes, to fist her hands. As she faced her master again, she tried to suppress what she could, but it was like trying to plug a ship made of rotting wood: something always leaked through.

A smirk spilled over Arzil's lips. "Should you betray me and run away like your friend Corsicanna, you'll find that you're more replaceable than you've realized."

Selene stilled, a shockwave rolling over her. "Corsicanna ran away?"

"Yes. Fled without warning or clue."

Why would Cori leave? That seemed so unlike her. Though Cori had never enjoyed her line of work, she'd often told Selene that it was her only option—a feeling Selene had always understood. Unless... she hadn't left. What if she'd been taken?

What if Cori's concern about the masked man had been a legitimate fear?

Concern Selene had brushed aside.

"You're dismissed, Selene. If your guard interferes again, I will know about it."

She left, only able to breathe once she shut the door behind her.

Cori was gone.

Chills washed over Selene's skin. Someone must have taken her. But why? To where? As trapped as she was in her own web of problems, how could Selene find her?

Perhaps some investigative work was in order. Since Cori had left no clues, Selene would start with discovering who had taken her friend. It was curious that Arzil didn't seem more concerned about Cori's disappearance, especially since Cori had spoken to Arzil about the cloaked man.

Selene strode back out of the Scorpio base, so numb she barely felt her boots hit the ground. Unless she did something differently, she was about to lose Raban *and* Cori, because she'd bet her life that Raban would interfere again, somehow. She hated that Arzil had gotten a rise out of her; she'd been trained better. It seemed she felt more strongly about Raban than she'd realized. But surely such feelings were harmless so long as she didn't act on them.

Her thoughts circled back to Cori. What if the masked man had killed her? What could Selene do then?

Vengeance came to mind. But the first step was to find out this man's identity and, if possible, hunt him down. Raban wasn't following her tonight. She'd take the opportunity to visit Onden, see if he knew anything about this masked man.

Selene quickened her pace, but Lyra materialized in front of her. They collided, and Selene barely caught herself against the stone wall.

"Lyra!"

Lyra popped up off the ground. "I am so, so sorry, Master."

"I'm not your—"

"One of the other apprenticelings told me you were here, and I wanted to see you. Since I haven't been able to accompany you on any more missions, I wanted to ensure that everything was going well."

Selene rubbed at the lines she could feel digging into her forehead. "Yes, everything's fine. I'm sorry for nearly running you over. Are you all right?"

"Of course." Lyra grinned. "And you probably already know what I'm going to ask."

Selene swallowed tightly. "I do. And I'm sorry, but I can't train or spar with you today."

The excitement in Lyra's eyes dimmed, but she managed to keep her smile. "Ah. I understand. You have that deadline for that big mission with the King coming up. Get it—*dead*line? I heard one of the other girls use that joke."

Lyra folded her arms and propped her hip against the passageway, and Selene suppressed a smile. That stance was, for whatever reason, in vogue with the other apprentices. "I can't wait to tell all the other apprenticelings that it was *my* master who assassinated King Alaric. You'll be famous. And after you've completed the mission, we'll spar again like you promised." Lyra winked. "Or maybe you can show me around the city since apprenticelings aren't allowed to go above ground by themselves."

When Lyra realized that Selene had left after killing the King, she would never forgive her. Selene's amusement dissipated. "I need to go, Lyra."

"Oh." Lyra pushed off the wall, shoving a loose lock of brown hair behind her ear. "What did I say?"

"Nothing. I just have a short time in which to accomplish a lot of tasks." Selene breezed past Lyra. She couldn't hear Lyra's footsteps pattering behind her, but she sensed her presence.

"Can I help?"

Selene shook her head. She wasn't about to pull someone else into the mess she'd created. "Just stay here and... train."

After a few seconds, Selene glanced behind her and found that Lyra had vanished. When Selene had first found that girl on the streets, Lyra moved so silently that no one noticed her—even in a crowd. Lyra had snatched bracelets from ladies' wrists and gold from pouches. It was why Selene had presented her to Arzil, in hopes that her skills could afford her a better life.

Selene jogged up the stairs, trying to ignore the heavy weight tugging at her chest. What the girl really needed was a mother, and Selene could never be that to her.

After a quick scan of her surroundings, Selene emerged

onto the streets above. She could worry about Lyra later. For now, Cori was her main focus. And the best man to go to for information would be the infamous bounty hunter, Onden.

Onden lived below deck on his boat. Selene had always admired the set-up. Enemies could only enter from the dock, and he could cut his ropes and flee if he needed to make a hasty escape.

The dock was empty, except for a few men unloading cargo and a handful of patrolling guards. She wasn't concerned by their presence; they were here to record which ships came and left and what cargo they carried. Nonetheless, Selene waited until one strolled by before emerging from the shadows of a warehouse.

The smell of salt and fish flooded her nostrils as she neared the ship. Lux lanterns dangled from poles above, swaying in the breeze and casting the harbor in swirl of shifting shadows and light. The river streamed past, its current tugging at the boats. The Lei River stole its salty water straight from the Anvinder Sea. As a girl, Selene had vacationed to the coast a handful of times.

Selene ascended the gangplank, careful to keep her balance as the ship rocked. She stopped just before boarding the boat, glancing down at a tripwire. Instead of sneaking past it she nudged it with her foot, making a little bell above chime.

If Onden was home, he'd appear momentarily.

She stepped over the tripwire and scanned the ship. If she needed to escape, she could go back down the gangplank or leap into the water. With her grappling hook, she might have even been able to board another ship. Other than a spool of rope, the deck was clear. But one could do much with a rope.

She strode to the ship's bow, watching the waters flow

beneath the boat. Gray clouds glazed the moon, muffling its light. The starlight was too weak to shine through the cloudy veil.

The river made a hushing noise as it flowed around the ships, from little fishing boats to majestic liners. They were opulently designed, with their crystal windows and golden railing. Guards patrolled their decks, protecting the ships from thieves and vandalism.

"Raven." Onden's steps made each shipboard squeak as he approached. "I thought you didn't plan on leaving to Arwa until at least next month. And I don't imagine you've come to make the payment yet, given the King is still alive."

She'd never told him how she would get the money, yet somehow, he already knew. "I've come for something else, information."

"What kind?"

"How much will it cost me?"

He joined her at the bow, leaning his forearms on the railing. "That depends on what kind."

Selene glanced at him, studying his profile. A new scar crossed his chin. Judging from its pink color, it was fairly recent. His jaw was roughened by silver and black stubble, his hair the same mix of color. Yet his face lacked the signs of age she saw in most others with salt-and-pepper hair. Weariness clung to him, especially in his eyes, but she suspected that was more from his line of work.

He still looked as strong as ever. Though he was slender, muscle corded his arms. He wore dark colors, as usual, with a crossbow strapped to his back and a variety of other weapons tucked into the strap he wore across his chest or dangling from his belt.

He cast a sidelong look at her. If another man had caught her staring at him, he would have suspected some attraction on her part. But not Onden. He knew what she was doing, how she constantly assessed the world around her.

"There was a masked man at the Maroon Maidens," she said. "I believe he's taken a friend of mine, Corsicanna. I suspect he's a bounty hunter."

"That's not much to go off of. Anything else?"

"His mask is black with two eyeholes. He wears it beneath a hood. He's tall—*very* tall. He was sitting at the time, but standing, I suspect that few Torvans would meet his height. His eyes are almost black, Taijese-shaped."

Onden leaned back against the ship, his hands on either side of him, his gaze tipped up to the starless sky. "There was a new bounty hunter rather similar to your description. Nobody knows anything about him. As you can imagine, some of the female bounty hunters find his mystique quite... appealing. He doesn't talk much. Word is he's searching for a blue crystal."

"No idea where he's from?"

"As you noted, he looks Taijese. But as a bounty hunter, he could be roaming Torva in search of work. They don't like to stay for too long in one spot."

"Except for you," Selene said.

"Well, I have a reputation here and a steady stream of clients. But after you... I might retire. There are only so many people you can snatch from beneath Arzil's nose before he starts taking notice."

And Arzil had already accused her of traitorous behavior. What if he knew more than he was letting on? What would become of Raban? And what would Raban do to her if he discovered she was playing him?

He glanced at her sharply. "Something wrong?"

Though Onden rarely showed emotion himself, he had an eerie knack for sensing it in others. Perhaps that was what made him one of the best bounty hunters.

"No."

Onden nodded, and she could see in his eyes that he knew better. "You're afraid."

"Assassins don't feel fear."

"Of course not." He reached his arms over his head and stretched them. "Is that all?"

Selene nodded. "Thank you. How much do I—"

"On the house. You're already paying me two fortunes to take you to Arwa."

"If I complete the mission."

Onden smirked. "Oh, you will. If you want to."

"What's that supposed to mean?"

"You're quite capable of completing your mission. But I'm beginning to doubt that you will."

"Why's that?"

He shrugged. "I would say that you should tell me, but I doubt you'd want to share such information." He headed back to the door leading below deck. "I trust you can show yourself out?"

"Yes."

The door clicked shut behind Onden. Selene spent another moment staring at the obsidian waves. Onden was wrong: she'd complete her mission. Once she had the money, she'd be sailing up this river, free to go and do and be whatever she pleased. She could finally make her own decisions, regardless of other people's allegiances and desires.

But without that money, such freedom would be impossible.

The Next Night

Though Selene had intended to eat well at dinner, she couldn't. Her stomach flip-flopped, churning whatever food she ate. And it hadn't helped that Shonn's eyes had burned into hers from across the table.

She had just reached her door, Raban behind her, when she turned to him. "Do you think Shonn suspects anything?"

He folded his arms, glancing at the ground in thought. The determined set of his jaw and the intensity in his eyes made his appearance more captivating than usual. She could easily see him as an assassin. No. He was too noble for that. Perhaps a warrior, ready to fell any who stood in his path.

"I don't think so. If he does... we'll just have to go from there." He shot her a soft smile. "And even if he reports you, I'll testify in your favor. Everything will be fine."

Selene nodded, drawing strength from his confidence. Her mission to kill the King would end in death, imprisonment, or freedom. And she was going to miss Raban in each of those scenarios.

Raban motioned toward her room. "You'd best go and get ready. I'll trail you until you reach Shonn's uncle's house, where I'll stop you from killing the poor old man." Raban shook his head. "Honestly, Selene. Think about his children."

She chuckled and shoved at his shoulder. "*Raban.* It's precisely his children I'm thinking about. That's why I asked you for help."

He stared, a look of surprise dawning on his expression. It took her a moment to realize why. She'd never initiated touching him before. Or with anyone, since Shonn had hurt her.

She was becoming far, *far* too comfortable in his presence. Maybe Arzil was right; perhaps she was fond of him.

She quickly retreated to her room. "That's an excellent idea. I-I'll see you soon."

"Good luck," Raban said, his voice muffled through the door.

Selene ran her hands through her hair, releasing her breath

in a sharp gust. So what if she was developing feelings toward him? It would be unseemly, nothing more. She wouldn't let him stop her from winning her freedom.

Selene scraped her hair back into a tight braid. As she reached for a drawer to find a hair tie, she saw a piece of paper resting on her desk. Selene abandoned her braid, letting her hair flow around her face, and picked up the paper.

Don't bother going out tonight.

12

MURDERED

Was this a threat? A warning? Perhaps Shonn had changed his mind. No, that didn't make sense. And if he had, he would have signed the note. But who else could know of her plans for tonight? Raban wouldn't have; he'd just tell her. And surely Shonn's spy was loyal to him.

Selene set the note back on her desk. She'd figure this mystery out later. She couldn't afford to delay the mission and make Shonn suspect that she'd never intended to carry it out in the first place. And if someone lay in wait for her, Raban would help her escape.

There was no need for stealth or creativity tonight. Selene braided her hair, secured the rope to her bed, and fashioned it into a makeshift harness. She stepped into the loops for her legs and rappelled down the house.

As soon as her feet touched the ground, a prickling sensation spilled across her back. Though she combed the shadows and rooftops, she couldn't spot anyone. But she knew Shonn's spy was out there. Was someone else out there as well? Someone besides Raban?

Selene made her way to the shed, changed outfits, and

headed downtown, toward Tyrus' house. The area was nice enough, even if the buildings weren't as impressive as those in the noble district.

The houses were three stories at most. Many windows were shuttered, and she knew from her scouting trip, that there weren't many made of crystal or glass. The people walking through the streets appeared to be hauling wares and coin after a long day at market. The few vendors who could afford it kept their stands open during the night.

Warm light escaped between cracks in shutters and beneath doors. The smell of fresh bread and cooked meat lingered on the air, though the people had probably finished dinner a few hours ago. Unlike her family, they had to sleep and rise early to earn their living.

Selene studied Tyrus' house, across the street. A dim light flickered between the shutters. Tyrus was probably still at home. She should probably sneak in through the back, giving Raban time to catch her. Ideally, Raban would "stop" her without Tyrus and his family even knowing.

Selene waited until the street was clear before sneaking across. She rounded the house, stopping at the back door, and crept through the grounds, acting like she was studying the lock or searching for another way in.

Why was Raban taking so long? If she piddled around much longer, Shonn's spy would become suspicious. She should have given Raban a map instead of relying on him to follow her.

After a few more moments, she delicately picked the lock. With a *clink*, all the pins glided into place. Triumph surged through her and she turned the knob.

The door opened, its hinges squeaking slightly. Selene suppressed a cringe.

She left the door open as she entered, not wanting to risk more noise. She'd let Raban silently catch her in here.

As she'd observed before, the back of the house was a workshop. Paintbrushes were left submerged in pots of water, and the room smelled like fresh wood and polish. Randomly shaped wooden objects littered the table.

Upon closer examination, Selene saw they were toys. How quaint.

She could use the door she'd come from as an exit, or the window, or the living room up ahead. There was a wonderful array of sharp instruments: chisels, saws, and knives. Some of the paint and polish could be thrown into someone's eyes to blind them.

Selene crept forward and peeked through the open doorway, into the living room.

There was a mismatched assortment of chairs: a wingback, a red stool, a patched divan, and a rocking chair. The embers of the fireplace glowed softly, casting the room in a dim orange. A staircase by the front door led to the second story.

Something about the wingback chair caught her attention. Though the chair was faced away from her, toward the fireplace, she could just barely see a round head poking above it.

Was the uncle seated there? Had he heard the hinges squeak when she'd entered?

But after a few moments, she relaxed. He hadn't moved or made a sound. In fact, she hadn't even heard him breathing. Could he know she was there?

The note's warning came to mind. She would have dismissed it as paranoia, but assassins survived by being cautious. She considered creeping forward but immediately dismissed the idea. What if Tyrus was asleep but then he awoke and saw her? Or what if this was a trap? At the very least, she should wait for Raban.

She crept back into the depths of the workshop, only to ram into someone. She swung around, dagger drawn.

A hand latched onto her wrist, and she relaxed when she

saw Raban's face. He put a finger to his lips, tugging her back outside.

But she planted her feet firmly, resisting him. At his confused glance, she stood on her tiptoes and whispered, "I think something's wrong."

His brows drew together. "What? Were you seen? And I apologize for the delay. I lost you for a moment."

"No one spotted me. I saw someone in the living room."

Raban shrugged. "Perhaps someone couldn't sleep."

"But I couldn't hear him breathing. Could you come with me and listen for a moment?" She attempted a smile. "Maybe I'm just losing my mind."

Raban rubbed his scruffy jaw and nodded slowly. "Very well."

She led him back to the doorway, giving them a view of the chair's silhouette with the man in it.

After a few moments, Raban's frown deepened. He put a hand on her shoulder, signaling for her to stay, and crept toward the chair.

Selene placed her hand on her dagger, prepared for a trap or ambush.

Raban stopped right behind the man, peering over the chair. He didn't speak or move. He finally turned toward her. "*Selene.*" His voice was coarse and harsh, as if it'd been dragged over jagged rocks before emerging from his mouth.

If he was speaking aloud, he obviously wasn't worried about being heard. She stepped nearer. "What—"

"Did you do this?"

Her blood ran cold, like river water rushing through her veins. She rushed to the side of the chair.

The man was dead.

13

SELENE'S BETRAYAL

The man didn't move. His skin felt cold and rubbery against her hand. Her gaze drifted downward, to the dagger planted in his chest. The surrounding fabric of his tunic was stained dark with blood.

Hang it.

How... Had Shonn hired someone else? Selene bent closer, squinting to make out the details of the dagger. There was a curved symbol carved into its handle. The sign for the Scorpio.

Someone had framed her.

Her face went hot, then cold. "Raban... I don't..." She shook her head. This was a nightmare. Perhaps she'd accidentally fallen asleep and dreamt of the plan going terribly wrong. She took a slow breath. "Why would I invite you to stop me if I was just going to..."

He paused for a moment, pressing his fist against his chin. "You're right; that wouldn't make sense—especially for you to call the man's lack of breathing to my attention. I'm sorry. But who else could have killed him?" He gestured to the dagger hilt, where the Scorpio insignia was inscribed. "A Scorpio assassin?"

"Possibly. Maybe this was all mere coincidence, and he

happened to be someone else's target... on the same night." Highly unlikely. And then there was the note.

"I should take you back to your room."

Selene nodded. She could show him the note later.

He pulled a coil of slender rope from his belt. "I thought it would look more convincing if I bound your hands."

Selene extended her wrists. He tied them securely but loose enough that they wouldn't chaff or dig into her skin.

"Come. And don't forget to put up a fight." Raban tugged her to the workshop, then out the back door.

As soon as they were outside, Selene began yanking back on the rope. "No, Raban. Let me go!" She kept her voice hushed, but loud enough for someone nearby to hear. "You have no right to—"

"Silence, Lady Selene." He jerked her forward rather convincingly. She nearly fell. "You're lucky that I'm not throwing you into the dungeons for trying to..." He shot her a glance, worry in his eyes.

That was right; now that the man was dead, their plans had to change. She could no longer tell Shonn that Raban had stopped her from killing the man. She would have to explain that she killed the man and *then* Raban had found her. But then Shonn would have questions, such as why would Raban only take her back to her room when she'd committed *murder*?

But it was too late now. Shonn's spy was out there, watching their performance.

Raban cleared his throat. "For *killing* that man. We will speak on this later."

They continued the rest of the way in silence, with Selene occasionally tugging against the rope or dragging her feet. Raban led her to the shed, where he untied her so she could change back into a lady's dress. After she emerged, he opted for gripping her upper arm instead of tying her wrists again.

Selene stumbled by Raban in a daze, a sick feeling in her gut. Who had killed the man? Would Shonn suspect anything?

A cloaked man approached them, stilling Selene's whirling thoughts. He appeared... familiar, something about the color of his cloak and his figure. She caught her breath. The masked bounty hunter who'd taken Cori.

Selene tore away from Raban to stand in front of the man. "Pardon me, sir, but—" A quick glance up into his hood revealed that he wore no mask—and his eyes were crystal blue.

He shoved her out of the way, and Selene stumbled back into Raban. The man continued on silently without a backward glance.

Raban glanced down at Selene, his hands on her shoulders to steady her. "Did you know him?" he asked, his voice nearly inaudible.

She shook her head. "I thought he was that masked man from the Maroon Maidens. Do you remember him?"

Raban rolled his eyes. "You were unapologetically flirting with him. How could I forget?"

Had he just been disgusted by her behavior? Or was he jealous?

Raban resumed his grip on her arm. "Come, let's keep walking."

Clouds dappled the night sky, bathing the city in shadow, then silver as they passed over the moon. Barrels and crates cluttered the side of the alleys, along with bone fragments and melon rinds from recent meals.

Selene cast another glance behind her. The man had completely vanished. It had been silly of her to expect the masked bounty hunter anyhow. If he had taken Cori, he'd likely fled. Unless he'd hidden her away somewhere in the city.

Or perhaps Selene's imaginings were too dark. Perhaps Cori had fallen in love with him and willingly left. But Selene knew

Cori; she wasn't the type to fall in love, or even believe in it, for that matter.

"Why are you searching for the masked bounty hunter, Selene? That sounds rather dangerous."

What could she tell him? If she said Arzil had told her, Raban would know she was still a part of the Scorpio. If she said she went back to the Maroon Maidens herself, Raban would be suspicious. If she truly had betrayed the Scorpio, going back would be unbelievably dangerous.

"The other night, when I was scouting, I'd hoped to set up a meeting with Cori, since I can't visit her at the Maroon Maidens anymore. But by the time of our meeting, she wasn't there. I fear something's happened to her, and a few days ago, she told me that she felt like the cloaked man was paying her too much attention, yet he never requested her services."

Raban nodded. "That is rather mysterious. I don't know what you could do to help her now."

"I can find that man."

"M'rithun likely knows that you've betrayed them by now. It has been a few days since you've last reported to him."

Selene ignored the pinch of guilt.

"Roaming the streets in search of this man is too dangerous."

She would be the one to determine that. But she nodded instead of arguing her point. "There's something else I need to tell you."

"What is it?"

"Tonight, before leaving my room, I found a note. It said, 'don't bother going out.' I didn't have much of an option, so I left anyway."

Raban rubbed his jaw. "Interesting. You'll have to show it to me tomorrow."

"Why not tonight?"

"Tonight, I have much to do. After dropping you off, I need to go report the murder to the city watch."

Fear pierced her chest. Surely Raban wouldn't report that she'd done it. But what if she'd left some evidence behind that pointed to her?

Raban stopped at the gate to her house. Once the guards had opened it, Raban shoved her forward. "Escort her back to her room. I have other matters to attend to tonight."

The guards seemed curious, but they escorted her back without questions. As they climbed the stairs, she grew tenser as she neared Shonn's floor. Would he still be awake? But when she passed it, the hallway was dark and silent. What if he was awaiting her in her room?

The guards stopped at her room, and she entered, all senses on high alert.

But nothing moved. The note on her desk drew her attention. She picked it up, rereading it over and over. She remembered the Scorpio knife embedded in the man's chest.

What if someone wasn't trying to frame her? What if it was another Scorpio member trying to do her a favor?

Her chest went cold. Surely Lyra wouldn't. The girl hadn't even made her first kill yet.

Selene pressed the button to open her secret compartment, preparing to stuff the note inside, but she paused. She could have sworn that she'd put Shonn's note in the same compartment. And now it was gone.

Who could have taken it? Tyrus' murderer? How would they know where to look?

Selene's mind felt thick and sluggish, as though her thoughts waded through sap. When no answers presented, she tucked the note in and shut the hidden drawer. Another mystery for another time.

She stripped off her dress, leaving it in a crumpled heap on the floor, and pulled on a free-flowing nightgown. It streamed down her figure, the fabric like the caress of water against her skin.

She tumbled into bed, drawing her blanket up to her chin. Perhaps Raban would have some insight to offer her. She closed her eyes, hoping she was too tired for nightmares to haunt her.

The Next Day

Raban shook his head. "I don't have the faintest clue as to what this might mean." He was bent over her desk, stretching the note out with both hands. Afternoon sunlight poured through her window, bathing his skin in gold.

Selene sighed. "Not helpful, Raban."

He shot her a smile. It was a lovely smile that made his features handsomer still. Not that she noticed, or even cared.

Perhaps she could search for clues when she snuck out today to meet that streetsweeper and find out more about Raban's past. Guilt slunk through her. It wasn't as if she'd use it against him—unless she didn't have a choice. Simply knowing the information couldn't hurt; it might come in useful in case he discovered her true allegiance and tried to report her.

One day, this whole mess would be behind her. She wouldn't have to worry about betrayal or feelings of guilt. She'd be free to do whatever she thought was right. But she'd also never see Raban again.

But that was for the best.

Still, she tried to return his smile.

Raban's smile melted, and Selene regretted that she'd caused its disappearance. "What is it, Selene? You look sad."

"Just thinking about the future."

"Is that so?"

She nodded. "You can't be my guard forever, you know. One

day you'll find a cute little wife and perhaps find a cabin in the mountains, where you'll have a large farm and a dozen children."

Raban stared at her, eyebrows high. "A farm *in* the mountains? You really think I'll become a farmer—not some legendary war hero?"

She shrugged. "It could happen."

"Unlikely, especially since I don't ever intend to get married."

She stared at him. "You don't?"

"No. I just... I'm not cut out for marriage."

He was noble and kind and patient. What better qualities were there for a husband? "Why?"

He fiddled with the note in his hands, folding it and unfolding it along the creases. "I used to think I would like to be married. But past experience has taught me otherwise."

"Let me guess," Selene grinned, "no woman out there is good enough for you?"

"On the contrary, I'm not good enough for any woman." He let the abused note drop to her desk. "I apologize that I wasn't of any help. I'm certain we'll get to the bottom of this, sooner or later." He practically fled from her room, shutting the door behind him.

He wasn't good enough? Why not? Could it have to do with something in his past? Perhaps the streetsweeper would answer some of those questions.

Selene stuffed the note back into the secret compartment and closed it. She was preparing to take out her mother's dagger to sharpen it when she heard raised voices from the other side of the door.

Selene crept closer. It sounded like Raban and Shonn were arguing, their tones low and pointed. It could be a while before they were done.

Selene's gaze shot to her window. She should go now, while

Raban was distracted. And he wouldn't expect her to leave midafternoon. She'd be back before he even thought to check on her. Selene dashed to her bed, tugged at the rope to make sure it was secured to her bedpost, and formed her makeshift harness.

She rappelled down the side of her house and sprinted toward the shed to change into her commoner dress. Raban knew about all of her dark secrets. This was her opportunity to find out about his.

Anger mounted in Draven's chest, like heaping coals onto a fire, as Shonn approached. He strolled casually, as if he owned the world.

This man had hurt Selene so badly that she still shied from any man's touch. He'd tormented her, threatened her, and nearly coerced her into killing someone. Draven hadn't reported Shonn yet, because he didn't want to implicate Selene. But as soon as Alaric arrived and Selene confessed, Draven would do everything in his power to ensure that Shonn was sent to the dungeons.

"Guard Raban." Shonn stopped before him. "What a pleasant surprise."

"Selene is unavailable." He couldn't keep the growl from his tone.

"I'm not here to talk to Selene, my good sir. I'm here to talk to you."

"I have nothing to say to you." Nothing that wouldn't get him fired, anyway.

"That's quite all right, because I have plenty to say to you. It seems you know Selene's secret occupation as well, and yet you haven't reported her. I wonder why. Could you, perhaps, be showing an unseemly interest in her?" If a snake could smile, it would have looked just like Shonn. "A guard pining after his charge? My parents would be most interested in this development."

Draven normally prided himself on his emotional control, but something about Shonn managed to irritate and annoy him in every fashion. "Perhaps I should report you. Hiring an assassin is illegal."

"But reporting me would draw attention to your precious Selene. And we couldn't have that, could we?" Shonn paced in front of him. "You have a very peculiar sense of honor, Raban, which makes me think there's more going on here than meets the eye. Have you, by any chance, convinced her to leave the Scorpio?"

There was no point in giving Shonn more information than necessary.

"And did she agree to this arrangement?" Shonn shook his head, *tsk*ing. "You should know better than to trust the word of an assassin, Raban."

"I would trust her word over yours."

Shonn's smile grew slick and sharp. "Is that so? Why don't we put that statement of yours to the test?"

Unease slunk through Draven. But he had nothing to fear. Shonn was simply trying to pry Selene's only friend away from her, so she'd be alone and helpless once more.

"By any chance, did you see where Selene went two nights ago?"

She'd been scouting out Shonn's uncle's house. Or so she'd said.

"My spy reported that she'd gone to my uncle's house briefly before visiting the Scorpio base."

"You have no proof of this. Why would I believe you?" Surely she wouldn't have returned to the Scorpio base after her promise.

A smirk tugged at Shonn's lips. "I'd be happy to show you

the location of the base myself. And speaking of Selene, where do you think she is right now?"

Draven's breath stilled. He hadn't heard any movement from Selene's room, but he'd been too immersed in his conversation with Shonn to pay it any mind.

Shonn sighed, shaking his head. "Poor Guard Raban. When my parents first hired you, I thought you were too clever to fall for her meager charms. I'd assumed she was too plain and awkward to ever tempt a man. It seems you've proven me wrong." Shonn strolled away, leaving Draven with an empty, cold feeling in his chest.

He turned to her door and knocked. When there was no answer, he opened it. The room was empty, the window open, and rope dangled from the sill.

Hang her. She'd escaped. And she hadn't told him why. She must be visiting M'rithun at this very moment.

Hurt curled around his chest, its claws digging deep. He'd been a naïve fool to trust her. He should have known better.

Draven strode to the windowsill and used the rope to descend. He would track her down and do what he should have when he'd first discovered she was a Scorpio.

14

RABAN'S SECRET

Selene entered the pub, and the smell of korosasth and cooked food washed over her, with the underlying scent of unwashed bodies. Ten tables filled the main area.

Empty wooden mugs and old fishermen—likely telling exaggerated tales—already cluttered the bar in the back. A variety of stools, chairs, and benches clustered around the tables, which appeared worn but polished and clean. Cheap paintings of women in tight dresses speckled the wooden walls.

The streetsweeper sat in the back corner, near the bar.

Selene made her way over to her and sat down. "I'm pleased to see you're here this early."

The woman, Faina, nodded, her eyes large and sparkling in her weary face. "Of course. I appreciate you meeting me, given that you're a lady and no doubt have many other tasks to attend to." She regarded Selene's commoner dress with raised eyebrows. "How did you manage to come here alone? I would have thought you'd at least have an escort."

Selene waved her hand through the air, as if brushing the comment aside. "Escaping wasn't too hard. And my primary escort is Raban. I thought it'd be best not to bring him."

After a short delay, Faina's eyes widened in recognition. "Raban? Is that what he goes by now?"

"He has another name?" Curiosity blazed within Selene, and she suppressed the urge to lean forward. She didn't want the woman to know how desperately she wanted the information.

"Yes. But first, I must ask, did you bring—"

"I did." Selene slipped forty aurum from her pocket and pushed it across the table.

Faina collected the coins in her palm and cupped them close to her chest, as if cradling a child. "Beautiful." She dropped them down her neckline, the clinking noise muffled by her shirt.

After picking up her mug, Faina took a deep swig of the drink. Judging by its dark color, it was something a bit stronger than korosasth. She set the mug down and wiped her mouth with the back of her hand. "Now, let's talk about... Raban, wasn't it?"

"Yes, but what's his real name?"

"I'll get to that. I would have you know that I wasn't always a poor streetsweeper." Faina propped her cheek on her hand, her eyes glazed as she peered into another time. "I used to be a chambermaid in the palace. It was quite respectable work. Well, it used to be. When your Raban came to visit, I gave myself to him, thinking that if he truly loved me enough to bed me that he'd make the honorable decision to marry me afterward. I was young and naïve at the time, and I had yet to learn that bedding someone rarely means love.

"When I awoke the next morning, the guards hauled me up out of bed—without a stitch of clothing on. I begged him to do something, and he simply watched as they tossed me out of the palace. Apparently the Empress wasn't about to have any wanton chambermaids. Because obviously wanton chambermaids are of greater concern than wanton dukes." Faina fisted her hands, her expression tensing.

Duke? Raban had been a *duke*? That was almost as unbelievable as him arbitrarily taking a woman's virtue and tossing her aside. Could that really be Raban?

Faina continued, "He made no effort to contact me after that. I was excommunicated and ruined. Though I could have become a prostitute, *he* had already made a prostitute of me once, and I wasn't about to become one again. Many years later, he returned to me, apologizing and practically begging that I marry him, so he could remedy the wrong he'd done me."

There was the Raban she knew.

"Judging from the look on his handsome face, I could tell that he expected me to accept his proposal. But I rejected him."

A smile stripped years from Faina's face. "After he'd ruined my life, I was determined that he shouldn't ruin anyone else's. I spat at him and called him foolish for thinking any woman would want him after all the mistakes he'd made. I told him I was worthy of a far better man than he—and so was every other woman in Torva. Nothing could come of wedding that man but pain and heartbreak for his poor wife. After a moment, he wiped the spit from his cheek, said I was right, and left."

Pity pinched Selene's chest—but this time, for Raban. "You rejected a duke? But didn't you want someone to provide—"

"Oh. No. By this time, he'd been stripped of his title. Without that, no woman in her right mind would want him. He no longer had anything to offer a bride."

Faina had likely told him that as well. Poor Raban. True, he'd made some foolish mistakes in his younger years and had acted callously... but he'd also done all in his power to make things right. No wonder the man thought he wasn't fit to wed anyone.

"And you asked for his name earlier." Faina sipped from her

mug and let it clank back onto the table. "When he was a duke, he went by the name of Draven."

Draven.

Her reality shattered like a mirror, the crystalline shards raining down upon her.

The man who'd betrayed the Scorpio.

The man who'd killed her mother.

The man she hunted.

He'd been under her nose all along. Hang it, she was a fool. Heat built in her chest, singed her skin. She should have known that a man cruel enough to thoughtlessly bed chambermaids was also ruthless enough to kill her mother.

She'd go back to her house immediately and do what she should have long ago.

Kill him.

15

TO KILL A TRAITOR

Selene shoved back from the table and whirled toward the exit.

"Wait!" A chair screeched as Faina stood. "I haven't finished telling my story. How I showed him that he couldn't just use a woman and discard her. That he's a poor excuse for a man. You should have seen his face when—"

Selene had heard all she needed. She rushed out of the pub, shoving aside anyone in her way. Evening light poured gold across the streets and buildings. Vendors advertised their wares with hoarse shouts, and shoppers rushed in a flurry, trying to make their purchases before day's end.

Selene darted into an alley, removed her grappling hook and rope from her pocket, and secured the hook on the edge of the roof. Adrenaline gave her a burst of strength, and she climbed to the top in record time. Rooftop to rooftop would be the fastest way back.

After crossing a few buildings, her initial burst of energy wore off, her sense of invincibility fading with it. Sweat gathered between her clothing and her skin, suffocating her. Perhaps she should go back to the Scorpio base first, get reinforcements. If this truly was *the* Draven, she'd need help. He'd been a very skilled assassin before—

"Selene."

Raban's—no, Draven's—voice rang out like daggers striking a target. A hundred emotions whizzed by her. That voice belonged to the man who'd comforted and protected her. But it was also the voice of a murderer who'd taken *everything* from her.

Selene turned and found him on top of a nearby building, crouching to keep his balance on the sloping red tiles. No smile on his lips, no softness in his expression. It was almost as if he was a completely different person.

She saw him through new eyes now. He must have changed his skin tone to disguise his Silvan heritage and dyed his hair to conceal its golden color. His green eyes were the only true thing about him.

Selene drew her mother's dagger slowly. The emeralds gleamed from the pommel and along its blade. "Draven."

His eyes didn't even flicker in surprise. "So you know." He rose. "I've discovered who you are too: a Scorpio assassin—even though you said you'd change. You never intended to turn yourself in to the King, did you?"

He knew. And no doubt he was going to kill her for it. Her heart thrummed so hard the tip of her dagger quivered; she hoped he didn't notice. "Not everyone can turn traitor like you, Draven."

"Is that how you justify extinguishing innocent lives? How you sleep at night?"

He drew two daggers and leapt across to her building. It took everything within her not to retreat. Even if she ran, she couldn't outrun him. This was to be her battleground. She quickly scanned the area.

This roof was flat stone. A door likely led down into the building. Laundry swayed on a clothesline, and a heap of wet clothes sat in a basket next to it. Otherwise, the roof was clear, a suitable place for a duel.

"Did you kill Shonn's uncle?" He stood where he'd landed, not advancing toward her.

Every muscle in her body was strung tighter than a bow string. She softened her knees and balanced her stance, ready for his attack. "No. I didn't ask for this kind of life. My mother was teaching me how to be an assassin when I was too young to think for myself."

"But not too young to take a life. And even if you didn't choose to become an assassin, you've chosen to continue this lifestyle, to accept the challenge of killing King Alaric—an innocent man who's done *nothing* to you."

Heat washed over her, her blood boiling in her veins. "He's taken *everything* from me—by releasing *you* when he should have *killed* you." Selene lunged forward, swinging the dagger toward his shoulder.

Draven deflected her blow, their weapons interlocking. "Because of your mother? Weren't you just complaining about how she forced you to become an assassin? Perhaps I did you a favor."

Selene darted backward, her chest heaving. "She noticed me. She *cared*. She could have—"

"Could have what? Changed? Like *you* have, Selene?" He stepped toward her, fluidly swinging his dagger toward her stomach, and Selene spun out of the way.

Her blood became so hot it frothed in her veins. Bubbled over until the heat consumed her heart. He'd been a spoiled duke. What did he know about being unloved? "You ruined my only chance at having a *real* mother. And now because of you, she's *dead*."

Draven assessed her coolly. While she seemed to be losing control, he held his in an icy grip. "I didn't kill her, Selene."

"*Liar!*" She lunged at him.

He dropped one of his daggers and caught her wrist, his grip tight enough to grind her bones. "I didn't. If you want to find a murderer to blame, you should look to Arzil."

"She was his *best* assassin, his best. He had no reason to kill her, and you have every reason." Selene drew out a second dagger with her free hand and swiped at his chest, nicking his skin. He stumbled backward.

"I've never seen your mother, Selene. Perhaps she decided to betray the Scorpio, and Arzil retaliated."

"No! I knew her, Rab—*Draven*. Do you know when I first saw her smile at me?" Heat surged to her eyes, blurring the world before her. *No.* She wasn't going to let him see her like this. Assassins didn't feel pain. She breathed deep, locking the emotions away. "It was the night of my first kill. My hands were bathed in blood, tears on my face, and she... couldn't stop smiling at me, telling me how *proud* she was. She'd never betray the Scorpio. Being an assassin was *everything* to her. How else could I win her love but to become what she loved? And I was almost there." She rushed at Draven, madly swinging with both daggers. "*You* stole that from *me!*"

He deflected them without blinking. "The need for revenge will rot your soul. It will tear you apart from the inside out. The only thing you'll accomplish in killing me is killing a piece of yourself. I learned that too late, Selene. Don't make the mistakes I did."

Her fury was liquid fire inside her veins. She channeled her anger into a swing, then jabbed at him. He dodged both strikes. Why wouldn't he just die already?

"Don't you see, Selene?" His expression softened.

She didn't want his patronizing pity. She didn't need it. He knew nothing about her life, yet he acted as if he knew everything. "All I see is a murderer who I should have killed a long time ago." She threw her dagger at him.

Draven used his own dagger to knock Selene's to the side.

His reflexes were faster than she'd thought possible. "The Empress tasked me to find the assassin in House Channing. To find *you*. After discovering who you were, I didn't turn you in. I couldn't. I'd hoped that I could change you—change you like I'd been changed."

Selene laughed bitterly. How could he have caused so much death, have been an assassin himself, and still be this naïve? "You were a fool to think so."

All the softness vanished from his expression. "Yes, I was. I assure you it's a mistake I won't make again." He advanced on her. Before, he'd attacked without passion and spent most of the time defending himself. But this time, there was strength in every blow, skill in every swing.

She found herself stumbling backward as she tried to defend herself against the onslaught. Her grip on the hilt of her mother's dagger was slick with sweat—and she nearly lost her hold more than once. His blades moved so quickly that they blazed gold from the sunset. He was a vortex of death. And she was a fool to have ever thought she could take him alone.

The back of her leg struck the roof's ledge. It was a short ledge, reaching knee high. A good shove would send her toppling to the ground.

This was how she was to die. At the hands of the man she'd vowed to kill. Though she was bathed in heat from the battle, a chill washed over her.

His dagger swung toward her face, and she leaned back just as she felt the air shoot past her cheek. Her balance wavered, and though she tried to straighten, it was too late. She tipped backward. Her heart lurched as her feet left solid ground. Draven's hand snapped out and grabbed the front of her dress.

For a moment, she was suspended five stories above the ground. She glanced at his eyes. Even as cold and guarded as they were, they remained kind. Throughout their entire fight, he could have injured or permanently disabled her. Yet he hadn't.

A wave of regret rolled over her. Perhaps... he hadn't killed her mother. Which meant she'd just made the biggest mistake of her life.

He wrenched her forward, sending her toppling to the roof's flat floor. The rock scraped against her cheek, the impact of her fall sending her mother's dagger flying from her hand. The jewels in the hilt and blade sparkled, flaring as the sun's dying rays hit it.

Selene began to crawl toward it, only to feel Draven grab her and flip her onto her back. She looked up just as she saw him tilt a glass vial toward her, a drop of liquid dangling from its rim.

"Goodbye, Selene."

She closed her mouth, but the drop snuck past her parted lips, its spicy taste unfurling against her tongue. The drug's effects washed over her, numbing her limbs and reducing her vision to a murky pool.

As Draven heaved her onto his shoulder and swiped her dagger from the ground, her heart twisted until she felt pain crackle across its surface. She wanted to share her regret with him, to ask him not to give up on her just yet. Perhaps she could change. But it was too late to beg for mercy now.

Instead of taking the second chance he'd offered her, she'd tossed it aside and ground it underfoot. Now she was going to die for her mistake. A strangely fitting end for an assassin.

People stared as Draven marched through the streets, Selene tossed over his shoulder. Her head swayed, her straight black hair rippling with it as her locks escaped from her braid. She occasionally muttered something incoherent. The Somnus sap had been enough to subdue her, but perhaps he should have given her more. This next part would likely be easier for her if she were completely asleep.

Not that he cared about making her imprisonment any easier.

A hint of unease nearly doused his anger. Alaric's arrival was still a few days away. What if the Empress decided to execute Selene before then? She was known to be impulsive, and her decisions weren't always sound.

Draven shook his head, as if to shake the thought loose. No. The Empress knew he was Alaric's half-brother. Hopefully that would be authority enough to ensure Selene was sentenced to a life of imprisonment instead of execution.

Draven stopped in front of the door to the secret passage and transitioned Selene to his other shoulder. She let out a little whimper and muttered something, but he couldn't catch any words. If someone saw her now, not knowing she was an assassin, they'd think she was a rather innocent-looking pretty girl.

Draven's hand wandered the wall until he found the button. He pushed, and the passage door swung out, seeming to appear from nowhere. Draven entered and closed it behind him.

As usual, it smelled musty and damp. Walking through with Selene was a pain. He continually had to hunch over so as not to let her back run into the low ceiling.

When he reached the end and opened the door, light spilling into the passage, the unease in his gut grew stronger. But there was no going back now.

The Empress lounged on her divan, her daughter at her side. Three noble men sat across from them, their backs to Draven. They were marquesses, judging from the copper threading in their clothing. It seemed like she was in the middle of entertaining them. Upon seeing him, the Empress paused mid-laugh, and the visitors swiveled to face him.

There wasn't a sound except for the dribbling water of the fountain.

"Is now a bad time?" Draven asked, trying to keep the sarcasm from his voice.

The Empress drew in a sharp little breath and swept her hand at the visitors. "Get out. All of you." When they shared confused glances, she said, "*Now.*"

The men nearly tripped over themselves trying to rush from the room, though they did cast a few curious glances at Draven. He was thankful that Selene's face rested against his back, hiding her identity. He'd hate for gossiping nobles to bring more shame to her family than was necessary.

The Empress straightened, a predatory smile gracing her lips. He was almost surprised her teeth were straight instead of fanged. "Now, what do we have here?"

Unease coiled more tightly in his stomach, and he knew, without a doubt, that this was a mistake. The Empress wasn't known for her mercy, and she would show Selene none.

When he didn't speak, she continued, "The assassin in House Channing?"

"Yes, Empress."

"Lovely. And is she unconscious because she's been drugged or because of a head injury?"

"She's been drugged, Empress."

"Set her down on the divan across from me. I would have a look at her."

Her eyes glittered as he set Selene down. The Empress rose, grasping Selene's chin and holding her face upward. "Well, well, well. Little Selene from House Channing. What an interesting development. As a lady, she should have known better than to oppose the Empress of Taijeng." The Empress' long nails dug deeper into Selene's jaw. "We'll need to send a message to her family to inform them of her arrest."

It took everything within Draven not to yank her hand

away. What had he done? Offered Selene on a silver platter to her tormentor? While he'd wanted to stop her from hurting anyone—especially Alaric and Evelyn—he didn't want this. He should have found a way to imprison her himself until Alaric arrived.

Draven cleared his throat. "Empress, I request that she live a life in the dungeons for her crimes."

"A life in the dungeons? Your heart is far too soft, Draven. It makes me wonder if you have a care for this girl." The Empress released Selene's face and patted her cheek. "No. For her, I have a special fate in mind. First, we need to discover the location of the Scorpio base. I doubt she'll tell us easily, so I'll hand her over to the tormentors. Once they've finished with her, we'll execute her." The Empress grinned, her smile thinning her red-painted lips. "After enduring the tormentors, she'll find death a rather merciful end." She raised her eyebrows at Draven. "I don't suppose you know where the Scorpio base is?"

Draven clasped his hands behind his back, so she couldn't see how hard he was fisting them. "No, I don't. Empress, as half-brother to the King—"

"*Please*, Draven. You're an illegitimate son; your connection to him has no significance. And I do hate to see you grovel like this for an assassin."

Draven closed his mouth so fast that his teeth clinked. If she wouldn't listen, he'd have to think of another way to aid Selene. Hang it, he should have taken time to slow down and think after capturing her. But instead, he'd let his anger and hurt prompt him to hand Selene over to the Empress.

To speed Selene's confession, he could give the Empress a truth serum, which was very hard to obtain—unless one knew where to ask. But doing so would only expedite Selene's death. It was best that he let her suffer for a while, giving him time to save her.

The Empress patted Selene on the cheek more firmly,

nearing a slap. "Poor, poor Selene. If only she hadn't betrayed her country and people." She straightened and pointed at a samurai by the door. "Tell the tormentors to ready their tools and to be in the interrogation room within ten minutes. And you," she pointed to the other samurai, "remove her from my sight at once."

The first samurai disappeared out the door, and the second picked up Selene.

Her eyes fluttered half open, her gaze lazily roaming the room. Her pupils were dilated, the dark brown of her eyes reduced to a thin band. She focused on the samurai's face, then Draven's.

"R-Raban?"

He glanced away from her. He couldn't afford to show her any more sympathy, not in front of the Empress. Or she might suspect that he planned to help Selene.

"Raban, don't let them take me. You said you wouldn't."

The samurai walked away with her, and Draven's traitorous eyes strayed to her once more. It looked as though she was struggling to stay awake, but she continued to stare at him, begging him to save her. The drug was still running through her system. Hopefully, she'd remember none of this upon awakening.

The samurai opened the door, and Selene struggled weakly. "No, Raban! Please!"

The door slammed shut behind them.

The Empress laughed. "It seems your little charge was quite taken with you."

An ache began in the center of his chest, spreading outward. Selene desperately needed someone to comfort and protect her. But this time, he couldn't.

Draven bowed his head, lest the Empress see the anguish crackling across his expression. "Am I dismissed?"

"Yes. You've done well, Draven. It's time to rest yourself."

Draven turned and headed toward the double doors, his footsteps quietly clacking against the marble floor. As soon as the door closed behind him, he quickened his pace, heading to his room. It was a few days yet until Alaric would arrive, but that would be a few days too late.

If Alaric wasn't here to save her, then Draven would just have to save her himself.

So long as Selene didn't reveal the location of the Scorpio base too soon, she'd be safe, unless... Draven stopped in the middle of the hallway. If Shonn revealed the location, they'd have no need to keep Selene alive.

Of course, if Shonn disappeared mysteriously, then Selene would be the Empress' only source of information.

A grin spread across Draven's lips, the sensation of smiling slightly foreign. He'd been wanting to do something with Shonn for a long time. This was his opportunity, and he had a perfectly practical motivation.

But if Shonn's spy still lurked about, he would need to be dealt with as well. Though Draven prided himself on his perception, Shonn's spy had proven incredibly stealthy. To catch him, he'd need to set out a trap. For that, he'd need help.

And Draven knew exactly who he'd ask.

16

THE TORMENTORS

Draven heaved himself onto the marble balcony and dislodged his grappling hook. He coiled the rope and dropped it into his pants' pocket. Dim light flickered through the fogged windows, revealing two people in a passionate embrace. Occasionally, they broke apart to speak in low murmurs, and the interaction was usually followed by a girlish giggle.

If Marquess Daiyu of House Feng was the same charming womanizer as he'd known, this could take a while. And Draven didn't have a while. Not when every moment was dragging Selene closer to her death.

Draven strode to the glass door and rapped on it.

The figures within froze. They spoke in hushed voices, before the larger of the two moved toward the door and swung it open.

Daiyu stood in the doorway, a candelabra in hand.

Draven pulled his hood back. "Come, Daiyu. Surely you could have armed yourself with something better than with a candelabra. At least call the guards."

After a moment of hesitation, he lowered the makeshift

weapon. "D-Draven. I haven't seen you in years, not since you were promoted to an official in the Octavian palace. And then there was that nasty business about you having your title stripped…"

Draven tensed over memories he'd rather not recall. "It has been a while, but hopefully not so long that you've forgotten neither what a phenomenal friend I am nor the favor you owe me."

Even in the dark, Draven could see Daiyu's cheeks darkening. "Of course I remember. Lady Renxiang was going to force me to marry her through blackmail."

"Until I found blackmail against *her* and persuaded her to retract her matrimonial demands."

Daiyu shook his head, his hair so dark it glistened blue. "I'll still never understand how you found such information."

That was all thanks to his truth serum. But an assassin never revealed *all* of his secrets. "Would you be willing to return the favor?"

"Of course. If you hadn't helped me many years ago, I'd never have found that lovely woman." He tipped his head back toward his room.

"Dai!" the woman yelled from within. "What's happening? Are you all right?"

Dai? Draven raised his eyebrows, and Daiyu flushed.

"She likes to call me that," he explained. "One moment."

He returned to the room. Their voices were hushed, though the woman's rose a bit higher. Finally, they both moved to the bed, and Daiyu returned to the balcony without the woman, closing the door behind him.

"Now, where were we?" Daiyu asked.

Though it was now dark within the room, Draven could see where the woman lay atop the bed. "You're letting her sleep here instead of returning her home?"

Daiyu's eyes grew wide, before his surprise melted into

mirth. "Draven. She *is* home." He chuckled. "You have been away for quite a while."

Draven forced a swallow past his suddenly dry throat. "You're... married?"

Daiyu ran his hand through his hair, which had already been thoroughly mused and ruffled. Perhaps by his wife. "Yes. Quite happily."

"It appears so," Draven muttered. "I thought you vowed not to be shackled to a woman. You said that having only one woman would be too boring for you."

Daiyu took a quick stride toward Draven, his expression stern. "Lower your voice, you hollow head. There's no need to speak such things in her hearing. I assure you, I've put her through quite enough and I don't intend to cause her any more pain. Only the pleasure and happiness that is due to someone as wonderful as her."

Draven's eyebrows rose. "Such flowery language. Now I know you love her."

"What man in his right mind wouldn't?" A smile softened his lips. "She's kind, patient, loyal, and utterly bewitching. There isn't anything I wouldn't do for her." He shook his head. "But as much as I enjoy this topic, you likely haven't come to hear about how delightful my wife is."

No, he hadn't. But he couldn't help but be intrigued that Daiyu loved a girl enough to finally settle down with her. "I take it you didn't tell her about any of the other women?"

Daiyu tugged at the hem of his flowing nightclothes. "Actually, I did. She was surprisingly forgiving, and she gave me the strength to forgive myself."

Could there be a woman out there who would forgive Draven for the mistakes he'd made? Selene likely wouldn't after he'd turned her over to be tortured. And she was the reason he was here. Draven's gaze zipped up and down Daiyu's figure. He was still of a similar build and height as Draven.

Daiyu's eyes narrowed. "What? What is it?"

"I was just thinking about that favor I mentioned."

"Ah. What exactly does it entail?"

Draven whipped off his cloak, extending it to Daiyu. "You'll see."

Draven entered House Channing wearing Daiyu's cloak, keeping his head down and hoping Shonn's spy would fall for the ruse. He patted his trouser pocket to ensure that he'd grabbed the vials of poison he'd need.

The guard recognized him, which he'd anticipated. Up close, he was still easily identifiable, but hopefully the spy would be fooled, since he was watching from a distance.

Once Draven explained to the guard that he needed to go upstairs to speak to Shonn on behalf of the Empress, he was quickly admitted. As soon as the guard had turned his back, Draven struck from behind, forcing the bottle of Manasseh between the man's lips. He went limp, and Draven slowly laid him on the ground. He couldn't have any witnesses know that he'd been there or they'd report their findings to the Empress, and she would wonder why Draven wanted to capture Shonn.

Draven raced up the spiraling stairs. He needed to render Shonn unconscious before Daiyu arrived. Daiyu had agreed to Draven's plans, so long as he didn't need to injure or fight anyone. He'd said his wife wouldn't approve.

By the time Draven reached the seventh floor, his chest was tight with the need for air. He drew in a few deep breaths before creeping through the hallway. The Lux lights above were glaringly bright, stretching Draven's shadow behind him.

He turned a corner and found two guards standing on either side of Shonn's door. Selene had guards, so of course

Shonn would as well. This presented a problem. He couldn't let the guards witness Shonn's capture.

The men stared at him silently, confusion flickering in their eyes.

Draven nodded in greeting. "I've come to speak to Shonn. I carry a message from the Empress, and it's imperative that I deliver it as soon as possible."

The guards shared a glance before one said, "Of course. Should I announce you?"

Draven shook his head. Better to catch Shonn unawares in his sleep. "That won't be necessary." He strode between them, to the door, and raised his fist.

Once he was certain that the guards weren't observing, he rammed his fist into the side of the first guard's face. He crumpled to the ground, and the other turned to face Draven, stumbling back a few steps.

As far as guards went, these seemed rather cowardly.

Draven darted forward and tackled him. His body thudded against the floor as well, and Draven hoped no one had heard the commotion.

He withdrew the vial and tapped out a drop. It landed between the man's lips. His eyes rolled back in his head, and he slumped onto the floor. Draven returned to the first guard and administered the Manasseh. If the Manasseh worked, they would remember nothing that had happened the hour prior to them falling asleep.

Draven tried opening Shonn's door, digging his fingers into the crevice to shove it aside. But it didn't budge. Locked.

He withdrew his pick and tension rod before delicately pushing each of the lock's pins upward. With a *click*, the lock twisted, and Draven slid open the door.

Shonn's walls were adorned with ornate weapons that Draven seriously doubted he knew how to use. There were several paintings of Shonn in various poses, attesting to the man's self-obsession, as did the mirrors. A spectacularly large one hung on the wall, a second stood beside Shonn's bed, and a handheld mirror lay on Shonn's nightstand. A thick rug softened Draven's footsteps as he approached.

Shonn bolted upright, his hair a mess of black clumps. "Who goes there?" He squinted in the darkness. "G-guard Raban? What are you doing here? In the middle of the night, no less."

Draven wondered if word of him had gotten around the house yet. The guards had seemed to know who he was. "I'm not Raban."

"O-of course. You're the Empress' spy, according to the messenger." Shonn nodded. "So kind of you to... grace our household. Again. You did my entire family a favor in rooting out the Scorpio spy, and I'd like to thank you. I know we had a few minor altercations—"

Draven snorted.

"—but surely you wouldn't report to the Empress anything that I've done, would you? After all, any treatment Selene received was well-deserved, given that she's an—"

In a flash, Draven gripped the front of Shonn's shirt, shoving him against his plump, silk pillows. His blood churned hot and fast beneath his skin. "No one could ever *deserve* what you did to Selene. I'll personally see to it that she's given an opportunity to testify against you in court."

Shonn had the audacity to smirk. "Be sensible. There's no evidence. What charges could possibly be held against me?"

Draven pressed Shonn harder against the pillow, until his smirk faded. "Everyone's guilty of something, Shonn. With some digging, I have no doubt that I could see you imprisoned. And then you won't ever be able to touch Selene again."

Shonn chuckled, though it almost sounded like wheezing. "A captor in love with his captive? I'd say that's even worse than a guard in love with his lady."

"Selene isn't going to be my only captive."

Shonn's eyes grew rounder than ever, and he opened his mouth, as if to scream. Draven reached into his pocket, removed the square piece of cloth—soaked in Somnus sap—and slammed it against Shonn's mouth and nose.

Shonn's scream was muffled against his hand, and he instinctively sucked in a breath. The light faded from his eyes, and his body thumped against the mattress. His chest rose and fell softly as he returned to sleep.

Draven heard a tapping at the window. He parted the curtains and swung the window open. Daiyu climbed the last scevola of rope and snuck inside, dressed in Draven's clothes. He wiped the sweat from his forehead. "That... was quite the climb." He huffed. "I have no idea how you do it." He glanced over at Shonn. "I never liked the boy anyway. But how in Torva am I supposed to climb back down with such a weight?"

Draven heaved Shonn onto his shoulder. "I'll help you tie him to your back. You'll be fine." Hopefully. If Daiyu plummeted with Shonn to their deaths, that would ruin tonight's plans.

Draven fastened Shonn to Daiyu's back, tying them together at the waist and looping Shonn's arms around Daiyu's neck before binding his wrists.

Daiyu carefully edged back out the window, gripping the rope with trembling hands. Just watching Daiyu made Draven break out in a sweat.

"You're doing great," Draven murmured.

"Easy for you to say. You don't have to carry him." Daiyu slipped over the windowsill, hiding him from view.

"If you'd rather trade places and catch Shonn's spy and subdue him for me, you're welcome to."

Daiyu grunted in reply.

Draven remained by the window, concealing himself behind the curtain as he scanned the skyline for movement.

Once Daiyu reached the ground, the tension from the rope easing, a black figure moved along the roof of a building. Hopefully that was Shonn's spy.

Draven waited until the figure began tracking Daiyu before escaping out the window and rappelling to the ground. He raced along the streets, keeping an eye on the spy as he lithely leapt from building to building.

He stopped at the base of a noble's house, judging from the gold paint rimming the roof tiles, and swung his grappling hook onto the edge of a balcony. He hauled himself up to the railing before searching out the spy once more. The spy had moved a block down the alley, still traveling on the rooftops.

Draven gripped the stones of the house, his slick fingers slipping, and climbed onto the roof. By the time he'd heaved himself up, his arms burned and his palms were glossy with sweat. He leapt from roof to roof, coming closer and closer to the spy.

When Draven was a building away, the spy suddenly whipped around to face him. The spy's eyes widened, and he changed directions, leaping onto a lower windowsill and nearly losing his balance.

Draven took a running jump onto the building, sank his grappling hook into a crack between the roof's tiles, and rappelled down the building. He was able to move much faster than the spy, who had to climb down by hand.

The spy's movements grew frantic, his fingers losing their hold. Just as the spy began to teeter dangerously backward, Draven caught the edge of his shirt. The spy flailed in his grasp, making the rope swing wildly. With one hand gripping the spy's shirt and the other holding the rope, there wasn't much else Draven could do.

If the movement slammed them into the building and knocked them unconscious, they'd both die. "Cease! You'll kill us," Draven said.

But the spy didn't seem of a mind to listen. The building swayed closer, growing larger until all Draven could see was its walls. A jarring pain crashed into his head, and his grip on the rope loosened, letting them drop several scevola before he tightened it.

Draven blinked hard, fuzzy stars prancing across his vision. Thankfully, the force of the hit had made the spy go limp. Draven relaxed his grip, letting them glide slowly to the ground.

Draven laid the spy down. With his slender figure splayed across the ground, he looked like... a woman. A second scan revealed his intuition was correct. Shonn had hired a female spy. How interesting.

He shook his grappling hook loose and bound the spy before tossing her over his shoulder. There was a cell tucked into the back of the dungeons where he could store Shonn and his spy. Although, knowing Shonn, he'd best place them in different cells.

With them locked away, Selene was the only one who knew the location of the Scorpio base, which meant that the Empress couldn't afford to kill her. He needed to find a way to free Selene before she broke.

Draven halted in an alley. Ahead, the palace towers rose between a gap in the buildings. "Hang on, Selene. I'm coming for you."

Pain set Selene's every nerve ablaze. She wondered if the bounty hunter was torturing Cori as Selene was being tortured. She hoped not. No one deserved this.

"Where is the Scorpio base?"

The question drummed against her mind, the words ricocheting beneath her skull. "I don't know."

A little shudder went through her as she anticipated the next bout of pain. The red-hot brand burned her back once more, and a scream erupted from her mouth, the jagged sound scraping past her raw throat.

She'd often wondered what would happen if she were captured and tortured. She'd hoped to be strong and take the pain with dignity. But here she was: screaming and crying and begging like a child.

She leaned her forehead against the wooden post she'd been tied to, Raban's name escaping through choked sobs. Raban had said that he'd be with her, that he'd save her. There were other thoughts circulating in the back of her mind, whispering that Raban wasn't Raban, that he'd betrayed her, that he'd brought her here so she could be tortured. But she shoved those thoughts away and clung to his name like a lifeline.

He was all she had left.

Breathing air came in unsteady jerks as her body spasmed with pain. She locked the location of the Scorpio base deep in her mind, even going so far as to rewrite it with other locations. She *couldn't* let them know where it was; Lyra's safety depended on her secrecy. She wasn't about to let Lyra endure pain and death at the hands of these men.

"Selene." One of the men rounded the pole to which she'd been chained and stood in front of her.

She'd been forced to kneel with her wrists bound around the pole, but if she'd been standing she would've collapsed by now. She steered her attention away from him, from the temptation to let the truth spill from her lips.

Thick, stone walls trapped her screams inside the room, where they would die with her. A blazing fireplace provided the heat for the brand. Various black metal implements hung from the walls. Under normal circumstances, she would have included them in her list of potential weapons. But used against her, they'd caused her more pain than she'd known she was capable of feeling.

The body's limit for torture seemed to be endless. When would it *finally* succumb to numbness and let her fade like a dying ember reduced to ash?

"Selene." From her peripheral vision, she saw the man step closer. "This will go on for *days* unless you tell us. You don't want that, do you?"

Days. The word devastated her. Enduring seconds more of this was unthinkable.

"Selene. Where is the Scorpio base?"

Another sob shuddered from her. "I..." More pain. More fire eating away at her flesh. More screams tearing at her throat. "I—I—"

"Tell us, and this will all be over."

"I don't know."

The man sighed and shook his head, like a disappointed father. "Remember, Selene. You brought this on yourself."

He strode behind her, and Selene pressed her forehead to the wooden pole. Searing heat warmed her back, and a scream built in her chest.

17

A FALSE RESCUE

Draven's hands trembled as he shoved more supplies into his pack.

He had five flasks of water. Would they need more? Where would they go? He had to hurry. Selene was dying at this very moment. First he'd need to sneak back into the dungeons to leave food and water for Shonn and the spy.

He forced himself to stop pacing, even though doing so caused an almost physical pain. He had to take time to *think*. The rescue and escape couldn't be sloppy or both he and Selene would suffer for it. Hopefully he had at least a few hours until she broke. Because as soon as they pried the location of the Scorpio base from her, they'd kill her.

The thought nearly sent him into another frenzied panic. He focused on taking deep breaths as he poured his money into a pouch and dropped it into the backpack. Selene would be severely injured, and she'd need time to heal somewhere. Likely, she wasn't going to be fit to ride horseback. He'd have to find a way to sneak her into a wagon without—

Abrupt banging startled him. He whipped around, his skin chilling like ice. Who would be knocking on his door? He grabbed the pack and stuffed it into a chest before slamming the lid shut.

"Draven! I demand that you open the door this very second."

The Empress. Draven rushed to the door and took a moment to put his hair in order and swipe the sweat from his forehead. He opened the door.

The Empress stood before him with her retinue of guards, flanking her like silent statues. It was strange to see her blazing red dress and flashy jewelry in this section of the palace. The hallway was plain stone, and usually only highly ranked knights wandered here. She appeared like a peacock in scrubland.

Draven dipped into a bow. "Empress. I wasn't expecting a visit so soon after—"

"Yes, yes, I know."

She swept past him, her perfume burning his eyes and nose. Her guards followed, stuffing his room to near-bursting. Draven watched her, hoping he was the only one who could feel how hard his heart was pounding. What did she want? Was she looking for something? Signs of his disloyalty, perhaps?

After a quick survey, she turned to face him. "Well? Close the door. We have much to discuss."

Draven shut the door, his palms damp. She must have found out about his plan to save Selene.

The Empress kept her gaze fused to his. "Selene has endured much in the past few hours."

It took every year of his training to not react. Was the Empress saying that Selene had finally revealed the location of the Scorpio base? That they were going to kill her?

"And she has yet to break," the Empress continued.

If he wasn't trying so hard to remain still, he would have slumped in relief. She was still alive, then. But why was the Empress telling him this? Was she going to ask *him* to be one of

Selene's tormentors? The contents in his stomach seemed to slosh, threatening to surge back up the way they'd come down.

"There's a new tactic I'd like to employ."

And it obviously had to do with him. "Oh?"

"She obviously cares for you." Mischief wreathed her expression. It was in the tilt of her lips, the glint in her eyes.

Cared for him? The thought made him hurt all over. He remembered how Selene had called for him when she'd been taken to the torture chambers. He couldn't imagine the pain and betrayal she must be feeling.

"At one point during the interrogation, the guards say she began calling out for you."

Agony knotted in his chest. Poor Selene. What had he done to her?

"I think that you're the only one that can coax the truth from her."

"You would have me interrogate her?" Just as he'd feared. If the Empress set a guard over him, she would soon find that he couldn't do it. He couldn't torture Selene. He knew that she was a danger to Evelyn and Alaric. But he couldn't, because when he looked at her, he didn't see an assassin. He saw a girl with beautiful veiled eyes and a sad smile.

"I didn't say pry the truth from her; I said coax. You are going to be the one to 'rescue' her."

He knew better than to feel hope or relief at her statement. She obviously had a plan for this "rescue," and he wasn't certain he'd like it. "What do you mean?"

"We could stage a rescue, where it appears as though you killed the guards and betrayed me in order to come to her aid."

Which he'd been dangerously close to doing anyway, whether or not the Empress sanctioned it.

"You could care for her, heal her."

Which meant that she'd been damaged enough that she was in need of healing. How extensively had she been injured?

Would she be permanently disabled? A wave of cold washed over him.

"And I suspect you could convince her to reveal the location of the Scorpio base faster than anyone."

"Empress, I'm not certain—"

"King Alaric's and Queen Evelyn's lives depend on you weeding out the last of the Scorpio."

So they did. But it was unlikely Selene would trust him after he'd turned her in.

"If you think the plan would be ineffective, we can continue with the interrogation as is. Even a Scorpio assassin must break eventually."

"No." His answer was too sharp, too quick—and both he and the Empress knew it. "I can't promise any results, but I can certainly try."

The Empress' lips curled into a smile. "It's in your best interest to provide results, not only for Evelyn's and Alaric's sakes, but also for Selene's. Should she not reveal the truth within a week, then we have no hope of ever getting information from her. She will be executed on the eighth day."

"And if she reveals the location? Then what happens to her?"

"Her fate will be negotiable... Perhaps if the idea is appealing to you, you could even take her to wife."

"No." Longing tugged at his chest, even as he knew it would never work. He could be her healer, her protector, her friend. But not her husband. That kind of lifestyle wasn't for him.

"Then a mistress."

Disgust twisted inside of him. "No." He would never dream of degrading her like that, especially with what she'd endured at Shonn's hands.

"Then, if she's sufficiently tamed, perhaps someone else's." Before Draven could protest, she raised her hand. "Think on it.

In the meantime, the captain of the guard will discuss her 'rescue' with you."

The Empress glided past him, all her samurai following but one. When the door closed, Draven turned toward the captain of the guard. He didn't want to manipulate Selene. But manipulating her was better than allowing her torture and subsequent death.

"So," Draven said, "how do you propose I rescue Selene?"

Draven stopped sprinting just short of ramming into the cobblestone wall. The keys on his belt jangled as he came to a stop. Those keys were Selene's ticket to freedom. His footsteps echoed through the passageway as his fingers ran along the crevices between the stones. He found a small stone, shaped vaguely like a fish, and pressed it into the wall.

The end of the passage opened, revealing the very lowest dungeons in Taijeng. There were only eight cells—four on each side—and two occupants.

The little female spy was crouched in a corner, and she glanced at Draven as he approached.

"What is the meaning of this?" The tiny stone room magnified Shonn's voice.

Draven glanced back at him. Shonn was clenching the bars of his cell on the other side of the passage. He didn't have time for an altercation with Shonn. Every moment he wasted here was a moment longer that Selene was being tormented.

He slid the heavy backpack off and unloaded the waterskins and sacks of food before passing them between the bars. "If you're careful, these should last you a month. I'll have someone come to check on you in three weeks' time if I can't myself." The female spy remained in the corner until Draven stuffed a blanket in between the bars and headed toward Shonn.

As soon as Draven was within arm's length of Shonn's cell, Shonn lunged for him, his fingers hooked and his arm fully extended. Draven smoothly stepped back, and for a brief moment, he considered setting Shonn's items on the ground, out of reach, and leaving.

But Shonn would die without water for three weeks. It would be no less than the man deserved, but Draven was not a murderer. Contrary to what Selene had assumed.

Draven set the items down, close enough that Shonn could grab them and pull them through the bars of the cell.

Shonn glared at him through narrow eyes. "You have no right to detain me. I have done nothing wrong."

Draven rose and headed back toward the passage. There was a system of secret passages that ran throughout the dungeons. The tormentors were about four levels higher. If he left through this passage and took a right at the first fork—

"Do you intend to leave us here indefinitely?" the soft question wafted from the spy's cell.

Draven turned toward her. She was cradling a water skin, her lips moist from a recent drink. "You'll both stand trial for your crimes."

Shonn snorted. "*Crimes*? You can't prove—"

"When will the trial take place?" she continued.

Draven felt a prick of guilt but ignored it. Selene was his first priority. "When I know Selene is safe. When this all dies down."

The girl's lips turned downward. "So indefinitely."

"I have a friend who's agreed to take care of you. You'll be all right." Draven sprinted toward the passage before the girl could pelt him with more questions. He pressed the small stone as he ran by, and the secret passage sealed. He stretched his legs, running toward the tormentors' room as fast as he could without tripping.

It wasn't fair to leave them here without an imminent trial

date. But for the time being, he didn't have a choice. And besides, Selene needed him. She'd suffered five hours of torment so far. If he traveled fast, she'd only need to endure two minutes more.

Selene was certain that the pain had finally addled her brain. In part, she was relieved. That meant the torture couldn't go on much longer before her body finally succumbed. But she'd also hoped that she was stronger than this.

The routine had begun like it always had, with them dragging her exhausted, tortured body to a cell and leaving her to bleed alone in the dark. It was its own kind of torment, though she much preferred it to beating and cutting and poking and whipping and branding. She would lie there, each breath a struggle, her body trembling with weakness and pain. She never knew how long she was left for. Perhaps seconds or minutes or hours or days. Time congealed together in an indistinct mass.

Then they'd come back, using the same torture methods on her and perhaps trying some new ones. At first, she'd endured the long walk to the torture chamber stoically. After a few sessions, she would weep and scream, begging them not to hurt her anymore. But this time, she only had energy for the next breath. Every inch of her body was in pain, yet something within her had gone numb.

They'd chained her to the pole, and then something peculiar had happened.

Raban came. He burst into the room and fought the men. One by one, they collapsed in front of him. And then he came for her, keys dangling from his hand. The chains jerked against her wrists, the links clinking together as he fumbled with the padlock.

Yes. She was most definitely addled. All this time spent screaming for Raban had finally brought about a hallucination of him. She must have passed out during the torture session; that was the only explanation. At least she could enjoy the reprieve while it lasted.

The lock finally released. Without the chain to hold her up, she toppled to the side. The impact felt like a kick to the chest, rattling every stinging bruise on her torso.

"What have they done to you, Selene?" Raban peered over her, his enchanting green eyes glowing with concern.

This was a rather lovely hallucination. She hoped she never woke up.

"And your *back*." She heard a string of curse words—some she understood and some she didn't. "This is all my fault, Selene."

A faint smile wisped across her lips. It was nice of him to say so. The real Raban would never admit to that, especially since he'd been the one to turn her in. In fact, she'd probably never see the real Raban again.

When he reached out toward her face, she grabbed his hand. "It's all right. At least you came for me."

Surprise exploded across his expression. "You—you forgive me?"

If that would make dream Raban happy... After all, there was no point in ruining a good hallucination. "Of course."

He brought her hand to his mouth and kissed her knuckles. And for some reason, the touch didn't make her feel ill. Yet another sign that this was a dream. "I'm going to give you some drugs now, to make the pain go away while we're traveling."

She sighed. And this was where the hallucination ended. She would either wake up or remain asleep forever. Hopefully the latter.

He held a cold glass vial to her lips. "Drink all of it."

She did as told—and felt a wave of bliss wash over her. She

couldn't remember the last time her body had felt so absent of pain. She felt new and fresh, like she could go anywhere and do anything. Drowsiness soon followed, and her eyelids drifted shut.

"You're safe now, Selene."

Yes, this had been a lovely hallucination. If she didn't die, hopefully she'd get to enjoy another one.

The sunlight glowed warmly against Selene's eyelids, in shades of red and orange.

The *sun*? There was no sunlight in the dungeons. Perhaps she was near the fireplace.

Selene opened her eyes. Pale light streamed in through a window, flooding the small room. Aside from the bed she lay in, there was a chair, a nightstand, and potted flowers by the door.

What? Had the Empress ordered her to be taken to the infirmary, perhaps? So that once she was better, she could endure more torture?

Selene ran her hands through her hair, only to draw away when she felt a row of stitches at her hairline. Had she finally cracked and revealed the location of the Scorpio base? She couldn't remember. Surely not, or she wouldn't still be alive.

Selene glanced out the window, ignoring how pain pierced her eyes at the bright light. It was nothing compared to the torture she'd endured in that tiny stone room. Outside, jungle foliage carpeted the sloping backs of mountains. Blue mists slunk around them, pooling into the lush valleys.

She blinked hard. The Taijese palace didn't have mountains nearby, nor a jungle. She must be outside the city of Renshi.

She glanced down at her body and found herself clothed in a soft white gown. There were laces in the back that went from her neckline to the bottom hem of the dress. A medical gown. She'd been taken somewhere and healed. But for what purpose?

Selene sat up. She felt weak, but there was no pain. None whatsoever. She reached to touch her back through the laces. Thick bandages covered her skin. She obviously wasn't completely healed.

The window drew her attention once more. It had been opened a crack, allowing the humid jungle air to trickle through. She could escape, before her captors returned. But where could she escape to? She didn't know where she was, and she was obviously still injured.

But she felt perfectly fine. And if her captors came back and saw that she was awake, they would restrain her. They would see that she was well enough and torture her again.

The thought was enough to make her whip the blanket off herself and swing her feet to the floor. She stood and found herself flailing for the bedpost. Her knees wobbled terribly, as though her legs would snap apart at any moment. She gripped the bedpost, her legs still vibrating so hard that they sent trembles up and down her body.

She eyed the chair. It was just barely out of reach. Perhaps if she shoved off the bed, it would propel her far enough that—

"*Selene!*"

She startled and let go of the bed post, thudding to the floor on her posterior. *Raban?* She glanced up at him as he approached, his expression dark and stormy. His skin was a shade lighter than when she'd last seen him. How was he here? She remembered the hallucination she'd had. It'd seemed like a mere moment ago.

He lifted her, one arm beneath her legs, the other high on her back.

She gaped at him. He'd actually rescued her? And betrayed the Empress in doing so? "Y-you saved me?"

18

A HEALING TOUCH

Raban's face pinked as he set Selene on the bed. His slightly fairer skin made his blush more apparent. "You don't remember? I thought you were somewhat conscious when I came for you."

"I thought it was a hallucination." She reached out and rested her fingertips on his arm, just to be sure. It felt solid and warm beneath her fingers. She drew away, her thoughts sloshing in her head. Why would he help her? He'd also been the one to turn her in. Perhaps because he... cared for her? Because he loved her?

Unlikely. Who would hand their loved one off to be tortured anyway? There must be something else, something he wanted from her. She wouldn't gain any answers by asking outright, so her best option was to wait.

Selene glanced around the simple room again, realizing that the walls weren't made of wood but rather bamboo. "Where am I?"

"We're in a Vism temple, with the monks. They're expert healers. They've made much progress on your back, *but*," he stared at her sternly, "that doesn't mean that you're fit enough to get up and walk around."

"If I don't, then I'm going to wither away in this bed." Although, it was a rather comfy bed, the cool white cushions like a caress against her battered body. And she was almost dizzy with exhaustion. She forced her drifting eyelids back up. "But... what happens if your betrayal is discovered?"

"It likely already has been."

"And what if they find you?"

"They won't." He pulled the blanket over her, tucking it in at the sides. "Now rest. That's the fastest way that you can heal."

"But if the Empress finds me—"

He tucked a lock of hair behind her ear, his fingers gliding across her forehead. "She won't. I'll protect you. You're safe here."

After what he'd done, she wasn't entirely sure that she could trust him. But his words brought comfort nonetheless, her body sinking deeper into the mattress. A thought flickered through her mind. Poor Cori. Who would save her?

Selene determined that she would. As soon as she got some more sleep...

Hands were crawling over her skin, touching her in places they shouldn't.

Selene jolted awake from her nightmare, only to find that the sensation didn't fade. She could still feel hands wandering over her body. She was laying stomach-down on the bed. Selene opened her eyes and glanced to the side.

The laces on the back of her gown had been loosened, and two men were touching her. Though her back was numb, she could still feel their hands. Her stomach lurched, and her entire chest squeezed until she was dry-heaving.

The men froze, obviously realizing they'd been caught. These perverted monks had obviously thought they could prey on a helpless woman.

Selene jerked upright, rolling into a sitting position. "Stay back!"

One man raised his hands and spoke in a low, lulling tone, as if calming a skittish horse. "Please, calm yourself. We mean no harm. We were just reapplying the ointment and changing your bandages." The first man gestured to the other, who raised a wooden container of green-brown goop. Dirty bandages dangled from his other hand.

"Oh." Perhaps she'd jumped to a conclusion too quickly. "I thank you, but I'm perfectly capable of tending myself." The thought of them touching her again was almost enough to make her shudder.

The men began shaking their heads, and the first said, "No, no, no. You're in no position to change your own bandages. Allow us to—"

"*No!*" Upon seeing the men's shocked expressions, she said, "No *thank* you. I'm sure the old bandages you put on are just fine."

A moment later, she heard how ridiculous the words sounded. She certainly didn't want her wounds to become infected. But the thought of those strange men putting their hands on her... She swallowed back the bile singeing her throat.

"If you leave the clean bandages and ointment with me, I'll manage."

The men shared a skeptical look with each other. They set the medical supplies on the edge of the bed and slowly crept out of the room, as if scared she would spook. Or pounce.

Selene stared at the ointment and bandages. Now she'd find out whether or not she was truly capable of doing it by herself. She touched her back, her fingers grazing moist flesh. She swiped them on her gown with a grimace. Even though the skin was obviously raw, she didn't feel a thing. They must be drugging her with something.

She was just reaching toward the clean bandages when Raban opened the door. She jerked back, feeling as if she'd been caught with her hand in the sweet bun bowl. "Raban."

He released a small sigh. "Selene... my name's not Raban."

She knew it. Yet she preferred Raban to Draven. Raban was her protector and friend. Draven was her tormentor and enemy. It was hard to reconcile the two men into one.

"I like Raban better," she replied.

Raban—or Draven—flinched. "Raban was a name I invented to disguise my true identity. You might not like who I really am, but I'd rather you use my given name nonetheless."

She scooped the clean bandages onto her lap, toying with the edges. "So everything you did as Raban was an act?"

He shook his head. "No. I did admit that I cared for you— under truth serum, no less." His face colored as he rubbed the back of his neck. "I know it must have frightened you when you discovered who I was."

"Not frightened."

"Then what?" He drew a chair to her bedside and sat.

"Angered. Hurt. I wasn't thinking clearly enough to be frightened. At least, not until you confronted me."

Regret lined his face, his gaze falling to her bed sheets. "Selene, I'm so sorry."

"For what? Capturing me?"

"Well, perhaps not that."

The hurt dug deeper, spearing through her heart. "Then you were well with me being tortured."

"Obviously not, or I wouldn't have taken you away. I wish I hadn't given you into the Empress' keeping. I wanted to stop you from hurting others, but that didn't mean that I wanted you to be hurt in their stead."

"What would you have done differently?"

"Taken you where you would have been safe, until I could have spoken to King Alaric myself."

Selene chuckled. "You have an enormous amount of confidence in the King's mercy."

"I do. I was the recipient of it a few years ago, you know."

When he'd betrayed the Scorpio. "Yes, I know."

"Betrayal isn't inherently bad, Selene. It merely signifies a change in loyalties, and thus a change in oneself."

But if she betrayed the Scorpio, she'd be expected to reveal the location of the Scorpio base. "You won't persuade me, *Draven*."

The light in his eyes dimmed. "You say 'Draven' differently than you say 'Raban.'"

Did she? She hadn't noticed.

"For the time being, all I want to do is persuade you to let me tend your back." He spread his hands, palms up, as if showing her that he was unarmed, that she had nothing to fear. She visually trailed the lines of his hands. Though his skin was lighter, it wasn't as pale as a northerner's should be.

"You don't have to keep making your skin darker, now that I know who you are."

Draven flipped his hand around, glancing at the back of it. "Once I stop applying the ointment, it takes a week to wear off. Then I'll return to my natural skin tone." He smiled at her. "If I didn't know better, I'd say you were trying to distract me. Would you allow me to tend you?"

She glanced at the door. "Those monks. They told you what happened, didn't they?"

His grin widened. "They said that the woman I'd brought was crazy and wouldn't let them tend her. They said that I should go in and settle her down."

As if she were a child. Anger sparked within her chest. "*Settle me—*"

Draven laughed, setting his hand on her arm. "Lower your voice, Selene. You're going to worry them. May I tend your back?"

And touch her? She hugged the bandages to her chest, as if erecting a barrier between them.

"I'll be gentle and touch you as little as possible."

She squeezed the bandages more tightly. Realistically, tending her own back would be rather difficult, especially when she couldn't see it. But better him than those monks. "I suppose so."

"Lie down then, please."

She was suddenly aware of the cool air at her back, how exposed it was. "How much of me will be uncovered?"

"Only your back. Don't worry."

Her breaths came faster, and she curled her fingers around the bundle of bandages until her knuckles paled.

Draven studied her face, intelligence and gentleness radiating from his jungle-green eyes. "You're all right, Selene. Even when we were fighting, I didn't hurt you."

"But then you let the tormentors take me. And they did hurt me."

He closed his eyes. "Yes, I know. I know that very well now." He opened them again. "As soon as they were dragging you away, I wanted to take you back, to ensure those terrible things wouldn't happen to you. But if I had, I would have been stopped. Then we both would have been handed over to the tormentors. And so I had to wait and plan our escape." He shook his head. "I'm sorry for ever bringing you there in the first place. With everything that's happened, I don't know how you're not angrier with me."

She couldn't help being suspicious. But she wasn't angry in the slightest. "How could I be? You might have turned me in, but you also saved me. And... I might have been wrong about you killing my mother."

His eyebrows leapt. "Why? What made you change your mind?"

"As you said, you didn't hurt me while we were fighting. I think you'd be more likely to change someone or capture them rather than kill them." She smiled softly. "Like you tried to do with me."

"And failed." But despite his words, he returned her smile. It slowly faded. "If I didn't kill your mother, who do you think did?"

She shrugged. "I still don't see how—or why—Arzil would." It had to be someone else.

"You have a lot of faith in his mercy."

"No. I have a lot of faith in his practicality. She was one of his best assassins. What could have prompted him to kill her?"

Betrayal, her mind whispered. She was also one of Arzil's best assassins, but as he'd recently reminded her, she was expendable. She remembered that conversation, where he'd accused her of being overly fond of her guard and told her that Cori was gone. The reminder dampened Selene's spirits.

"Don't think on it too much, Selene. I didn't mean to upset you." He lifted the heap of clean bandages from her arms. "Now lie down. I won't take long."

19

WATCHED

Though Selene's heart began a nervous pitter-patter, she lay down on her stomach, turning her face to the side so the pillow didn't smother her. She felt Draven settle a blanket over her legs and rear before brushing her hair over her shoulder. He further opened the back of her gown, since the monks had already unlaced the fabric.

The air chilled her bare skin. Selene dug her nails into her pillow. She felt so vulnerable like this. She'd never let anyone see her with so little clothing.

"It's all right, Selene." He touched her arm briefly, his palm warm and calloused. "Thankfully, they finished cleaning it before you woke up. All I have to do is reapply the ointment and bandages."

From the corner of her eye, she saw him tip the jar, a glop of goo landing on her back. It should have felt cold and slimy—or set all of her raw nerves on fire. But she barely felt it. "Are they drugging me?"

Draven nodded as he washed his hands, using the basin on her nightstand. "To help with the pain. Otherwise, you'd be in perpetual agony." He lightly glided his fingertips over her back.

Her heart pounded frantically, as if trying to escape the confines of her ribs. She tried to slow her breathing, hoping he hadn't noticed her reaction. Thankfully, she didn't feel nauseous.

"When I first brought you," he continued, "they had to remove some of the dead and mangled skin from your back. That's when they administered the first dose of drugs."

She didn't like the idea of being drugged. But for the most part, her mind felt clear. "Are there any side effects?"

"Yes. It has been known to make people more impulsive. And since it's very effective at numbing pain, the recipients have a tendency to feel invincible, like they're healed and well when they're not. That was probably why you were trying to make your escape earlier today. If you'd been more clear-headed, you would've realized that you wouldn't have gotten very far."

Selene's cheeks tingled with fire. In hindsight, that decision did seem rather impulsive.

His hands ran up and down her back, spreading the ointment across her skin. Her heartbeat gradually slowed as he worked. The repetitive motion of his palm working from the center of her back outward was almost relaxing.

"There. All done."

Selene startled and blinked, not remembering when she'd closed her eyes. "Oh. That didn't take long."

He grinned as he wiped his hands on a towel. "I believe you were asleep for most of it."

Heat surged to her face once more, and Selene glanced aside. Assassins weren't supposed to blush—and definitely not so frequently.

Draven curved his arm around the bowl and picked up the jar of ointment with the other. "I was in the middle of getting your dinner when the monks came to me in a panic. If you'd like, I can go back and see if there's any more broth left."

Typically, she hated broth. It was weak and watery, unlike stew with chunks of meat and vegetables or porridge with cream and fruit. But suddenly, it sounded rather delicious. "That would be lovely."

Draven grinned, not even attempting to hide his enthusiasm. "I'll return shortly, then."

Selene wound her arms around the pillow, letting her cheek rest against its softness. How long would she and Draven stay here? Until she was well? What then? Draven would be a wanted criminal by now—because of her.

Her earlier suspicions returned. There was no way he'd give up everything—his life, his status, his reputation—to run away with her. He had to have some ulterior motive, because if he didn't, then that would mean... he loved her.

The Next Day

Selene's legs wobbled as she clung to the wooden bed post. They were so weak and thin. It was hard to imagine that she'd lost so much muscle within a few days of lying in bed. After she'd steadied herself, she took a handful of tottering steps forward.

Draven hovered nearby, like a worried mother bird ready to swoop in and save her hatchling should it fall. "You're doing wonderfully, Selene."

"I can barely walk."

Draven extended his hand toward her. "Allow me to help."

She eyed his hand. He'd checked on her back this morning, and his touch had only stirred a slight sense of discomfort. If such an intimate touch barely bothered her, it was unlikely that handholding would either.

She reached toward him. He tucked her hand beneath his arm, letting her lean heavily against him as he strolled around the room in a tight circle. The little walk was more tiring than she would have liked to admit, but she could feel the exercise strengthening her legs.

Draven seemed to sense her exhaustion and seated her on the edge of the bed. "Why don't you rest?"

She narrowed her eyes at him. "Who said I needed to rest? With your help, I'm certain I could take a stroll outside." She looked at the window, then back at him.

He flashed a grin at her, and she tried to ignore the strange feeling in her chest. He'd been smiling at her much more today. "Would you really like me to describe how heavily you were panting? Or how you nearly tripped twice? Or—"

"No, no, no. I'm fine, thank you." She lay down, resting on her stomach. She couldn't wait until the day when she could lie on her back again.

"I'll leave you to your rest, then." Draven dipped into a bow and closed the door behind him.

Selene stretched out across the bed and watched the shadows slink across the room as the sun traversed the sky. After an hour, she was ready to try walking again. But Draven hadn't returned.

Selene sat up. Since when did she require Draven's assistance to do everything? If she were smart, perhaps she could take a walk on her own. Draven's cloak was draped over the chair, perfect for disguising her gown. She rose to her feet —and was pleased to find that she felt steadier this time.

Selene walked to the chair and whipped the cloak around her neck. She glanced at the window again. Perhaps she could take a very, very short walk. She'd be back in her room before Draven realized she was missing.

Selene took a few slow steps forward and opened the bedroom door. There was a long hallway with another room branching off from it. At the end, the hallway turned sharply to the left. Square tatami mats covered the wooden floor. At least if she fell, it'd be a soft landing. Selene staggered forward, using the bamboo wall as support. By the time she made it to the end, she was breathing more heavily than the exertion should have warranted.

She considered turning back until she glanced around the corner. There was a tiny side door, just ahead. It appeared different from the other doors. What if that led outside? Or it could merely lead to a storage closet. Perhaps she'd just check the door before returning to her room.

Selene neared the door and tried the handle. To her delight, it swung inward, revealing an orderly raised herb garden, with rows of thick, leafy green plants alternating with tiny sprouts, barely visible against the dark soil. Vertical bamboo rods fenced in the area, and a lush, tangled jungle lay beyond. Puddles of mud dappled the ground from recent rain, and the air was thick with warmth and moisture—even in the middle of winter.

Selene closed the door behind her and wove around the puddles before sinking next to the bed of herbs, her chest heaving from the exertion.

She rolled onto her stomach and rested her cheek against the ground, examining the herbs, breathing in their fragrances. She couldn't wait until she'd regained her strength. Without it, she felt like a weak husk of herself.

Selene snapped off a stalk of tart-smelling lemonweed and placed it on her tongue, chewing it until she could smell nothing but lemons. This place was so peaceful and serene, with the jungle birds chirping and chatting in the distance, the scenic greenery carpeting the mountains. But she knew it wouldn't last. As long as she remained in Taijeng, the Empress would find her.

Unease skittered across her skin, and Selene looked beyond the fence—just in time to see leaves stir, but not from the wind.

She caught a flash of black clothing, a pair of eyes staring back at her.

Panic burst within her, wiping the last of her exhaustion away. Tuteno. It seemed the Empress had found her sooner than expected. There was no way that she could fight anyone off in this state.

Selene lurched to her feet and raced back toward the temple. *"Draven!"* Her foot splashed into the middle of a mud puddle, and she slipped forward and fell, warm brown water staining her gown and Draven's cloak.

Selene glanced back at the forest. Nothing. There was absolutely nothing there. But she could have sworn—

A door slammed open, and heavy footsteps pounded toward her. "Selene! What are you doing out of bed?" Draven lifted her from beneath her arms and raised Selene to her feet. He examined her dripping clothes with a frown.

"I—I was going for a walk." She glanced at the jungle once more. Still no signs of the person she'd seen earlier. As Draven picked her up, she placed her mouth by his ear. "Draven, I *saw* someone in the jungle. Watching me."

Draven headed inside. "Likely just a monk out for a stroll."

"But monks don't wear black. It has to be one of the Empress' spies."

A few monks rushed through the door, though they stopped upon seeing Draven and Selene.

A short one with heavyset brows stared at her. "Are you well?"

Before she could answer, Draven replied for her, "She's fine. She merely fell when walking in the garden. Perhaps she could have a bath?"

The monks both nodded, and the short one said, "Of course, of course." They hurried back into the temple.

Draven strode into the hallway. Selene's clothes dripped brown water spots onto the floor and she grimaced. Poor monks. She was probably one of their worst patients, yelling at them when they tried to tend her, then making a mess inside.

She glanced back at Draven. "It was *not* a monk. Draven, you're in danger here. I know I might not be able to travel, but you should find a horse and flee—"

"I'm not leaving you." His voice was steady, his response without hesitation, and Selene's heart did a little flip. "And it wasn't one of the Empress' spies, Selene. This area is safe, secluded—"

Her chest squeezed. If something happened to Draven because of her, she would never be able to live with herself. "Draven, please believe me. I'm an assassin. My instincts are rarely wrong."

"Like they were when you thought I'd killed your mother?"

Shame washed over her. She glanced down at her stained gown, wishing she'd put the pieces together much sooner.

"Forgive me. That was cruel." He loosened his grip on her legs to open the door to her room. "I shouldn't have brought it up again." He set her on the chair, positioning her sideways so that she wouldn't lean her back against the furniture.

She threw her right arm over the chair, setting her chin on the top of it. "You can bring it up anytime you please. It was a mistake on my part."

"But it's in the past." Draven knelt before her, taking her wet hand in his. "I just don't want you to worry about your safety here. I know you said you trust your instincts, but in this situation, I'd like you to trust mine."

How was that fair? He refused to trust her instincts but wanted her to trust his? Selene nodded nonetheless.

"Thank you." Draven rose. "And I'll ask the monks about who was wandering in the jungle, if it would make you feel safer."

Selene nodded more enthusiastically. "Please do. And thank you."

"Of course." Draven began walking toward the door. "The tub is heavy. I'll bring it in here and help the monks haul the bath water. I wouldn't be taking good care of you if I let you look like a pig, now would I?"

Selene's mouth dropped open. She snatched a spoon off the nightstand before flinging it at him with the accuracy of an assassin throwing a dagger. He closed the door, chuckling, and the spoon clinked harmlessly against it.

She tried to let the light-hearted moment pierce through the darkness, but the unease wouldn't leave her. Regardless of what Draven said, she knew she should be wary of the man in the jungle.

20

FALLING

A few hours later, Selene was clean, her soggy bandages changed, and wrapped cozily in clean sheets. To keep her restlessness at bay, Draven had found a scroll for her to read. It was about some local myths and legends, but the writing was dull and the phrasing confusing, rendering it horrendously boring.

The door opened, and a monk peered into her room. "I—I have come to bring you supper, if that's well with you."

Poor monk. She'd likely frightened all of them after her episode with them changing her bandages. Selene set the scroll down. "That sounds wonderful. Please, come in."

The man practically tiptoed to the nightstand and set the bowl down. He appeared like he was about to bolt when Selene said, "Pardon me. Do you know which monk was wandering in the jungle today?"

He glanced up at her and blinked. The lashes rimming his eyes were surprisingly thick. "Wandering the jungle? You saw someone?"

"Yes. Hasn't Draven told you?"

The monk shook his head.

Selene's suspicion flared, but she tamped it down with

rationale. Draven likely hadn't had time to tell them yet. That was all. "I saw someone in the jungle today, dressed in black, when I was in the herb garden."

The monk's gaze skittered to the side. "Ah, yes. That must be Brother Furvus."

"He wears black?"

"Yes. And he likes to forage in the jungle for fruit and nuts."

A reasonable explanation. Yet there was something vaguely bothersome about his answer. She'd never seen a monk wearing black. But she hadn't seen all the monks of the temple either. "That makes sense. Thank you."

He nodded and practically sprinted from the room.

She wanted to believe that the monk was telling the truth— and that she could trust Draven. She wanted everything to be as idyllic as it appeared. But she knew better. Something was going on—and neither the monks nor Draven were being honest about what it was.

If the man in black was the Empress' spy, then the monk was covering for him. Could the monk be in league with the Empress? What if all of the monks were?

And what about Draven? Even though she'd told him she'd seen a stranger hiding in the jungle and his life was in mortal danger, he'd seemed completely unconcerned. What if he was also in league with the Empress? But why would he have brought her here? Perhaps because the Empress ordered him to? And the Empress had likely sent other men with him to ensure that Selene didn't try to escape.

That meant that Draven hadn't truly rescued her. He hadn't risked his life or betrayed Taijeng to save her. Somehow, that seemed more believable than the idea that he'd sacrificed so much for her, an assassin who had been trying to kill him. She crushed her pillow against her chest as she lay face down on the bed, hoping to stifle the ache in her heart.

Of course, this was all based on several assumptions. But

her instincts whispered that she was right. And that realization broke her. It felt like a physical crack had run down her middle, ripping her apart. Tears flowed freely down her cheeks, blotting her pillow with dark spots.

Draven was still in league with the Empress.

He had ulterior motives for helping her.

And he certainly hadn't rescued her because he loved her.

The Next Day

"You're quieter today, Selene." Draven was sitting in the chair by the window, his eyes fixed on her.

She opened her eyes, weary of pretending to be asleep. "I'm just tired."

"But you were so adventurous yesterday."

"Exactly. It wore me out." She turned toward the wall, away from Draven. Yesterday's realization had sapped her energy and strength. She knew she should be plotting her escape if her assumption was right. But she couldn't work up the motivation to do anything. Even opening her eyes was laborious.

She heard Draven rise and walk to her bedside. "I found this stunning view overlooking a cliff. Why don't we visit?"

"Walking exhausts me." Her words were partially muffled by the pillow.

"The spot isn't too far. I can carry you."

What did he want from her? Why did he care? She lifted her head off the pillow and glanced back toward him. "Why do you want me to go out so badly?" She would have suspected an ambush or attack. But given her condition, anyone could attack her at any time, and she'd be helpless.

He knelt by her bed, his face level with hers. "You seem low on energy today, and it concerns me. The more you're up and about, the sooner you'll recover. Surely you don't want to be abed for any longer than necessary."

Selene stretched out until her toes nearly touched the footboard. "Tomorrow I'll get up."

Draven narrowed his eyes and rose to his feet. "I think it'd be good for you to get out of this room."

"But I don't want to." She raised her eyebrows at him. "And there's nothing you can do to change my mind."

"Who said anything about changing your mind?" Draven smirked, mischief glinting in his eyes. Before she could ask what he intended, he tugged her into a sitting position and scooped her into his arms.

When she began to struggle, he tightened his grip. "Don't—or you'll injure yourself."

"If you were concerned about that, you should have left me in bed!" But she relaxed against him. Fighting him took too much energy.

It took a moment for her to realize how much he was touching her. And how much she didn't mind it. It was even... comforting.

He strode down the hallway to a spot where the flooring changed abruptly from bamboo to stone. An older wing perhaps? Here, mosaics—occasionally interrupted by narrow arched windows—covered the walls. Monks strolled by, their cowls over their heads. The scent of incense made her eyes water.

The hallway opened up into a circular room with a domed ceiling. Beneath it, footsteps echoed like pattering raindrops. In the middle of the temple, a few monks were seated on the floor in a ring, their eyes closed as they meditated. Multiple bamboo hallways branched off from the main temple. It appeared one led to a library, another to a storage room, and a third to the monks' personal rooms.

The only side of the temple that didn't extend into a

bamboo hallway was the front entrance. It was wide enough for at least ten men to enter shoulder-to-shoulder. And there was no door to guard the area from blood-sucking skimmers or intruders. It was open to the hot, damp air, and stone steps streamed from the mouth of the entrance to a dirt road that vanished into the jungle.

Draven descended the stairs and walked along the temple's wall. The perimeter of the temple had been cleared to a path a few scevola wide. It made it easier to traverse. They passed the stables as they walked. It was identical to the other bamboo hallways except for the musty smell of horse manure.

When they'd reached the back, Draven walked through a clearing, the long grass swishing around his legs. There were a few places that the grass had been flattened. It seemed that Draven wasn't the only one who came here.

Within a few scevola, Draven had brought her to the edge of a cliff. Mountains tumbled beneath them as far as she could see, the blue mists complementing the viridian green of the jungle. The mountains faded into vague silhouettes in the distance until they blended into the sky completely. Their rolling curves were mesmerizing. It was like having an enchanted map splayed out at her feet.

She glanced back and saw the temple on the other side of the clearing. It was reassuring that it was nearby. It had become her safe haven. And in a way, Draven had become her safe haven too. She desperately didn't want to lose that.

Draven set her onto a flattened patch of grass. "Aren't you glad that I dragged you out here?"

"Perhaps. But that doesn't mean that I'd give my consent for you to do it again." At his disappointed look, she flashed him a smile to let him know she jested.

He grinned and lay back onto the grass. His green eyes reflected the gray sky, lightening their color. Though he appeared relaxed, there was tension in his expression, a tightness about his jaw and eyes. Even so, he was devastatingly handsome. It was as if a sculptor had designed the planes of his face, the edges of cheekbones, the straight line of his nose.

Draven's lips quirked into a smile. "You're supposed to be staring at the scenery, my dear."

Heat stormed across her face, and she glanced away, lest he see her blush. "I was just thinking that you looked tense." Among other things...

"Oh?"

She could immediately hear the guardedness in his voice. She glanced back at him. "You're hiding something from me. And I fear it will lead to death or more torture."

"I'd never allow that to happen, Selene. *Never*." He propped himself on his elbows. "What I did a few days ago... that was a mistake. I wanted to protect Evelyn and Alaric, but not at the expense of your life."

Selene directed her focus toward the view in front of them. He wasn't going to tell her what he was hiding, so she might as well change the subject. "You address them rather casually, given that they're royalty."

He released a one-beat laugh. "I've become rather familiar with them. You know I was formerly a duke, serving as the public relations official in the King's palace." At Selene's nod, he continued, "While there, I was also serving the Scorpio. My mission was to get rid of Queen Evelyn. But instead of getting rid of her, I fell in love with her."

A raging current of heat flowed through Selene, her stomach tightening into knots. It took her a moment to realize that she felt... jealous. Ridiculous. She didn't have any claim on Draven.

"My plan fell through when she chose Alaric over me. I'd cared for her a lot, more than I had for anyone else, so it took me a few years to let the pain of that loss fade. But in the meantime, I also realized that I hadn't loved her. What I'd felt for her was selfish; it was based on what I wanted instead of what was in her best interest."

The tightness in Selene eased slightly. "Then you don't possess any romantic feelings for the Queen?"

"None." Draven stared directly at her, unsaid words twinkling in his eyes. Then he looked away. "As far as my connection to the King goes, he and I are half-brothers."

"*Half-brothers*?" Now that, she hadn't known. "What? How?"

"We share the same father," he said it without emotion, as if he were trying to make small talk about the weather.

"The late King Vulcan?"

"The very one."

She felt a wave of shock roll over her. "Draven. You're royalty."

Draven shook his head. "I was born of an affair. I might have royal blood, but I am not royalty." He chuckled bitterly, his gaze falling to his lap. "You must think me horribly selfish and thoughtless."

"Draven, I don't know who you used to be, apart from what Faina's told me. But I know who you are now. You're honorable and noble and kind." Even if he did keep secrets from her. But could she blame him? She'd been plotting to kill his brother.

His brother… She squinted at him, mentally comparing his features to a poster she'd seen of the King. Now that she thought of it, she could see a resemblance between the King and him.

"So you know who Faina is?" he asked.

Selene nodded. "The streetsweeper. She met me the night I discovered you were Draven. She's the one who told me."

"I thought so. If you don't mind me asking, what did she say about me?"

Selene grinned. "She didn't seem to think very highly of you."

"It's what I deserve."

Selene fell silent for a moment. He also didn't think that he deserved to be married, all because of Faina. "She was wrong, about a lot of things."

He peered up at her, his eyes aglow with hope and curiosity. "Really?"

"Yes. She said you were a fool for thinking any woman would want you because of the mistakes you'd made. She said all the women in Torva deserved a better man than you. She said that without your title, you had nothing to offer any woman."

"And... she's wrong?" he asked.

A quick glance to the side revealed that Draven had gone completely still. She couldn't even see his chest rise and fall with breath.

"Yes," Selene said. "What she said was a load of tuteno. Any woman in Torva would be lucky to have you. And while you may no longer be noble in status, you're noble in character. And in my opinion, character is far more valuable than status."

Draven still didn't appear to be breathing as he stared at her, his expression radiating warmth.

Her heart thudded strangely against her chest. "Draven?"

21

FLEEING THE TEMPLE

Draven's gaze swerved away from Selene, snapping back to the view. "Thank you, Selene." His voice was soft, his words almost lost to the light breeze.

"Of course. I'm only speaking the truth." Selene scooted herself back around to face the drop off. "Faina said that you proposed to her?"

"Yes." His posture sagged slightly. "I thought that I could make amends for what I'd done. But nothing can erase the past."

Selene pounded her fist against the ground. "*Draven!*"

Judging from his wide eyes, she'd startled him.

"We just spoke about this. Do my words mean nothing to you? You might not be able to change the past, but you can choose your present, and in doing so, change your future. And you have. Even if Faina refuses to acknowledge it, you are a different man."

Draven plucked a blade of grass, winding it around his index finger. "I could say the same of you, Selene."

"P-pardon?" What in Torva was he talking about?

"You don't have to let your past define your future. Just

because you've previously been an assassin for the Scorpio doesn't mean that you always need to be."

She snorted. "I know that." She'd been plotting for the past year to leave the Scorpio, after all.

He shot her a quizzical glance. "You do?"

Her plan was on the tip of her tongue, but she swallowed it back. After she was healed, she'd still need to find a way to evade both the Empress and the Scorpio. And she might still need to kill the King to have enough money for that.

The thought didn't sit well with her. In fact, it made her feel disgusting. The one thing Draven wanted was to save his half-brother. Selene didn't know if she could stomach that particular assassination. She'd be too distracted by thinking of Draven's grief. Perhaps she could ask Arzil for a different mission, to kill someone more worthy of death.

But who was more worthy of death than she?

The thought was abrupt—and deeply disturbing. Was she worthy of death? She'd merely taken the only options available to her. Her mother had been the one to first bring her into the Scorpio, and then Arzil had made her stay. To leave would have meant death, which was why she was trying to save enough money for a proper escape.

But Draven had been presented with the same options as she: remain with the Scorpio or leave and be hunted by them for the rest of his life. She'd just told him that he'd made a choice to have a different future than his past. Couldn't she do the same?

Selene shook her head, trying to dislodge the wayward thought. Before Draven had come, she'd been so certain of her beliefs. To think that they could all be wrong made her uneasy.

"Selene? What's the matter?"

"I'm just tired."

"Would you like me to take you back inside?" He began to rise, but Selene waved him back down.

"It's all right. I want to remain out here for a while longer." Selene set her chin onto the back of her hand, studying how the blades of grass danced in the breeze.

Flowers speckled the greenery around her, like shimmering jewels adorning a crown. There were Sassithorn flowers, which would glow silver under moonlight. Dew Drop flowers sparkled like radiant diamonds. Evanescence flowers dangled like little bells from ground vines. White glowed from the middle of the flowers, darkening into fuchsia at the tips. It was strange to see them in their natural form, before they'd been liquified into poison.

It seemed like seconds later when something brushed against her face. Selene opened her eyes. She must have truly been tired. Thankfully, she felt refreshed and couldn't remember having any nightmares. She suspected the drugs they used on her for pain helped her sleep dreamlessly.

Draven was at her side, nudging her shoulder. "Selene, wake up."

She swatted his hand away. "I'm awake."

"We should go back inside. It's nearly dinner time, and it looks like it's about to rain."

She glanced at the dark gray sky, and droplets flecked her cheeks. That must have been what she'd felt against her face earlier. She rolled to her side and sat up.

When Draven reached for her, she wound her arms around his neck. She barely even thought about touching him now; it came so naturally. And she'd fallen asleep by his side—in the middle of the jungle with enemy spies about. Enemy spies who were likely his allies.

By all standards, she shouldn't trust him. Yet she did anyway.

Perhaps Draven was right, and she had only seen a monk wandering in the jungle. Perhaps he truly had betrayed the Empress to rescue her.

Once Draven had returned her to her bed, he retrieved bowls of broth for both of them. Selene sat up and swirled the wooden spoon through the broth. It was still too hot to eat.

Draven blew on his and sipped a spoonful. How did the broth not set his tongue ablaze? "Do you ever think you'd return to the Scorpio, Selene?"

An excellent question. She stared into her broth, waiting until its surface was smooth enough that she could see her reflection. "I honestly don't think I'd be able to. Arzil would think me a traitor."

"And you're not a traitor?"

"Not in action..." But in feeling. She felt far too much for Draven, and Arzil would be able to sense that as soon as he saw her.

"Then how?"

"It doesn't matter."

"So in an ideal world, would you still be back at the Scorpio base?"

"No. I'd never join in the first place." If she didn't ever intend to kill King Alaric, perhaps telling him her old plan would be safe. "I was planning to leave the Scorpio, which was why I needed to kill King Alaric."

He cast her a doubtful look. "You needed to kill the King to leave the Scorpio?"

"If I'd killed the King, I would have been rewarded 80,000 aurum. There's a bounty hunter in Renshi that smuggles former Scorpio assassins out of the country. The only ones who've escaped Arzil alive are those that he helps. I would have been able to afford his services, had I killed the King. Once you join the Scorpio, it's hard to leave."

Draven nodded. "I understand. I had my master leave the Scorpio, which made it easier for me to leave. If he hadn't, he would have aided in tracking me down."

"Your master was Sephtis, wasn't he?" She asked as if she

didn't know. Every assassin knew. Sephtis had been a famous assassin—for both his skill and betrayal of the Scorpio. Draven was equally legendary.

Draven nodded. "I was apprenticed to him not too far from Octavya. We were in an enormous base, with moving and changing passages. I've never seen technology like that before, at least, not in Torva. Did you ever see it?"

"No, only the one here, in Taijeng."

"And what's the base here like?"

She didn't like to remember what it was like. Her memories of that place were as dark as the passages. "Cold. Tight spaces. I tend to feel far too claustrophobic when I'm down there." The description leapt off her tongue, and her mouth snapped shut. What was she doing? If he learned the location of the Scorpio base and was still allied with the Empress, Lyra would be in danger, as would the other apprenticelings.

"Claustrophobic? It's underground?"

Selene clenched her jaw tighter. She'd said far too much. "Why do you want to know?"

"I'm merely curious." Draven offered her a small smile, but she saw past his innocent façade. There was an intensity in him that had been absent during their time by the cliff. He was pumping her for information.

And then suddenly, it made sense that the Empress would allow Draven to "rescue" her. Selene had been crying out for him all throughout the torture session.

She wasn't certain whether she ought to laugh or cry. How pitiful was that? That the only one she could have imagined caring enough to save her was also the one who'd allowed her torture in the first place?

The Empress had supposed that Draven was the only one Selene would trust enough to reveal the location of the Scorpio base to. And she'd almost been correct. She was still being interrogated, just in a different way.

And Draven had agreed to this. Pain burst in her chest, and Selene pressed her hand over the aching area. It felt like the little threads holding her heart together were snapping in two, leaving the rest of her to unravel.

"Selene?"

She should pretend to be ignorant, that she didn't suspect that anything was going on. But she'd spent her entire life pretending, and she didn't have the energy to do it anymore.

Selene set her bowl of broth on the end table. "I've lost my appetite—and I'm rather tired."

"Of course. You've been active today." As she lay down, he strode to her bedside and drew the covers over her. "Rest well."

Though she closed her eyes, she couldn't sleep. Her thoughts were swirling inside her head like a whirlpool, a never-ending vortex that vanished into the darkness of her mind. She'd just given Draven an enormous clue about the whereabouts of the Scorpio base. What if he reported to the Empress' spies tonight, and they left to tell the Empress? What if everyone in the Scorpio base was slaughtered by the time she got to the city of Renshi?

When Draven finally left her room, she sat up in bed and flung the covers off. She had to go back and warn them. But there was no way that she could walk back in time. She'd need one of the horses. She remembered seeing the stables outside, along the temple wall.

She used the nightstand to steady herself as she rose. The broth still sat there, probably cold by now, but she'd need energy for the journey. Selene picked up the bowl and placed the edge between her lips before pouring it into her mouth. It was cold, and the watery texture made her shudder.

But once she set the drained bowl down, she did feel stronger. She could probably ride hard at least until tomorrow. Perhaps she could beat the spies back to the Empress.

Draven, unfortunately, had not left his cloak draped over

the chair tonight. He'd likely taken it when he'd gone out to meet the spies.

Selene hardly had to use the wall as she strode through the hallway. There were a few Lux stones glowing dimly from the ceiling, but she didn't see anyone. Apparently, the monks had an early bedtime.

Selene reached the main part of the temple. She didn't see any hallways that led to the stables. She'd just have to retrace her steps from earlier. She padded down the main stairs leading to the dirt road.

She didn't realize that two guards were standing on either side of the entrance until she was standing by them. She suppressed a startle and continued walking, as if she were supposed to be going outside this late.

The guards didn't even move. She would have thought that they were statues, except that she hadn't seen them in the daylight. They were likely incredibly skilled to have escaped her notice until she was nearly upon them.

As Selene followed the wall of the temple, the grass brushing against her calves, pain shot up her foot. She paused and look down. She'd stepped onto the pointed end of a twig. She should have thought to bring shoes. No matter. She'd be on horseback anyway.

Selene picked her way to the stables, careful to place her feet away from pointy objects. She feared the stable door might be locked, but the latch yielded easily, and the door opened, revealing stalls of horses. Each was glancing over its gate at her, their ears perking up.

Some were *very* old—nearing the age of retirement if not death. Others were sized between a horse and a pony. One horse in particular caught her eye. It was tall and sleek, its brown coat glistening like a king's crown. Its legs were long and graceful, its eyes gleaming with intelligence.

Yes. This one would get her there quickly.

She entered the stall and set a saddle blanket and saddle on the horse. She looped the cinch around its belly and a halter around its neck. She grabbed a spare saddle blanket and pulled the thick fabric over her shoulders. It wasn't a cloak, but hopefully it would prevent anyone from examining her short white gown too closely. After clipping reins onto the halter, she opened the stall gate and led it outside.

It took a few tries to mount it—and a few falls—but when she did, she felt like a giant. Selene thrust her arms forward and dug her heels into its sides. It walked forward. And when she didn't slow it down, it sped into a trot, then a canter. Selene swayed with its smooth, long strides. She didn't think she'd ever been on a faster horse. It was thrilling, with the humid air whipping past her and the ground blurring beneath her.

After three hours, it was much less thrilling. She was *exhausted*. The jungle surrounding her was pitch-black, and though she heard strange creaks and howls and snaps, she couldn't see anything in its depths. Silvery moonlight spilled across their path, which was broad and well-used, making it easy to follow. The horse had slowed its pace, its coat lathered in sweat.

All her energy from earlier had been sapped away. Pain twinged in her back, and she removed the saddle blanket to glance behind her. The bandages had turned pink. Which meant she was bleeding.

Selene gripped the saddle horn, leaning heavily against it as she tried not to fall asleep. What was she doing? She hadn't packed food or water or bandages. And hadn't Draven said it was a two-day ride? And now she was bleeding. It was only a matter of time before she attracted all the local predators in the area.

She recalled what Draven had said about the drugs making her more impulsive. Until now, she hadn't felt the pain in her back at all. They must still be drugging her food. When she'd drunk the broth earlier, she'd felt a burst of energy, even a sense of invincibility. Except now it was wearing off.

What if the Empress had *wanted* her to run away? To reveal where the Scorpio base was? Dread settled like a rock at the bottom of her stomach. Her best chance of survival—and keeping the Scorpio base a secret—was heading back to the temple.

Selene steered the horse back the way they'd come. She was such an idiot. How could she have gone this far without taking the time to think? She needed to get off this drug as soon as possible.

A twig snapped sharply by the side of the road, and the back of Selene's neck prickled. Could the Empress' spy have followed her? Surely not. No one could take a horse through that jungle, and he couldn't have followed on foot.

"Show yourself!" Selene shouted.

The jungle seemed to quiet at Selene's words.

"I said 'show yourself'!" Selene reached toward her waist, only to realize that she didn't have any daggers on her.

But apparently the motion was threat enough for whoever was there. A man stepped out, his arms held high. He was heavily cloaked, his face masked. But she recognized those eyes.

It was the bounty hunter who'd taken Cori.

22

CONFESSING

"*You.*" Selene trembled with anger. It seared her skin, scorched her chest. This bounty hunter had captured—and possibly killed—her friend. "What have you done with Cori?"

"I don't know who you're talking about."

"Corsicanna," Selene ground out. Whatever he'd done with her, he'd pay for it.

There was no flicker of recognition in the man's eyes. Maybe he hadn't captured her; maybe Corsicanna had run away of her own accord. But Selene couldn't believe that. Cori was adamant that prostitution was her only means of earning money, that she had no other choice. A likelier story was that the man's mask made him harder to read.

"As I said before, I don't know who you're talking about," the man said. "Now, if you'll excuse me, I'll be on my way."

"No, not until—"

Horse hooves pounded in the distance, and Selene's heart lurched. Who was coming down the road? She glanced that way.

There was an explosion of sound in front of her: snapping

branches, crunching leaves. Selene looked in time to see the bounty hunter disappear into the jungle.

"Stop!" Selene spurred the horse forward, but it halted at the edge of the jungle, releasing a nervous whinny.

The foliage was thick enough that riding on horseback would nearly be impossible. Fine. She'd just have to get off. There was no way that she was letting this coward escape—

"Selene!"

She swung her head around, looking sharply at Draven. She dug her teeth into her lower lip, unsure whether she ought to make a break for it and give herself in. Would he keep her in a cell after this? Turn her back to the Empress for torture?

Draven whistled sharply, and her horse trotted toward him —even though Selene tugged on the reins.

As she neared, she saw how Draven's green eyes blazed in the darkness. "Selene. Are you insane?" He dismounted and stood at the side of her mount. "Get off my horse."

His horse? That was why he'd responded to Draven's whistle. "But—"

"*Now.*"

Selene glanced longingly at the jungle. The masked man would surely get away now. But she couldn't have chased him down in her condition even if Draven hadn't detained her.

Pain flared in her back as she dismounted. Draven caught her at the waist, lowering her the rest of the way to the ground. He didn't release her, and she felt unease knot within her abdomen. Even if he was angry at her, he wouldn't hurt her. Would he?

"*What* were you thinking? You could have been killed. You could have fallen off the horse, or you could have gotten lost, or you could have been chased down by predators or bled out..." He tugged her closer and wrapped his arms around her, keeping them by her shoulders so he didn't touch her back.

Selene stiffened in his embrace. She couldn't remember the

last time someone had touched her like this. "You're not angry?"

"Angry at your stupidity, perhaps." He held her away from him, gripping her by her shoulders as he scanned her figure. Then he turned her, so her back faced him. "You're hurt." He sighed heavily. "Selene, if you're going to escape, at least don't kill yourself in the process. And what were you thinking? Confronting a man alone in the middle of the jungle? What if I hadn't come?" He spun her to face him again.

"Then I would have caught him!" Even as the words left her mouth, she knew them to be a lie. A child could likely win a fight with her right now.

"What if he'd overpowered you and hurt you?"

"I'm a highly trained assassin." Her voice was softer this time. He was right. If not for Draven's timing, she might very well be that man's captive, like Cori.

"And a highly injured assassin, you hollow head." Draven picked her up and helped her onto the smaller horse he'd ridden. Then he unhooked one end of the horse's reins, likely to keep hold of them as they rode back.

"But that man, he's the one I spoke to at the Maroon Maidens. He captured Cori."

Draven paused. "What would he be doing all the way out here?"

"I don't know. Can we go after him?"

"Absolutely not." Draven mounted his horse, and with a slight squeeze of his legs, his horse walked forward. Hers trotted behind, its strides much shorter. "You can't make it on foot—"

"Then you could go after him."

"And leave you alone in the jungle? Or give you an opportunity to escape and further injure yourself?" He didn't turn to face her as he spoke.

"So you admit that I'm your prisoner." Selene folded her

arms. Though the adrenaline rush from the past few minutes had kept her awake, exhaustion began to outpace her.

"Until you develop enough sense not to kill yourself." He twisted in his saddle to glance back at her. "Selene, when I came back and saw that you weren't abed, I was so worried—"

"Worried?" Was that what a captor was supposed to feel for his captive?

"Yes. If something had happened to you..." His grip tightened on the reins.

"And yet, you were willing to bring me to the Empress, who was intent on torturing me or executing me."

"I assure you, that was a grave mistake. And I rescued you, didn't I?"

"*Did* you, Draven? Or did you just lead me into another trap?" There. She'd finally voiced her suspicions.

She expected Draven to deny it immediately. But instead, he remained silent. The silence stretched so long that she feared he'd never answer.

"I would have done it anyway, Selene." His voice was so soft that she had to strain to hear it.

Her heart thudded, and she gripped the saddle horn tightly enough to leave indentations. "Done what anyway?"

"Rescued you, regardless of whether or not the Empress had sanctioned it."

"The Empress ordered you to rescue me?" Just as she'd feared. Last evening's broth sloshed inside her stomach, the swaying of the horse suddenly making her feel sick. Of course he wouldn't have rescued her because he cared. After all, who would care for her enough to risk everything?

He released a long breath. "I agreed because it was the only way to save you."

"And the only way to coax me into revealing the location of the Scorpio base." Her chest felt fragile, ready to fracture at any moment. Letting herself care so much about this man had been a mistake.

"I only want to save Evelyn and Alaric. And you." He ran a hand through his hair. "Please understand. The Empress said that if I didn't get you to reveal the location of the base within a week's time that she would execute you. I didn't want to take that chance."

Then he hadn't saved her just to interrogate her—or because the Empress had ordered it. "Why?"

He slowed his horse's pace, so that it trotted alongside hers. "I've told you before that I care for you."

"Romantically?" For some reason, she wanted him to say 'yes.' It was a silly wish; she'd never desired a romantic relationship before.

He drew in a slow breath. "I wouldn't marry you, Selene."

She wasn't expecting anything like a proposal. But the rejection still stung. "Because of what I let Shonn do to me?"

His jaw firmed. "No. First of all, it's not what you let Shonn do to you; it's what *he* did to you. And that's not your fault."

She'd carried the guilt of that incident for years. It was a relief to hear from someone else that she wasn't responsible. "Then?"

He glanced down at her, his eyes widened in surprise. "Why the insistence? Do you *want* me to marry you?"

Did she? The idea certainly wasn't without appeal. She hoped her face didn't look as hot as it felt. But doing so would be impractical anyway. They were still on opposite sides in the same war. "I was just curious."

"After what happened with Faina, I've already told you that I don't intend to be a husband. I'm simply not that kind of man. I'm certain that one day you'll find a kind and gentle man who would deserve to be your husband."

Kind and gentle. Like Draven. Even when he'd discovered

she was an assassin, even when she'd tried to kill him, even when she'd fled from him.

Selene tried not to sag forward in her saddle. The stinging pain in her back intensified. "You likely think me despicable for protecting the other assassins." For some reason, she wanted him to understand her perspective, to know that her goal in withholding the information wasn't purely evil. "If I reveal the location of the base, people will die."

"If you don't reveal it, you will die. And possibly Evelyn and Alaric too."

But as soon as the Empress had the information, she'd slaughter everyone in the base. Including Lyra.

"Selene, who among them is worth saving?"

"All the children. And my apprentice-to-be."

To her surprise, a smile graced his lips. "You have an apprentice?"

"Not yet. But I was going to. Her name is Lyra. She's yet to make her first kill, and she's completely innocent in all of this. I won't be the cause of her death."

Draven's face brightened in recognition. "Lyra. Is she Sparrow? The girl who accompanied you when I was caught and you put me in that stable?"

She'd nearly forgotten that Draven had been awake that entire time. "Yes, that's her. Though she accompanied me, I can assure you that she wouldn't harm a skimmer."

Draven nodded. "I thought she seemed rather innocent when I saw her. Do you not think M'rithun is worth saving?"

M'rithun? Oh, he meant Arzil. "No."

He rubbed his jaw. "What if I could ensure no harm befell the others? The children and Lyra?"

Hope flared inside her chest. Could he? But how? "You're telling me that the Empress would agree to let them go?"

"No. The Empress needn't find out. I would go and warn them."

And Draven would have to put his life at risk to help her. If the Empress found out, he was a dead man. And if Arzil spotted him... "Arzil is there. What if he sees and recognizes you?"

"I'd be happy to take that risk if you would tell me the location of the base." His expression was solemn and sincere. She shouldn't trust him again... yet she did.

What if he could save the children and Lyra? Would she be willing to tell him where the Scorpio base was? To save others' lives? But how much longer did she have left? He'd said seven days. They had to be reaching the end of her time. She swallowed past her suddenly tight throat. "You said I had a week's time. How long ago was that?"

Draven glanced at the sky. The moon had passed its zenith. She blinked hard, trying to not let her eyes stay closed lest she fall asleep. "Seven days ago. She said she'd kill you on the eighth day. Do you understand why I asked for details about the Scorpio base today? I didn't want you to feel interrogated... but your life depended on it."

Then she was to die tomorrow. Except for the pain in her back, her body felt numb. How was she to be killed? With more torture? She couldn't endure more—she physically and mentally couldn't. She simply wasn't strong enough. Just thinking of all those metal tools, of the fireplace glowing at the end of that stone room—

Selene barely slid off the horse in time to fall to her hands and knees and heave up the broth. The watery yellow liquid dampened the dirt beneath her.

Draven dismounted and was at her side in an instant. "You'll be all right, Selene. I won't let her take you again."

She spat the sour taste of bile from her mouth, and Draven wiped her face with the edge of his cloak.

He guided her to her feet, even as she shook and trembled. "Perhaps you should ride with me."

She was too exhausted to protest as he helped her climb

into the saddle. He positioned her legs so she rode sidesaddle and mounted up behind her.

He pressed her shoulder, so she leaned into him. "Rest against me."

She slumped to the side, dizzy with nausea and exhaustion. "What would happen to me if I did tell you?"

"The Empress said your fate would be... negotiable."

"What does that mean?"

"One of the options she presented was to give you to me as a wife. But I told her 'no.'"

Selene crumpled inwardly. Of course he wouldn't want to forever bind himself to her, just to save her life. "Then I'll be thrown into the dungeons."

"No. I wouldn't let that happen."

"You wouldn't have a choice." Selene ran a hand through her hair. "So I'll be killed tomorrow. And I won't even be able to fight back, not in this condition." Dread clamped around her heart. The situation was truly hopeless. It was either death or reveal the location of the base.

"You wouldn't be fighting them alone."

He was saying that he would fight with her? For her? She stared into his eyes and saw the same sincerity she'd glimpsed earlier. This didn't make any sense. He'd been hired to hunt her down, not to help her—and certainly not to care about her. "Why, Draven? What did I do to earn such loyalty? Or is this part of your scheme to gain my trust?"

His smile was brilliant, nearly glowing beneath the moonlight. "You mystified me from when we first met. I pride myself on my ability to read people. But I couldn't read you."

She raised her eyebrows. "And that's enough of a reason for you to risk your life for—"

"Patience, Selene. I'm getting there." His fingers grazed her forehead, brushing her hair back from her face. "As I guarded you, I realized how much you reminded me of... me. You didn't have anyone to confide in, to protect you. You were caught in a web of lies spun by the Scorpio.

"My strong desire to help and protect you soon grew into admiration for your strength and your skills. I saw a light inside of you that refused to be snuffed. I thought you plain at first, but then, slowly, you became beautiful." He tipped her face up toward his. "Now I wonder how I ever saw you as anything less."

She couldn't speak, could barely hear his words above the rush of her heart. Beautiful? When was the last time she'd heard someone call her beautiful? "You love me," she breathed.

"Yes."

She couldn't stop staring at him, joy and sorrow welling up within her. Something about his declaration made her unspeakably happy. But nothing could come of it, especially with her impending execution.

But if he loved her so much... "Yet you find the idea of marriage abhorrent. Is that because you fear you'd never be able to consummate a marriage with me?"

"Of course not. After the mistakes I've made... I don't think it's a good idea."

"Regardless of the things I said earlier, you're going to continue to let Faina's opinion dictate your life?"

He stared at her for a long moment, a smile playing with the edges of his lips. "Are you saying you *want* to marry me?"

Would she? For once, she could imagine marriage with a man—and a pleasant marriage at that. But she was an assassin... then again, so was he. Or he had been. "I—I don't know. But even if I did know, marriage between us would be impossible, especially if I die on the morrow."

"As I said earlier, that won't happen." He gripped her hand with his. "Please, Selene. Let me save you—really save you."

No one had ever cared so much about her wellbeing, not

even her mother. "You really love me, don't you?" The thought was still hard to believe, much less verbalize.

"If Evelyn and Alaric hadn't shown me mercy, I doubt I would've changed. I think you just need an opportunity like I had." He squeezed her hand. And she found his touch comforting rather than unpleasant.

She smirked. "You're trying very hard to convert me." And, if he could truly save Lyra and the children, he might just succeed.

"No." At her look of surprise, he continued, "I don't need to. You already know that M'rithun's way isn't right—and you're seeking to escape it. But you're seeking the wrong way. If Alaric dies, chaos would ensue. Thousands would die. In the following battle for control, those who are weak and unable to defend themselves would be trampled underfoot. Telling me the truth is the right thing to do, Selene."

It wasn't the easy thing, however. But sometimes there wasn't an easy way out; just the right way out. The thought resonated within her. All her life, she'd been avoiding the right decision by choosing the easy one. And she'd justified it by telling herself that she didn't have another choice. Perhaps she'd always been able to make the right decision. She'd just refused to because she'd feared the consequences.

Selene drew in a fortifying breath and nodded. "All right."

"What?" Draven stared at her, his expression slack. Despite all his convincing, it seemed he hadn't truly thought he'd be able to persuade her.

"I'll tell you. But promise me—"

"I promise. I will do everything in my power to protect the girl and the children." His grip on her hand grew tight. "Or I will die trying."

23

SNEAKING INTO THE SCORPIO BASE

Selene rested her forehead against Draven's chest, hoping she hadn't sentenced him to death by asking him to save the children.

"The Scorpio base is in the southern slums, five blocks west of Dragon's Den Inn," she said. "There's a one-story house with a red X on the door. They marked it to look like the house had been infected with Bloodburn so no one would enter. There's a bookshelf in the backroom. Pull on the side, and it will swing outward to reveal a downward spiraling staircase. If it helps, I can draw a map."

Though she'd agreed to tell him, her stomach still gave a sharp twist. The offer felt traitorous, even though she knew it to be the right decision.

"That would be most helpful. Thank you." He kissed her cheek. "I'll take care of you, Selene. I promise."

A tiny flutter of pleasure whisked through her chest, then vanished like a firefly's light winking out. What was that? Had she *liked* him touching her? Not just tolerated it but... enjoyed it? Selene stared down at her hand and found it still entwined with his. What was happening to her?

They continued the rest of the ride in silence, and with the gentle lull of the horse's gait and Draven's solid warmth to lean against, she found her eyes drifting closed. Even though the night's events troubled her, she couldn't resist the call of slumber. Draven had said he'd take care of her. Now she would discover whether or not he spoke true.

"Darnell, Raz, Velius, Amun."

Selene startled awake. Sunlight pierced her eyes. The pain in her back had sharpened, now impossible to ignore. She closed her eyes again and a gentle hand touched her shoulder. She instinctively tensed at the unexpected touch.

"It's all right, Selene." Draven's voice. Which meant it was Draven's touch.

She relaxed back against him.

But who was he calling? A rustling noise caused her to force her eyes open. They were still on the dirt road and had almost reached the temple. Four men dressed in form-fitting black emerged from the surrounding jungle. She must have seen one of them in the garden.

Draven wheeled his horse around to face them. "I've found Selene."

"We see that," the man on the left said, his chilly gaze boring into her.

"We've come to an agreement. Selene will reveal the location of the Scorpio base under certain conditions, which I must go fulfill first. In the meantime, I'll leave her in your care."

Selene tightened her grip on Draven's hand—only to realize he was no longer holding hers. He must have pulled it away while she slept. He was going to leave her alone with them? What if they grew impatient and resorted to torturing her again?

The shortest one narrowed his eyes. "An agreement with a Scorpio assassin? The Empress wouldn't approve. If she's willing to tell us the location, she should tell us now. If not, today is the eighth day." The man placed his hand on the hilt of his sword.

These men obviously wanted to see her suffer and bleed. Surely Draven could see that. She glanced up at him, silently begging him not to do this.

But he didn't bother glancing down at her. "She has refused to tell us otherwise. And I don't believe killing her would be wise. She's our only lead. Without her, it may be many more years until we discover the base." Draven guided the horse forward a step. "The Empress has assigned me to lead this mission. Would any of you like to challenge my authority?"

The one on the left shifted, and for a moment Selene feared he would speak up. But he remained silent, studying the ground. More than likely, they knew of Draven's past as a Scorpio and a high-ranking noble. To think that she'd even tried to take him alone...

"Excellent choice." Draven guided his horse toward the stables.

Selene curled her hand around a fistful of his shirt. "Draven, those men will kill me as soon as you're out of sight."

Draven didn't reply or even glance down at her. Once he'd stopped in front of the stables, he dismounted and helped her do the same. Her knees wobbled like they were about to come loose at any moment. She'd been on the horse so long that her legs felt numb. If only her back was numb as well. It burned with pain, and her head throbbed from lack of sleep.

Once it was clear that she wouldn't be walking on her own anytime soon, Draven picked her up. But instead of cradling her in front of him, as he'd done previously, he carried her over his shoulder, which dug mercilessly into her abdomen.

Draven was treating her more like a captive than someone

he'd professed to love. Perhaps that had only been a means of manipulating her into telling the truth. Perhaps he wasn't concerned about whatever those men would do to her. Her stomach dropped like a rock.

He didn't need her anymore.

When they entered the stables, Draven handed his horse off to a monk, offering him a few aurum in return. Then he gingerly set Selene down and she leaned against the wall of one of the stalls for support. When he glanced down at her, she made no effort to hide her fear or despair.

"D-Draven?"

His thumb brushed over her trembling lower lip, and he gripped her upper arms before pulling her closer, letting her lean against his chest. "It's all right, Selene. I'm sorry. I didn't mean to frighten you."

She released a shuddering sigh, letting him bear more of her weight.

His hands chafed her upper arms. "It'll be all right, Selene. You're all right." He pressed a light kiss to the corner of her eye. "I said I'd take care of you, and I meant it. You won't ever have cause to fear me." He rested his cheek against her hair, his warm breath stirring the strands. "I don't want the spies to think that we've come to this agreement because I love you. If they think that my feelings are clouding my mind, they might ignore my plan, take you to the Empress, and make you her prisoner once more."

"And I'm not her prisoner?"

He laughed. "You likely won't be free to leave until I return. But you'll be treated well, like a guest. Once I come back, you can tell the Empress the location of the Scorpio base, and she'll take care of the rest. When Alaric arrives, we'll explain the situation to him, and he'll grant amnesty to the children, Lyra, and you. And then you'll live happily ever after."

Selene glanced up at him. "And what about you? You'll continue to be the Empress' lapdog?"

"Hey." He grinned and poked her side. "I'll do what I can to best serve Torva."

Then they would continue on, living their separate lives. "Would I ever see you again?"

"Perhaps. But with establishing your new life, free of the Scorpio and your family, I might never cross your mind."

Selene went on her tiptoes and wound her arms around his neck. "Impossible." In this position, she was completely pressed against him. There was a tingle of unease, but for the most part, she felt comfortable.

Draven laughed. "I would give a lot to be able to hold you right now. While I'm gone, make sure your back heals more quickly, understood? I expect a proper embrace when I return."

"As long as you return, anything." She was surprised at the sincerity of her own words.

"Perfect." He smiled so broadly that she could barely see the green in his eyes. "Let's get you to bed. You can rest today and remain here while you heal. I'll ride to Renshi."

She loosened her grip and rocked back on her heels. "I wish I could come."

"You're in no position to travel." He twirled a strand of her hair around his finger. "I'll send a messenger ahead of me, so you'll know when I'm coming. I'll tell the spies and the Empress not to expect my return for two weeks. If something goes wrong, Alaric will be in Renshi by then. Make your case to him, and he'll protect you from the Empress' whims."

If he didn't come back... Her chest squeezed so tightly that she couldn't breathe. "If everything goes right, when can I expect to see you?"

"I'll need two days to travel to Renshi and one day to sneak out the little ones. On the third day, I'll send news that I'm at the palace. If you're well enough, you can travel to the palace with me and reveal the location of the Scorpio base. If not, you can send a letter with the information."

"How will I travel to the palace with you if you're already there?"

"I'll come back for you, of course. On the fifth day, I'll be here. And perhaps you'll be healed enough for an embrace."

"I would like that." And she meant it. Though anyone else's touch upon her aroused disgust and fear, his touch aroused... something else.

He picked her up, one arm beneath her knees and the other high on her shoulders. He carried her to her room and seated her on the bed. "I have one request of you."

"What is it?"

"I want you to allow the monks to tend your wounds. I know it will be uncomfortable, but it's the only way you'll heal. And I'll be very disappointed if I don't receive an embrace upon my arrival."

She sighed, then nodded. "Very well."

"Thank you." He pressed a kiss to her forehead. "I'm going to rest for a bit before I begin the journey."

"Will you come in to tell me goodbye?"

"If you wish it."

"I do."

Judging from the softening in his expression, her answer pleased him. "Then it'd be my honor. Now sleep."

When she lay down, he drew the blanket over her shoulders. And then he left to seek his own rest. Selene gripped a fistful of her pillow. She hoped he'd return to her within five days' time, safe and whole.

Draven cracked Selene's door open. It was evening, and

though golden light poured into Selene's room, she was sound asleep.

Dark shadows swept under her eyes, a sign of her exhaustion. Her face was smooth and uncreased by worry. A black lock of hair rested against her cheek, and she gripped her blanket to her chin. Her lips were slightly parted. Though they weren't the plumpest pair of lips he'd seen, they appeared incredibly soft. The urge to kiss her jolted through him, and he raised his focus higher, to her perfectly imperfect nose and the thick lashes shadowing her cheeks. Just by looking at her, one would think that she was helpless. But that was far from the truth. Even in her injured state, she was a force to be reckoned with.

He snuck into her room, unable to take his eyes from her. A myriad of emotions washed over him. The urge to protect her. Admiration of her beauty and strength. The longing to touch her again. Delight that she even allowed such touches. Fear that this would be the last time he saw her.

Waking her seemed almost cruel, but he knew she'd be livid if he didn't. And he needed this goodbye more than she did.

He knelt by her bed. For the past week, he'd been dreading this day, unsure if he could really fight off the spies and protect Selene. If she hadn't told him about the Scorpio base, today could have been a very different day.

A sheet of paper rested on her nightstand. He picked it up. A map of the Scorpio base. He'd forgotten about it. It was a good thing she'd remembered. If not, he'd have been blindly wandering through the dark passages, hoping not to run into M'rithun. In the map's place, he left Selene's dagger. He slid it from its sheath to better study it.

Strange spikes curled out from the ornamental pommel, adorned with four oval emeralds on each side. Tinier faceted emeralds dotted the top of the blade, each about a finger's width apart from each other. It was a beautiful dagger, but it was unfortunate that it was the only thing of value her mother had given her.

Selene sucked in a breath, drawing his attention to her, but she didn't wake. Her brows lightly furrowed as her breaths grew faster.

Could she be having a nightmare? Draven sheathed the dagger before rubbing Selene's arm. "Wake up, Selene."

She nearly startled awake, her chest still rising and falling sharply. "Draven?"

"It's all right. You're safe." He rubbed his hand down her arm again, this time in a caress. "Were you having a nightmare?"

She nodded.

"About... Shonn?" Anger kindled inside his chest. Throwing Shonn into the dungeons was too merciful an end for him.

To Draven's surprise, she shook her head. "Sometimes I have dreams about him. But mostly about my kills." She glanced at his collar, as if she couldn't bear to make eye contact.

"I used to as well. They'll get better over the years." He nearly ran his fingers through her hair to ease the guilt in her eyes. But he didn't want to push her too far and ruin their last night together. "I woke you to tell you 'goodbye.'"

"You're leaving? So soon?" She rubbed at her eyes.

"Yes. But I'll be back." He hoped. If he were caught in the Scorpio base, there wasn't any chance that he'd be able to fight off all of the assassins. But he'd go in disguise and be cautious.

He wanted to return to Selene more than anything, to see if she'd truly embrace him. He remembered when she'd gone on her tiptoes in the stables to wind her arms around his neck, the curves of her body against the planes of his.

"What is it?" Selene sat up, tossing a frizzy lock of hair over her shoulder. "Why are you smiling?"

Was he? He hadn't realized. "I'm just thinking of the

greeting I'll receive upon my return. I'm hoping for at least a strong embrace."

Selene blushed but returned his smile. The sight knocked the breath from his chest. She was stunning when she smiled. How was he going to stand being parted from her? Perhaps he should take the Empress' suggestion and wed the girl. But there was no need to be hasty in such a decision. He'd think on it more when he returned and decide if he was truly fit to wed her.

He tapped the weapon he'd left on her nightstand. "I'm returning the dagger I stole. I thought you'd find it comforting."

She grasped the dagger, running her thumb along the facets of the emerald. "Thank you."

"Of course." He grasped her hand and kissed the back of it. "I'll return for you, Selene. And I won't allow anyone to hurt you again."

She shook her head, her smile remaining on her lips. "Draven. No one can guarantee that."

"Then I'll be the first." He rose. When he released her hand, a physical ache gripped his chest. When would he touch her again? Or see her again? What if he failed?

No. Failure was not an option. He'd return to her within five days.

He headed toward the door, stopping to look at her one last time, impressing her face in his memory, so he would remember it no matter what happened.

"Goodbye, Selene." The words "I love you" lodged in his throat. He'd practically already told her so, but he'd never said it plainly. But what was the use in saying it when they might not remain together? He'd best let another man say those words to her.

"Goodbye, Draven." Her smile was weaker this time, the kind one wore to incite courage, or to say that everything was all right even when it wasn't. Her fingers tightened on the dagger's hilt. "Come back soon."

"I will." He turned and left, leaving a piece of his heart behind him.

Three Days Later

Draven swung the bookshelf open, revealing the secret passageway. He stared into its black depths, dread hanging from him like a physical weight. Once he'd left the Scorpio, he'd never looked back. And now he was about to enter their last stronghold. Would he emerge alive?

Draven released a sharp breath and entered the passage, pulling the bookshelf shut behind him. After a few seconds, his eyes adjusted, allowing him to see the passage in shades of gray. He crept down the stairs, sweat dampening his clothing. He wore the form-fitting outfit of an assassin with cloth wound around his head to disguise himself. Hopefully none of the other assassins would look at him too closely.

The frigid passage seemed to spiral downward for an eternity, until his thighs began to warm from the exertion. Brushing against a stone sent a jolt of cold through him.

He reached a landing and took out Selene's map. The second landing housed the children.

After descending to that location, he halted and entered the hallway. An assassin approached, and Draven's heart lurched, feeling as if it could burst from his chest. He kept his eyes fixed forward but offered a nod. The assassin mimicked the movement.

Once he'd passed, Draven's heart slowed to a more manageable rate. He stopped in front of the first door on the left and tucked the map away. He reached into his cloak and pulled out a glass vial of off-white Caecus powder from the inner lining. Known for temporarily blinding its victims.

Draven tapped a bit of the powder onto his hand, returned the vial, and knocked on the door.

A female assassin opened the door, her height nearly matching his. "Who are—"

He threw the powder, and she clapped her hands to her eyes, releasing a guttural yell. Hopefully none of the other assassins had heard that.

24

TRAITOR OF THE SCORPIO

Draven entered the room, closed the door, and tackled the woman. A few of the children screamed or whimpered. He could comfort them after he handled her.

Before the woman could grab her dagger, Draven drew it from her belt and sent it skidding to the other side of the room.

She tried to rake her nails across his cheek, but he caught both her wrists in one hand. With the other, he withdrew a vial of Manasseh and poured a drop between her lips.

In a split-second, she stopped struggling, and Draven rose to his feet and turned his attention to his captive audience. "Greetings."

The children regarded him with wide, wary eyes. They were all clean, but their skin was a ghostly pale from their time below ground.

He would see to it that instead of being locked in an underground base and taught how to extinguish life, they'd live as normal children should. They'd see the sun shine every day, be taught seemingly useless subjects such as science and math, and think more about life than death.

"I'm here to save you," he continued. "Later today, the

Empress is going to send guards here. You all need to come with me if you want to—"

The door burst open behind him.

Tuteno. Someone must have heard the commotion.

Draven spun to face the intruders. Two male assassins stood at the doorway. They took one look at the crumpled female and charged toward Draven, daggers drawn.

He drew his own daggers. He dodged the first man's attack and parried the second. He *was* a skilled fighter, but two-versus-one was hardly fair. He shoved one man backward, just as the second man came in for another attack.

When a third man appeared at the doorway, Draven knew this was a lost fight. If he were fighting anyone else, he would have dropped his daggers and surrendered, saving his strength for later rather than a futile endeavor.

But they were Scorpio assassins. And there was nothing they hated more than cowardice. If he surrendered, they'd likely beat him more for it before turning him over to M'rithun.

M'rithun. Nausea writhed in his stomach. A throwing knife sliced through the edge of his shoulder and clanked into a stone wall behind him.

Draven gritted his teeth against the burst of pain. There was only one entrance into the room, and the three assassins stood between him and the door. He was tempted to use the bunkbeds behind him to dodge his assailants for a while longer. But doing so would endanger the children.

The assassin closest to him attacked in a frenzy, as if unleashing a maelstrom of suppressed anger. His moves were sloppy, his stance too wide. Draven swept his foot across the ground, and the man fell to the floor. The next assassin was small and swift. He landed on Draven's back, one arm curling around his neck, the other clapping a Somnus-sap-soaked handkerchief to his mouth.

Draven exhaled slowly, pulled the man's arm away from his

neck and tucked his chin. His heart beat harder as he held his breath. He ran backward, slamming the man on his back into a wall.

Though the man grunted, his grip remained firm.

The third assassin side-kicked Draven's leg, right against his knee. With the man on his back, weighing him down, he wasn't fast enough to jump out of the way. His knee buckled, and he toppled to the ground.

The pressure in his chest was building, his lungs screaming for air. But he'd been trained for this. He had at least a minute or two before he actually blacked out.

While he was on the ground, Draven rammed his head back into the assassin's nose. His grip on Draven finally loosened, the handkerchief streaming past his fingers. Draven drew a deep breath just before receiving a kick to the head.

His vision wavered as pain needled his senses. Hang it, that hurt. Draven caught the man's leg as he aimed for another kick and pulled, letting the man fall to the ground.

Just as he rose to his feet, the room wobbling around him, another assassin swung his dagger hilt at Draven's face.

It hit his temple, his vision exploding with stars. A sharp stinging sensation tore into his skull as the world dimmed.

No. He wasn't going to black out. He couldn't afford to.

As he fought back dizziness, someone shoved him from behind, and he fell. He tried to gain his feet or fight back, but there were arms around him, pinning him, restraining him, binding him. He seemed to be holding his own until he felt the cold metal of a dagger against his neck.

"You keep struggling, and I'll cut your throat. It would be easier to bring you in dead anyway."

Draven stilled. If he wanted to escape, his best hope was to avoid further injury and wait until they least expected something. And by this point, he'd proved that he was no coward.

They yanked his arms behind him, his shoulders bending so far that he feared his joints would tear. Draven clenched his teeth to hold back a grunt. They hauled him to his feet, keeping a dagger against his throat, and marched him down more stairs. As the chill in the air intensified, Draven stiffened his muscles to keep from shivering. They entered a hallway and strode to the very end before opening a wooden, water-damaged door.

M'rithun sat upon a wingback armchair that curled slightly around him to cradle his form. His hair was an unnatural white, his locks brittle and long. Draven's stomach plummeted at the sight of him. It was the same lurching sensation he felt at the beginning of a fall.

Spread out in front of M'rithun lay a map of Taijeng. Draven couldn't help but stare at it. Passageways through the city were lined in blue. Red circles highlighted various houses and the palace: the sign for a target's residence.

Short candles lined the room, and various paraphernalia—such as jewelry, bones, and a doll—cluttered the walls along with a wide assortment of weapons. If Draven could manage to get his hands on one, he'd have a chance at escaping.

M'rithun rose and strode toward them. "Draven. What a pleasant surprise."

"M'rithun. Or should I call you 'Arzil' now? It seems you've made quite a few changes in my absence." Draven's voice didn't waver. It was a victory, given that he was terrified. He knew what awaited him as soon as this conversation ended.

M'rithun's smile was even whiter than his hair. "I could say the same of you. I heard you were in Taijeng. Recently, I discovered you were posing as Selene's guard. Given your loyalty to the Empress, it makes me wonder if you're responsible for Selene's disappearance."

Yes, he was. And he hoped M'rithun never laid eyes on Selene again.

"And yet some things never change." He extended his hand, and one of Draven's captors handed over his daggers. "You still prefer to use these, I see. If only I had killed you with a dagger when I had a chance instead of teaching you how to use them. All sorts of unfortunate accidents happen during weapons training anyway."

For a split second when Draven looked at him, he saw the old M'rithun, with a joke upon his lips and long raven-black hair. Back when they were apprentices, the other assassins had teased and mocked him for not cutting it. So M'rithun challenged them to a duel and bested them. But now they were no longer apprentices; Draven had become a traitor and Arzil had become a master.

"Well, Draven? Nothing to say?"

Draven firmed his jaw. "Only that I have no regrets." Not for taking Selene away—and not for coming here on her behalf. But that wasn't completely true; he did have one regret. Now the words he'd wanted to share with Selene would be left unsaid.

He loved her. And he'd never gotten to say so.

Maybe that was for the best. Maybe it would make it easier for her to move on once she received word of his disappearance.

M'rithun laughed gleefully. "Oh, we'll see about that. For your first punishment, you will be whipped. Assassins, let's show him to his room for the remainder of his stay here, shall we?"

The three assassins shoved him out of the room, down the hallway, and back to the stairwell. Arzil's steps tapped behind them as he followed. They strode down the steps, so far beneath the surface that he could almost feel the tons of rock and dirt above him, weighing him down and crushing him.

A whipping. He'd been whipped before. He could likely

handle that. But how many more punishments were to come? How much could he take before his body was left irreparably tattered and broken?

If only he'd remained in Selene's embrace and never left. He would sacrifice everything if he could just see her one more time, ask her to wrap her arms around him again. He would savor the sight of her fathomlessly dark eyes until his dying breath.

The stairs finally leveled out; they'd reached the bottom. This hallway led to one metal door. The assassins heaved it open, revealing a torture chamber. It wasn't all that different from the torture chamber in the Taijese palace, except this one had a few more metal tools and contraptions: A device that slowly pulled the victim's limbs out of socket. A chair of needles. A bed of coals.

"Gag him and bind him to that pole," M'rithun's voice snapped through the air like the crack of a whip.

They strapped him to a wooden pole in the corner, much like the one he'd found Selene chained to when he'd 'rescued' her. He never should've brought her to the Empress.

They left Draven's ankles tied together and fit a scratchy cloth around his mouth, pulling it so tight it stretched his lips back at the corners.

There was a metallic ringing as someone drew a dagger and sawed off his shirt. The air chilled his bare back. Draven closed his eyes and focused on his breathing. He was tempted to take sharp, ragged breaths. But he forced them to come slow and smooth, as if he were meditating.

In. Two. Three. Four.

Out. Two. Three. Four.

The whip whistled through the air and snapped some-where behind him. An intimidation technique. Draven didn't flinch.

And then the first lash landed on his back.

One Day Later

If Draven were alive, he'd come to Selene tomorrow.

Selene sat on her chair, staring out the window, scenarios rolling through her mind. Was he being tortured? Or on his way to see her? The anxiety stole her appetite, and though there was a bowl of stew on the end table, she couldn't bring herself to look at it.

Finally she rose, her joints creaking. She wanted to look well when Draven came for her, and that meant she had to eat —even if her food tasted like ashes. Selene strode to the end table, thankful that her strides were smoothing out as she healed. Walking came easily as she grew stronger.

She curved her hands around the bowl's rim, preparing to bring it back to her seat, but a prickling sensation trickled down her spine.

She turned around. A man's figure was silhouetted against the window—inside. He stood a few scevola from her. Selene gripped the bowl, preparing to fling it at him.

"Selene, wait."

She recognized the bounty hunter's gravelly voice. "Onden?" Why was he here? Did he mean to attack her? "How did you find me?"

Onden strode toward her, and she tightened her grip on the bowl of soup. He glanced down at her. "You don't look so well."

Selene shrugged. "I've been better, certainly. Why have you come here? And how? If you mean to attack me—"

"No, of course not." He slipped out a piece of paper from an inner pocket in his cloak. "This should explain things."

Selene set the bowl of stew down and took the note. Arzil's

seal was on it. Her heart plummeted. He knew where she was—
and that couldn't be a good thing.

She broke the seal and read the note.

Selene,

You filthy little traitor.

A chill washed over her. Arzil knew everything.

25

HOW TO SAVE A LIFE

Selene continued reading Arzil's note:

I've captured the man you were supposed to kill: Draven. It seems you've fallen in love with him instead. Though you've disappointed me immensely, I've decided to show you mercy. I've paid this man enough money to smuggle you into a remote village in Arwa. Leave with him, and your life will be spared. I won't pursue you, and you'll be out of the Empress' reach. You can leave this whole debacle behind you and begin a new life.

-Arzil

Arzil had to have known, somehow, that she'd been planning to leave the Scorpio.

And he'd captured Draven. Which meant that he... he was lost to her.

The thought made her want to retch. She was a hollow head. She should have never sent Draven on that suicide mission. But how could she have sentenced Lyra and the others to their deaths? She couldn't have... but now she'd sentenced Draven to death instead. What had she done? Perhaps she never should have revealed the location of the Scorpio base.

It seemed she had no option other than to go with Onden.

But she wasn't ready to give up on Draven. She carefully folded the note along the creases. In truth, going with Onden wasn't her only option, but it was the only easy one. Any other route would require immense sacrifice on her part. But Draven was worth sacrificing for.

She nodded at Onden. "I agree. But I'll need time to prepare. We'll leave tomorrow morning."

"It's imperative that we leave as soon as possible. You have four of the Empress' spies watching you, Selene, and I don't want them to detect my presence."

"I understand, and I would leave this very moment with you, but I... have unfinished business."

The bounty hunter huffed, then nodded. "I suppose I'll have to defer to your judgement." He headed back to the window, then paused. "Selene. I know that you're too smart to refuse Arzil's offer. To do so would mean suicide."

"I know." Her words came out heavier than she'd intended.

"I hope this Draven character is worth it," he said. And then he disappeared out the window.

The grief within her spilled over as soon as she was alone. Selene sank onto the bed as the tears slowly came, following the curve of her cheek and dripping down her neck. When she drew her hand under her jaw, the back of it came away wet and glossy.

He couldn't be dead yet; there was no way that Arzil would let him die so soon. But how could she possibly rescue him? Even if she was fully healed, she was in no position to fight off all the assassins in the base. She didn't have enough money to hire people to help her. Outside of the Scorpio, she didn't know anyone who could fight well enough to be a good ally.

The Empress had an entire army at her disposal. She easily had the manpower to rescue Draven. But doing so would mean sentencing herself and all of the assassins to death. She doubted giving the Empress the location of the base would be enough to earn the Empress' mercy. She would die, and Draven would live.

Her throat grew painfully tight as she loosed another sob. She couldn't just let the Empress kill her and Lyra and the apprenticelings. But neither could she let Arzil torture Draven to death.

The King was due to arrive soon. But not soon enough to save them should the Empress decide to host a mass execution. Perhaps if she asked the Empress to wait to judge the assassins until the King arrived, she would listen. After all, there were severe penalties for disobeying the King of Torva.

Selene rose, scraping the last of the wetness from her face. This was the best way to save both Draven and Lyra. She had to at least try. And if Draven had been rescued, surely he wouldn't let her be executed.

Selene released a shuddering breath. Enough weeping. It was time that she found some paper to write down the location of the Scorpio base. Tonight she'd set out with the spies to the Taijese palace.

A chill struck Draven's back, making his skin blaze in pain. A weak moan escaped past his lips. He couldn't even remember all the instruments they'd used on him yesterday. It was all a blur of agony. And today they'd do it all over again.

Something cold and slimy rolled over Draven's skin, and he startled, his eyes flying open. He was chained to a cot, stomach-down, his arms stretched around the cot, and judging from the chill damp in the air, he was still deep underground in the Scorpio base. The room was small, about four times the size of his cot. The thick wooden door, with its small latticework window, appeared to be the only escape.

He glanced over his shoulder and found a girl cleaning and

treating his back. He knew better than to assume this was kind treatment. They were piecing him back together so they could tear him apart again. They didn't want him to die of infection before he'd received the torture due to him.

The girl's gaze flicked to him. "Tuteno. You're awake." Something about her eyes and her voice seemed vaguely familiar. He tried to pinpoint the memory, but it remained elusive.

"You wanted me to remain asleep?" he asked.

She nodded, making more of her brown hair escape from her braid. "This would hurt less that way."

"And why do you care?"

Only when she flinched did he realize his tone had been harsher than he'd intended. "Not all assassins are evil people. Some don't even like hurting others and can be quite kind."

"Like Selene," Draven murmured, his chest aching terribly at the thought. When would he see her again?

"Selene?" The girl's dark eyes widened. "You know Selene? Where is she? What's happened to her?"

Draven stiffened. He shouldn't have said anything. He couldn't reveal Selene's location, lest they go after her.

The girl turned her attention to the jar of ointment, pouring some more on his back before rubbing it in. It stung against his raw skin, like someone had dropped a lit match on his back.

"I only ask because she's my master," the girl said. "I've been worried about her ever since she's disappeared. You don't have to tell me where she is, but is she all right?"

Selene's apprentice? His mind seemed rather slow as of late. But he'd had other things on it, namely surviving M'rithun's torture. "You're Lyra, aren't you?"

"Yes. We've met once before, though I doubt you remember. How do you know my name?" She ran her fingers down his back, her skin slick with ointment.

"I remember, *Sparrow*." He grinned. "You were the one who

was kind enough to check on my ribs after that man kicked me. And my head after he dropped me."

She was about to reach into the ointment jar but paused, her hand frozen midair. "But... weren't you asleep by then? Selene had given you Manasseh."

"I have my ways." He winked at her. "I overheard your name, and Selene told me about you recently. She said that you were going to be her apprentice."

Lyra flashed him a smile, and Draven caught a glimpse of mature beauty beneath her youth. "Really? She talked about me?"

Draven nodded. Maybe he could still fulfill his mission from within the Scorpio base and convince Lyra to smuggle the children out. "She wanted me to get you to leave. The Empress is going to invade the Scorpio base. Selene wanted to ensure that you would be spared and the children. Take the children with you and leave while you can."

Lyra smothered his back in another layer of ointment. "But then who would look after you?"

Draven chuckled, only to stop abruptly when he found it painful. "Saving your life and the children's is my first priority."

"That's very kind of you." She finished smoothing the ointment into his back and wiped her hands on a towel. "But if you're here, who's going to tell the Empress where the Scorpio base is? Selene?"

Highly unlikely. After all, she'd be risking the lives of Lyra and the children. She certainly cared for him, but he couldn't imagine her betraying everyone she'd known and loved by revealing the location of the base.

"I was going to tell the Empress," he said. "After I evacuated you and the children."

"If you're here, then it doesn't seem like I'm in much danger by remaining." She removed a strip of linen and laid it on his back. "Perhaps if you escape, I'll heed your warning."

That was even more unlikely than Selene telling the Empress the location of the Scorpio base. "But there's a better life for you out there. Do you truly want to be an assassin? To kill people who've done nothing wrong? The profession of healing seems to better suit you."

She put another strip of cloth on his back and sank onto her haunches. "I would like to be a healer. But to attend the schools would take money that I don't have. Before Selene found me, I lived on the streets." She laid the last few strips of cloth down. "I was fairly successful at picking pockets, but finding a way to sell the items I stole was difficult. I had to do so without arousing suspicion, and even when I managed that, I often had people take advantage of me because of my age and buy the item for a fraction of what it was worth." She stepped away, surveying his back. "Not too bad."

Draven managed a smile. "Thank you. Your kindness is appreciated. Might I ask for one more act of compassion?"

Lyra had begun gathering her supplies and glanced up. "What is it?"

"If you have any water, I'd be further indebted to you."

Lyra unlatched a flask attached to her belt and held the opening to his lips. She poured slowly until he'd had his fill. She tossed the spare strips of linen over her shoulder and picked up the basin of water and the jar of ointment. "Anything else?"

"Aside from my freedom, no."

Lyra shot him a sympathetic smile. "For what it's worth, I'm sorry. I have to say the torture is my least favorite aspect of being an assassin." She strode to the door and rapped twice. "I'll see you tomorrow."

"Tomorrow?"

She nodded as someone opened the door from the other side. "I'll tend you once a day to help keep you alive until you —you—"

"Die?"

"Yes." She glanced down, but not before he saw her eyes darken.

Such a soft heart. An endearing trait that was completely at odds with her occupation. Draven smiled broadly, as he would if he were greeting a friend. "In that case, Miss Lyra, I'll see you on the morrow." He bowed his head. "Until we meet again."

Lyra smiled back, dipping into a shallow curtsey. "Until then."

Two Days Later

As Selene and the spies neared Renshi, the jungle gave way to fields of rice plants, their green tufts poking above the water. A few workers were harvesting alongside each other. Cloth sacks looped diagonally across their chests, filled with green bundles. They stopped and stared as Selene passed with the spies, who were still wearing form-fitting black.

Despite the heaviness pooling in her chest, Selene smiled and waved at them. The smallest, a young girl with two braids, enthusiastically waved back. Shaded areas with thatched roofs dotted the fields.

Some of the taller buildings of Renshi rose up ahead. As they neared, the traffic thickened around them. Farmers taking their goods to market. Traveling caravans of pilgrims roaming the country. Foreign visitors gawking.

Selene had never been outside Taijeng, but she'd heard that their style of buildings was quite different, with their curved roofs of green and red, their lean, towering structures, the generous flourishes of gold adorning the wealthier nobles' houses.

As they neared the palace, Selene's heart beat harder. How would the Empress react to the revelation of the base's location? Would she believe Selene? If she didn't, it would mean Draven's death.

They passed the open gates, the guards' eyes following them. In fact, everyone in the crowd seemed to be watching them. It wasn't often that one got to see the Empress' spies in broad daylight. Once they'd entered, they rode to the back of the palace and dismounted at the stables.

She received as many stares from the servants as the spies did. She had exchanged her plain knee-high gown for a spare commoner dress the monks had. The servants were likely wondering what common woman would travel with a retinue of spies.

The spies led the way through a small wooden door, nodding at the guards by the entrance, and emerged into a servants' hallway, judging from the plain stone floor and wooden walls. The servants here were clothed more like merchants, their clothing made from fine fabric and deep colors with leather belts cinching their waists.

A servant passed by her with a covered dish. The aroma wafting from it was rich and savory. Selene's stomach tightened. She'd hardly been able to eat on the journey to the palace. Perhaps she should have forced herself to eat more. If she were imprisoned, who knew how long it'd be before she got a decent meal again?

But if she were executed instead, it wouldn't matter.

They left the servants' hallway for an ornate one with golden designs inlaid in the floor and tiny glass tiles forming mosaic-style stained-glass windows. There were marble benches and tapestries so lovely that they appeared like portals to other worlds. If Selene looked closely enough, she could almost see them moving, the water wavering, women's hair rippling in an unseen wind.

They stopped in front of a pair of white-and-gold doors, the broad arched handles gleaming like golden rainbows.

Selene's stomach leapt and twirled like a foreign dancer. Part of her dreaded going in, but the other part *needed* to know both her and Draven's fates.

The samurai standing in front of the door stared down at her. "Who am I announcing?"

Selene lifted her chin. "Lady Selene."

The samurai squinted at her. "Lady Selene. The Scorpio spy?"

"Yes." Dampness unfurled on her palms, and she pressed them to the fabric of her dress. "Are you going to admit me or not?"

He opened the door. "Announcing the arrival of Lady Selene."

No one was within. There was a fountain in the middle of the room, chairs and divans placed in a circle, and decorative red curtains draping the wall. Side hallways branched out from the main room, a door at the end of each. Somehow, this room seemed hazily familiar, as if she'd dreamt of this place.

Selene strode in, pushing the thought aside. Where was the Empress? Surely the guard wouldn't have announced her if she weren't within her chambers.

One of the side doors flung open, and the Empress emerged in a dressing robe, a green gel covering everything on her face but her nose, mouth, and eyes. Her hair was tugged back into a braid coiled around her head.

The Empress stopped within arm's reach of her, and Selene could feel all the guards in the room tense. The Empress' eyes flashed like lightning, her lips slashing into a smile. "Draven was here three days ago, saying that you would only reveal the location if he fulfilled some mission. He has yet to return. I have a feeling you're responsible for his demise."

Selene's heart pounded faster, and she removed the piece of paper from her pocket. "He won't die if you act quickly." The paper trembled slightly, and her outstretched arm refused to be still.

The Empress shot her a quizzical look. "If this is a trick—"

"This is the location of the Scorpio base. Draven is likely being tortured as we speak, and time is of the essence if you want to save him. My one request in giving you this is that you show a few of the Scorpio assassins mercy, mainly the children and a girl named Lyra."

The Empress walked toward her with short, quick strides, her movements losing their grace. She snatched the paper from Selene and unfolded it. After a moment of studying it, she lowered the paper. "You finally revealed the location of the Scorpio base, all to save your greatest enemy. Had I known *that* was what it'd take, I would have skipped the torture and threatened Draven's life instead."

Selene's fingers physically ached for the dagger she'd strapped to her thigh—unknown to the spies. She didn't want to risk having such a precious item left behind or confiscated. It would take her a second and a half to reach it. But she needed the Empress alive if she was to save Draven. "Then you'll save him?"

"Only because in doing so, I also have the ability to eradicate the last of the Scorpio. But killing them immediately would be too merciful. Better to make an example of them and execute them publicly."

A tremor went through her. "And the children?"

"Of course. If I want to eradicate the Scorpio, I'll have to kill *all* of them." The Empress returned to a cushioned chair and leaned into its embrace. "Those children will grow up to become assassins. I won't allow that to happen."

"*Not* if you give them into the care of loving families."

"And what families would want children who have been trained to kill? Such an idea would be foolish, and I am not a fool."

Selene's anger bubbled up to the surface, and she glanced at the ground, hoping the Empress wouldn't be able to read her eyes. "Of course not, Empress. Perhaps if you simply forestall the public execution until the King arrives, you can ask for his—"

"No. I'd rather get this dirty business over with before the King's arrival. And it's such a trivial matter; I doubt he'll care one way or another." Selene opened her mouth to speak, but the Empress snapped her fingers. "Silence. I've had enough of this. I don't need to justify my decisions to an *assassin*. Samurai, take her to a cell, where she'll await the others."

26

ON DEATH'S BRINK

The samurai left their posts to approach her, and Selene knew she had to make her case quickly. "Then you would execute me as well? Even when I've enabled you to rescue Draven and defeat the Scorpio?"

"That hardly makes up for all the wrongs you've done over your life," she replied coolly. "Tell me, Selene. How many lives have you taken? One? Five? Twenty?"

Selene's stomach lurched. With her high-ranking in the Scorpio, she'd stopped counting after fifty.

"That's what I thought. This is hardly justice, given that I'll be taking one life as recompense for dozens. But you only have one life to give."

"What about Draven? Do you think this is what he would want?"

The Empress wrapped the end of her robe tie around her finger. "I suspect he'll be severely injured when he arrives. After the healers treat his wounds, I imagine they'll give him a draught to help him rest. I wouldn't be surprised if he slept past your execution."

Save for Arzil, Selene had never met anyone this cruel. The

anger burned so hot within her that she could have sworn that her skin was on fire. "*How* could you do this? To me, I understand. But to him? You know he wouldn't want this, that he's risked everything in his service to you, yet you're going to disregard his wishes anyway."

The Empress raised her eyebrows. "And you would be so presumptuous as to claim that you know what he wants?"

"He certainly doesn't want me *dead*." Selene shook her head. "As a reward for discovering the Scorpio base, you offered me to him as a wife. Now he's done what you've asked, and you decide to execute me instead? Tell me, Empress, where is the justice in that?"

The Empress' face mask crinkled as her eyebrows rose. "He told you that, did he? Most interesting. Perhaps he also told you that he most passionately refused my offer. And if he ever wanted to wed you before, he certainly doesn't now. You're the reason he's suffering in the first place. That's all the Scorpio do: cause innocents to suffer."

"I have a proposal." Selene lifted her chin.

The Empress pointed a long fingernail at Selene. "*You* aren't in a position to make one."

Selene spoke before the Empress could stop her, "Let me see Draven when you bring him back. Instead of guessing what he wants, we'll ask him."

The Empress rose to her feet. "As told, he'll be asleep for a few days. If you truly cared about him, you wouldn't want to interrupt his healing."

Selene's arms trembled. It took all of her willpower not to lunge toward the Empress. "Allowing him to wake for a few minutes won't interrupt—"

"We're done here." The Empress flicked her hand in Selene's direction. "Guards, take her to the dungeons. Lock her away in the largest cell, so that there's enough room for all of the Scorpio assassins once they've been captured. After her betrayal, I'm certain they'll want to see her."

Nausea bubbled up within Selene's stomach, bile stinging the back of her throat. All of a sudden, she was glad that she hadn't eaten much. If the other Scorpio assassins got to her, she'd likely die before the execution date.

The samurai by the doors calmly walked toward her.

Perhaps if she were fast enough, she could escape and see Draven once he was brought back to the palace. Draven wouldn't allow her to be killed. Selene bowed her head and remained still, acting as if she'd comply. When they were nearly upon her, Selene darted out from under their grasping hands and sprinted toward the door.

She hauled the door open—and barreled into one of the awaiting spies. He grasped fistfuls of her dress, and the other spies were quick to pin her down. She couldn't even reach her dagger now.

The samurai rushed up to her and bound her hands behind her back, the rope so tight that Selene feared it'd draw blood. They hauled her to her feet and searched her. Two pairs of hands ran up and down her body—her torso, her legs, her arms.

Her chest suddenly heaved, and Selene doubled over as she spewed vomit onto the marble floors.

The samurai waited until she was done and continued searching her, their faces expressionless and cold. They relieved her of her mother's dagger and hauled her toward the dungeons. There would be no more opportunities to escape. She glanced longingly at the dagger on the samurai's belt. She likely wasn't going to get it back; now it was truly lost to her.

Hope withered and died; the light burning in her chest snuffed out. Her last few days would be bleak. She'd either be beaten to death by the other assassins or executed publicly alongside them. And Draven would only discover her death upon his awakening.

After a few turns through the halls, they halted in front of a pair of gigantic metal doors. It took three of the samurai guarding it to heave the gate open. The only light within the dungeon came from the Lux-stone torch her guard carried. Some of the cells were empty. The others held a range of people—sirens with steel devices around their heads to clamp their mouths shut, little children huddled in corners, deranged people with clouded eyes hunched over their meals, well-muscled men with malice in their features.

At the end of the hallway stood a locked wooden door. Once the door was opened, they dragged her down the stairs to a second hallway. Then a third. By the fourth hallway, Selene had no hope of escaping—or seeing the light of day until her execution. If she survived that long.

A large cell that could easily fit fifty people dominated the end of the fourth hallway.

The cell had a system with two metal gates. The samurai unlocked the first gate with the key, pushing Selene within. Trapped between the first and second gate, it was like she was in her own tiny cell. The samurai opened the second gate by pulling on a chain that dragged the gate upward.

"Get in," the samurai said behind her. Something sharp pricked her back, and she moved forward into the main cell, before the samurai's blade could slice any deeper.

The second gate clanked shut behind her, and she whipped around toward it, gripping the bars. The samurai's steps were silent as they strode down the hallway. She likely didn't have long before she was joined by the other assassins. A few hours at most. Though she'd mostly healed, she wasn't in a position to fight all of them.

She sank to her knees, still holding the bars. They would realize that someone had revealed the base's location and, upon entering the dungeons, they would see that she'd been the first to be captured. They'd know their betrayer.

Selene sat there, her legs doubled beneath her, dread eating away at her sanity. She wouldn't be surprised if they beat her to death. And with fists and feet as their only weapons, it could prove to be a very slow, painful death. If only she'd gotten to see Draven one last time. She hadn't realized how much she missed him until after he'd left. She'd taken their time together for granted.

She wasn't certain how much time had passed when she heard the shuffling of dozens and dozens of feet. They must have finished raiding the Scorpio base. Maybe she could persuade one of the guards to tell her if they'd successfully retrieved Draven.

Surrounded by heavily armed guards, the group finally came into view, their hands chained behind them. She recognized their ripped black clothing and faces, even if bloodied and filthy. Scorpio assassins. They stared at her silently, and she shivered. This must be how a mouse felt when watched by a cat.

Selene remained where she was, too frightened to move. A cold sweat chilled her skin. The assassins likely smelled the fear wafting from her. One by one, the guards unchained them and shoved them into her cell. Neither Lyra nor Arzil were among them. A potent mix of fear and relief washed over her.

As more assassins crowded the cell, Selene backed slowly into a corner, hoping that they would forget about her. But their eyes remained trained on her. At least none of them had approached her...

Her luck ran out when a male assassin entered the cell, heading straight toward her. She recognized his long, narrow face and straight brown hair. Mace.

He stopped in front of her. "Welcome back to the Scorpio, traitor."

Selene forced herself not to shrink back. Instead, she held her shoulders level and took a step forward. "Mace, I—"

Mace gripped the collar of her dress. "Wouldn't it be a shame if the little raven broke her wings?"

He threw her to the ground, pain bursting in her head. The first kick landed on her back, and agony rippled across her freshly healed skin. It didn't take long for other assassins to join him as they entered the prison. Selene instinctively curled into a ball, unsure how many more kicks she'd have to endure before they left her alone—or until her body couldn't take any more.

The Next Day

Soft hands upon his face. A sweet, feminine voice, urging Draven to wake up.

Selene.

She'd heard about his torment. She'd come for him, to the Scorpio base. Or perhaps he'd died and there was a Selene-like being in the next life.

He forced his eyes open. His cheek was squished against a pillow, and he lay stomach-down on a bed. He raised his head. No Selene. His dream vanished like a mirage in the desert. He sank back into his pillow, his heart sinking with him. Where was he? And where was she? The last thing he remembered was Lyra tending to him after another torture session.

Draven tried to roll to his side, only for pain to ignite in his back. He dug his teeth into his lip and winced when he found his lips already scabbed and sensitive. That's right. He'd been biting his lip to keep from crying out while M'rithun was torturing him. Little good it had done in the end.

He settled back on his stomach, his gaze combing the room. Wall screens divided the area, light shining through the paper from outside. His bed was plain, unadorned, but the mattress was denser than Coran cake and softer than a sea breeze. Nothing adorned the room besides the bed and a small end table.

One of the wall screens slid to the side, revealing a balding Taijese man in a healer's white robe. His black hair formed a partial ring around his head. "You're awake. How are you feeling?"

"Better than I was previously." His voice croaked as it scratched against his dry throat.

Though it felt like someone had set the ends of his nerves on fire, it wasn't the overwhelming, all-consuming pain he'd endured while actively being tortured.

"You must be thirsty. It's been quite some time since you've had a real drink."

"Quite some time? How much time? And where am I?"

"In the Empress' palace." The healer picked up a pitcher from an end table and poured him a goblet full of water.

"And the Empress was responsible for my rescue?"

"Yes. She sent guards to retrieve you. And you've been healing here for the past two days."

"How did she know where to find me?"

"A Scorpio traitor revealed the location of their base."

Draven rolled to a sitting position, ignoring the sensation of acid being poured down his back, frying the skin off his flesh—if he had any skin left. "Selene." It had to be her.

"Yes, I believe that was her name. Now, you mustn't get too worked up. Lie back down. You don't want to impede your healing. I heard a rumor that the Empress planned to execute her along with the other captured Scorpio."

Draven's feet were already on the floor. "Execute her? Then she's still alive. Where is she?" His heart pounded fast and hard, like a galloping horse. If anyone had harmed her, he'd see her avenged.

"It matters not. Your healing is my first priority."

"And Selene is mine." He gripped the edge of his mattress, his fist curling around the sheets. "If you don't tell me, I'll wander all of Renshi until I find her."

The man's eyes tightened in concern. "Now, now. There's no need to get all excited. Just lie—"

"No need? A woman is going to die—all because she chose to help me." Draven pushed off the bed, straightening to his full height. "I'm one of the Empress' most highly ranked commanders. You can either tell me where Selene is or I can report you for your insolence."

The small man trembled. In any other circumstance, Draven might have felt pity for him. "I see. This way, this way. She's nearby, actually. They brought her to the infirmary this morning."

Draven's heart lurched, his chest constricting until he could barely breathe. The only time they brought death row prisoners to the infirmary was when they feared that the prisoner wouldn't survive until their execution.

The healer opened the screen door and entered a hallway. He strode a few scevola before stopping and pushing another screen door aside, revealing a tiny room much like Draven's. Except that instead of a luxurious bed, the patient was chained to a cot. With the large swath of white bandages wrapped around Selene's head, he barely recognized her.

27

A PETITION FOR THE KING

"Selene!" Draven darted toward her as fast as his injuries would permit. He knelt by her side, ignoring the jolt of pain the abrupt movement caused.

Her eyes were closed, her lashes dark against her cheeks. Her skin had lost its darker Taijese coloring, looking more like the pale skin of a northerner's rather than her normal milk-tea complexion. Bruises marred her battered face, coloring it in dull shades of green, purple, and yellow. Her left cheek was swollen and red beneath her eye. The bandages around her head covered her forehead and most of her silky black hair.

Draven speared the healer with a glare. "Who did this to her? The guards?"

"No." Selene's voice answered, soft and hoarse.

Draven glanced down at her. With her swollen face, her deep brown eyes were barely visible. And what he could see of them crushed his heart and ground it to dust. The sparkle and mystery that had so entranced him upon first meeting her was gone. They were dull, filled with sadness and deprived of hope.

And yet, there was something about her that remained

untouched, ethereally beautiful. Like an angel with broken wings.

She smiled, only to wince at the movement. "You're—you're alive."

He cupped her face gently, so as not to press against her bruises. "You didn't know I was alive?"

"I knew the Empress was going to attack the Scorpio base, but once they placed me in the dungeons, I received no news about whether or not you'd been successfully rescued." She gently placed her hand atop his. "I was hoping that I'd get to see you... one last time. This almost feels surreal."

One last time. Before her execution. He would *not* allow that to happen. His thumb caressed her soft cheek. "Selene. I am so, so sorry. Whatever has happened, I'll fix it."

She smiled faintly, but he saw more sadness in it than joy. "It's all right, Draven."

"No. No, it's not." He closed his eyes. "You've sacrificed so much for me, Selene."

"As you've done for me." Her cold hand touched his cheek. He opened his eyes. The chain on Selene's wrist was stretched taut. "I couldn't allow Arzil to continue tormenting you, not when I had the power to put a stop to it."

"So you told the Empress where the base was, and as a reward, she had you imprisoned and beaten."

Selene shrugged, only to flinch violently at the movement. "This beating is courtesy of the Scorpio."

"The other assassins?"

She began to nod, only to inhale sharply and still. "I keep on forgetting that I can't move anything right now. And yes. They know I betrayed them, that I'm the reason we will all be executed in three days' time."

"All?" He interwove his fingers with hers. "Then you're to be executed with them." Unless he could convince the Empress that doing so was a bad idea. He refused to even contemplate Selene's death until he'd exhausted all other options.

"Yes. I'm sorry, Draven. I tried to reason with the Empress, but she wouldn't listen. She said that this is justice. And perhaps, in a way, it is."

"Justice is important, Selene, but so is mercy. If I'd only received justice, I would have been dead a long time ago." He rubbed his thumb over her knuckles. "Your injuries must have been quite severe for them to bring you here."

"I'm just relieved to be out of that cell." She smiled weakly, and Draven promised himself to do all he could to see that she wasn't returned to it. "There was a cut on my head and I have a broken rib. The rest are just bruises."

Draven fingered the hem of her gown. "May I?"

At her nod, he drew it back to reveal her stomach and lower ribs. Her torso was bandaged tightly, and the exposed skin he could see on her stomach was bruised even worse than her face. "Tuteno."

"That bad, hmm?"

He smoothed her gown back down and met her eyes, twinkling faintly with humor. "Worse," he answered. He rested his forehead against his palm. "You must think me the worst sort of man for saying I'd take care of you and then allowing this."

"Draven, you weren't even conscious when I came here. There was nothing you could have done." She settled her hand on his fist, which he'd rested on the edge of the bed. "You have no idea how highly I think of you, how much I admire you."

Her words kindled warmth within him, and he glanced up at her. She was amazing. To think that she could endure torture, his betrayal of her trust, a beating—and yet, she spoke to him of her admiration. Not hatred or bitterness or blame. Nothing even remotely like Faina.

He'd met many beautiful women over the years, those with dew-kissed skin, wide shimmering eyes, and lips perfect for pouting and kissing. But Selene was beautiful in a way that they would never be. Her beauty was a radiance that glowed from within her. Just glancing at her face made warmth burst inside him. Her features might not be remarkable to most, but there was no sight dearer to him.

"I never could have asked you to sacrifice so much for me, Selene. Thank you. I will see to it that you're not returned to that cell."

She glanced down at her hand, stroking his. "The Empress doesn't seem to be very persuadable at the moment."

"You doubt that I'll see you released?"

"I doubt I'll be alive within three days' time." Her voice was steady, but he caught a flash of sadness in her eyes.

He released a sharp, ragged breath. "Selene, I beg you not to speak like that."

"I know better than to pretend that everything will work out, Draven. But if I die, promise me one thing." Her gaze searched his. "Promise me that you won't mourn me for too long—and that you'll marry a woman who loves you deeply, like you deserve to be loved. No one like Faina."

Marry someone who wasn't Selene? He froze. Somehow, without realizing it, he'd entertained the idea of marrying her. How could he wed anyone else? He loved her and trusted her and admired her. A simple common girl or a spoiled noble girl wouldn't understand him and what he'd been through. Selene did.

He pressed a kiss to her knuckles, then a gentle one that barely grazed her cheek. His mouth hovered above hers. "May I?"

She wasn't breathing, and for a moment, he was concerned that he'd made her afraid. But then she nodded.

He dropped a light kiss on her lips. "I promise you I will do everything I can to save you. I'll get the King involved. He'll help us."

Selene pursed her lips, and he could sense she wanted to disagree. But instead she glanced aside, to the wall screen. "I'm just tired of my hopes being dashed to nothing. If you have the fortitude to hope, you should do so. But I do not."

"Then mine will have to be enough for the both of us." He brushed his fingertips against her cheek. "Rest well, Selene. This will not be the last we see of each other."

She tried to smile at him, but it wavered uncontrollably, tears glossing her eyes. He squeezed her hand, rose, and left her room. Now, it was time he paid the Empress a visit.

When Draven arrived before the doors to the Empress' chambers, his entire body was trembling. It seemed the muscles in his legs had disappeared while he'd slept. Thankfully, the healer had managed to procure a walking stick for him to steady his steps.

Draven leaned more heavily against the walking stick and nodded to the samurai. "Announce me."

"The Empress is not within her chambers," the samurai said. "She's listening to petitions."

"Then allow me in, and I'll wait for her."

The samurai hesitated but finally nodded. He opened the door, and Draven hobbled past him. He sank into the nearest armchair, a sigh spilling past his lips. He leaned against the armrest to avoid touching his back to the chair. This was how Selene must have felt.

It seemed like seconds later when a door slammed open, startling him awake. The Empress strode in and stopped at the sight of him. She was dressed in several layers of gowns, her hair twisted into an updo with golden bands.

"The samurai told me you'd entered. But that didn't prepare me for how haggard you'd look." She strode to her divan, slipping off her shoes and stretching on top of the cushions. "I was under the impression that you'd be asleep for the next five days."

His exhaustion vanished amidst a blaze of anger. "Long enough to miss Selene's execution?"

The Empress removed the golden bands from her hair, letting it spill down her shoulders. "The little assassin that nearly got you killed?"

"You said her fate would be negotiable."

"That was before she was responsible for you coming to the brink of death. If not for my healers, you wouldn't be alive right now."

"If not for Selene, I wouldn't be alive right now. I want to see her released. I've endured much, and you owe me at least that."

The Empress sighed and ran her fingers along her scalp. "I'm really not in the mood for this. If finding a wife is your concern, I'm certain we can find many women who are a good deal prettier."

Hang her. She was lucky there wasn't something nearby that he could throw at her, such as a knife. Or a vase. He wasn't picky. "You never intended to release her, did you? Once you had the location of the Scorpio base, your intention was always to kill her. She has changed, Empress. Just like I've changed."

The Empress' jaw tightened. "With your newfound loyalty to a Scorpio, I'm not sure you have changed."

Draven stared at her. The rumors said grief had driven her crazy. But there was a gleam in her eyes, of intelligence, of awareness. She wasn't crazy, but perhaps there was something else driving her unreasonable behavior. "What do you have against the Scorpio, Empress? What happened to make you so bitter toward them?"

She closed her eyes, and in that moment, Draven saw all her hidden grief written plainly across her expression. "Who do you think was responsible for my husband's death? And my miscarriage?"

Tuteno. He was still angered that she would harm Selene, but he couldn't help but feel sympathy for her. "Empress, I'm terribly sorry. I had no idea."

"Few did. After they murdered my husband, they poisoned me. I survived; my child did not." She placed her hand on her flat stomach. "It's been years, yet sometimes I'll reach toward the other side of the bed, only to find it empty. Other times, I'll caress what once was the bulge of my stomach, only to find it equally empty.

"Emptiness, Draven. That's what the Scorpio assassins have left me with. I'll never know who the assassin was for certain, but if I wipe out all of them, I know I'll likely have killed the one responsible. And I'll prevent others from experiencing the same heartbreak that I have."

Draven didn't want to understand, but he did. He remembered feeling such grief when his mother had died. But even so, there was always a reason to turn from one's bitterness. "Empress, what about your daughter? You say you're left with emptiness, but surely she helps fill the void."

The Empress simply shook her head. "The void is one that is too wide to be filled. And after her broken engagement, I have no hope of grandchildren to carry on my legacy."

His sympathy melted into pity. Yes, she had suffered, but instead of focusing on what she had, she focused on what she'd lost. And that was the true tragedy. Oily, cold dread pooled in his stomach. If the Empress was this bitter toward all Scorpio assassins, what was the likelihood that he'd be able to convince her to spare Selene?

But even if he couldn't, perhaps he could find a way to buy her time and keep her safe until the King arrived.

"Empress, I can see why you'd be reluctant to free a Scorpio assassin. However, I do have one request."

The Empress collected herself, casually lounging on the couch like she didn't have a care in the world. "Don't think that by revealing my story to you I'll be any more sympathetic to your cause."

"Of course." He leaned forward, ignoring the painful twinge in his back. "If you place Selene back in the cell with the others, she won't survive until the execution date. You'll have to either remove her again to take her to the infirmary or the graveyard. All I'm proposing is that you keep her in a different cell."

The Empress narrowed her eyes. "Somehow, I don't think your primary goal is for Selene to live long enough to be executed. But your rationale makes sense. I'll have her housed in a different cell."

Draven bowed his head. "Thank you."

"Is that... all?"

"Yes." He rose, gripping the walking stick with his sweat-slicked hand. "Thank you for your time." He hobbled back out of her room, each step more difficult than the last.

Evelyn and Alaric were going to arrive a day too late to stop the execution, and he was in no position to ride out to them. Not yet, anyway. He'd give himself two more days to heal first. Once he reached the royal entourage, Alaric could fly back ahead of him and stop the execution.

Draven entered the infirmary and peeked in on Selene. She was fast asleep. He was tempted to wake her again, but instead he slid the wall screen shut and limped the last few scevola to his room.

She would need all the time to heal that she could get. And if everything worked out according to plan, hopefully he'd have many more opportunities to spend time with her.

Two Days Later

Draven was already much stronger than he'd been two days ago, and his walking stick aided his movement immensely.

He'd told the healers that he was going out for a stroll. Thankfully, none of them had noticed the small bundle of cloth he'd taken with him, filled with bits of food he'd saved over the past few days. He tugged the hood of his cloak further down to conceal his face from any passing servants and entered the stables behind the palace. The salty tang of human sweat mixed with that of the horses. The scent of hay and manure drenched the area.

Draven locked eyes with the Empress' unicorn—the only mount fast enough to take him to Evelyn and Alaric in time. The unicorn's sleek coat was pure black. Its white horn emerged from the star on its forehead, appearing opalescent even in the dim stable light.

Its stall was more spacious than the other horses' in order to accommodate its larger size. A bucket of oats and berries sat adjacent to the water trough. A unicorn could only be confined if it wanted to be. As an expression of gratitude—or perhaps as incentive to stay—they were treated like royalty.

The unicorn continued to stare at him, its eyes a striking pale blue and eerily intelligent.

Draven scanned the passage and saw a few stable workers watching him. He'd have to make this quick. He folded his forearms on the top of the stall. "Greetings... unicorn." With a flush of embarrassment, he realized he didn't know its name. Hopefully it wouldn't be too offended.

The unicorn tilted its head.

"I'm sorry. I don't know your name." Draven rubbed the back of his neck. "To be fair, we haven't been properly introduced."

The unicorn stepped forward, nodding its head toward the nameplate on its stall, which read *Amaya*.

"Amaya. It's a pleasure to meet you. I'm Draven."

The unicorn stamped her foot, blowing out a snort.

She was an impatient one. He should have taken time to befriend the unicorn sooner. If she didn't let him ride her, he was sunk—and Selene was dead. "I'll get to the point, then. There's this girl, and I love her. She's going to be executed two days from now by the Empress' orders unless I can ride to King Alaric and Queen Evelyn before then. They're the only ones with enough power to stop this. You're the only horse—"

She snorted again, shaking her head.

"Pardon me, the only *mount* fast enough to reach them in time. Would you please help me save her?"

The unicorn gave him a brisk nod and leapt over her stall and Draven, thudding to the ground behind him.

Draven suppressed a startle. "Thank you." He glanced back into her stall, where her saddle and reins hung. "I'll have to saddle you first—"

She shook her head, stamping her front foot.

"All right. No saddle, then." He staggered to its side, only to pause. Even fully healed, he'd have difficulty mounting it. "Could you help me? I've been recently injured and—"

The unicorn knelt on her front legs.

Draven leaned his walking stick against the stall and swung his leg over her back. Amaya rose and immediately lurched into a gallop, even though they were inside the stables. She deftly wove around the stable workers, into the courtyard, and out of the Taijese palace gates.

The guards watched as they left but made no move to stop them. Everyone knew better than to try and stop a unicorn when its mind was made up.

Amaya's muscles rippled beneath Draven's legs. He'd never gone so fast in all of his life. He could scarcely see the buildings and people as they whizzed past.

Draven held onto her mane and bent low over her neck, trusting that she knew where she was going. The air buffeted his face, making his eyes sting, and he closed them. Occasionally, he opened them to see where they were.

The outskirts of Renshi.

A path through the jungle.

The broad stone highway leading to Octavya.

The sun hovered above the horizon, painting the clouds in swatches of blush pink, when the unicorn let out a high-pitched whinny. Draven raised his head. Just up ahead was a small army of guards and warriors. No doubt the royal carriage was ensconced in the middle.

The line of guards halted, drawing out their weapons. The unicorn came to an abrupt stop in front of them, nearly throwing Draven from her back. She stamped the ground, lowering her horn to the same level as their swords. Her aggressive posturing would likely set them on edge.

Draven raised his hands. "We mean no harm. I simply want to speak to King Alaric and Queen Evelyn."

The carriage door swung open, and Alaric emerged from it, his enormous green wings at his sides. Sometimes Draven still forgot how big they were; it was a wonder that he fit in the carriage.

"*Draven?*" Alaric's expression was completely unreadable, and Draven felt every muscle within him clench. Pain danced along his back. After their last meeting, he didn't dare expect a warm welcome. But with Selene's life on the line, he had no other options.

28

THE SCORPIO IN HOUSE CHANNING

Draven dismounted the unicorn, only to clutch her mane when his legs trembled and he nearly fell. He tried to kneel but found he didn't have the strength to do it slowly. His grip on the unicorn's mane weakened and his knees slammed into stone. He tried to clear the pain from his expression. "My King."

Alaric strode toward him, the guards parting to make a path. He stopped, staring down at Draven. "You're injured. What's happened?"

Draven let out a one-beat laugh. "It's a long story."

"You needn't stay on the ground. Rise and come with me."

Draven grimaced, regretting that he'd left his walking stick behind. He tried shoving off the ground, but found his strength failed him halfway, and he began trembling uncontrollably.

Alaric was quick to grab Draven's hand and hoist him up, tossing Draven's arm around his broad shoulders. Alaric was shorter but had no problem assisting Draven. The man was built with the strength of a dragon.

As they neared the middle of the party, occupants in the carriages alongside the royal one curiously peered out their windows.

Alaric set his hand on Draven's back to steady him, and white stars popped in his vision. He would have collapsed if Alaric weren't supporting him. Heat stormed across his face. This wasn't the best impression to make after seven years.

Alaric froze, glancing sharply at Draven. "Hang it, Draven. Your entire back is bleeding. What happened?"

"*What*? Draven's bleeding?" A shrill voice cried from within the carriage. Evelyn poked her head out, her long, dark-blond hair flowing down to her hips. Gone was the red she'd previously dyed it when he'd first met her.

"*Evelyn*. Get back in the carriage—now." Alaric's voice was nearly a growl, and his tone left no room for argument.

But apparently Evelyn didn't think so. She narrowed her eyes at him. "I swear, you get bossier and bossier the longer I'm—"

"*In*. Please," Alaric said, a note of pleading in his voice.

Evelyn huffed but disappeared back inside.

Alaric guided Draven into the carriage. Evelyn was perched on the seat, studying Draven through wide eyes.

"Lie down," Alaric said to him. "I'll bring one of the healers to attend you, and you can tell us what in Torva happened."

Draven settled himself onto the carriage floor, sandwiched between the two seats, and sighed in relief. It was a miracle he'd ridden so far without collapsing.

Evelyn sucked in a breath. "Your *back*, Draven. It's bleeding. What happened?"

Apparently blood had soaked through the bandages. It seemed not so long ago that Selene had done the same thing. "I don't mean to be disrespectful, but could we wait for Alaric to return? I can already feel my energy waning, and I'm not sure I'll be able to tell the story twice."

"Of course. Forgive me for my thoughtlessness."

He laughed. "Evelyn—I—I mean Queen Evelyn—"

"Just Evelyn. We're friends, after all."

Friends? After all that had happened? He was deeply grateful that she was willing to forgive him so completely. "Thank you, but I fear the King would be—"

"The King would trust his wife's judgement," Alaric answered from behind him.

Draven stiffened until Alaric's words sank in. Had Alaric forgiven him as well?

"If you'll move onto the bench," Alaric continued, "the Healer will see to your back."

Draven shoved off from the floor and practically crawled onto the bench, embarrassment once again warming him. The cushions on the bench were so soft that Draven's weight nearly compressed them in half.

Golden curtains hung over the windows. Evelyn sat on the bench across from him, snuggled in a nest of blankets and pillows—almost an excessive amount. Apparently the rumors about Alaric spoiling his queen were true.

Alaric squeezed into the carriage, and Evelyn scooted to the side. A blanket shifted off of her, revealing a very well-rounded belly.

Draven's mouth fell open, and he barely stopped himself from saying something idiotically obvious, such as *"you're pregnant."*

Evelyn caught his look and grinned. "The baby is due in four months." Interesting. Judging from the size of her stomach, Draven would have thought her farther along.

Alaric's brow pinched with worry as he curled his wing around Evelyn. He didn't appear nearly as thrilled.

The Healer crowded into the carriage, carrying rolls of bandages and jars of ointment. She set them down, tucking a lock of long silver hair behind her pointed ear. Draven remembered hearing a rumor in the Octavian palace that she was a half-elf and over a thousand years old. He believed the rumors.

"Draven," she said, her melodical voice almost like a song,

"I'm glad to see you here. Alaric has been meaning to reconnect with you over the past few years. Unfortunately, he has been rather hesitant to do so."

Alaric was suddenly looking everywhere but at Draven.

Alaric had *wanted* to see Draven again? In truth, Draven had expected Alaric to resent him.

Evelyn giggled. "The Healer is dead set on starting a bromance between you guys."

Bro... mance?

"Oh, never mind." Evelyn drew her blanket up to her chin and snuggled into Alaric's side. "I keep forgetting that not everyone knows Earth speak like Alaric does."

Alaric cleared his throat. "I believe Draven traveled all this way to talk about something of great importance."

The Healer tucked a cloth beneath Draven to cover the cushions and sliced open the back of his shirt.

Draven stiffened as she peeled the blood-dampened cloth away. "Yes. I was captured by the Scorpio and tortured. The only reason I was rescued was because one of the Scorpio, Selene, told the Empress the location of the assassins' base. But now, regardless of Selene's change in allegiance, the Empress is going to execute her in two days' time, along with everyone else who was captured from the base—even the children." Draven hung his head. "I know I don't deserve—"

The Healer scrubbed at his raw back, and he sucked in a sharp breath. It felt like someone had set his skin on fire.

Once the pain subsided, he continued, "I know I don't deserve any special favors from either of you. But you showed mercy to me, and I was hoping you'd do the same with Selene —and some of the other Scorpio. She sacrificed everything to save me, and I would trust her with my life."

The words had come out in a gush, and he'd barely had time to take a breath in between. Now he breathed deeply, watching Evelyn and Alaric's expressions.

To his surprise, Evelyn was smiling. Grinning actually, mischief twinkling in her pale brown eyes. "So this assassin is a woman? And you would trust her with your life? Sounds like you really admire her."

Alaric shook his head. "Was that really *all* that you took away from what he said?"

"I heard all of it. I'm just paying attention to the important parts." She redirected her attention to Draven, and he suppressed the urge to squirm. "And judging from what he just said, he found a girl that he really, really loves. And she loves him back. *And* she's a former Scorpio, just like him." Evelyn waggled her eyebrows at Alaric. "Are you thinking what I'm thinking?"

He stared at her flatly. "Enlighten me."

"They would be perfect together. I totally ship it."

What was she shipping? And to where?

Alaric glanced at Draven. "You're in no condition to ride back to the Taijese palace."

Draven clenched his jaw as the Healer spread a cold gel across his back. "I'll do whatever is necessary to save her."

Evelyn let out a little squeak, holding her hand to her heart. "Alaric, we have to help her!"

"We will." Alaric pressed a quick kiss to Evelyn's temple. "But we have to think of logistics. We could send someone back on the unicorn—"

"If you flew back, that would be the fastest way." Evelyn's expression lit up. Aside from Draven, she seemed the most excited about Selene's rescue.

Alaric combed his fingers through his hair. "And leave you? I can't. What if something were to—"

"Alaric. We have armed forces—five times as big as they need to be—surrounding us. I'll be all right. The baby will be all right." She tipped her head up toward Alaric, and Alaric obligingly lowered his face to hers. She pressed a quick kiss to his lips. "Now, go be a hero and save Draven's girl."

Draven felt a sharp pain reverberate through his chest. What would it be like to hold Selene like that? To have her press a kiss to his lips? Would he ever have the opportunity to kiss her again?

Alaric's fingers grazed Evelyn's cheek. "If you were to be hurt in my absence, I would never forgive myself. And I don't know how I could bear to be parted from you for the next day." The sparkle in his eyes suggested that he was half-joking.

"We'll just have to make up for that when we're together again." She nudged his nose with hers. "Go."

"All right." Alaric glanced at Draven. "As Evelyn has suggested, I'll fly to Renshi. I should get there in time to stop the execution. You'll remain with the party."

Draven swallowed, his throat suddenly aching. "I thank you, both of you. I can't describe how deeply grateful and indebted I am. And please thank the unicorn on your way out."

Alaric nodded. "Of course... brother." He tugged on Evelyn's arm. "Would you walk with me as I gather some supplies for the journey?"

She rose, the blankets pooling by her feet. "I can't think of anything I'd like to do more." They left together, and judging from how they were looking into each other's eyes, they intended to do much more than gather supplies.

The Healer rebandaged his torso. "So long as you remain in a carriage and engage in no more strenuous activity, I'd say you're well on your way to making a full recovery."

"Thank you. Your kindness is most appreciated—and most undeserved."

The Healer dismissed his comment with a smile. Though he suspected her to be ancient, her skin was smooth and flawless, likely a result of her elfish heritage. "Of course. I've been tending to Alaric since he was a small child. I'm happy to tend to his brother as well."

As she left, Evelyn reentered and seated herself across from him. The carriage lurched forward, and the entire party resumed their journey to Renshi.

Draven laid his head on the cushioned seat, hoping this would be a restful trip. Though his worry for Selene ate at him, he was exhausted. He needed sleep.

"So," Evelyn said, "tell me about this girl."

Draven opened his eyes and found Evelyn leaning as far forward as her swollen belly would allow.

"And don't leave out any details." Evelyn grinned, her eyes aglow with excitement. "I want to know *everything.*"

Two Days Later

This was it. The day of Selene's execution.

This will not be the last we see of each other. Draven's words drummed against her mind, pulsed within her heart. He'd said it so sincerely. Yet those had been his last words to her; she hadn't seen him since. Even if he had failed to persuade the Empress to release her, she wished he'd have at least visited her in the dungeons.

Selene waited in her solitary cell, conveniently situated across from the main cell, where the other assassins could shoot her venomous looks but couldn't touch her. It was a small mercy that she tried to be grateful for. But a part of her wondered if being beaten to death would really have been more terrible than execution.

She hoped Draven wouldn't be there to watch. Even though it would be one bright spot in her final day, the thought made her sick.

She closed her eyes, summoning up her last vision of him.

His skin had been significantly paler. Whether it was from the ointment wearing off or loss of blood, she couldn't tell. But his green eyes had been as fierce and vivid as ever. A shade that stole her breath. She remembered his tender expression and gentle touches. And now he would never touch her again.

She hoped that Cori—wherever she was—didn't feel this alone. Selene gripped the bars of her cell tightly. Now she'd never help rescue Cori or discover what had happened to her. If only she'd thought to ask Draven to search for her.

Guards slowly marched into the dungeons, their footsteps clapping like thunder. The majority of them waited outside the main cell. Using the two gates, they drew the assassins out one by one and weighted their ankles and wrists with shackles.

Three guards came her way. Perhaps three would have been understandable were she in peak physical condition. As weak as she was, she wouldn't have been able to fight off even one of them.

One drew near, his eyes hard and cold. "Either you come to us or we'll come to you—and you won't like the latter option."

A brief spark of rebellion flared within her, tempting her to choose this last act of defiance. But pain already wracked her heart. She didn't need to deal with any more today.

Selene rose and stumbled toward the gate of her cell. They unlocked it and wasted no time chaining her. They shoved her into line behind the other shuffling assassins.

Some appeared angry, as though they'd kill all of the guards if given the chance. Others appeared empty of life and hope, their dead gazes crumbling to the ground.

The line slowed abruptly when the assassins reached the stairs. It seemed that she wasn't the only one who'd grown weak with inactivity. Her body felt heavier with each step, her thighs burning until they quivered. It almost would have been better to live out her last days in good health, strong and vibrant, and die abruptly than to be in this pitiful state.

Level by level, the assassins stumbled upward, guards occasionally prodding sluggish prisoners. Finally, they emerged into the palace. Only guards frequented this section; Selene didn't see any servants. These guards watched the procession with a mixture of disgust and curiosity.

Only when Selene felt her chest grow heavy with disappointment did she realize that she'd been expecting to see Draven. If not at the execution, then at least here. But perhaps the sight of her shuffling to her death was too painful.

Selene suddenly wished the line would move faster. She wanted to get this over with. If she wasn't going to see Draven, there was no need to prolong her suffering.

But they continued their slow march, swaying from one side to the other as they tried to walk with their heavy chains. By the time they reached the palace gates, the remains of Selene's commoner dress were drenched in sweat, gluing it to her chest and back. Even in winter, the Taijese air was hot and humid, thick enough that it seemed she could only coax a little into her lungs.

They marched through alleyways and streets, every single person, commoner and noble alike, stopping to stare at the Scorpio assassins. Many had likely only heard rumors—or perhaps frightening bedtime stories.

A young man was holding his horse's reins and talking to a vendor. After his eyes skimmed the line, he smirked and turned back to the vendor. "They don't look so fearsome after all. It's a wonder they weren't all captured sooner."

A few assassins shot him nasty looks, but most didn't bother.

Selene thought the rest of the trip would be uneventful, but she was soon proven wrong.

"Selene!"

She jerked to a halt, looking toward the voice. Her grandmother raced down the street, cloak flapping behind her and a worried expression pinching her face.

The guard jabbed Selene's side with his sword, slicing through her dress to cut tender skin. "Keep moving."

"No! Wait!" Her grandmother reached the line, placing her hand on the guard's forearm. "This is my granddaughter!"

The guard shook her off. "I don't care if she's your dog. Today, she's to be executed."

Her grandmother gave him a flat look. "I know that, you dimwit."

Surprise washed over his expression.

"As her family, I have a legal right to have a last word with her." What could her grandmother possibly have to say to her? They'd been on friendly terms but never particularly close. "If you would deny me, we will take this case to court, and I'll—"

"Fine, fine. You can have your last word." The guard grabbed Selene's arm and hauled her out of line. The other prisoners shuffled past her. "Just make it quick. We can't delay the execution. And I'll need to remain with—"

"Of course, my dear." Her grandmother patted his cheek. "You're more than welcome to witness our last moments together."

Once again, the guard seemed at a loss for words.

"Come, come. I'd rather not all of the guards and Scorpio listen in on us." Her grandmother shuffled into a nearby alley and stopped, just out of hearing distance of the rest of the guards and assassins as they continued their march.

The guard dragged Selene, following her grandmother. "Remember, you'll only have a few moments—" He jerked backward, blood gushing from his neck, a small dagger protruding from his skin.

"No, my dear." Her grandmother strode forward, jerking the dagger from his neck. "You're the one who only has a few moments."

29

BACKSTABBED

Outwardly, Selene couldn't summon the energy to react. Had her grandmother really just killed that guard? Was this some crazy dream to help Selene cope with reality?

"Come, my dear. We have no time to lose." Her grand-mother looped her arm through Selene's.

Selene's gaze fell back to the guard as he spluttered and choked on his own blood. Who would miss him when he was gone? Who would mourn his death? Did he have a girl he was seeing? Parents? A family?

"Selene! We must hurry. The other guards will soon notice his absence and come to investigate." Though her grandmother seemed eager to leave, she appeared very calm about the whole situation. Unsurprised.

Selene stared at her grandmother. How had she not seen it before? Her mother had trained Selene. That left the obvious question of who had trained her mother. "How long have you been a Scorpio? And why didn't I know?"

Her grandmother's laugh was musical, sounding as if it belonged to a much younger woman. "Longer than you've been alive! Arzil insisted that I spend as much time away from him and the base as possible. After all, as an intelligence agent, it was imperative that my identity remain a secret."

"Serpent," Selene breathed.

Her grandmother's smile was infused with pride. "I'm glad that you've heard the stories about me. Now come, we must make haste."

"To where?"

"Arzil has a new Scorpio base, deep in the jungles. He's gathering the remaining assassins to seek revenge on King Alaric. With our combined skills, we can—"

"No."

Her grandmother's smile withered. "I—what? What did you say? My old hearing must have failed me."

Selene took a step back. "I said 'no.' If killing King Alaric is the price of my freedom, then I want no part in it."

Her grandmother went very still. "You're assuming you have a choice in the matter."

Selene's blood chilled her veins. A choice. Did she really not have one? Or was this another moment where she'd have to decide between the easy way out or the right way forward? "I won't. I'd rather die by my values than live without them." She wasn't going to betray Draven's trust again. Wasn't going to let others make her decisions for her anymore.

"Foolish girl. Just like your mother."

Her *mother*? Breath stalled in her lungs. "What about my mother?"

"She betrayed the Scorpio, and for it she died." Instead of sorrowful, her grandmother's expression was smug, her eyebrows raised, her mouth tilted in a smirk.

All the pieces clicked into place, and Selene's heart pounded. Had her mother tried to leave the Scorpio? Was that why she'd died, for making the right choice?

Draven had been right about one thing: Arzil had had a

hand in killing her mother. And apparently her grandmother had as well.

"You... killed her? Your daughter?" Selene was too stunned to be angry. Her entire life, she'd been told that Draven, the famed Scorpio traitor, had killed her mother. But instead the leaders of the Scorpio had done the deed.

Her grandmother jabbed a thin finger into Selene's chest. "Do you have any idea how much I've sacrificed for you? I made excuses to your father and stepmother to help you sneak out. I specifically instructed the guards to let you escape. I've made life as an assassin as easy as possible for you—and this is what I receive in return?"

Tuteno. Her grandmother was a murderer—and she knew Selene wasn't loyal to the Scorpio. Selene needed to report this to the guards, before her grandmother and Arzil could assassinate the King.

Selene turned and raced back toward the line of shuffling prisoners—only to slam into the ground. Something sharp pricked her neck, and her legs refused to work, like limp sticks of rubber. Her grandmother plucked a blow dart from Selene's neck. As Selene's vision and hearing faded, her grandmother leaned over her, face crumpling in disappointment.

"So much potential. Such a shame."

The Next Day

If Draven had to spend one more moment in the carriage, he was going to burst.

The ride had been comfortable, and Evelyn's company pleasant, but he needed to know what had happened to Selene. Had Alaric arrived in time? Was Selene still alive? Had the Empress again imprisoned her with the rest of the assassins?

Had she been further injured by the prisoners? Even if Alaric had saved her, what if she was mortally wounded?

He kept his face by the window, peering between the curtains as they entered Renshi. They marched through the lower district on the outskirts of the city, the opulence of the royal entourage in sharp contrast to the squalor of the slums. Many commoners stopped what they were doing to gawk at the party.

A woman with a pinched face watched the procession, her expression guarded, and her children huddled behind her threadbare skirt. An elderly man peered at them through a cracked monocle. A little girl wandered dangerously near the horses, a wooden toy hanging limply in her hand as she stared in open-eyed wonder.

Draven let the curtains fall closed, willing the carriage to go faster. If only Alaric had flown back to them to give them news of what had transpired.

"We're almost there, Draven," Evelyn said softly, stroking her round stomach.

Draven nodded but couldn't stop the impatience from thrumming inside of him.

Finally, the group slowed at the palace's back entrance, used for royalty and servants. Draven was out of the carriage door before it had stopped. He bounded up short stone steps and nearly ran into Alaric.

Draven searched Alaric's eyes, trying to read what had happened. "Selene. Where is she? Did you stop the execution in time?"

Alaric drew in a deep breath, sorrow darkening his eyes. "I did stop the execution, but I didn't find Selene."

What? Draven's chest swelled and deflated with each breath, making his heart swirl with dizziness. Had she died before the execution? What had happened to her? "Wh-where is she? Did you find her—" *body*. The word lodged in his throat. She couldn't be dead. Not when he'd tried so hard to save her.

Alaric removed his crown, running his fingers through his hair. "The prisoners and guards say that her grandmother appeared, demanding to have a last word with her granddaughter. The guard that accompanied them was found dead in an alley, his neck slit. The grandmother is at House Channing and reports that Selene killed the guard and escaped. No one can find Selene. In addition, the Scorpio leader, Arzil, has escaped capture as well."

Selene had... escaped? Willingly? Or had someone captured her? Could the grandmother be involved in something he wasn't aware of? Perhaps this was part of a scheme to aid Selene? Or perhaps the grandmother was completely innocent and Selene had taken advantage of the opportunity.

Draven sank onto the stone stairs, and Alaric darted past him, heading straight toward Evelyn's carriage. He couldn't blame Selene for escaping when the opportunity arose. But slitting the guard's neck? If she had to choose between her life and his, he supposed her motivation made sense. He couldn't help but be... disappointed. He'd thought she was different. That she'd changed.

Draven laughed at his naivete. He thought he'd finally changed her. He'd fallen for her charms once more. He'd believed what he wanted to see.

But this time... this time, she'd truly seemed to care for him. She'd revealed the location of the Scorpio base to save him, after all, resulting in her imprisonment and near-execution. Had she planned to escape all along? Surely not... Unless the grandmother had been involved.

Whatever had happened, he needed to find Selene. And he had a feeling that the first step would be paying her grandmother a visit.

It felt like centuries had passed since he'd first come to House Channing.

Draven paused in front of the gates, recalling the times he'd dragged Selene through them. He hoped that—somehow—she was innocent of the guard's death. Between that and escaping, it was becoming less likely that Alaric would grant her mercy.

One of the guards appeared suddenly at the gate, his eyes bloodshot, his breath stinking of korosasth. "Who goes there?"

"You would know me as Guard Raban, but I'm Draven, the Empress' commander."

The man tugged at his gnarled beard and then his eyes brightened. "Ah! Raban. Yes, I remember. You were the only one that could keep that twit inside come nightfall."

Draven clenched his jaw, resisting the urge to chide the man. "I have rather urgent business here."

"Right, right." The man unlocked the gate. "Say, put in a good word for me in the palace, will ya? I've always wanted to be a guard there. I've heard they pay well."

The man wouldn't even survive the entry test. Honestly, Draven had never seen lazier guards than those at House Channing. If he didn't know better, he'd have thought Selene handpicked them herself.

Draven climbed the twirling stairs to the fifth level. He strode down the hallway, the tatami mats softening his steps. Which of these doors could belong to her grandmother? He'd never had a reason before to visit this floor.

He knocked on the first door. When there was no answer, he went to the second. On his third try, the door swung open, revealing Selene's grandmother. Now that he was familiar with the curves and contours of Selene's face, he could see the echo of her appearance in her grandmother. She had near-black eyes and a slight bump in her nose, just like Selene.

Her smile faltered only for a split-second upon seeing him. "Why, Guard Raban, to what do I owe the pleasure of your visit?"

Draven tried to read her expression to discern how she truly felt about his visit. But her eyes were veiled, much as Selene's had been. A pang went through his chest at the thought. Would he ever see her again? "I wanted to speak about your granddaughter."

Her grandmother's face tightened, making all her wrinkles more pronounced. "It's a shame, what happened with Selene. I expected better from her."

Draven glanced down the hallway to ensure that no one was privy to their conversation. "Due to the sensitive nature of our topic, would you mind if I came in?"

"Of course, of course." She stepped aside, sweeping her hand to indicate Draven should enter.

As he passed her, he caught the scent of lotus blossoms from her silver hair. She wasn't dressed in the same flashy, opulent manner as Selene's stepmother, but neither did she chose Selene's drab style of clothing. Her butter-yellow silk dress was simple but well-tailored. Silver and gold bangles jingled from her wrists as she closed the door.

Her room was smaller than the solar but spacious enough to accommodate a fire pit, sitting area, and bed. There were three windows along the wall and vases of ferns scattered throughout the room.

Selene's grandmother seated herself onto a thickly cushioned green chair.

Draven sat across from her. There was a small table between them with a half-filled teacup on top. "I hear you were the last to see Selene before she escaped."

Her grandmother nodded, her eyes large and sorrowful. "Indeed. It was so tragic to witness the man's death. I never would have thought Selene capable of such violence."

"Why do you think she killed the guard?"

Amusement tilted her lips. "To escape, of course. And to get rid of any witnesses." She picked up the teacup and took a delicate sip.

"If that's the case, why didn't she kill you as well?"

She spluttered, then coughed, firmly setting the teacup down with a clank. "I'm her grandmother. She wouldn't kill me."

"Or perhaps she was confident that you wouldn't reveal any of her secrets. Perhaps you knew exactly what would happen when you asked for a last word with her."

"That's preposterous." Her grandmother leapt from her seat faster than any person her age should be able to move. "If you've just come here to insult and accuse me when I'm grieving over the loss of—"

"Forgive me. That was not my intention." Draven folded his hands and leaned back in his chair. Instead of giving him a real answer, she'd blustered. His best hope was to conceal his suspicion and act as if he'd offended an innocent person. "I care for your granddaughter deeply, so you'll have to excuse me if I seem on edge or jump to conclusions. I would just like to find her."

"You care for her? Even after she's killed someone?" The grandmother's eyes sparkled with intrigue.

"In her defense, she was trying to escape with her life." And perhaps her grandmother had played a more involved role than anyone else had realized. "After she killed the guard, what did she do? Where did she go?"

"She told me to tell no one. I agreed to it at the time, but I was only lying so that she'd spare me. Then she climbed up on the roof of a building and left."

"And how did she kill her guard? Did you not try to stop her?"

"It was too late; her movements were so fast, likely from her experience in killing so many others." She shook her head as if disappointed, but a different expression rippled over her features.

Draven nodded slowly and asked again, "*How* did she kill him?"

"She threw a small dagger at him, and it sank right into his neck." The grandmother gave a delicate shudder. "And then she used the dagger to free herself."

Draven stared directly into her eyes, not wanting to miss any signs of conflict or discomfort. "She freed herself afterward? How would she throw with her wrists bound?"

The grandmother blinked, her face coloring slightly. "Oh. You must forgive my poor memory. I seem to miss more the older I become. She freed herself first, then killed the guard."

Another inconsistency stuck out in her words like a glaring red flag. "Is that so?" Draven kept his tone light as he leaned forward.

He caught a flash of fear in her eyes. "Yes, as far as I can remember. I might have forgotten some tiny details."

"Selene was bound in chains; she couldn't have sliced those with a dagger. So how did she have enough time to pick the lock on her manacles and kill the guard without him noticing?"

The grandmother opened and closed her mouth, the color on her face rising higher. "H-how am I possibly supposed to know such particulars? She obviously used one of her assassin tricks."

"Interesting. And I wonder how she acquired the dagger."

The grandmother simply shrugged and took a sip of tea, hiding behind the cup.

Sensing he wouldn't pry any more from her, Draven rose. "Thank you for your time, my lady. This visit has been most informative."

She rose shakily. "Well. I'm so... pleased that my information could be of... use to you." The words seemed forced from her lips.

Draven had never heard someone sound so falsely polite in his life—which was impressive, considering he'd once worked with many scheming nobles in the Octavian palace. Given her behavior, he'd request that Alaric set a few guards near House Channing to watch her.

Draven left, tossing a glance over his shoulder to ensure that he didn't find a dagger in his neck. He had a hunch that Selene hadn't been the one to kill the guard.

The world faded in and out of existence. Selene fought the darkness, yet it swept over her every time she opened her eyes. She was weak. Utterly helpless. Not strong enough to resist its pull.

The blindfold and gag were finally torn from her face, the abrasive fabric leaving light burns on her skin. Her mouth felt like sand and tasted like death. Her head sagged to one side, too heavy to lift upright.

She was tied in a chair, in a tiny, empty cabin. The floor was made of dirt. The walls and roof were wooden logs. No windows. Judging from the chirping around her, they were deep in the jungle.

Where no one could hear her scream.

A cold sweat washed over her skin until shivers wracked her body. Dread pooled in her gut, settling there like liquified rock. What in Torva would happen next? Couldn't she just skip this chapter in life and move onto the next one, where she slumbered in the arms of death.

The door swung open, offering her a glimpse of the jungle.

The light outside blinded her from seeing anything but the

silhouette of the person standing in the doorway. But she didn't need to see his features to know.

A tall, muscular frame.

Strands of long, brittle hair.

Air froze in her lungs.

Arzil.

He strode in and slammed the door behind him.

Her heart hammered. How many more minutes, or hours, or days would she had to endure his torture until she died?

"Selene. How good to see you again." He approached and trailed his fingers down her cheek. Nausea lurched in her stomach. "You're already shaking. That didn't take long."

30

TO SEE HIM ONE LAST TIME

Selene clenched her jaw. It was all right to be afraid, so long as she didn't let that fear become her master.

"We're over two days' journey into the jungle. Far, far away from any civilization. From anyone who could help you. Anyone who could hear you." When she didn't respond, Arzil continued, "If you cooperate, my earlier offer still stands. You can leave Taijeng and live out the rest of your life in peace."

She swallowed tightly, her dry throat aching. "What does cooperating entail?"

Arzil drew back and paced around her. It was rather unnerving to blindly feel him pass behind her. "I want you to lure Draven into a trap for me. Write a note to him, telling him to meet you one day's travel from the west gate, along the path leading to the Lei River. You'll tell him you no longer love him, and you'll plunge a dagger through his heart. If you refuse, then you'll die—very, very slowly." Arzil withdrew a syringe from his trouser pocket. With its finely-shaped glass barrel and metal needle, it must have cost a fortune. The Scorpio reserved syringes for a special kind of torture.

A pearlescent liquid swirled inside the glass vial.

She recognized it instantly: Evanescence flower.

She'd lived just like her mother. Now she would die like her.

Arzil twisted his wrist, letting shimmers race across the liquid. "This would be a rather fitting way for you to die, considering that your mother passed in the same manner."

A sick feeling sloshed in her gut. To think her grandmother was at peace with how her daughter had died. She wasn't sure whether she should vomit or cry.

Being disintegrated from the inside out would be an unpleasant way to die. But saving Draven would be worth every agonizing moment. And if her mother had endured it, so could she.

An adamant refusal was on the tip of her tongue, but she swallowed it back. She could never kill Draven. But playing along was her best hope of escape. Selene bowed her head. "If I do this, you promise me that you'll spare my life and give me my freedom?"

"Yes."

Selene released a long sigh. "It seems I don't have another option, then. I accept."

Arzil laughed, patting her shoulder. "That's what I always liked about you, Selene. You'd do whatever it took to pursue the easy path and save your own skin. A desirable quality in an assassin." He whipped out a dagger, and Selene flinched before realizing he was planning to release her. He sawed away at the ropes binding her.

Once Selene was free, she stood and nearly toppled to the ground. She gripped the back of the chair to steady herself.

Arzil withdrew a folded piece of paper, an ink pot, and a quill. He set the writing implements on the seat of the chair. "Now, write him the letter."

Selene slowly lowered herself to her knees and dipped the quill pen into the ink pot. "Any particular day or time?"

"Excellent question. Ask him to meet you two hours before sunset on Vyenembre the second."

As Selene tapped the pen against the side of the pot and began writing, Arzil let out a low chuckle.

"Finally," he said, "Draven will pay for his betrayal. And I can't think of a more painful death that he could endure than one by your hands."

Selene gripped the quill a bit tighter. Not if *she* had anything to say about it.

The Next Day

Draven stared at the note between his hands, trembling so hard he couldn't read. Evelyn and Alaric stared at him expectantly, and he felt their stares burning into him. Moments earlier, he'd been summoned to Evelyn and Alaric's chamber, and they'd handed him the sealed note.

"What does it say?" Evelyn asked, quite literally on the edge of her seat.

Alaric's expression was much less eager, but he was leaning forward as well.

Draven swallowed, saliva scraping his dry throat. "Dear Draven..." He was hardly going to tell them that the first line read *My Love*. "I am safe and well—for the time being. However, I fear this will change soon. Two hours before sunset on Vyenembre the second, please meet me one day's travel from the west gate, along the path leading to the Lei River. Once there, I trust that you can safely escort me back to the palace. In addition, I have information that will be of interest to you. I know I haven't given you cause to trust me in the past, but please do so now. My life and the future of Taijeng hang in the balance." Draven folded the note, tucking it into his pocket. "It's signed by Selene." Specifically, it was signed *Ever Yours, Selene.* But once again, there was no need to share the particulars.

He was tempted to pull the note out again, ensuring that she'd signed it as he'd read it. There was still hope that he could save her, that they could be together.

Alaric's expression had darkened, as if to compensate for Evelyn's brightened one. "How do we know this is from Selene?" Alaric asked.

"It's her handwriting," Draven replied.

"Judging from what you told us, her grandmother might be partially responsible for the guard's murder. Speaking of her, one of the men you sent out reported to me this morning that the woman had left. They lost her somewhere a few blocks south of the house. They suspected she used a secret passage or tunnel."

This did cast her grandmother in somewhat of a suspicious light. Perhaps there had been two assassins in House Channing, and he'd been tracking the wrong one all along. "We should have her grandmother's possessions searched. Perhaps they will offer a clue."

Alaric nodded. "An excellent idea. But Selene's note still appears suspicious. You're certain that she's trustworthy?"

Draven clenched his jaw, resisting the urge to defend her. After the visit to her grandmother's, his faith in Selene had been restored. In addition, why would she have revealed the Scorpio base and risked her life for him if she didn't love him back? The thought warmed his chest and renewed his determination. "I'm going after her. I'm not asking for your help."

Alaric rose, wings rustling. "I intend to help you, Draven. I'm not going to let you charge off into the jungle alone. I'm simply trying to warn you to be careful. You really think we can trust this girl?"

This girl. At least he hadn't called her "this assassin."

Draven nodded. "I'd trust her with my life, and I'd happily

sacrifice it to save her." Well, perhaps not happily. After all, if he died, there would be no embrace or victory kiss.

"I see. In that case, I'll send half of my forces to accompany you." Alaric reached out slowly and placed a hand on Draven's shoulder, as if afraid that he'd trespassed. "I know you're in love with her, but try not to do anything idiotic."

Draven bowed his head. "Thank you, King—"

"Just Alaric. Or brother. Whichever you prefer." He withdrew his hand and didn't quite meet Draven's eyes, perhaps fearing Draven's response.

Alaric was extending him an offer—an offer of family. Draven hadn't had a family since his mother's death—or suicide, rather. Gratitude swelled within him. Alaric's forgiveness was inspiring and completely undeserved. "Thank you. Brother."

A smile flickered across Alaric's lips. "The date on the note is for tomorrow. I take it that you'll leave soon to meet her?"

Draven nodded. "Given that we'll need an entire day for the journey, and I need to meet her just before sunset, I'd best set off soon."

"Then I'll instruct my men to ready themselves." Alaric glanced at Draven's frame, as if he could see the wounds there that marred his skin. "You're certain that you're well enough to travel?"

"Well enough. Better than when I rode to see you, certainly. If I were to engage in combat, that could pose a problem, but hopefully the need won't arise, especially with so many of your men accompanying me."

Alaric's brow furrowed, but he nodded.

Draven chuckled. "It seems you are behaving more like the older brother."

The tension in his expression eased slightly. "It seems so. Be careful. I have gained my brother only in recent years, and I would not lose him."

Draven nodded, once more surprised by a swell of emotion. "Thank you." The words seemed a paltry exchange for what he'd received. "I'd best prepare for the journey."

Alaric nodded. "When you return, I have a few propositions I'd like to discuss with you."

What could Alaric possibly want from him? "What kind of propositions?"

"I've been meaning to restore your noble title. I know that you rejected such an idea before, but leaving you ripped of your title makes it appear that you're being punished and shamed. In addition, Evelyn and I have noticed that the Empress is a little..." He glanced over at Evelyn.

She twirled her finger around her ear. "Cuckoo for Cocoa Puffs."

Alaric chuckled, seeming to understand whatever Evelyn had just said. Sometimes, it seemed like Evelyn was intentionally using Earth speak. Perhaps she found the Torvans' confusion amusing.

Alaric said, "Quite right. In case you were in need of a job, once we've removed her, we thought you might like to be the new Grand Master. My previous Grand Master, Elmir, would like to retire from the position for personal reasons."

Grand Master? He wanted Draven to be in charge of all of his armed forces? All across Torva? "That's a tremendous honor. One I hardly deserve."

"You've more than proven your merit. All I ask is that you think on it. We can discuss it later, once Selene is safe."

Draven bowed his head. "I will. Thank you."

As he left the room, Evelyn called out, "We're looking forward to having you back, Draven. And to meeting this girl of yours."

Draven stroked the unicorn's mane, honored that she had once more allowed him to ride her. Though she was likely going to find the pace tedious when they slowed down for the many horses accompanying them.

He double-checked the supplies in his pack. Two blankets —one for him and one for Selene. It was best to assume that he would retrieve Selene successfully. Coran biscuits. Jerky. Three flasks of water. Fire starters. A few throwing daggers, including Selene's emerald dagger. He'd found it in the armory. Likely it'd been taken when she was captured. No doubt she'd want it back.

Alaric's men stood next to their horses as they packed their last few items and checked their supplies. Three of Alaric's healers were accompanying them, lest anyone was injured on the journey. His best healer, *the* Healer, was to stay with Evelyn and attend her.

Once Draven ensured none were looking, he retrieved Selene's note and reread it, delighted over it, puzzled over it. She was very vague about why she was in danger and needed him to meet her. Was it possible that she'd been forced to write the note? Perhaps by her captors?

He hoped Arzil wasn't among them. Simply imagining his pale face, his features contorted with wicked pleasure as he tortured Draven, was enough to make shivers trail up and down his raw back. What if Selene had written this under threat of torture? What if she had been tortured? What if—

"Draven."

Alaric's voice rumbled surprisingly close, and Draven scolded himself for not being more aware of his surroundings. He pocketed the note and glanced up. "Alaric. Come to see me off?"

Alaric was holding the reins of a mighty horse, its size rivaling that of the unicorn. "I've come to accompany you."

Draven's sudden intake of breath swelled his chest with air. "You're coming? But Evelyn—"

"Encouraged me to come. I offered to stay with her, lest something happen with the baby." The worry lines crinkling Alaric's forehead deepened. "But she assured me that she's as safe as possible in the palace and that I could be of more use by your side." His sudden grin eased the worry from his expression. "I would have argued, but at this point in our marriage, I know better."

Draven laughed. "I don't know whether I ought to look forward to that point or dread it."

Alaric's grin softened, though if anything, it grew more genuine. "Most definitely look forward to it."

Draven already looked forward to it. The realization hit him like a blow to the stomach. He already looked forward to marrying Selene, to seeing her slowly wake in the mornings, to challenging her in sparring matches, to showing her what a man's touch should feel like.

He'd made mistakes, but he'd grown past them. With Selene, perhaps they could both have a new beginning. There were still so many uncertainties. Her captors might still be trailing her and might pursue them. He didn't know if both he and Selene would make it back to the palace alive. But what he did know was that he loved her. And if he had the opportunity to see her again, he was going to woo her until she agreed to be his.

Alaric gripped his horse's mane and mounted, tossing his leg over to the other side. "Are we going to rescue your love or remain idly chatting?"

The men around them did the same, mounting soon after Alaric had.

Draven only had to contemplate trying to climb onto the unicorn for a moment before she knelt. Draven mounted her, thanking her with a pat to her flanks. "Let's ride."

The Next Day

Selene paced in the jungle clearing, hoping that those watching nearby would think her hands formed fists out of anxiety rather than to conceal something. Over the past few days, she'd snuck glimpses of a map in Arzil's new study, charting out the location of the new Scorpio base. She had the exact coordinates written on a slip of paper.

To her surprise, Lyra had been one of the assassins in the new Scorpio base. Selene was too closely watched for them to speak privately, but occasionally, Lyra shot her a wink. Selene had a feeling the girl was up to something. She hoped Lyra wouldn't endanger herself. Draven was already in enough danger, and she didn't think she could handle losing both of them.

This was likely to be her last encounter with Draven. But at least something good could come of it. The thought made an ache squeeze her chest, until she could scarcely breathe. She wanted to find a way to escape this together. She wanted to tell him how much she loved him and that when he touched her, she felt what no man had made her feel before. Safe. Cherished. Loved.

But she refused to entertain such a possibility. There were assassins posted around the entire perimeter, and she knew that if she failed to do the task assigned to her, they'd strike her down. Or Draven. And she would do whatever was necessary to protect him, even should it cost her life.

Sweat gathered on her back, dampening her bandages. At least she was wearing her tattered dress rather than the skin-tight suit of an assassin. Broad jungle leaves arched over the clearing, letting light occasionally speckle the ground. Exhaustion slowed her movements, and she strode over to a tree, leaning her hip against it as she rested.

Within a few moments, she heard a faint rumble, felt it vibrating the jungle floor. The birds stopped chattering as the sound grew louder. She recognized the rapid tattoo as the beat of horses' hooves. Selene pushed off the trunk of the tree, her heart thrumming. It sounded like Draven had brought an army with him. She wasn't sure if that was a good sign or a bad one.

She heard them stop beyond the clearing, just out of view. She caught hints of movement and rustling as the men spread out, and she tried to mentally keep track of where they were concealing themselves when Draven stepped into the clearing.

Her heart stopped and the world with it.

31

TO HAVE LOVED AND LOST

Draven appeared a bit tired, dark circles beneath his eyes. But he was as handsome as ever. A slight scruff roughened his jawline, and a hint of golden hair gleamed at his roots. His face immediately brightened upon seeing her, and after a few strides, he went still.

She took another moment to absorb the sight of him: the attractively slender build of his body, the dear sight of his face, the warmth in his eyes. Selene's feet moved of their own accord, dashing toward him as fast as they could manage.

She flung her arms around his neck, hugging him close to her. She kept her right hand fisted to conceal her note. "I promised you an embrace, didn't I?"

The tension seemed to melt from him, and he leaned into her, carefully wrapping his arms high on her back. "You did. And that was a better embrace than I could have ever hoped for." He pressed a kiss to her forehead, and a bolt of warmth raced down to her toes.

She leaned back to look up into his face, a wide grin stretching her lips so fiercely that her cheeks ached. "If only we could remain like this forever."

Draven's tender expression made her heart constrict. He cupped the side of her face. "And why can't we?"

Her smile vanished, a heaviness weighing down her chest at the reminder. This moment was to last for a few seconds. And then she'd likely never see him again—if she even survived this encounter.

"Selene? Selene, what is it?" He pressed his forehead against hers, their noses barely brushing. "You can tell me. Are you worried about being imprisoned for killing the guard?"

She forgot her sorrow amidst her confusion. "What guard?"

"The guard you killed upon your escape." He watched her carefully, his attention swerving between her eyes.

"The guard *I* killed?" Indignation stormed through her, and she would have torn away from him if not for his strong grip. "Do you truly think so poorly of me? My grandmother killed him. And when I refused to come, she used a poison dart to knock me unconscious."

"Calm yourself, Selene. I suspected as much. I merely wanted to hear the confirmation from your lips." He glanced around the clearing, his eyes narrowed. "Let's move this conversation elsewhere."

He threaded their fingers and began to pull her into the jungle, but she tugged back. As soon as they stepped foot out of the clearing together, the assassins would realize that she had no intention of killing him. In fact, judging from the impatient energy buzzing around her, perhaps they were already beginning to become suspicious.

Confusion flashed across Draven's features. "Selene?"

She drew him near, unfurling her hand in his. "It's the coordinates of the new Scorpio base," she whispered. "Now run. I'll cover you."

"Run?" He grabbed the crumpled piece of paper and tightened his grip on her hand. "No. Not without you. I'll not be separated from you again."

Selene could almost feel a palpable shift around them as the assassins stirred. Unless Draven left very soon, he was going to die. "Leave me. It'll be all—"

From the corner of her eye, she saw the glint of an arrowhead in the trees. As she stared at the foliage, she saw Arzil's eerily pale eyes, staring at her in shock and anger. Arzil had seen her hand him the note. She didn't have long until he released that arrow. Selene released a slow breath, focusing on Draven. She would make the right choice, even when it cost her everything.

Draven's gaze remained on her, steel resolve shining in his eyes. He hadn't noticed.

Selene pulled him close, wrapping her arms around him, and positioning her back toward Arzil.

Draven placed his hand on her shoulders. "Selene, what—"

The violent thud of an arrow striking her back made her whole body jerk.

Draven glanced over her shoulder. "*Selene!*"

The jungle seemed to erupt in chaos as Draven's men fought against the assassins. Selene only caught a few glimpses of the battle around them before her grip on Draven loosened and she fell.

Draven caught her and knelt with her in his arms, his hands carefully avoiding the arrow. He glanced down at her, his eyes raw with pain. "Selene." His voice was hoarse and jagged at the edges. "What have you done?"

"Saved your life." She managed a smile. "I expected a bit more gratitude." A sharp, delayed pain pierced her chest, and she stiffened, gripping the front of Draven's shirt as tightly as she could.

She'd saved Draven. And now she was going to be torn from him. She'd known this would happen, but it still made sorrow swell in her chest. She hadn't wanted her story to end like this.

Draven lowered his head, leaning his forehead against hers. "Why, Selene?"

"Because I love you." She placed her palm on his forehead, wishing she could massage away his worry lines. Her words to her grandmother echoed through her mind. She didn't want to die, but she certainly didn't regret her choice. "I'd rather die for my values than live without them. You were right; I've always had a choice. And I've always made the wrong decisions—the easiest ones—until now."

Draven clenched his jaw, his eyes falling closed. "I love you too. And if we both make it out of this, I'd be honored if you'd be my wife."

Laughter spilled from her lips, as sorrowful as it was joyful, and the movement made agony wrack her chest. "There's nothing that would make me happier." But they both knew that was impossible. The pain in her back grew hotter, and she felt fresh blood seeping through the bandages.

Draven simply held her, as her body went numb, as the sounds around her grew distant and muffled. His expression, filled with a gentle sorrow that made her heart break, was the last thing she saw before her vision blurred, then faded.

Though Selene breathed shallowly, she'd gone pale and still in Draven's arms. He closed his eyes as a fresh wave of agony raked over him. He'd never felt so utterly helpless. The woman he loved was dying in his arms, and there was nothing he could do to bring her back.

Within a few moments, he became aware of his surroundings again. The fighting had died down. Alaric stood beside Draven, his sword at the ready. It seemed he'd been protecting them during Selene's last moments.

Draven pressed a kiss to her forehead as her skin lightened

with each passing second. Her slender lips were white, nearly vanishing into the rest of her skin. If not for her unnaturally pale skin, she could have been asleep. But she wasn't. She was bleeding out, her life slipping from between his fingers like sand. He could feel himself unraveling; the frail threads holding him together were snapping apart.

A heavy hand gripped his shoulder, and Draven glanced up at Alaric. He'd hoped that Selene and Alaric's first meeting would have been different than this.

Alaric knelt beside him, examining the wound in Selene's back. "The healers might still be able to save her."

Draven's chest swelled with hope. "Where are they?"

Alaric rose. "I'll go find one." He ventured into the jungle, where his men were either capturing the assassins or piling their corpses.

Draven glanced back at Selene, willing her chest to continue to rise and fall. "Stay with me, Selene. Just a few moments more."

"Selene! Draven!"

Draven glanced up as Lyra limped toward them, favoring her left foot, her expression contorted in pain, her brown hair dangling over her face.

"Lyra?" What was she doing here? Why had she joined Arzil? Speaking of the man, Draven hoped that he'd been caught.

Lyra lowered herself next to Draven, her wide eyes fixed on Selene. "Will she... will she make it?"

Draven forced a swallow past his tight throat. "Possibly."

Lyra gently drew her fingers through Selene's hair. She glanced up at Draven. "You probably hate me for remaining with Arzil and not trying to run away and aid the both of you."

"I don't blame you for wanting to avoid capture by the Empress. You likely hate *me* for being the reason the Scorpio base was discovered."

She shook her head. "You were trying to get me and the children to leave before the Empress came, after all. And as I've told you, I don't agree with everything Arzil does." She stretched out her leg with a grimace.

Beneath her form-fitting black pants, he saw a knot swelling on her shin. "What happened?"

"I fell out of one of the trees. I was fighting Arzil, and he just shoved me." Lyra made a face. "Assassins have a terrible habit of not fighting fair."

"You were fighting Arzil? I thought you were loyal to him."

She stared at him flatly. "I've told you that I don't like what he does. The only reason I joined him here was because I overheard him talking about how he'd use Selene to hurt you. I thought it might be helpful for you to have someone on the inside." She huffed, blowing a lock of brown hair. "Little good I did. Thankfully, one of the King's men saw me fighting the assassins or I'd probably be clapped in chains right now." She scanned his face. "You're looking better than when I last saw you."

"That's what happens when you stop torturing someone."

Lyra flinched. "I heard they treated Selene no better."

He sobered immediately. "Unfortunately, no. But she's strong. She survived that ordeal. Perhaps she'll survive this one as well." Unless that healer didn't get here soon. He would have gone to haul the man over to her, but doing so would require disturbing Selene's body and leaving her side. Whether she died today or in several hundred years, he didn't want her to face death alone.

"Pardon me." A surprisingly young man knelt down beside Selene, effectively shoving Draven to the side.

"You're the physician?"

"I am." The man set down an armful of bandages and a bowl of water. "I'm going to remove the arrow and see whether or not there's damage to her organs. If so, she's not likely to survive,"

Draven's stomach churned, his skin prickling with cold. "You're her best chance."

"Sir Draven," a man said from behind him.

Draven glanced over his shoulder, simultaneously irritated and thankful that someone would distract him from the procedure. Arzil was held captive between two knights. Judging from Arzil's flickering eyelids and bruised face, he appeared close to blacking out. A third knight stood beside them, a steely calm in his eyes as if he fought these kinds of battles on a daily basis.

Draven grinded his jaw back and forth for a few moments, battling with the desire to kill the man here and now. This man had nearly tortured him to the brink of death and then nearly killed his bride-to-be. If Selene died, her blood would be on his hands. But Draven knew telling him so would only bring about satisfaction, not remorse. The realization made him feel both disgusted and further angered. "Take him to the King. He would know if we should keep him imprisoned to host a trial later... or not." A part of Draven hoped that Alaric would spill Arzil's blood onto the jungle floor. So long as that man was alive, he was a danger to both Draven and Selene.

The men nodded and dragged Arzil away. The third man remained behind, his hand resting comfortably on the hilt of his sword. "We sighted her grandmother during the battle, but she escaped. Perhaps we can send out a small party to track her."

"Excellent idea. We can't let her run away—or worse, find her way back here to hurt someone else."

Draven turned back just in time to see the healer pouring powder into Selene's mouth.

Lyra studied the healer through narrowed eyes. "What was that?"

"To keep her asleep," he explained. "I don't want her waking up in the middle of this. And the procedure might take a while."

Draven nodded, keeping his eyes fixed on her face and clasping her hand tightly in his. If she died, a part of him would die with her.

32

MAKING HER CHOICE

Pain. Then the blissfulness of darkness. Draven's voice floating down to her where she lay in the abyss. He was somewhere far, far above her. Out of reach. She feared she'd never be able to touch him again.

Which was strange. How could someone who feared touch be afraid to never touch someone again?

She nearly surfaced into the light a few times, long enough for him to brush her cheek with a kiss and say, "I love you." And then she would be pulled back under. Sometimes it was because she lost her strength. Other times, she could feel her victims clawing at her ankles with bloodied, crooked fingers, reminding her that she didn't deserve to live. And then she'd be submerged once more, until all she could see was...

Darkness.

It took a moment for her to realize that this wasn't the darkness of unconsciousness; it was the darkness of night. She could see the room she was in, the thick rug flowing across the floor, the fireplace dominating one side of the wall, the canopy of the bed looming over her.

She glanced left. There was a small table with a bowl of

powder, a glass of water, a folded piece of paper, and her mother's dagger. Draven had found it for her? Her heart surged within her chest. She'd like to do nothing more than embrace Draven. Among other things.

But the chair by her bed was empty. She'd been certain that was where Draven had sat when he'd said, "I love you." But he wasn't there now. She scolded herself as her heart plummeted like an anchor into the sea. But what did she expect? That he'd watch her night and day without rest?

She began to sit up, only for pain to blaze through her back. She cried out and collapsed back against the bed, pressing her hand against her mouth to muffle sobs.

Movement stirred at the end of her bed. Someone was there. A man sat up. Draven. He'd been lying down at the end of the mattress; she just hadn't seen him.

"Selene?" He crawled over to her, cupping the side of her face. "You're awake. What's wrong?"

She stared into his eyes, her heart feeling like it was about to burst within her aching chest. "You're here. You saved me."

"Of course." He pressed a light kiss to the tip of her nose. "I'm so sorry, Selene."

She shook her head, only to wince as pain throbbed through her torso, especially her back. "Not your... fault."

"You need more medicine." Draven slipped off the bed and returned with a spoonful of powder.

Selene shook her head. "I just got you back, Draven. I want to be where you are."

"I'm right here." Draven held the spoon closer to her lips.

Selene swallowed, her throat suddenly tight. "D-Draven?"

"What is it, love?"

"Could you hold me? Please?" Her chest grew tighter as her heart ached with longing. "I didn't think I'd ever be able to touch you again. I thought that embrace in the jungle would be our l—" Her throat clamped shut.

"Of course." Draven slid in beside her, his movements slow and gentle enough that they didn't cause her pain. He wrapped his arm around her shoulders and pressed a longer kiss to her cheek. "How is this?"

"Perfect." She sniffed and leaned her head against his shoulder. "Draven?"

"Yes?"

"Do you still want to marry me?"

"We might have to wait a few months, until you're fully healed. But yes. More than ever." He nudged her forehead with his. "I love you."

She ventured a smile. "I love you too. I know I can't control everything—I couldn't control Arzil's actions or my mother's choices—but I have control over the things that matter most, like doing the right thing. And loving you. And that's a decision I want to keep making for the rest of my life."

Draven smiled. "I would tell you how happy I am to hear that, but I don't think words would do my feelings justice. Speaking of your mother, there's been something I've been meaning to show you." He leaned over, snatching the piece of paper from the table. He unfolded it and handed it to her. "When Alaric's men went through your grandmother's possessions, they found this among them."

The script on it read, *Selene*.

Her mother had written a letter to her. Selene took it, goosebumps racing up her arms. She unfolded it. A quick glance revealed that it was written the day she'd died.

Selene,

I am sorry.

I have led you astray. I trained you up in the way that I was trained. I never questioned what I'd been taught—for years. And now I've infected you, ensnared you in this way of life. The only way out is death. How fitting. I would call it justice, but those assassins who have yet to see the light, yet to realize that life is precious, yet to understand that we shouldn't control who lives and dies—they're the ones who live. I fear that I am to die soon—in the same manner that many of my victims were killed.

I told you that the Scorpio were not to be defied, not to be questioned. I told you that anyone that they commanded us to kill was worthy of death. I told you that you had no option but to take the road presented to you. I was wrong, Selene.

We always have a choice to do the right thing. Oftentimes the right choice is the hardest path. Sometimes choosing the right thing means choosing death. But pursuing that decision is worth dying for. It's better than living a life in which you're willing to sacrifice your morals and hurt others in order to sustain your own existence.

I've made my choice, Selene. What will yours be?

Now I only need to garner enough courage to give this letter to you, before my time runs out.

Your Mother, Kaili

Selene swallowed past her tight throat. Her eyes felt heavy with unshed tears. She'd made a choice, just like her mother had. A choice to do the right thing, even if it came with risks.

She let the letter fall to her lap, and Draven squeezed her hand. "Are you all right, Selene?"

She nodded. "I'm glad that my mother made the right choice, even if she ultimately died for it. I'm proud to be her daughter." She set the letter back onto the table and turned toward Draven. "I've been so focused on the things in life that I couldn't control. Now I think it's time to focus on what I can. I can do the right thing. I can forgive my mother." She brushed her lips over his. "And I can love you."

He smiled against her lips. "Not nearly as much as I love you. Now, ease my concern and take your medicine, won't you? The next time you awaken, you might be healed enough for me to give you a few pointers on kissing."

She narrowed her eyes at him. "Are you saying I'm bad at it?"

"No. I just want an excuse to kiss you." He pressed another light kiss to her forehead.

Draven's lips were soft against her skin, his body warm next to hers. "But I don't want this moment to end," she said.

"We'll have many more moments just like this one. And when you're well, we'll start planning that wedding. If you recover quickly enough, perhaps we can have it in the summer."

The thought of marrying Draven in a few months—and being held by him whenever she pleased—was pure bliss. But a few months seemed so far away. Perhaps she could persuade him to marry her a bit sooner.

"Trust me, Selene."

She drew a deep breath and nodded, opening her mouth. Draven placed the spoon between her lips and dumped the powder onto her tongue. She swallowed and immediately felt her consciousness beginning to wane.

The last thing she remembered thinking was how comforting it was to be held by Draven. And how she couldn't wait for him to hold her again.

33

CHOOSING TO LOVE HIM

Six Months Later

Selene could scarcely breathe for the excitement fluttering through her. She'd dreamt of this day for months, agonized over how slow it seemed to be approaching.

And now, all of a sudden, it was here.

Her wedding day.

Selene glanced at the foreign face in her vanity mirror, uncertain about the creams and paints they'd applied to her. Black lined her eyes, making them appear bold and striking. Red coated her lips, making them seem plump and lush. Pink dusted her cheeks, giving her an innocent blush.

She wasn't used to wearing items that would intentionally draw attention to herself. But in a way, she liked it. She hadn't taken the opportunity to dress up since she was a little girl.

"Selene? You all right?" Evelyn nudged her side. "Are you thinking about Draven again?"

Selene's grin widened. "Yes. And about how excited I am that we're *finally* getting married." She huffed. "He set the wedding date out so far that if I didn't know better, I would have said that he was delaying the wedding."

The six months had crept by at a snail's pace. She'd enjoyed spending time with Draven, but as the King's new Grand Master, other duties often stole him away. Shonn had been sentenced to life in prison for charges of assault and purchasing illegal substances, though his spy was released. Arzil had been tried, found guilty, and executed.

Her grandmother had seemed to vanish off the face of Torva. Sometimes, Selene even wondered if the woman had fled to Earth through a portal. Draven had spread the word to knights around Torva to watch for someone with Cori's description. But no one had found her. Selene often feared they'd find her body rather than her person.

Evelyn grabbed Selene's hand and squeezed it, bringing her back to the present. "Draven just wanted to make sure that you were recovered and ready before the wedding. I sure would have appreciated Alaric delaying our initial wedding... at least a little." Evelyn rose from her chair to adjust Selene's veil.

"Evelyn, sit back down. I'm not the only one who's been recovering." Selene pressed a hand down on Evelyn's shoulder.

"I'm fine. It's been two months since the delivery." But she sat down nonetheless, a testament to her exhaustion.

Evelyn had gone into labor for twenty-four hours, delivering a baby that was on the verge of being too large for her small frame. Honestly, Selene was surprised that Alaric had let Evelyn come to Taijeng for the wedding. According to Evelyn, Alaric had been concerned enough after the birth to take her to the healers on Earth.

"Stop looking at me like that." Evelyn smiled, taking the bite out of her words. "I'm not some weak fragile human to be pitied."

"No. You're very strong. I don't think anyone would dare say otherwise."

Evelyn laughed softly. "At least not in Alaric's hearing. He's been rather protective lately."

ELIZABETH NEWSOM

With good reason.

"He's even suggested that I don't have any more children." Her expression sagged in disappointment.

Selene grasped Evelyn's hand. "It's nothing you did, Evelyn. He's trying to protect you like Draven's trying to protect me."

"I know. Speaking of Draven, this is *your* wedding day." Evelyn's smile was bright and genuine this time. "Don't let my little pity party rain on your parade."

Pity party? Rain on her parade? Must be Earth phrases. Before Selene could reassure her, the double doors to the room slammed open as a mob of fairies engulfed Selene like a fog, touching up her hair and makeup, smoothing out wrinkles in the dress. It was rather kind of Evelyn to lend her fairies-in-waiting to Selene for the day.

They all stood back. The purple fairy nodded—her name completely escaped Selene. "You look... halfway decent."

The green one grimaced and shot Selene an apologetic look. "Believe it or not, for Zinnia, that's a compliment."

Lyra crinkled her nose, appearing as if she were seriously considering flicking the purple fairy across the room. "Well, *I* think she looks stunning." Lyra took both of Selene's hands in hers. "Are you ready, mas—Selene?"

Selene shook her head with a smile and bent close, her lips by Lyra's ear. "If you call me 'master' in public, there will be some serious concerns about our relationship."

Lyra giggled. "I know. It's an old habit."

Selene gave Lyra a small shove. "Now go. The ceremony's about to start, and I expect to see you seated in the front row."

Lyra's smile was blindingly bright as she skipped from the room. Selene had never seen her so happy and carefree. She was glad Draven had suggested keeping her at the palace with them.

After a few more moments of fussing over her, the green

326

fairy fluttered back and nodded. "Perfect. Now, it's time for you to make your grand entrance."

Selene rose. Everyone gasped and whispered as the folds of the dress smoothed, revealing golden streaks and shimmers. Beneath sunlight, the fabric looked like it'd been set afire. Selene glanced up at them, only for a sheet of hair to swing over her face. This was why she hated leaving it down.

Selene raised her hand to tuck it behind her ear, and the purple fairy was quick to slap her hand away. "We spent hours on that hairstyle. Don't you even think about touching it."

But it was *her* hair. Selene refrained from saying so and lowered her hand. The fairies lowered the veil over her face and Evelyn placed a bouquet into her hands. It was a long trek out of the palace and into the gardens. The air was thick with humidity, almost too thick to breathe. Perhaps they should have gone for an indoor wedding. The ceremony commenced on a wide swathe of grass, lined by bushes thick with flowers. A few pews had been placed on both sides, leaving an aisle down the middle.

And at the end of the aisle, Draven.

The expression on his face made the morning of preparations worth it. His smile was wide and polite. Fake. Until his eyes landed on her. He laughed softly and glanced down. When he looked up again, his eyes were bright and glossy, the whites slightly reddened. He took a deep breath that filled his chest and gave her a second shakier, softer smile.

Selene felt her own face warm as tears gathered in her eyes, on the verge of spilling down her lower lashes. She quickened her pace, doing her best not to trip over her own dress.

"You got this, Selene," Evelyn said as Selene passed her.

Selene glanced back and saw Lyra seated beside Evelyn. Her former apprentice winked.

Selene returned their smiles as she dropped the bouquet

into the waiting hands of some attendant. In the next instant, Draven's arms were around her.

This was where she belonged. And where she always wanted to be.

Alaric cleared his throat. "It's going to be hard for her to say her vows, Draven, if you keep her face pressed to your chest."

Draven released her—slowly—before shooting a glare at Alaric. He took a half stride back, keeping ahold of her hands.

Alaric gave a relatively short speech about Torva and the significance of weddings before asking them to give their own vows. They had agreed not to have a Hand Binding ceremony, since Draven had argued that it would impede him holding her when they kissed.

And then—finally—Alaric said, "You may now kiss the bride."

Draven swept her into his arms, and she felt no fear. Only a thrill that began in her chest and radiated outward. When he kissed her, she parted her lips and clung to him tightly, willing him to never let go. And for a long time, he didn't, slanting his mouth to deepen the kiss.

Only when her chest started to tingle with the need for air did he draw back, still keeping her wrapped tightly in his arms.

"Whoooooo!" The purple fairy shouted. "Keep it going!"

Draven chuckled and stole another kiss before the crowd descended on them, wishing them congratulations. Though it was their wedding, ironically, she didn't spend nearly as much time with Draven as she would have liked to. Despite her lack of close relatives, she still had plenty of guests to speak to. Some of the palace servants had befriended her over the past months, and Draven's friends and extended family from Silva were all clamoring to talk to her.

Somehow—eventually—she made her escape into the depths of the garden, where she could breathe and think. If she was lucky, Draven would notice her absence and meet her. But perhaps that was just wishful thinking on her part.

"Selene."

Not Draven. Selene reached for the dagger hidden up her sleeve and whipped around. She'd only intended to wear her mother's dagger ceremonially, but now it appeared she'd have to put it to use.

A slight woman peered out from behind a tree, her silvery blond hair pulled back into a disheveled ponytail. Ocean blue eyes stared at her, darkened by the shadows sweeping beneath them.

Cori.

She'd been looking for Cori for months. But Selene hadn't actually expected to find her, especially to be face-to-face on her wedding day. She appeared thinner than before, her skin slightly tanned, her hair cut jaggedly short.

Cori smiled thinly. "I wanted to congratulate you. And ask for your aid."

"Where did you go Cori? Where's the masked man? What happened to you?" Selene lowered her dagger and stepped nearer, only for Cori to dance back a step.

"I don't have much time." She ran her hand through her hair. "Coming here was probably a bad idea. But I thought that you could help me."

"What's going on?" Selene would have stepped forward again, if she didn't fear that Cori would further retreat. "I'll gladly help you if you'll explain what happened. Draven is going to be King Alaric's new Grand Master over his entire army and guard." Not to mention that he was Alaric's half-brother. "And as my husband, I'm sure he'd be willing to help as well."

Cori drew in a breath, only to expel it in a rush. She glanced down at her forearm, which was covered by a sleeve. "Tuteno." She scanned the gardens, her pale blue eyes wide and haunted.

"I—I have to go. They could be anywhere, and without guards here, I won't endanger you as well."

"Endanger me?" Selene stepped forward. "Cori, explain yourself. What—" Cori shot into the garden, and Selene sprinted after her. "Cori, wait!"

"*Selene!*" Draven shouted from behind her.

If she were to stop, she'd lose Cori. Possibly forever. Within a few turns, she'd lost her anyway and had to slow down.

Draven halted by her side and caught her hand. "Selene. Why were you running? Is something wrong?"

She glanced around the garden. No sign of Cori. "I saw my friend, Cori."

Draven's eyebrows rose. "Is she all right?"

"No." Selene pressed her hand to her forehead. "Draven, she said she was in danger, that she needed help. But then she froze, said someone was coming for her, and ran away. She said she didn't want to stay and put me in danger when there were no guards around."

Draven tugged Selene a bit closer, combing the gardens warily. "That's most troubling. I'll have guards search the perimeter." He squeezed her hand. "And after that, they'll search the city for Cori."

Selene's chin nearly dropped to her chest. She was briefly surprised at the low neckline before remembering why she wore such a dress. "But we're moving to Octavya. If she needs our help again, how will she find us?"

Draven squeezed her hand. "With Alaric putting a new steward in charge of Taijeng, she'll always be welcomed at the Taijese palace. Other than that, there's not much we can do, love." He strode forward, tugging her along with him. "I'll have the guards search the gardens. Then, perhaps, we can find a secluded area within the palace." He winked at her, and she felt a warm fizzy feeling cascade through her.

Draven led her back to the main area where they'd held the

ceremony. People were still meandering around, socializing, and filling their plates high with food from the buffet. Draven strode over to a guard, taking a few seconds to murmur something to him in a low tone.

The guard nodded and approached another guard.

Draven led her around the outskirts of the group, lest someone try to talk to them and impede their escape.

Once within the palace, Draven guided her down a few corridors before he found a quiet one with a small bench in the alcove. He seated himself, pulling her onto his lap.

His eyes flashed, and his smile made heat flush her face. "Now, where were we?"

"I remember." Selene smiled and brushed her lips against his.

He returned the kiss with a passion that made her head light. She wrapped her arms around him, twining their bodies together. Somehow, she wanted to be even closer. And tonight, she would.

When Draven finally drew back—because she didn't have the willpower to—they were both breathless, their chests heaving against each other. She smiled up at him, happiness pouring into her soul.

So much had happened to her, so much that she couldn't control. Yet the only choices that mattered were those that were hers to make. She could always make the right choice even when she didn't feel like she had one.

And loving Draven had definitely been the right choice.

She cupped his face, wishing she could express all that she felt. "I'm glad I chose you. And I'm glad you chose me."

He chuckled. "As am I."

As he leaned in for another kiss, Selene had never been happier to have failed a mission. She would not only get to choose to love Draven today, but every day for the rest of her life. As excited as she was, she knew choosing love wouldn't always be easy. But life wasn't about making the easy choices that cost her nothing. It was about making the right ones that could cost her everything.

And if that meant better loving Draven, it was a price she was gladly willing to pay.

COMING IN 2021...

"That man. He's staring at you again."

Corsicanna straightened from wiping the table and glanced toward the hooded man. He was in the same spot he'd been in all night, his gaze locked to her. He was swathed in darkness, from his black eyes to the mask concealing his face to the hooded cloak casting him in shadow.

Mei bumped Cori's hip with hers. "Aren't you going to approach him? I would, but it seems he has eyes for only you." She trailed a hand down her curvy hip and sighed. "It's too bad. He just won't know what he's missing out on."

Goosebumps trailed down Cori's arms as she returned her attention to the table, scouring its surface until it gleamed like a smooth sea. Surely that man couldn't... suspect anything. What if he knew about her past? Or what if he was here for her necklace.

Cori glanced down to ensure the piece of jewelry was still there. The golden chain trailed over her pale skin and disappeared beneath her neckline. Though she couldn't see it, she knew the charm that hung from the end. It was a golden snake, clinging to the necklace chain with its fanged mouth, its mismatched blue and green eyes penetrating.

She almost reached up to touch it beneath her dress until she glanced up and found the man's gaze glued to her.

"You should go to him," Mei said. "You haven't been getting as many customers as of late, and Arzil said that if you don't increase your weekly quota—"

"I *know* what Arzil said." Cori scrubbed in circular motions until her shoulder burned. Arzil was the owner of the brothel… and some other shadier businesses. In truth, the brothel was just a means of disguising his true line of work, as the leader of the Scorpio, an assassin's guild.

He was such a despicable Torvan. It never ceased to confuse her how people could voluntarily work for him. Like her friend, Selene, who was his apprentice in the Scorpio. It'd been quite some time since Selene had come to the Maroon Maidens to visit Arzil. Cori couldn't understand how Selene justified her work, just as Selene didn't understand Cori. Nonetheless, Cori hoped Selene would visit soon.

"We're not paid to serve and clean, Cori," Mei continued. "If you don't start bedding more men, Arzil won't hesitate to ship you off to Cade."

Cade. The only country in the United Countries of Torva that allowed slavery. And if they ever found out that she was a siren, there was no way she'd escape. She'd be kept under lock and key at all times.

Cori touched her throat. Sometimes she even wondered if her song worked. It had been so long since she'd last used it…

"*Cori.*"

"I know." Cori tossed the rag, letting it slap back onto the table. "I'll talk to him."

Mei stalked off to another customer, likely to charm a few coins from him.

Sometimes, Cori wasn't certain whether Mei was insanely

jealous of her or looking out for her best interests. She supposed it depended on the day.

Cori straightened and drew a lock of hair down her cheek. Men loved it when her hair was in easy reach. She tugged her dress down, drawing her neckline a bit lower, and glided toward the hooded man.

She could feel the numbness starting at her fingertips and creeping upward. This was why she'd been avoiding clients for the past few weeks. A part of her wondered if this was all there was, if she'd spend the rest of her life doing this until she was too unattractive for men to bed her.

She stopped in front of the hooded man and wiped all thoughts from her head. Smile. Tilt her head. Jut her hip out to the side. "Good day."

He stared at her, then his gaze dropped to her neckline. Another chill raked its frosty fingers down her arms. Was he looking at her bosom? Or the necklace?

"Is it?" he asked.

Cori blinked. Swallowed. "Is it what?"

His lips thinned in disgust. "Prostitutes. All the same."

Her skin burned with shame and anger, but she kept her smile affixed to her lips. It wasn't unusual for men to treat her poorly, especially if they were paying high sums to do so. "Do you require my services or not?"

He blinked up at her in surprise. She must have used a sharper tone than she'd realized. "I do not."

Relief coursed through her veins, even though she knew that was a bad sign. She desperately needed another client. But somehow, she couldn't find the motivation to provide her services for yet another night. She could feel a strange hollowness in her middle, and it seemed to expand with each passing night.

She swiveled on her heel and left the sour man to his bitter thoughts. Yes, she should work harder to find a client.

But she was thankful that her client for tonight wouldn't be him.

Tynan had to fist his hands to keep from reaching out and snapping the necklace off of her slender neck. She must keep the jewel somewhere on her necklace. But before he did anything rash, he'd have to be certain of it. After all, he'd only found one man, one of the girl's previous clients, who had claimed that he'd seen the sapphire-eyed snake charm on the necklace as she slipped it off.

Now that he'd seen the girl himself, he was certain that she was a siren—and that her necklace was exactly what he was looking for. He would see if he could find any more of her clients who would offer up information for coin. And he'd return every night to study the girl, get a better idea of his opponent's strengths and weaknesses.

He remained in the chair for a few more hours, his gaze trailing her. Though she never even glanced at him, he could tell she knew she was watched by the tenseness in her jaw and the set of her shoulders.

She likely thought he was a drunkard who had nothing better to do. What she didn't know was that her fate was in his hands. He was a siren hunter. And she was his next target.

ACKNOWLEDGMENTS

Another year and another book published. Woohoo!

I went through a very different process writing this book compared to the last one. First of all, it didn't take between four and five years—thank goodness. I also did the bulk of my writing during the school year, which was definitely challenging. Though the process was different, what remained the same was how many people played such a big role in creating this book, critiquing it, and encouraging my writing.

First of all, as I've said in the beginning of this book, glory and recognition should go first to God for gifting me with this mission and passion. Writing is *so* hard, but it's taught me so much about God and His character... In fact, be on the lookout for a book about something along those lines.

Thank you to my parents for continuing to fund my writing endeavors and encourage my passion. You guys are my number one cheerleaders, and I'm eternally grateful for how you've built up my confidence in my own writing abilities and told me to chase my dreams... even when those dreams aren't particularly profitable. You're amazing.

Coleman deserves my gratitude for a lot of things—one of

those being how he's spent hours helping me write. Thank you for all the times when you've told me we can't watch movies together until I've finished my writing, when you've read my book aloud to search for typos, when you've let me call you for hours to brainstorm plot ideas, and when you've listened as I've complained about stupid reviewers. I remember, with perfect clarity, a moment when I was sitting in your apartment, my head pounding after staring at my computer screen for hours. You made me tea, wrapped me in your arms, and told me that I was doing great. You happen to know just what I need and when I need it. I'm so lucky to have you in my life.

And just like in the last book, Jamie Foley deserves another HUGE thank you. Thank you for telling that reviewer off on my YouTube video (reading it still makes me laugh), for taking the time to endorse my books, and inviting me to the super cool Fayette Press group. I'm so thankful to have a friend who's walked my writing journey alongside me.

Sarah Grimm, you are the *bomb*. Thank you for being a top-notch editor and friend. I've so enjoyed getting to know you through Realm Makers, and your editing has been so valuable to me. Your suggestions are always on point, yet you manage to communicate them in a way that builds me up and encourages me.

Thank you to my other endorsers, Morgan Busse and Tricia Mingerink. I know both of you keep busy with your writing careers—and life in general. Thank you so much for taking the time to read my book. I deeply appreciate the support. Please let me know if there's anything I can do to help you out in return.

Thank you to my beta readers and proofreaders: Selina Struzik, Marvah Yousuf, Shelley, Breann Hill, Katherine, Emily Lim, Gabriela Kaisheva-Fartsova, Ceylan Gunduz, Ariel Whyte, Christina C., Lindy Fourie, Christie Olson, Sophie Bea Louise Overton, Katherine Canales, Hannah Joyce Pardo, Kimberly A.

Pacheco, Sabrina Sgoda, Anita Kinclová, Kimberly Ann Pacheco, and others. And thank you to my print proofers and close friends, Taylor, Brenna, and Alli. You guys are amazing, and I deeply appreciate your help and encouragement.

I'd also like to thank Cassandra Hamm for all she's done to promote this book and my last! And Kendra Ardnek—thank you for including my book in so many of your posts. I love seeing them. And RJ, you did a fabulous job with your photos —I loved the ones with the lights.

Kiff, you're a fabulous cover designer, and I'm so lucky to have you as both a cover designer and friend. Somehow, you have a way of magically extracting the vague ideas in my head and creating something amazing.

Thank you, Anne-Marie, for taking so much time to draw an epic, mind-blowing map. I love showing it off whenever I get the chance. I guess talent just runs in the family.

Thank you, Curtis, for your clever cover design idea... *wink wink*

A huge thank you to the numerous friends who bought my book and praised my writing efforts, like Taylor (both the one with the beard and without), Caitlyn, Yemile, Adam, and Madi —to name a few. Your words of encouragement mean so much to me. And thank you to my relatives who have bought and read my book, like my GG (I'll miss you), Grandma, Aunt Susie, and Aunt Naomi. I'm so honored that you've taken the time to read a book that means so much to me.

Finally, thank YOU for reading my book—and this far in the acknowledgments. It's impressive, really. If you're interested in further supporting this book, please take the time to review it on Amazon! You have no idea how much it would help.

If you ever want to reach out to me, I'd love to hear from you! Feel free to contact me at elizabethpnewsom@gmail.com

ABOUT THE AUTHOR

Elizabeth Newsom is a marketing major at UT Tyler. While she's going to Texas for college, she visits her family in New Mexico over breaks. Elizabeth's first complete work was a Jelsa fanfiction that she published on fanfiction.net, then WattPad. Encouraged by her small successes on those platforms, she then began to pursue a career as an author. While other authors typically use this part of the biography to talk about their husband and/or dogs, Elizabeth has neither of those. However, she does own a pretty great succulent that currently resides in her dorm room. Visit her online at elizabethnewsom.com or connect with her on social media:

Pinterest: @authorliznewsom
Wattpad: @ElizabethNewsom
Amazon: Elizabeth Newsom
Facebook: @authorelizabethnewsom
Instagram: @elizabeth_newsom